NIGHT

NIGHT

ALEXANDRIA WARWICK

ANDROMEDA
PRESS

Published by Andromeda Press, LLC

Cover illustration by Faryn Hughes
Map art © Alexandria Warwick

978-1-7330334-1-1
First Edition

*To those who look for light
in dark places*

The North

Tor
The Western Sea
Iniga For
Nalwa
Northe
Lun
Talguk
Western Territory
River Mitka
Unana
Centra
The Atakana
The De
Kesikan Pass
Souther
The Banished Lands
Auk

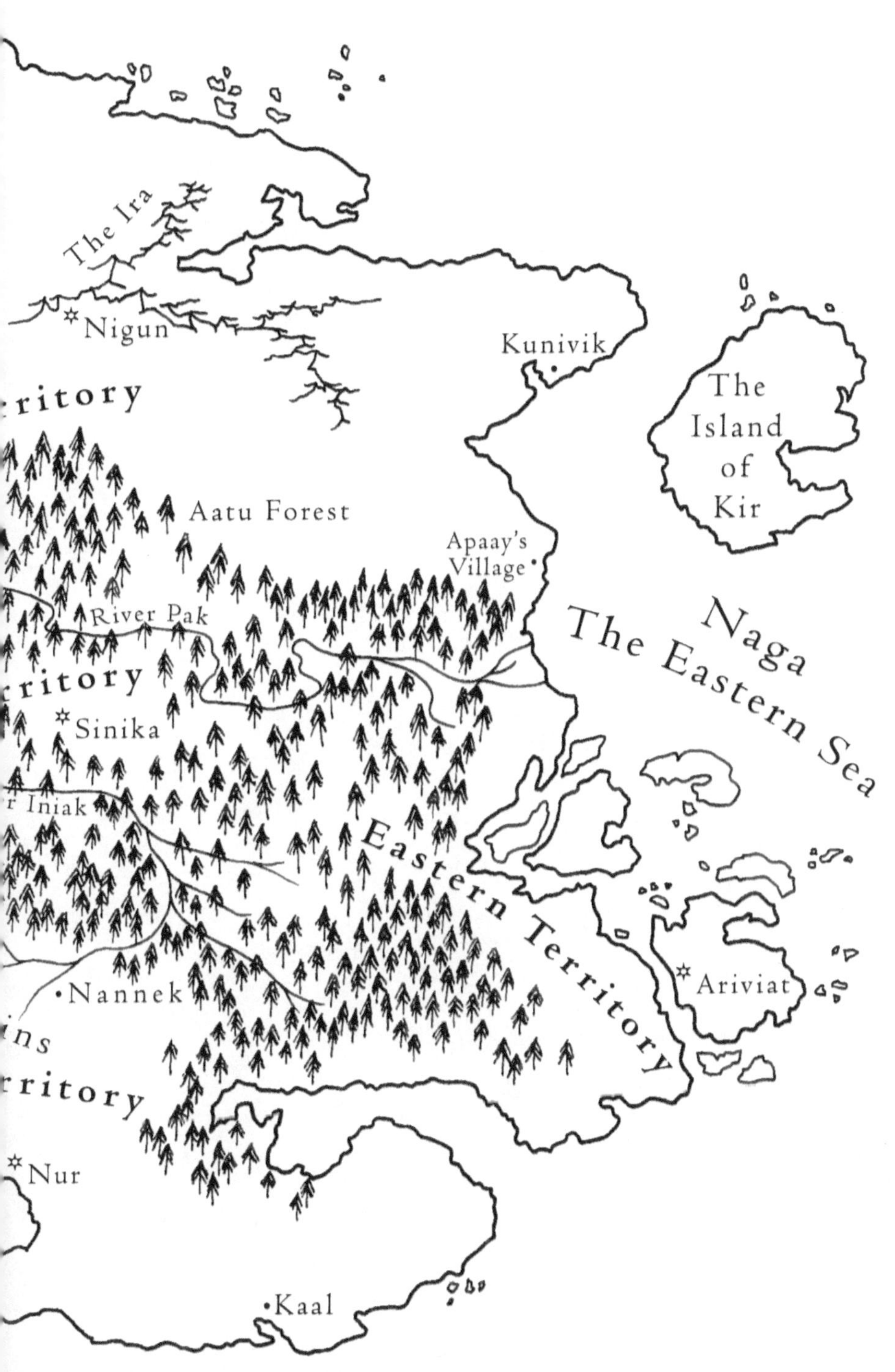

The Ira
Nigun
Kunivik
The Island of Kir
ritory
Aatu Forest
Apaay's Village
Naga
The Eastern Sea
River Pak
ritory
Sinika
r Iniak
Eastern Territory
Ariviat
Nannek
ins
ritory
Nur
Kaal

There was a wolf in the distance, a dark shroud beyond the trees, and it had been watching Apaay for five days now.

Five days—and five nights—the darkness like eternity.

When the shape had first materialized beyond the mouth of the cave, Apaay had convinced herself it wasn't alive. It was a tree or rock, or a shadow cast by the dim half-moon. But then it moved. Prowled through those pale hills, dark as a spot of ink. Always, it was there: in the corner of her eye, slipping between the woods, never lingering for long.

A storm was approaching. Apaay smelled it on the air, the wind swelling to a howl and scattering snow around her legs. Naga lay far to the east of her, beyond the sprawl of the Aatu Forest. The Atakana lay to the west. And to the north—

Ice and screams and blood and death.

So much death.

Some days, she swore she heard Yuki's cruel voice dripping poison into her mind. Apaay reminded herself it wasn't real. They had escaped the labyrinth, she and Ila and Masuk. She had gotten them out, had returned to her village.

My fault, my fault, my fault.

Her eyes snapped open, and the screams cut off. The flurry swirled, frost glittering on the cave walls. She didn't see the wolf. It must have returned to its den.

As a child, Apaay had once discovered a wolf with its foreleg caught between the jaws of an iron trap. It had snarled at her with such ferocity, shaking as it bled, but Apaay hadn't faltered, her heart surprisingly free of fear. She could never understand what kind of person would want to chain something free.

Lips peeled back, the predator had watched Apaay as she crouched down, making herself less of a threat. The animal stilled as she reached for the jaws and—carefully—pried them apart.

The wolf bolted. Its leg hadn't appeared broken. She liked to think it had survived.

Apaay didn't realize she had closed her eyes. Without sight, the howling crested and broke, over and over. Snow thumped atop her legs.

But strangely, she felt warm. Heat seeped through her furs and soothed the ache in her joints, and she sank deeper into the warmth, not knowing where it came from, but grateful for its presence. Not a nightmare, then, but a dream. She was home, curled up in the bedding furs with her family. Her limbs were loose, her mind utterly at peace. *Eska,* her heart whispered into the dark.

It was so nice being warm after spending eighteen years in the cold.

PART ONE

NIGHT

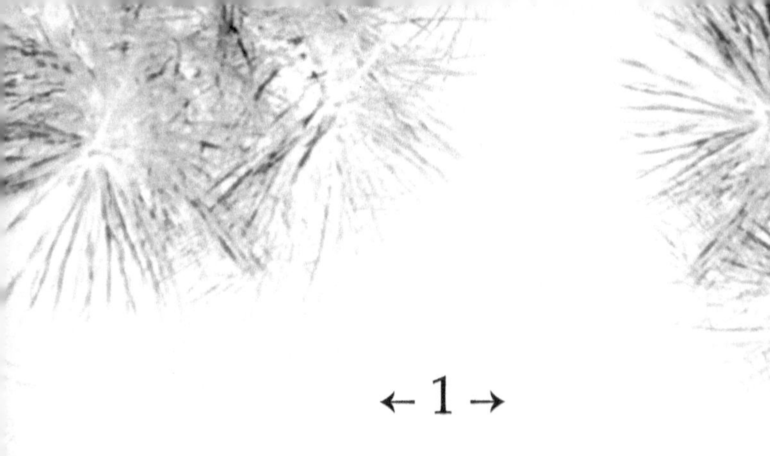

← 1 →

"**I**s she dead?"

Callused fingers brushed her icy cheek and traveled to the pulse point in her neck, a sear of heat. Apaay hadn't the strength to brush them away, hadn't the strength to waken. She was firmly within the pit of a hot, ravenous nightmare. Her breathing shallowed out as awareness trickled through. She wasn't sure where she was. Couldn't remember what had come before unconsciousness. It must be Eska trying to wake her because she had overslept, and it was hunting day, except . . . why did she smell the earth when Eska always smelled of the sea?

"No," said the second voice, equally deep. She didn't recognize either. "At least, not yet."

The man brushed at something around her shoulders. Then she remembered. Snow. The storm must have passed. How long had it been since she'd fallen asleep? Apaay hadn't meant to sleep. She had only intended to rest for a while.

"How long do you think she's been here?" the first man asked.

Her hood was pulled forward to better protect her face. "Too long. I don't know how she's still alive." He removed one of her mittens and swore. "We need to get back."

"Wait. See these tracks? Something else was here."

"A little help, please?" snapped the second man.

They began to dig.

"Is this her, do you think?" said the first man.

"I'm not sure. We'll let the elders decide her fate."

"She's lucky Qannak found her."

A soft whine sounded, and then a warm tongue licked Apaay's cheek, thawing it out. Her facial muscles twitched in pain.

"We're miles from the village," said the second man, pulling her into an upright position. "There's no way she could have known this girl was here."

"A miracle, then."

He hefted Apaay into his arms. "Miracle," he said in puzzlement. "Right."

← →

When Apaay next awoke, it was to a shimmer of low embers and slumbering heat.

A groan slipped free as she rolled onto her side and unlocked her bent legs, wincing at the flare of pain in her knees. Her mouth was so dry she could feel the bark-like texture of her tongue. She lay on a pile of furs, naked beneath the musk of animal skins. Apaay remembered nothing from the moment she had closed her eyes until now.

"You were lucky, you know."

Her attention slid toward a man slicing a root into fine strips near the hearth. The fire was a strange sight. Wood was scarce along the coast, salt-bitten and waterlogged, which was why light generally came in the form of lamps, moss soaked in oil. The slow, deliberate scrape of the knife lifted the hair on her nape.

"Very lucky," he continued, as if he hadn't noticed her lack of response. "Another hour of exposure and you would have died."

Apaay drew the blanket up to her chin, the fur tickling her neck. The man's back was to her. He wore an undercoat of deep russet, a white strip coloring the bottom hem. A hare, she guessed, for the pelt appeared silken. Trousers and slippers, though not made of sealskin. A beautifully ornate comb secured his long black hair away from his face.

It took multiple attempts for Apaay to speak. She hadn't used her voice in so long. "Who are you?"

"Who I am doesn't matter. But I am curious as to who *you* are."

Panic lodged hotly in her throat. She couldn't see this man's face. A quick glance around the snow house showcased the sparsity she would expect from her own people. It smelled slightly medicinal. Out of curiosity, she wiggled her toes. They were all still attached. Lucky, indeed.

"It's been some time since we've had a visitor from the coast." He still didn't face her, for whatever reason. "How long have you been traveling?"

"Six weeks." Maybe more, maybe less. She'd tried keeping track of the days. Eventually, she had stopped caring.

The man nodded, as if that explained something. "The sea still clings to you."

Setting down the knife, he finally turned around. Fine facial lines marked him as middle-aged. "What were you doing out in that storm? It nearly killed you."

His eyes were so dark she could not distinguish his pupils from his irises. They fell to her shortened hair, the shame she bore. The brown-black strands were only a few inches long. Apaay wondered what he assumed of her. The air in the room pinched with the knowledge they shared, that yes, she knew the danger of such squalls, knew she had walked into certain death.

Before Apaay could respond, a girl entered the snow house through the tunnel, bearing a basket of roots and herbs. Apaay saw this place for what it was: a healer's room. In her village, there had been such a place, a structure as large, and as wide, the air tinged with herbs.

After setting down the basket, the girl knelt at Apaay's side. "Glad to see you're awake," she said in a clear, quiet tone. "I'm Qin."

"Don't let her leave," the man told the girl with a hard look.

Apaay watched him exit the room. "Where is he going?"

"Can you sit up, please?"

Apaay did as she was asked, clutching the blanket to her chest as Qin began kneading the muscles of her back, hands, and feet. Apaay nearly cried out. It had been so long since she'd been touched with gentleness. Somewhere in the foggy cavity of her chest, her heart was weeping.

The girl sat back. "Drink this." She passed her a skin of liquid.

Apaay recoiled the moment the coppery fluid drifted across her tongue. Her body's reaction to the taste of blood was so swift she barely had time to snatch a nearby bucket before upending the meager contents of her stomach. Her skin prickled, and she was shivering, shivering as she sweat, as she found herself back in the labyrinth's arena, strands of silver hair drenched in the blood oozing from the woman's torn throat.

Apaay squeezed her eyes shut, unable to look at the girl. She hadn't been able to eat meat since her escape, only roots and bark. "I'm—" Choked breath. "I—"

"It's all right," soothed Qin, a hand to her back. Apaay flinched away. "We'll get you cleaned up."

The girl wiped the blood and sickness dribbling down Apaay's chin, then tucked the blankets around her shoulders. "They say there is a girl targeting the Analak communities."

Apaay inhaled sharply at the news. "I know who it is."

The girl watched her with a guarded expression. "Hm."

"You don't believe me?"

"What I believe doesn't matter. The elders have already spoken."

"What does that mean?"

It was a hard sort of silence, one of guttered whispers when one passed too closely.

Qin said, "They think the girl is you."

A chill crept across her skin. Wood cracked loudly. "Me?" Something crumpled in her chest. But there was fury, too. This girl didn't know a thing about Apaay and what she had endured.

"Why would I attack my own people?" she growled, curling her fingers into the blankets. "What reason would I have to do such a thing?"

"I don't know. The motives of others are often clouded."

A furious heat closed Apaay's throat as she glared at the girl, who studied her with equal parts mistrust and wariness. "Yuki," Apaay spat. "That's who destroyed my village."

"Yuki?" Her eyebrows lifted. "No one has ever heard of her."

Apaay shoved aside the blankets and reached for her folded clothes. They were dry, thankfully. "I'm not going to listen to this."

Qin backed up a step. Fright rounded her eyes as she watched Apaay struggle to dress herself. Then she disappeared through the tunnel.

Only when Apaay was alone did her fury extinguish, and she sagged against the wall. These people thought *she* had destroyed her village?

Tugging Eska's face from her pocket, Apaay studied the familiar features. The scar across the temple. The dimple in her chin. Though she had not seen her sister in four and a half months, there was no doubt Eska lived. This Apaay knew. The skin of Eska's face was both elastic and warm, an indication, she guessed, of breath flowing through her sister's body, and maybe hope, too, that they would find each other again.

She returned the face to her pocket with a shaky hand, tucking it against the wolf carving she was never without. Weeks ago, Apaay had knelt in the ashen earth of her home. Her family had managed to escape Yuki's destruction. Others had not been as lucky. Forgiveness was a grace she would never deserve. What had occurred—she would carry it all her life.

By the time Apaay was fully dressed, sweat clung to her skin in a light sheen. Crawling through the short tunnel, she braced herself for the slap of cold as she reached the outside.

Interspersed between the white domes, small firepits dotted the trampled snow. Towering pines huddled like caribou in a winter squall. Families laughed and skinned animals around the fire. Somewhere close, a beating drum. Though Apaay didn't know these people, she *knew* them. The Analak were not a monolith, but they had been birthed from the same father, the same mother, the land and the sea. The twinge in her heart, the flutter in her soul. It felt too much like home.

Equal parts curiosity and animosity greeted her. Word must have spread of her presence. Among the hushed tones, Apaay picked out one that gave her pause. She looked around, a cloud of confusion descending at the voice. "Muktuk?"

From across the way, a man lifted his head.

Chena's brother.

He came toward her in puzzlement. "Apaay?"

Her knees folded, and he caught her around the waist. She forgot Muktuk had moved inland with his wife a few weeks before the Face Stealer had infiltrated their village. "It's so good to see you."

"What are you doing here? You can barely stand. Here." He lowered her onto a log stripped of bark, the wood smooth and moon-pale. Then he sat beside her, gripping her hand fiercely.

His confusion transformed into something far more ominous as he noticed how her clothes bagged around her frame. Apaay had always been thin, a coil of untapped energy, but there was that, and then there was this: an erosion of oneself.

The man from the healing room appeared, his gaze cool. "This is her," he said. "The one they found."

Muktuk glanced between Apaay and the man. Uncertainty and hesitation warred.

"There's been word," Muktuk finally said to Apaay, "of a girl attacking Analak villages." He searched her eyes. "That's not you, is it?"

Apaay stiffened and tried to jerk her hand free. Of all the people to doubt her, she would never expect Chena's brother to be one of them.

He tightened his grip. "I'm sorry. Two of our men found you unconscious. No one knew who you were or why you were here." His face grew somber. "Why *are* you here, Apaay?"

The question sent her pulse into a stumble, and it kept stumbling as it gained speed. Muktuk hadn't any idea of what had happened to their village. The horror of those two months in the labyrinth, the six weeks wandering the North. Apaay did not think she had the strength to tell this man what had befallen his family.

"Maybe you should sit down," she said.

He didn't break eye contact. "I'm already sitting."

She blinked, came back to herself. He was right. They were both sitting. Well, that was good.

"Where's Chena?" he asked, an edge to his voice.

"I don't know," she whispered.

A feeble laugh, coarse with disbelief. "Apaay." He looked away to gather himself, took a breath. "Where's my sister? Where are my parents?" He turned back to her. "Why are you here by yourself?"

"The Face Stealer came."

"For Chena?" Horrified.

"For Eska." She stared into the fire and did not feel the slightest hint of warmth. "I went after him."

So she told him of Yuki and the Face Stealer and their cavern of darkness. She told him of Eska's stolen face, but nothing beyond it. There was no mention of the polar bear Unua she had killed, nor of her shaved head. No mention of Masuk, the scarred, forgotten prisoner, or Ila, with her gentle soul. No mention of Nakaluq, whose life she had sacrificed in exchange for Chena's freedom, and who she had buried in the frozen earth. But she did mention Chena. And she mentioned her unborn child, too.

For long minutes, Muktuk did not speak. This knowledge dragged at his handsome face, worry tightening his jaw. The older man, thankfully, had made himself scarce. "So Chena's alive?"

"Yes. At least, I believe so." The Face Stealer had said as much, promising to take her to a safe place when Apaay had agreed to the blood oath. Then again, he'd said many things.

"And my parents?"

Apaay couldn't say it. She dropped her eyes.

Muktuk recoiled as if she had slapped him across the face. Hunching forward, he pressed his fists into his eyes, the strain of his body evident. Apaay almost touched his back before deciding against it. "I'm sorry, Muktuk." Her voice thickened, but she had cried herself dry. "I'm so sorry."

"Give me a minute," he managed.

He needed time. They all did. Apaay would have given him space were she not too weak to stand. So she peered into that edge of dark pine, the shadows shrinking in fear of the firelight, and tried to ignore the sense of someone watching her.

"You're sure you don't know where she is?" Muktuk asked.

"Somewhere in the Atakana." Maybe. She couldn't be sure if Chena was in the same location as Ila and Masuk, who she had last seen in one of the wide, sloping valleys of the great mountain range, or her family.

He rose and speared his fingers through his hair. "I need to go after her. What if she's hurt? Or the baby?"

Apaay touched his arm, pulled him back down onto the log. "You need to stay here with your family."

"She's my sister."

"Yes, but your wife and son need you more." Apaay fought the churning in her stomach. *I'll find her.* She almost said it. It would be the most convincing lie.

"You don't even know if she's alive," he said. "She could be dead."

"Chena's not— She's not—" The words collapsed noiselessly. How did she know her friend wasn't broken at the bottom of a ravine? She didn't.

So she said, "We'll figure out a way to bring her back." Whether alive or dead, Chena's body would be returned to her remaining family. As for Yuki and the Face Stealer, she didn't know where they were. She knew nothing of his motives, or hers. But they had been born from the same waters, the same darkness. "There's something else."

He waited, fear glinting in his eyes.

"The girl who destroyed our village is still alive." Needles hissed as the wind threaded through the trees. "You need to prepare for the worst."

The fire was dying, and neither made any move to tend it. *Let it die, then,* Apaay thought numbly. *Let it be surely, quietly smothered.*

He rose to his feet. "I need to warn the other villages."

She struggled to stand as well. "I'll come with you."

"No." He pressed her back onto the log. Apaay couldn't fight the strength of his hands. "You've done enough. More than enough. You would be doing me a huge favor by helping Kia with the baby while I'm gone."

It wasn't what Apaay had hoped for. And what had she hoped for? It wasn't as if she had the strength for a long journey.

But that made sense, she supposed. It might even be wise to remain here for the time being. She could help Muktuk and his wife until she thought of a way to find Chena and Ila, until her courage returned, until her faith rebuilt, until she rid herself of the shame surrounding what she had done.

Yes, she supposed she could.

← 2 →

This was the Wood: cool shade; a spread of trees; the beautifully warm, beating heart of perpetual summer.

A haven.

After weeks spent exploring the grounds, Ila had a clearer idea of what, exactly, the Wood was. In the most basic sense, it was a world contained from the outside, tethered to the Face Stealer's power. Beyond its barrier, winter raged upon the North. Inside these protective walls were high meadows and creeks running through lowlands, places to get lost in, places to find oneself. There was warmth and sun and summer, as though the long night did not exist, not here at least. Ila had come to understand it well enough to know she'd never learn all of its mysteries.

It was a forest, yet a vast, complex edifice, too, with rooms and hallways and cozy chambers draped in vines or carpeted in tender grasses. A symmetry of nature and man. As well, the land itself was sentient, for it sensed her intentions. If she desired to wash, all she had to do was step onto a path, and moments later, a break in the trees would reveal a slow-moving river. If she desired to sleep, she would cross miles in a single step and appear at her shut bedroom door.

The refugees had explained this to her during her first week here. Many had come to the Wood following the war decades ago, but the newest arrivals were Apaay's very own village. They had calmed Ila, ensuring her the Wood was safe, that the Face Stealer was not a threat here. There was food to eat, and shelter. There was no pain here, they said.

She had believed them.

Now Ila stood before the Wood's heart-tree—an ancient, towering pine that commanded the forested clearing from which it grew. She had returned to this tree every day for the past six weeks, ever since escaping the labyrinth with Apaay. Ila had spent her life without direction, and now she was seeking it out by feeling, the way one does in the dark. Or rather, seeking out someone in particular.

Ila circled the trunk until she came to a clearing on its other side. Light spilled through the forest opening, splashing against the grass, striking the edge of a young woman's jaw as she slashed her staff through the air, around and around in some particular pattern. Tulimaq, she was called.

They had met weeks ago. Sweaty and soiled and dragging a half-conscious Masuk up the mountain, snow clinging to her legs and boots, Ila had reached the frozen lake where the Face Stealer had told them to go. There, they had waited, fatigued, yet free of Yuki's reach. Two massive doors had materialized before them, the ivory of bone. Ila shoved, and they tumbled through the doorway into the place she now knew as the Wood, breathing hard, half-frozen, unable to move.

Moments later, boots had appeared by her head. Ila had blinked. Blinked again. It was light, not dark. Green, not white. Warm. A young woman scowled down at her, hands on hips. She had thin lips, a heavy square jaw, and broad shoulders that blocked out the sun. Her hair was pulled back so severely it looked as if her head had been shorn.

She'd yanked Ila up by the front of her parka. "Who are you?"

Ila, too exhausted to articulate clearly, had spelled out her name with one hand.

With no change in expression, the girl released her and pointed down the hall. "There's a bathing room the second door on the right. The water is hot." Then she'd left.

Now Ila was here again, subject to that chipped gaze as Tulimaq whirled and halted, hardly out of breath. Her gaze rested on Ila, whose cheeks flushed from the attention. In the shade, Tulimaq's skin looked dark as earth, with pink undertones. Then she turned her back, telling Ila without words to leave.

Ila should have left. It was obvious Tulimaq wished to be left alone.

She stayed. It had taken her almost two weeks to gather the courage to approach. This woman was strong. She could protect herself. She was not afraid.

Ila watched, intrigued, as Tulimaq handled her staff, which had a sharpened blade attached to one end. Together, they whirled and blurred, not separate, but whole. Tulimaq's stance was wide; it was rooted. Her soft-soled boots shifted the dirt as she stepped forward, back, side to side. Her sealskin clothing—the sleeveless top a mottled gray, with white strips cutting through the bottom hem—had been cut well for her frame.

Watching Tulimaq move confidently, Ila was strikingly aware that she did not move in such a way. She didn't walk through life without fear.

But oh, how she wanted to.

Fifteen minutes passed, and Tulimaq was again before her, strands of damp hair having pulled free to curl around her face. "Why are you still here?"

Ila dropped her gaze, lifted it when she remembered why she had come: to ask if Tulimaq would teach her. *You're very good,* she signed. *How long have you trained for?*

Tulimaq glared, and Ila bit the inside of her cheek to stop herself from inching away. What if Tulimaq didn't understand sign language? But she'd been surprised to learn that many who had taken refuge in the Wood were fluent, whether deaf or not. Apparently, hearing loss was not an uncommon occurrence in the North. She marveled at how large everything was—the world, this girl—and how it made her feel so small.

A vibration of the staff slamming into the dirt buzzed through Ila's soles. "You come here, interrupt my training, waste my time with menial conversation, and yet war grows closer with each passing day. Do I look like I'm interested in discussion?"

As if she'd been slapped, Ila lurched back. The shame throbbed through her. Perhaps Tulimaq was right. She had opened a door that had clearly been shut and entered a place she did not belong. The fault was hers.

I'm sorry was all she could say.

Ila turned into the trees and fled.

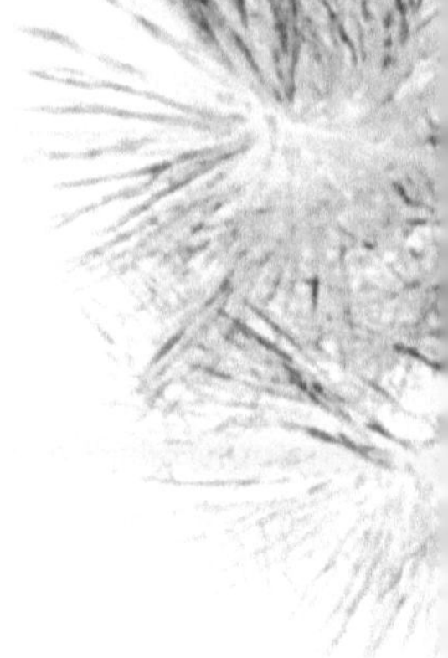

← 3 →

The cold touch of darkness jerked Apaay awake. With a gasp, she bolted upright, shaking so hard she almost toppled backward. Bracing a hand against the wall, Apaay hung her head as she fought for breath, sweat prickling her brow.

She had orphaned those boys.

Apaay hadn't meant to do it. Hadn't known it was a polar bear Unua she had fought in the labyrinth, one of the shape-shifting races that inhabited the North. She had tried to protect Ila, deaf and blind with the scarf extinguishing her vision, while Yuki and the Face Stealer devoured her fear with their eyes.

More than anything, Apaay wished she had the ability to move past those two months caged below the labyrinth, but it always came back to this: a memory. Ash and splintered bone.

Glancing around the snow house, she found Kia and her son still asleep. During the day, she helped Kia care for the baby, who'd been named after Kia's late father. In the evenings, she would rock him and murmur, "Little father, little father." Nearly eight months along with her second child, Kia had a limited range of motion. Apaay helped tidy their home and tended their clothes, stitching up the holes in their trousers and boots so Kia could sew more outerwear for the baby, who was growing daily.

The day after Apaay had spoken with Muktuk, he and a few villagers met with the elders about warning the other communities of possible threat. "I can help," she'd said, trailing him as he gathered firewood and dumped it in the communal pile, which families would use for their own cooking fires. Even if she didn't have the courage to go after Chena herself, she could still help in some way.

Exasperated, he turned to her. "Apaay, you can barely stand. You won't be able to make the journey. It's too far."

"Not true."

He looked to where she leaned one hand against a tree.

She snapped upright. "I can ride in the sled."

"We don't use sleds."

"What?" Come to think of it, Apaay realized she hadn't seen many dogs. "Then how will you reach the village?"

He pointed upward. "Through the trees."

The trees?

Following his hand, she tilted back her head and squinted through the dark. "I don't see anything."

"There are lines running through the trees. The momentum makes us go."

Apaay then spotted wooden platforms lashed to the thickest boughs, partially concealed by the shadowy canopy. Lengths of rope stretched between the platforms, bearing hanging slabs of wood, which she finally realized would carry the passenger at a declining angle to the next platform. "Why don't you use sleds? It would be faster."

"We don't have whale bones to use for the runners, and wood rots when it's damp. Plus, the tree roots get in the way."

That had been nearly two weeks ago. The party had yet to return.

As for everyone else, there was no news of Yuki or the Face Stealer. The pitied looks sharpened into ones of skepticism. Who was this slip of a girl swallowed by furs, with stooped shoulders and mistrust in her eyes? What had *really* brought her so far inland, so far from the sea?

She tried to explain to anyone who would listen that the in-between was not of this world. A labyrinth with shifting rooms, mirrors that allowed travelers to leave one place and reappear in a different one entirely. They tossed question after question at her, and when they asked why she hadn't been killed as well, why, out of everyone in her village, she had escaped, Apaay told them the truth. *I don't know.*

Lies, they said.

Apaay couldn't help what she had done or what had been done to her. She could only try to swim as black water closed over her head.

← →

"I don't know if I should stay here," she confided in Kia one night after the woman had put her son to bed. They sat on the wide shelf in her snow house, surrounded by the thickest, softest caribou pelts. Apaay knew they had been harvested during the month of sea ice forming, when the fur was too thick for clothing, yet perfect for blankets. Light gleamed along the concave ceiling, the snow tinged a silvery blue, like the heart of a flame.

Kia, who was sewing up a hole in her husband's trousers, paused and lowered her hands to her lap as Apaay kept watch over the oil lamp. "Why do you say that?" Silver threaded through the woman's long, wavy hair. She was close to ten years older than Muktuk, who was seven years older than Apaay. Relationships with large age gaps were not uncommon for the Analak, especially considering how small the communities were.

Apaay trimmed the mossy wick to even out the flame height. As they were inland, Apaay hadn't expected a lamp in Kia's home. Muktuk must have brought the lamp over from the coast when he moved. "In case you haven't noticed, no one believes anything I tell them." Without Muktuk's return to support her claim, why should they?

The woman's eyes were kind, and maybe a little guilty, too, at her own beliefs. "You have to admit, it's a vast claim."

Apaay sat back, unable to protect herself against the sting of Kia's words. It seemed she could still feel some emotions. "You don't believe me?"

"I do. I definitely do." Kia laid a hand on Apaay's knee. "Give them time. If what you say is true, then we must hope this girl didn't reach the other villages. But no one has ever heard of such a person. Don't you think it's a little odd?"

Of course it was odd. Yuki was like no one she had ever met. She was a girl, and yet so much more than a girl. Who was she, Apaay wondered, and where had she come from?

"I don't have all the answers," Apaay said, returning her attention to the lamp. It was a thing of precision, lamp tending, for it must be nurtured at all hours of the day to ensure it did not extinguish. "If I did, do you think I would be here?"

"I know. You're afraid for Chena and your family." The lamp's yellow flame warned of poisonous air, so Kia poked a hole through one of the snowy walls until the fresh air returned the color to a healthy white. The temperature was not cold enough in the Aatu for ice houses, which were what Apaay was used to. "Will you go after Chena if Muktuk returns with information on the Face Stealer's whereabouts?"

That had been her intention, long before she'd ever come to this place. Apaay had told herself she would find the people she loved, and they would flee beyond the Face Stealer's reach. But that had been months ago. The guilt and shame of what she'd brought upon her village had broken that promise, because it was her fault, all of it.

It had been fragile to begin with. Sometimes, she was afraid to *breathe* too hard for fear that all would come crashing down. Finding Muktuk had been happenstance. She had sought death in that cave.

Kia awaited her answer.

Last she had seen Chena, chains weighed down her wrists and ankles. They had been so free before, that day on the ice. What if Apaay went to save her and she failed—again?

"I don't know," she whispered.

"Apaay." Leaning forward, the woman grabbed her hands so Apaay was forced to look into her eyes. "No one else knows how to find them."

"I don't know where they are." Somewhere in the Atakana, that she knew.

Kia frowned, shoulders slumped in quiet defeat. It was true. To uncover any sign of life among the Atakana's exposed peaks, least of all a pregnant girl and a shadow demon, would indeed be an ordeal. "If what you say is true and these people do have Chena, who will save her?"

Tugging her hands away, Apaay pulled her knees to her chest. She desperately wanted sleep. But more than that, she wanted to feel awake again. "What if I try to help Chena and something worse happens to her? I don't want to risk her life, or the baby's."

Quietly, Kia said, "So you will do nothing?"

Apaay lifted her dull-eyed gaze. Stared for a moment. If doing nothing prevented her from imparting additional harm, wasn't that the better choice? "I'm going to collect more wood."

Kia didn't try to stop her, but Apaay sensed the woman's concern as she slipped on her mittens and drew the parka hood tighter around her face, still too ashamed to reveal her shorn hair to Muktuk and his family.

Once outside, the central fire drew her near. The pit of char was so large she could lie stretched across its center and not touch the ring of stones. Muktuk had informed her the central fire was never extinguished. Always, it burned, a light for those lost, and for those to welcome home.

Forcing herself to turn away, Apaay headed deeper into the forest, snow crunching underfoot. In the time it took her to walk two miles from the village, Apaay did not pick up a single fallen branch. She kicked at them with her boots, a burn warming her legs as she pushed herself into an aggressive walk, feeling a strange desire to run until she collapsed. She had recovered from her hypothermic encounter weeks ago, but the weakness lived inside her these days.

Since fleeing the Face Stealer, she'd wondered if things could have turned out differently. It had begun with Eska. It had ended with the ruination of her home. What would have happened if Apaay had played by Yuki's rules? Bartering for Chena's freedom— had that been the point of no return? Or her escape?

The tree cover was so thick it blotted out the moonlight. The scrape of branches sounded like the stricken caw of a bird, and the temperature continued to drop.

Apaay decided she had gone far enough, quite far enough, and was heading back when she heard a snap.

She froze. Breathed deeply to clear the lightheaded tendrils invading her awareness. Something watched her, though she could not see what it was. She did not know these woods.

Apaay began retracing her steps, walking faster, clambering over a fallen tree.

The second snap sent her running.

The swift crack, the plunge into silence, was final, both a question and an answer. Where? Here. When?

Now.

She was running on instinct alone. It was hard enough navigating the snow without falling, but trying to locate the shadowed impressions her boots had made? She could think of nothing but the cold. The blister as it filled her lungs, and the respite as it panted out of her mouth. Apaay hadn't considered taking a weapon with her, and not because she didn't think it was important. She had not touched a weapon since sliding that bone dagger into Nakaluq's still-beating heart.

The snow gave way beneath her. No footprints. She must have taken a wrong turn.

Fighting to pull free of the snow suctioning her legs, Apaay clamped down on a flare of feeling. A bottomless, glassy fear. The wave of emotion was so unexpected it shoved her up and out of the drift, and she bolted, running toward the fire that was too far off. She spotted an outcropping of stone: a cave.

Apaay scrambled up the rise faster than she thought was humanly possible and crouched behind a rock, the air smelling of ice and animal musk. Shadow coalesced inside the cave, and it took a moment for her vision to adjust. She closed her eyes to listen. Nothing. Then—

Her eyes snapped open on a sudden inhalation. Winds boomed beyond the mouth of the cave.

She was not alone.

A wolf, its coat a pure and unending black, snow dusting the slope of its shoulders, stepped free of the tree line.

Apaay grabbed a rock near her feet and shrank against the wall. Eyes of palest yellow gleamed. Its long legs were like swift-running waters, the dark head ducked against the score of wind. It closed the distance between them with predatory intent.

Apaay inhaled silently through her nose, teeth clenched to prevent their chattering. By nature, wolves were not aggressive toward humans, but this one was separated from its pack. It must have stalked her all the way from the village. She hadn't noticed. Why hadn't she noticed? Back pressed against the wall, she considered her options. The only way out of this cave was through the entrance, where the wolf stood.

Apaay tensed in anticipation of an attack. The rock sat heavy in her hand. She would drive it into its skull if needed. "Stay away from me," she growled with surprising viciousness. "Stay—" Abruptly, her voice cut off. She gasped as the wolf shifted.

And became man.

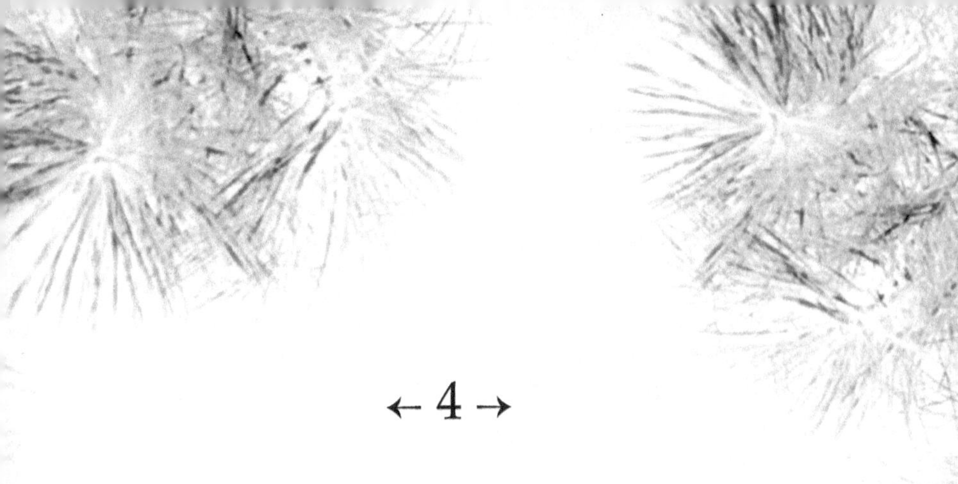

← 4 →

The eyes were no longer yellow, but green.

And violet.

And gray.

A rumble of power swept through the cave, shadowy tendrils wrapping around Apaay's legs and arms, another swath draping over the back of her neck, close as a lover. She couldn't move. Those eyes pinned her against the wall, their shifting hues visible in the watery gray light. She had a rabbit's heart.

"You—" The word shriveled and died.

Slipping his hands into his pockets, the Face Stealer stepped farther into the shelter, the movement thrumming with honed focus, a quiet lethality. Only when he stopped in front of her did he murmur, "Hello, wolfling."

Apaay swallowed to bring moisture to her mouth. He was exactly as she remembered. Hair black as the sea in winter. Bone structure that looked as if it had been forged by some dark god. She had traveled for weeks through multiple blizzards in an attempt to mask her trail. It hadn't done a thing. The cave, which was already small to begin with, now felt downright claustrophobic in his presence. Who was he? Cunning. An animal and a monster. Cold. So cold she wondered if even a fire could warm his heart.

"Aren't you going to say hello?" he asked, smoothing the wrinkles from his parka. "I traveled all this way to see you, after all." He peered at her from beneath soot-black lashes, and wicked laughter flowed from his mouth.

The smoky tendrils floated away from her limbs to cling to his upper torso. It had been so long since she had felt anything. She welcomed the adrenaline even as she loathed its source and the reminder that were it not for him, she would not have escaped the labyrinth alive. This demon, who had destroyed *everything*. And he was here.

With a burst of speed, Apaay bolted for the mouth of the cave. Never again would she find herself in one of his webs. She would seek safety elsewhere. She would vanish, become nothing, become wind.

She was there, on that edge of ice and stone. The wind tugged at her clothes, ruffling the fur of her hood as Apaay lunged forward.

And smacked into a wall of depthless shadow.

Apaay staggered back, chest heaving with confusion and something uglier, something that raked claws down her spine, drawing from her a cold sweat. She could no longer see outside. Darkness blocked her way out, trapping her here—another hell, a prison of stone.

"No," she whispered. "*No.*"

Apaay launched forward, clawing at the barrier, the strange, insubstantial material shifting where she made contact, like ripples in a pool. She could feel it, the resonant hum of its power contained in the opaque layer. Her fingers curled into hooks, gouging into the substance to reach the other side. She would rip a role through the void, shred this otherworldly fabric until her nails were bloody and her fingers nubs of skin, but it wasn't working, and she was near frenzied with panic. Apaay rammed her shoulder against the surface. The taste of iron was sharp on her tongue.

Apaay whirled around to face the demon, hand fisted against her tightening chest. "Let me out," she croaked.

His smile had vanished. "I want to talk."

"I don't want to talk to you," she spat, trembling so hard she knew he noticed. "I don't even want to *look* at you." But she was. She was looking at his dark, alluring beauty, and hated herself for it.

The Face Stealer's attention drifted down her body in a closed assessment, bumps puckering her skin where his eyes touched. He tilted his head, focusing once again on her face. Another smile, sharper, crueler than before. "Now, we both know that's a lie."

She would kill him. She would really, truly kill him.

A hair-raising shriek rang in the enclosed space as Apaay lunged. Weaponless, near collapse, it didn't matter. She wanted him to *feel*, as she did. How her heart was a clenched fist that would never dare open again.

But as Apaay's fingers brushed his chest, he had already materialized in another area of the cave, enfolding himself into the shadows to move from place to place. Momentum sent her crashing into the opposite wall, and the force ripped through her joints. Apaay whirled with a near-feral growl. His eyes glittered with what might have been mirth.

She had promised herself back in the labyrinth that she would kill him, and she had come to pay her dues.

She ran for him again with the same result, only to find him gone, her hands clasping around air where his neck had been moments before. Apaay grew short of breath. Now he was at the back of the cave. Now the front.

"We can do this all day," he said, winking in and out of existence. He moved so fluidly there was only a shroud of his materialization before he flickered out like a lamp flame.

Apaay braced her hands on her knees, fighting the water's cold drag. Then his breath ghosted along her nape.

She whirled, fueled by a vengeance so blistering, she was less surprised by the flat of her hand making contact with his cheek and more surprised that he didn't incinerate at her touch. Her palm stung through her mitten. That felt good. *Really* good.

Apaay snagged him by the collar before he could overcome his shock and sent them tumbling head over heel onto the ground, grappling for control until she straddled his waist and shoved his head against the floor, the fingers of one hand curling inward, nails biting into his forehead and scalp. In the other she held a knife, its point digging into his throat.

His pupils expanded, trying to swallow the chill, distant green of his irises as he studied the dagger she'd snatched from his waistband. They both knew he could vanish at will, yet he did not. It was that curiosity of his. A sick fascination. "You're not the first person to want to shove a knife through my throat, but like I told you before—" The smile twisted from one of cruelty to one of mockery. "I am very hard to kill."

She wondered briefly why that was as he leaned forward, forcing the knife deeper. Flesh split and peeled.

Her hand trembled. She wished it wouldn't. Apaay didn't want to appear weak to someone as powerful as him.

"Do it," he whispered, challenge blazing in his eyes.

Her fingers twitched against the hilt. "You don't know how badly I want to," she said lowly. A drop of blood rolled down his warm brown skin, disappearing below his neckline. She had to look away. "But I'm not like you," she seethed through her teeth. "Because when given the choice between love and fear—" Keeping her hand steady on the knife, Apaay leaned forward. "I choose love."

The knife clattered onto the ground.

He clucked his tongue. "Pity. I would have thought you'd enjoy carving me up. That was certainly the case with that polar bear Unua."

Apaay's breath stilled. "You sick, horrible—" A sob tore from her mouth. "*Thing.*" Her fist shot out and connected with his cheek, snapping his head sideways. Apaay did it again. Faster, harder, bloodier, she drove more force behind her blows, into his face, his chest. Skin split along her knuckles, a welcome pain.

She caught his temple, the bridge of his nose. Then his chin and jaw. Words poured from her mouth. Monster, thief, nightmare, poison, filth, horror, demon, demon, *demon.* The next strike slammed the back of his skull into the stone, and still he did not raise his hands. Apaay's blood crackled through her.

"Fight back." The words were a hoarse scream. "Fight back, you bastard!" His face was a bloody sight. The fury felt like it was burning holes through her lungs, but Apaay knew that no matter how much she hurt him, it wouldn't take back time, wouldn't bring her people back, wouldn't make this shame go away.

She drove another punch into his jaw. The Face Stealer didn't try to stop her. He took the beating, every painful, bloodied pounding to his flesh in utter silence. His nose streamed blood, as did his lower lip, split from where she had smashed it into his teeth, where red now sank into the crevasses between. It wasn't enough. She wanted to break his face. Apaay waited for the crunch of cartilage, but it never came. She was too weak.

The punches slowed as exhaustion finally set in. Shoving away from him, Apaay tripped toward the back of the cave and collapsed, bowing over her bent knees, feeling as if she was coming apart at the seams. The Face Stealer was truly the most hideous, revolting man she'd ever had the displeasure of meeting. Ever.

But he was not fully man, was he?

The Analak did not interact with the five Unua nations. It was less of a peaceful coexistence and more of a pretending their worlds were separate, though they shared the land. The shape-shifting races had lived in relative peace alongside one another until the Polar Bear Empire had begun expanding its territory two decades ago. Suddenly a life of peace became a life of war. A year of fighting led to a scarred earth, a divided North. Mistrust and dissent poisoned the waters. The Polar Bear Empire left rubble and bones smoking in its wake. And Nanuq—

Apaay's eyebrows tugged together. The name rose from a hole in her memory.

She remembered why that name had sounded so familiar when Yuki first mentioned it in the labyrinth.

Her people considered Nanuq the master of all polar bears. Only he had the power to decide whether a hunter succeeded in killing one of the large white carnivores. If her memory was correct, he had played a significant role in the Polar Bear Empire's invasion of the Western Territory. The once-great Wolf Kingdom had been razed to the ground for reasons unknown, their people slaughtered.

Except, it seemed, for this demon.

What did this mean, that he had revealed his true form? She assumed the Face Stealer would not expose his heritage to anyone for his own safety, but maybe it wasn't a secret. Maybe Yuki had known who and what he was.

"You were the one watching me through the trees," she said, and took a breath. A hard thing with the constriction in her chest. "You are both animal and man."

Steeling herself, Apaay pushed to her feet and turned to face him. Blood smeared his face, the skin split along his brow bone, the swelling beginning to take effect. His eyes, an electrifying blue, brimmed with white heat, the color brilliant against the nut-brown hue of his skin. She saw what she had not seen before, unaware of his true heritage. The predatory intensity of his gaze. Predatory, because he *was* a predator. It was unearthly, his beauty.

But perhaps that was his curse. To hold such terrible beauty, and to be hated and feared by all.

"You," she said, "are wolf Unua."

Shadow pulsed in time with his breath, twitching as if agitated. "I am."

"I thought the wolf Unua had been wiped out."

"We were." A pause, as if he was considering how much to divulge, though his expression remained blank. The Face Stealer was nothing without his secrets. "Some, however, managed to escape."

"How many?"

His eyebrows lifted, then drew together. "The Wolf Kingdom was once a nation of one hundred thousand strong." Wrath uncoiled behind his eyes. Apaay took a startled step backward. "After the war, I estimate less than ten thousand survived."

So few. "Where are they now?"

"In hiding."

Apaay crossed her arms and stared at the wall. "Why did you follow me?"

"You mean you haven't guessed? How disappointing." A wisp of darkness grazed her leg, and he smiled as she recoiled from the touch. "I'm here," he said, "to call in your blood oath."

← →

Hours later, Apaay leaned against the cave wall, near sleep. The Face Stealer reclined against the opposite wall, one leg outstretched, the other bent at the knee with his wrist placed atop it, utterly at ease aside from the swelling of his bloodied face. His eyes were shut, his chest rising and falling. Clearly, he did not share the same worries of lowering his guard in her presence.

The mouth of the cave remained cloaked in shadow. She had refused to comply with his request, so he had refused to let her out.

Apaay should have known the demon would call in his debt. Upon learning of Chena's capture, she had asked him for aid. A foolish, albeit desperate request. Blood to blood and palm to palm, Apaay had vowed a blood oath, binding her word to his blood in exchange for Chena's freedom from the labyrinth. So long as he was alive, she was bound to carry out her promise.

On bare feet, Apaay padded to the ever-shifting curtain. She'd removed her boots earlier, as their dampness had grown uncomfortable. Now that the way outside was obstructed, the cave had warmed from their body heat and breath. Apaay set her jaw. They would likely remain here until she agreed to fulfill the blood oath.

She lunged. The substance sucked around her with a humming power before spitting her back out. She tried again, scoring the fabric-that-was-not-fabric. Ambient light kept the cave from a total eclipse, but being trapped in the dark, with *him*— Panic clamped rough hands around her.

"You'll wear yourself out doing that," the demon drawled from behind her.

"I'm not going with you." Whatever horrible favor he wanted from her, she would take no part in it.

"Don't tell me you're going back on your word." His laughter made her want to smash something. "No matter how many times you try to leave, it won't let you pass."

"Why?" Apaay looked at him, her gaze as flat as her voice. The back of his head rested against the wall, the column of his throat deepened by the shadow cast from his chin and jaw.

He watched her through a slitted gaze and shrugged. "Because I don't will it. My power is but a handful of clay. It is my mind that shapes it."

Apaay touched the barrier, watched it shy away before it poured over her hand. It was no longer cold, but warm. "Are the shadows a part of you?" They didn't seem separate to her. Often, they trailed him or made an appearance when he experienced a stronger emotion, she'd noticed.

"As much as your breath is a part of you."

His tone drew her attention back to where he sat. It had almost sounded guarded.

"Fine. I'll just wait until your power drains." Nothing in this world was infinite. Sooner or later it would deplete and she could escape.

"Then you'll have a long wait," he said. "The source of my power is so vast that it will replenish itself long before it runs out."

Pulling away from the barrier, Apaay strode back to her side of the cave. "So you're wolf Unua," she stated, gauging his reaction, "but you're also a demon. How is that possible?"

"I was wolf Unua before I became the Face Stealer. I'm still wolf Unua, but now I have this other responsibility to uphold."

"Responsibility meaning ruining lives?"

He didn't respond, not at first. "I chose this life. So whatever burden I must bear, I won't turn from it."

He chose it? To become . . . *this*? Then his mind was even more debased than she had first believed. She thought of Eska. Apaay had never, not once since leaving home, stopped thinking of her sister. "Do you choose the faces you steal or is it random?"

"It depends." He stretched out both legs, crossed them at the ankles. "Often, Yuki would order me to take certain faces. I could not refuse her. Aside from that, I can take any face I wish, can give any person any face I wish, at any time I desire."

"And my sister's face? Did Yuki tell you to take it?" She waited, poised on an edge for his answer.

"If I say no, will you attack me again?"

Apaay swallowed, feeling ill. If she was interpreting things correctly, why had he targeted Eska's face? What need did he have of it? "I'm not carrying out your damn blood oath."

"You can't escape the bargain you made, Apaay."

For a moment, all was quiet. Originally, she had intended on carrying out the blood oath. She would have done whatever it took to free Chena. And then, slowly, it hadn't been about survival. She hadn't cared anymore. She had only wanted things to end, to be at peace. "And if I refuse?"

He made a sweeping gesture before him. "Try it, if you're so inclined." The faintest smile curled the edges of his mouth. "I dare you."

Maybe this was one more of his games, but Apaay wanted to crush him so badly that she did not care if she was playing into his hand. "You can't force me to do anything, not without my agreement."

"That's the thing," he murmured. She thought she might catch fire from how brightly his eyes burned. "You already gave your agreement."

Apaay remembered exactly how that conversation had gone. He'd taken advantage of her desperation when she hadn't been in a position to consider the consequences. "I didn't have a choice."

"There's always a choice."

"What was the choice? My friend's death and the death of her unborn child, or Nakaluq? Is that the choice you're talking about?" Apaay tried to smooth her ragged breathing. She felt too close to breaking completely. "Whatever I chose, it would have always ended in death. I won't do it."

"Will you not?" Abruptly his eyes changed, became fervent and knowing, as he slowly rose to his full height. "You will carry out the blood oath," he intoned. The air shuddered. It wasn't the darkness of fear, but of a coaxing, gentler quality. One that Apaay *wanted* to listen to. "Your promise was given to me, and this debt will be repaid."

She felt it then. The first stirring in her blood.

Whatever it was—the demon's power, his will, the tether connecting them through the blood oath—it flooded her veins, taking control of her body with frightening familiarity.

She felt its intention as if she could see the Face Stealer's guiding hand. He could compel that will to curl around her bones, make her limbs move any way he wished. He could sink claws into her mind and force out of her mouth a scream, or a song, or babbled nonsense, or her shameful secrets and fears. It had been only seconds, but already Apaay was fighting that pull, struggling to remain separate from the power encompassing her body.

Say no, she thought. *Tell him you will not carry out the blood oath. That it is severed and no more. That he can take that oath and shove it down his throat.*

At his soft chuckle, her chin snapped up. As soon as their eyes clashed, power slammed into her like a battering ram, buckling her knees. The pressure in her mind pushed against her eye sockets. How was he not destroyed by the power contained in his body? It was tearing her apart with little effort.

Say yes, said the voice, *and all this will end.*

Sweat dripped down her face from how strongly she fought the intrusion. *Refuse,* her mind whispered.

Apaay shook her head. She opened her mouth to speak the words, but her throat constricted, forcing the air back into her lungs. She tried again and choked. Tighter and tighter, his power squeezed. Her grip was slipping.

A muscle popped in her jaw. "I—" She bowed farther over her knees, the last of her resolve crumbling under a wave of despair. He was too powerful. "I accept."

His power released her. Strange, how parts of her felt empty where that rush had filled her.

Apaay turned away, her stomach churning. She did not realize how tightly fear had twined with her grief, neither distinguishable from the other.

"What is it to be, then?" A muted question. "Will you force me to strip as Yuki did, toss me out into the snow?" She swore the wind pounded on the other side of the black divide, demanding she be cast out. "Will I fight an opponent I cannot best? You can't take my hair, as that's already gone." The dark strands fell messily across her forehead.

The Face Stealer was uncharacteristically somber. "I know you don't believe me," he said, thumb pressed to his lower lip as he studied her, "but I do not desire to torture you. Do you not think you've suffered enough?"

She said nothing.

Pressing his fingertips together, he regarded her with a cool gaze. "Yuki, as you know, stole something of mine, something of value. I need your help in retrieving it. In return for your efforts, I offer you my protection."

It surprised her, the favor he asked. She had expected something a little more bloodthirsty. "I don't want or need your protection."

"And your family? What of them? I find it strange that you have not asked after their well-being since I arrived. They are safe and in my care, in case you were wondering."

It felt like pieces of herself were being slowly frozen over. She hadn't asked because she was too afraid of facing them. Knowing they were safe put a fraction of her mind at ease. She assumed Chena, Ila, and Masuk were in his care as well. "You will bring me to them?"

"They are housed at the Wood. That is our destination."

"The Wood?"

"My home."

Apaay had not realized he had a home.

Breathe, she thought. To look into her parents' eyes and see disappointment, disgust—it would break her. "What exactly did Yuki steal from you?"

"That is the question of the hour." He gave a resigned shake of his head. "Unfortunately, I can't tell you. And before you decide to gouge my eyes out," he said, and she didn't think he was joking, "let me explain. Yuki cursed me. Until the object is retrieved, I can't tell you anything about what led to its disappearance, nor can I tell you what it is."

"But I can't find it unless I have that information."

"I know. It's quite clever, actually. Yuki does have a flare for the dramatic, in case you hadn't noticed."

Oh, she'd noticed.

Apaay rubbed at a spot on her forehead, frowning. Why was he coming to her now after all this time? Why not as soon as they'd escaped the labyrinth? If Apaay thought she'd get an honest answer, she would have asked him. "So, what, I'm supposed to look for something when I don't even know what it is I'm looking for? That's impossible."

"And? Don't tell me you're not up for the challenge."

"Like I said, I don't really have a choice, do I?" Apaay muttered, reaching for her damp boots. Except she found them dry and warm, as if they had been sitting before a fire.

Apaay glanced over her shoulder. The Face Stealer stared at a point on the wall, seemingly deep in thought. As if sensing her gaze, he turned. Saw her holding her now-dry boots, having not slipped them on yet.

"Can't have you suffering from frostbite," he explained. "You'll need both your feet in order to carry out the blood oath."

After a moment, Apaay tugged on the boots with shaky hands. No matter how deeply she breathed, it didn't feel like she could get enough air. The only person Apaay loathed more than herself was this demon, and the only thing she hated more than her pathetic existence was his power over her. The fact remained: The only way to free herself was to complete the blood oath.

And then? When all was said and done, what came after? She didn't know. But above all, Apaay and her family would be free. She swore it.

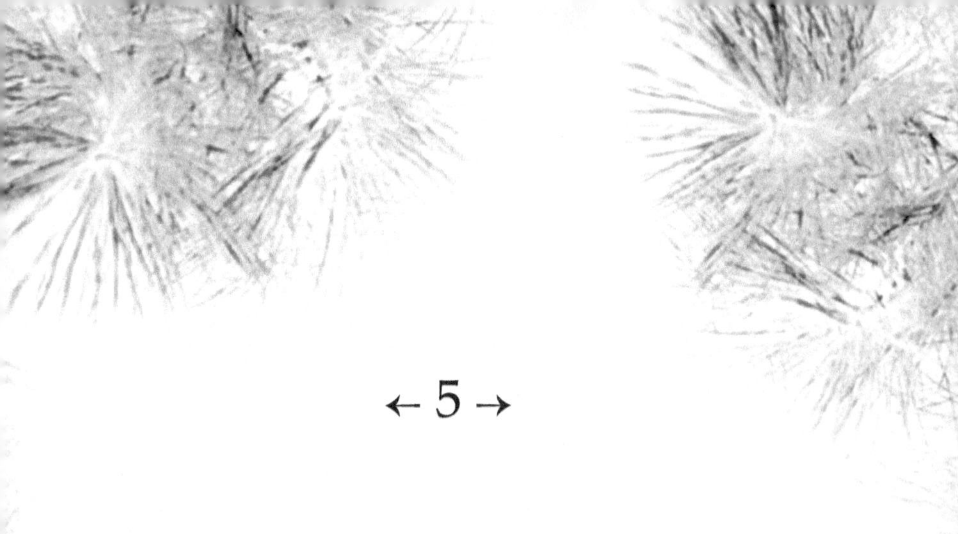

← 5 →

After waking with the sun, Ila was hungry. She was always hungry these days. The slight fullness of her face was new but not unwelcome. She could still count her ribs through her skin.

The spread of food in the breakfast chamber was fresh and inviting. The space itself housed small round tables covered in dyed cloth, and chairs that were actually oversized mushrooms in various sizes, some tall and slender, others squat, with caps wide enough to seat five people. There were wooden bowls heaped with shiny blackberries, ripe and swollen with juice. A second piled high with blueberries, which had the most pleasing sweetness. An assortment of nuts. And of course, thin strips of seal, whale, and caribou meat. Ila hadn't known any other foods existed aside from meat until her arrival at the Wood.

She was reaching for extra blueberries when a tiny creature appeared—one of the Keepers of the Wood. No taller than her hand and generously plump, it had a miniature leaf hat perched lopsided on its head. This Keeper in particular wasn't fond of Ila, for she had accidentally broken a glass her first day, much to its frustration.

As she dropped the berries onto her plate, the Keeper lurched forward, slapping her wrist with its miniscule hand. "Save some for everyone else."

Ila returned its glare with one of her own. She imagined its voice to be high and squeaky. *No one is here but me. And the food refills itself.*

"It won't if you eat it all!"

A pause as she considered how to respond. In her opinion, it was always best to speak the truth. *I don't like you.*

Its beady eyes widened. "I don't like you, either!" Its violent outburst sent the leaf hat tumbling.

At least they could agree on one thing.

With a huff, she strode toward her table and spotted Masuk hovering in the doorway, looking reluctant and uncomfortable. Ila set down her plate.

"Have you seen Apaay?" he asked.

Slowly, Ila shook her head. *She's not back yet.* Eight weeks had passed since she had seen her friend. Ila was starting to worry something had happened to her.

"If you see her, can you tell her I'm looking for her?" His unscarred eye watched her, the pupil narrow as a speck of dirt.

She hesitated only a second. *I can do that.*

He left before she could wonder about his arrival.

It wasn't that she disliked Masuk. How could she dislike someone she didn't know? But he was shrouded in secrets, and that made her cautious. She'd barely seen him since their arrival. He kept to himself and didn't engage in conversation. Ila, meanwhile, spent her time exploring the Wood or helping around the refugee camp. Sometimes she gathered firewood or collected water from the creek. Other times she watched the Analak women participate in their tattooing ritual. They were all healing. She tried not to judge Masuk too harshly over keeping his distance.

Once Ila finished her breakfast, she sought a new path to explore. As it was summer here, she wore lighter skins and the soft boots she'd found in her bedroom, cut to exactly her size. Ila had been walking for nearly ten minutes when she paused, the air wavering around her. She looked over her shoulder to where the trail bent out of sight.

Something was telling her to go back.

Ila hurried back the way she had come, taking care not to trip over the exposed tree roots. She emerged from the green tunnel in front of where two figures stood. The first she recognized as the Face Stealer, who she hadn't seen in weeks, his expression quietly livid. Snow, already melting in the heat, dripped down his arms. The second figure she didn't recognize.

Then Ila peered closer. No, she *did* recognize her. As the girl's head lifted, Ila rushed forward, short of breath. Apaay was . . . She was . . .

Apaay? she signed in uncertainty.

The Face Stealer vanished in a blot of darkness.

Placing her hands on Apaay's shoulders, Ila drew the girl toward her. She pushed back the hood. Looked into her eyes. There was nothing. No spark of recognition. Her face was little more than skin stretched over bone, gaunt, haunted. Her lips were dried and cracked with blood.

As she drew Apaay into an embrace, Ila noticed how much weight her friend had lost. She could feel the girl's shoulder blades and the vertebrae of her spine through the parka. Apaay did not embrace her back.

She held Apaay for a long time, fighting the feeling of something being wrenched open inside her, and the panic at having no idea what to do or how to help. *What happened?* Ila asked as she drew away. Gentling her touch, she brushed fingers across her friend's cheek and tried not to take it personally when Apaay flinched. Something had happened in the time since they had last seen one another. In the labyrinth, there had still been some fight to her. Now there was not even an inkling of that.

Apaay's chin wobbled before she turned away, staring off into the distance. "I need to see my family. He said they were here."

Gripping Apaay's shoulder, Ila turned her back around. She did not appreciate the sight of her friend's back. *I can bring you to them.*

A vague nod was her only reply.

As Ila took her friend's hand, she noticed Apaay still wore her mittens. She slipped them off and stuffed them into Apaay's pockets, as one would do for a child in need of undressing. Then Ila drew her down the path that led to the edge of a meadow. The lavender flowers were as tall as their knees, rustling sweetly as they parted the sea of yellow-green stalks.

We're almost there, Ila said. *It's just over this hill.*

They began their ascent. When they topped the grassy knoll and looked down at the scatter of tents, Apaay froze beside her.

What is it? Ila asked.

Apaay looked like she had seen a ghost. The pulse ticked in her neck, and her breathing shallowed out, a tightness drawing near her mouth, the skin pallid. She thought Apaay might faint, but then she blinked, shook her head. "Nothing." Fingers alighted on her pocket. They trembled. "I was reminded of something. A . . . different hill."

← →

Ila's hand in hers barely registered to Apaay. She remembered a situation very much like this one, in the white, in the cold, with smoke in the air and a fear like she had never known turning her blood to ice. Her stomach, heaving and roiling. Sweat dripped down her armpits as a feeling of suffocation swept over her.

"I need a minute." Apaay jerked away, covering her face with her hands. Her back expanded with a halting breath, a shudder, the air choked.

Less than two hundred yards away, her family waited. She had not seen them in nearly five months.

How did she begin to explain to them why it had taken her so long to come home? They would see her blood-soaked hands, smell the ash of their ruined village on her skin, and know she had brought about its destruction. Her shame had driven her far, far away, yet the promise she made to them had brought her back: Return Eska's face no matter the cost.

The cost had been too great, in the end. Her greatest fear was that they would look at her and see a stranger.

Did they know of her debt to the Face Stealer? Now that she had reached the Wood, he would send for her, though she didn't know when that would be. How would her parents react knowing she was subject to the demon's power?

Gently, Ila turned her around. Apaay dropped her hands.

You don't have to meet with them today, Ila said, compassion in her gaze. *If you need more time, they will understand.*

"No." Her throat worked, and she touched her shortened hair. "It's time I face them." With that, she descended the hill, leaving Ila to follow.

With each step closer, Apaay grew stiffer, her steps leaden, slower and slower. Her people had built their community here, at the far reaches of the meadow. The tents butted up against the tree line, which provided shade. The dizziness grew worse with every step, past and present colliding. The meadow grasses were gone, the ground gray, and the people gone, too, the air eerily still.

Yet here they were, those who had managed to escape. Strangers in a strange land.

The only thing grounding Apaay was Ila's hand in hers. She gripped fiercely, holding tighter than she ever had before, and still it felt as if she would float away.

They came to the central fire, which flickered in the center of the village. Beyond the fire were her parents. Mama, stitching what looked to be a new pair of trousers, and Papa, carving a new knife. They were full-bodied, compact where Apaay was malnourished.

It felt like something out of a dream. Their surroundings were all wrong. Their faces, hammered into hard things. The slump to their postures suggested they carried the weight of the overhanging sky upon their backs. Apaay stopped and stared, and she was still staring, waiting to *feel* something.

Then Mama looked up. The hide slipped from her hands. "Apaay?"

Hearing Mama's voice snapped something in her chest. She bit the inside of her cheek, held her ground, though she wanted to flee. Her knees knocked together. Mama's eyes, a beautiful brown, and her sleek hair. And beside her, Papa, his head lifting, hope in his features, but also fear, the exhaustion that came with obsessing, questioning, picking apart this one thing he couldn't control: *Will I ever see my child again?*

Mama lurched forward and ran, Papa not far behind. Apaay let them come. She heard Ila suck in a breath as her heart kicked up, then slowed. Relief. Worry. It was all there, spilling out of them.

And there they were, arms around their daughter, Apaay's ear pressed to another beating heart, each thump saying *alive, alive.* Apaay fought to swallow and whispered, "I'm sorry."

"No, naaja," whispered Mama. "There's nothing to be sorry for."

Papa's hand came to rest on her shoulder. He'd wrapped his arms around both wife and child, his face buried in his wife's neck. They clutched their daughter so tightly. They would not let go.

Other refugees had gathered to watch. The Analak, their hair long and full of shells and bones, huddled in a smaller group.

"Naaja. My naaja," said Mama, weeping openly.

Resting her head on her mother's shoulder, Apaay closed her eyes. She still hadn't returned their embrace. "I know, naajaluk. I know."

Apaay wished it did not have to be this way: her, them. The line, however, had been drawn. She did not know by whom, but there it was.

Papa said in shock, "Your hair."

Apaay flinched and pulled away. She couldn't do anything about it now. It was done.

A few moments passed before she spoke. "I did it," she whispered hollowly. "I got Eska's face back." They had not believed she could do it, but Apaay had proven herself ten times over.

Mama gasped, hands lifting to cover her mouth as Papa gaped and said, "You . . . got it back?" He stumbled, nearly collapsed at their feet. "How?"

A cold, thin smile curled Apaay's mouth. "It doesn't matter." Not now. Not anymore.

"And this will work?" Mama asked with so much hope Apaay's heart would have shattered were it not already broken. "She will be saved?"

"She will be." This promise, followed by a slow, glassy blink. "Where is she?"

The flaps of a nearby tent flew open, and out stumbled Eska, faceless, followed by Chena, who was swollen with child. Chena held back as Eska shuffled forward, waving her arms to feel out her surroundings. Apaay made a soft sound. The Face Stealer had done this.

The moment Eska fell against her body, Apaay touched the crown of her sister's head. "Naajatikaaq." Real. This was real.

Apaay pulled Eska's face from her pocket, staring at it for a moment. She had kept it safe all these months.

Gently, she pressed the limp skin to her sister's bone structure.

Now there were real tears on Eska's cheeks, a quivering mouth as she burrowed into Apaay's thin embrace. In her periphery, Mama and Papa shoved forward. They took Eska into their arms. They sobbed and promised never to leave her. They thanked the gods for returning their daughter to them—both of their daughters. It was a beautiful moment, truly, yet Apaay could hardly stand it. She tried to linger for as long as she could. The truth was, being in her family's presence hurt more than anything.

She pulled away. "I'd like to lie down. I'm tired." She and the Face Stealer had traveled far.

Mama exchanged a worried glance with Papa. "Our tent is right over there," she said, pointing.

The tent wouldn't do. Apaay needed space.

That's when Ila came forward. *There's a room set up for us, if you'd rather stay there.* Ila looked uncertain. Her eyes darted from Apaay's parents to her sister and back to Apaay.

It sounded better than the tent. She nodded. "Thank you."

Ila said, *Down that path, the last room on the right.*

The feeling of eyes on her back trailed Apaay until she reached the far side of the hill. Then she ran. Faster and faster, she tore through the tangled halls, with the trees acting as pillars, and a closed ceiling of light-dappled leaves. The first door she came to, Apaay shoved it open.

Masuk looked up from where he sat on a bed low to the ground, a glen of golden light surrounding him. Apaay must have entered the wrong room. And yet, it was the first time she had breathed all day. Masuk knew of the caged life. He understood, somehow, the shame of her lack of hair. But most importantly, he did not know her at all. That was significant. If he did not know her, he could not know how far she had fallen. He knew her only as she had been, a prisoner in Yuki's labyrinth, not quite an animal, and desperate enough to do terrible things.

Apaay made it only a few feet into the room before her legs folded. It was too much. She sucked in one breath, and the next one was harsher, and the next one even more so. Facing her family had been the hardest thing she had ever done. She thought there would have been *some* relief.

"Please," Apaay gasped, shrinking further into herself. She did not realize she was sobbing, one palm pressed to the floor to stop herself from falling over, the other covering her face. "I can't— I need—"

What did she need?

To not feel so alone.

Masuk came forward to touch her chin, gently. His ravaged face pinched in concern, the scarring along his left cheek shiny in the morning's glow.

"My family." She fell against him, clutching his arms so fiercely it felt as if her fingers were claws, digging into his skin to keep him there, as if she might burrow inside him and become someone else. "It hurts. It hurts so badly."

"I know," he said, and rocked her as they knelt. "I know."

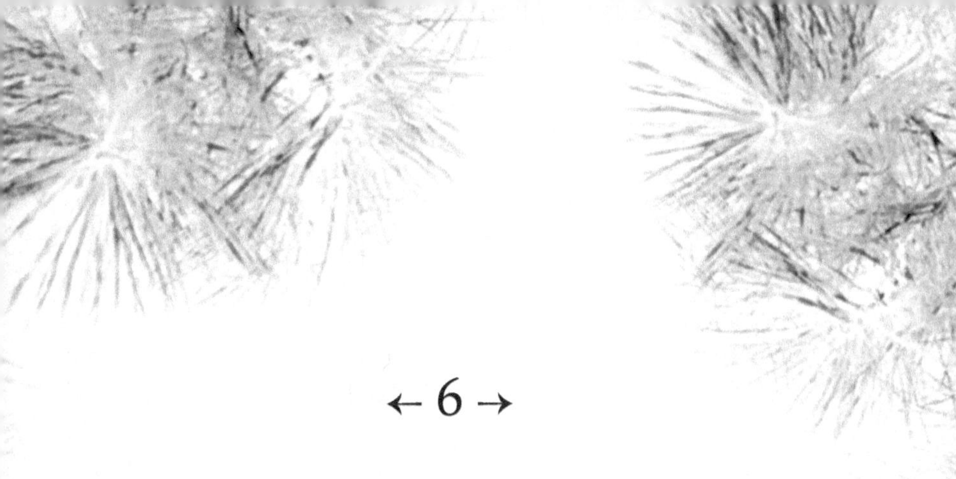

← **6** →

In the following weeks, Ila gave Apaay her space. She did not seek her out. She did not stop her when their paths crossed in the labyrinthine passageways, the ones with vines climbing the walls and roots crawling along the ground, and the air smelling of a thousand leaves. If Apaay did not join Ila for breakfast, then she must be eating with Masuk. If she did not return in the evenings, then she must be with her family. Ila told herself these things. But it felt wrong, as if she had fallen asleep to the sun and woken to the moon.

Their reunion had been reduced to a dark, seedy thing, unspoken and unacknowledged, something one let slip and disappear. Ila let it rest, partially because she didn't know how to broach the subject, and partially because of what she'd heard of late. Rumors. Apaay's community left in ruin, save a handful of people who had survived, now refugees of the Wood. Yuki, a terror of a girl, whose eyes were far, far older than the child she appeared to be.

Ila didn't think she had a right to complain. She hadn't lost what Apaay had. Still, this was a large, swallowing place, full of enchantments, and she was a girl without family. The loneliness was never far off.

One night, Ila didn't return to their bedroom until sundown. Shadows engulfed the area near the trees, but moonlight puddled onto their bedding furs, turning the browns and reds and golds into colors of the earth. Out of curiosity, she touched Apaay's bed. Cold. The flower she'd left on her friend's pillow remained untouched.

Ila wondered so many things. She wondered why Apaay sought Masuk when they had fought together in the labyrinth. What could Masuk give Apaay that Ila couldn't? Had Masuk lost family as well? Or could he simply navigate the world in a way she could not? That was half the reason Ila hesitated in reaching out. If she did not know what Apaay experienced, how could she know how to help?

After everything Apaay had endured, Ila should be happy her friend had found relief in someone, but the thought brought a weight to her chest. Apaay had not grown up needing Ila, but in such a short time, Ila had grown to need her.

Ila stared at her friend's mattress, no longer tired. Instead, she returned to the hall, the corridors lit by orbs containing many of the glow bugs, the ground strewn with leaf litter. Across the hall, Masuk's door was shut. He must be asleep.

Choosing a path at random, Ila moved through the tendrils of light and darkness. With a brief thought, Ila found herself at the heart-tree where Tulimaq had been training when she'd stumbled across it weeks ago.

In the gray dusk, light settled on the forest floor, backlighting a silhouette of fluid movement.

Feeling bolder than she had in recent months, Ila strode into the clearing with more confidence than she felt and planted her hands on her hips.

With a liquid spin, Tulimaq whirled around and skimmed the end of her staff along the floor. She did it again, faster. The blade was a piece of bone, curved as a crescent moon, swift as it descended toward the earth. "What do you want?" she asked without stopping her exercises.

Ila stepped forward, hands moving before the question was finished. *I want to learn how to fight.*

Tulimaq slowed, stopped, her square jaw etching a deep shadow against her neck. Sweat stains bled beneath her arms where the thinner cloth had dampened. Ila noticed that the girl's arms, while thin, were bare and well-muscled, bronze beneath the sheen of moisture.

Ila pulled her gaze up to Tulimaq's. A scowl stared back. "Don't waste my time, girl." She resumed the pattern of exercises.

Ila retreated a step before remembering she didn't want to be that person anymore. She would have to retrain herself to react differently. It started with believing she deserved this chance, no matter her upbringing, and ended with a push against the invisible ties binding her. *How am I wasting your time? I want to fight. I want you to teach me how.*

The staff was whirling, whirling, then the butt flicked out and smacked Ila in the abdomen, sending her into a bush.

Branches caught at her clothes and hair. She struggled to disentangle herself, well aware that she must look the fool. Ila didn't want to be cowed anymore, or weak. She had been born into the life of a mouse and wished she had been granted life as a serpent so that she might shed this old skin. If she did not take a step forward, she would always be in the same place.

The spins slowed, became lazy, almost insultingly so. "You're not ready."

Eventually, Ila freed herself from the bramble. *I am ready.* Adamant.

"No." Firm. "You're not."

Tulimaq spoke with a surety Ila didn't have. *You know nothing about me.* Suffering had made her strong. It hadn't hardened her, not like this.

The end of Tulimaq's staff hit the dirt. "You can train your body to become strong, but if your heart is weak, it will make no difference."

The first flicker of uncertainty. *My heart isn't weak.*

"Yes," said Tulimaq. "It is."

When Tulimaq next turned her back, Ila didn't try to stop her. She left without a word, pressure pounding at her temples and behind her eyes. Hurrying back down the path, Ila rounded a corner and abruptly plowed into a hard object.

She would have fallen if large hands hadn't come to rest on her shoulders. She tensed. "Steady," said the Face Stealer.

Concealed beneath the broad-leafed trees, the shadows were so clustered Ila couldn't read his lips without squinting. Only his eyes punctured through, silver as the moon.

He began to move around her, but Ila shifted to block his path. Additional light filtered through the canopy, offering her a clearer view of his expression. Not closed like Tulimaq's, yet not completely open, either. *Something on your mind?* he asked, switching to signing.

The better question was, what wasn't on her mind?

Ila studied the demon with new eyes. She had barely seen the Face Stealer since his return. Admittedly, she had avoided him, still unsure of how she felt about discovering Irnik had been but a mask. Even if his face was different, some part of her remembered the security of speaking to him in the labyrinth over the years. Ultimately, it came down to this: She wanted to be heard.

A lot of things. She couldn't get the words out fast enough. *I'm worried about Apaay. She won't speak to me. Doesn't seem to speak to anyone, really. Except maybe Masuk. I don't know. Sometimes I want to talk to her, but I'm afraid she'll push me away.*

My dear girl. He gazed down at her with a raised eyebrow. *I asked a simple question. I did not ask for your entire life story.*

Ila met his bland look with a furious one of her own. *If you didn't care for the answer, then why did you ask?*

A smile played upon his mouth. There was nothing but cold calculation in the curve of his lips. "You used to be so timid. What happened?" Despite the obvious condescension, he appeared more delighted than offended by her waspish reply.

Life happened. And death.

This man wasn't Irnik. Irnik had been generous with his time. The Face Stealer had an agenda. She'd be much better off seeking advice elsewhere.

She'd started to brush past him when he caught her arm, tipping his head toward a side room she swore hadn't existed a minute ago. After some consideration, she followed him into a densely wooded area with a star-studded sky of deep midnight. The Face Stealer led her to one of the cushioned chairs before settling across from her on a low-seated couch in a comfortable recline.

Ila swallowed, tapping her thigh with the tips of her fingers. She didn't have any reason to fear him, she told herself. If he wanted to hurt her, he would have done so a long time ago. *I want to learn how to fight, but Tulimaq won't train me.* The next statement did not come as readily. *She said I wasn't ready.*

There was a pause. *He.*

What?

The demon slung an arm across the back of the cushioned seat. *Tulimaq uses "he."*

A moment passed as Ila tried to process the Face Stealer's statement. *But Tulimaq is a woman.*

Tulimaq is not a woman, he said simply.

Ila sat back, a shaky breath catching in her throat. Her face warmed as her eyes burned. She truly did not understand the depth of the world she lived in. It made her want to crawl into a very large, very deep hole.

The Face Stealer's chest rose and fell on an impatient sigh. Black tendrils of power shifted across his shoulders. "You're not going to cry, are you?"

No, she snapped. Irnik had never been so callous, so conniving, so cruel.

He regarded her. "Well, go on." He waved a hand. "Why did my combat master say you weren't ready?"

It was such a small thing, spoken by someone who she neither knew nor cared for, but it hurt. *He said my heart was too weak.*

And what do you think?

She thought maybe Tulimaq had a point. Here she sat, speaking her worries to the Face Stealer and not standing up for what she believed in. Reverting to that helpless state. The young man had been right. She was running when all she really wanted was to be seen. And to be remembered when she was gone.

Briefly, Ila closed her eyes. She was finding it hard to look at this man, because when she did, she saw a different face. One she had believed to belong to a friend.

Her hands trembled. They hadn't shaken when she demanded that Tulimaq train her, but they shook now. *All those years I spent in the labyrinth.* She closed her eyes against the memory. It was an age before she opened them again. *Was it you? Were you Irnik the entire time?*

His response felt careful. *And if I was?*

All I want is the truth.

"The truth." Head tilted, finger tapping against one of the cushions. "The truth can be so many things."

The answer is simple: yes or no.

He shrugged, mouth a faint curve, as if he didn't care one way or another. "Yes."

She had to know. Had to know what had driven him to impersonate a guard, befriend her, lie to her and help her, comfort her and betray her, and, in the end, save her, save them all. *Why did you help me?*

In the striped shadows of the overhanging branches, he was like the fireweed flower, beautiful until one touched its poisonous thorns. In all the years in the darkness, Irnik had been the only bright thing. Something precious had been stolen from her at discovering she had grown to love a lie.

Ila wished she felt fury toward him. He had taken that brightness away from her. But she didn't. She felt only confusion. Where he had taken away one brightness, he had given her a light far more radiant: freedom.

"Because you were alone," he said, gaze heavy. "I didn't know how else to help you except by offering my friendship."

And were you my friend? she demanded, remembering how Irnik's face had changed to this one right before Apaay had been thrown into the water to drown. *Or was it just another one of your games?* There was cruelty in him, made sharper by time. She wouldn't put it past him.

He switched back to signing. *It was not a game to me.* Light cut across the bridge of his nose. The smile was gone. *It never was.*

The truth in that statement made her throat tighten. She didn't know what she would have done if it had been a game. *You could have helped me.*

Leaning forward, the Face Stealer propped his elbows on his thighs, long legs bent, hands clasped and hanging loosely between his knees. There he remained, a pillar of shade, motionless but for the rise and fall of his chest. Time trickled out, and Ila wondered whether the Face Stealer would, in fact, respond when he straightened and said, *I can see you are upset over the idea that I kept you in that cell, but I assure you, it was not done out of cruelty. If you must know, I did attempt to get you out of there once. You probably don't remember it, as you were very young at the time. I thought of bringing you here. I even went so far as to give Yuki a sleeping draught.*

She searched his face for deception, found chilling rage instead. *Did something go wrong?* Obviously, the escape attempt had not been successful.

No. He leaned back, though his eyes never left her. *I realized it wasn't the right time to leave. I had to wait. It was too dangerous to travel between the territories. I thought it safer to keep you in the labyrinth. At least there, I knew no one would harm you.*

Ila had no idea what he was talking about. She knew, however, that the matter was far more complicated than it appeared. *As Irnik, you said you found me, brought me into the labyrinth. Was that the truth?* She didn't want to hope. Thought it might be better to accept she'd never had a family instead of discovering her family had abandoned her.

Tilting back his head, he studied the moon. It was full and bright. Ila didn't think she'd ever get tired of looking at it. "It's getting late," he said as a shift came over him. "Don't you think?"

Ila sensed the change in the air but didn't know what it meant. She was wide awake. *No.*

"Well, I'm tired." He stood, giving her no room for argument. "This was a nice chat."

A hand to his arm stopped his exit. This was someone she could only push so far, and she was not willing to test his patience any further tonight. *Thank you,* she said.

He glanced at her hand before stepping aside. "Let's not make a habit out of this, shall we?"

Ila stayed long after he had left. It comforted her to know the Face Stealer had, at some point, attempted to save her from the labyrinth. His words confused her, though. Had he helped her escape, it would not have been the right time. He'd had to wait. Why? Wait for what?

Or . . . who?

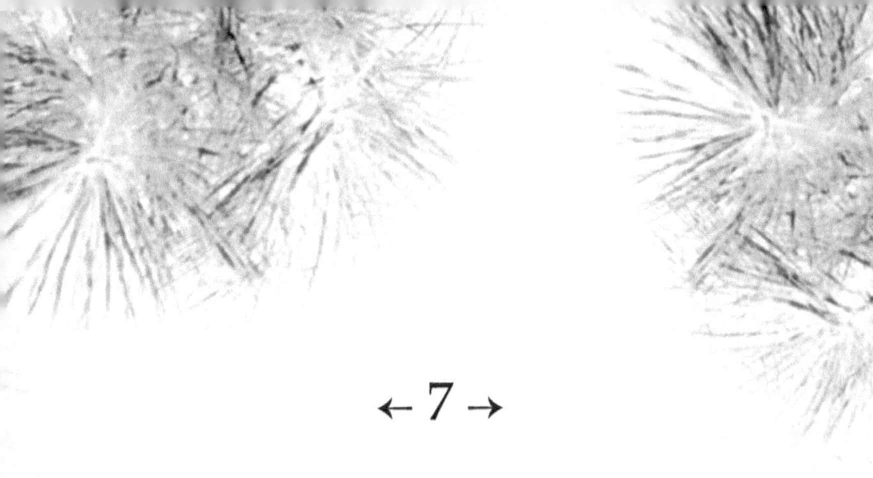

← 7 →

"Naajatik?"

Apaay jerked awake, a scream cramming her throat. Frost bit at her skin against the heat of pooling blood, an explosion of engulfing darkness. Already, her arms were swinging. Even after everything, a deep-seated instinct demanded she fight, though for what, she could not say.

"Naajatik. Naajatik!" Soft hands caught her swinging fists and lowered them against the blanket until her vision cleared and her struggles ceased.

Eska gazed down at her in concern. Quick, snapping eyes and a clever mouth. The face Apaay had returned to her.

A churning sensation claimed her gut, and Apaay had to turn away. She could barely look at her sister without remembering that she had almost been too late.

Inside their tent, five warm bodies slept atop a heap of blankets, the caribou-skin tent walls stirring in the warm summer night. Papa's snores leaked through the smoke of the nightmare.

Apaay fought down the heave of her stomach, not wanting to spew what little she had eaten for dinner across the ground. With the help of the other refugees, her people had managed to fell a caribou not far from their camp. The kill had been for all.

Apaay hadn't eaten until Eska demanded she put something in her stomach, voice shrill with mounting fear. So Apaay had swallowed a handful of berries. A mistake. The red juice had stained her fingers, and no matter how hard she scrubbed, she could not remove its lingering color.

A long moment passed before her stomach settled. The air did not hold the stale taint of mildew, but pine, fresh and crisp and utterly free. She was not in the labyrinth. She was lying on the grassy earth with her parents and Eska and Chena.

"You were having a nightmare," Eska said, fingers tightening on Apaay's.

Her throat ached to the point of pain. Originally, she had intended to sleep in the room she shared with Ila, but after spending so long apart, she thought it important to stay near her family, at least for a few nights. "Go back to sleep," Apaay whispered, tucking the blankets tighter around Eska's frame. Her eyes burned with fatigue, yet she was fully awake in her mind, fighting the exhaustion of her body.

She felt Eska settle against her back. "Whatever it is," her sister said in sadness, "you know you can tell me, right?" A touch to her shoulder, of trying to call someone back when they were too far gone to hear.

Apaay watched the tent rustle as another gust blew. It was not Eska's burden to bear. Neither was her anxiety surrounding the blood oath. "What was it like," she whispered, "after . . . you know."

Her little sister released a slow exhalation. "It was empty."

The swallow caught in Apaay's throat. Somehow, she forced it down.

"I did not know hunger, but I remembered what it felt like. I could remember colors, and pictures and smells, but the memories were faint. I could hear Mama and Papa and the people of our village, of course, since I still had my ears, but I didn't go outside. I didn't want anyone to s-see me." Another breath. Eska was so strong. And Apaay was so proud.

"I knew you would come back for me," Eska said, her voice wobbling. "I knew you would."

"That's a lot of faith to put in me."

"I believed you could do it." Fierce and unwilling to bend beneath Apaay's doubt. "You fight until the end, Apaay. You do."

She didn't have the heart to tell Eska that she had almost not returned. Had it not been for Ila, she would have given up.

"I'm sorry about Lusa," Apaay whispered. The girl was not in the Wood. Neither were her parents. "I know how much you loved her."

"I only hope the end came swiftly for her. She did not deserve to suffer."

Eska fell silent, unaware of how those words slowly choked the life from her older sister. She could not have known Apaay blamed herself for the deaths of their people. How to explain? She didn't want to drag them into her dark world, didn't want them touching the filth of her memories. Time seemed to rush forward and pull back all at once, so much like the tides she hadn't seen in months. She couldn't seem to find her way back to the person who had once dreamed.

"I will carry your heart in my heart," Eska whispered, the words a painful memory.

Apaay could not stop the flinch and forced herself to remain still.

She did not respond.

← →

After Eska fell back asleep, Apaay sat up, taking care not to jostle Chena in the process, and crawled outside of their tent, into a night that was as clear as it was warm. As soon as she escaped the tent walls, the tightening in her chest eased. Sweat slipped down the curve of her neck as she moved through the tents dotting the clearing, toward the path leading to her secret grove.

When the sadness became too heavy, she came here to quiet her thoughts. She would kneel at the edge of the shallow pool, dip her fingers into the chilled water, and beg the gods to help her forget.

It had become clear her village did not plan on leaving the Wood anytime soon. She'd spoken to Mama and Papa about the issue. For every reason she gave to leave, they gave her a reason to stay. The Face Stealer had saved them from Yuki's slaughter attempt. There was plenty of food here. Protected by the barrier, they did not have to worry about additional attacks.

Apaay had just turned a corner when movement caught her eye, and she found Masuk picking his way through the brush. As he lifted his head, he spotted her and froze. "Apaay?"

She couldn't muster up a smile. "I just—"

Immediately, he stepped forward and gripped her hand. "I know."

With Masuk, she never had to apologize or explain. Most days, words weren't needed. They would sit in his room in companionable silence, or walk among the stones smoothed from the river, each deep in their own thoughts. It was enough.

He shifted nearer, his eyes catching the light. The shadows on the ground crept atop his boots, making them appear as if they were damp from snow.

"Couldn't sleep?" she asked.

A slow shake of his head. Masuk didn't fare much better these days, plagued by his own nightmares. He often wandered as she did, exploring the grounds.

Moonlight bathed the wide planes of his face, the puckered hills of his scarring, shiny with sweat. "I've been thinking," he said quietly as she followed him through a field of wildflowers. Soft white petals opened to the sky. "When we escaped the labyrinth, do you remember if the Face Stealer took any faces with him?"

She did not need to close her eyes to return to the cramped room with the low stone ceiling. It resurfaced almost immediately. "Yes."

Five faces had hung on the austere wall: Eska's, two young women, and two young men. The Face Stealer—posing as Irnik— had slipped the faces into his parka. "There were five. One was my sister's. I don't know who the others were."

"Do you remember what they looked like?"

She thought back and said, "One man had a cleft chin. Another had scarring on his face." *Like you.* "There were two young women.

One had a red mouth. The other was . . . I don't know. Gentle?" Upon touching that face, the skin had warmed beneath the pads of her fingers.

A bead of sweat slithered down Masuk's temple. "That's her," he said hoarsely. "The one with the red mouth."

She went still at the quaver of emotion. "Who?"

"A girl I once loved. Her name was Ain."

Without realizing it, Apaay touched the edge of his sleeve. "Why would the Face Stealer take her face?"

A corner of his mouth twitched, almost as if he might smile. "Why do the tides rise and fall? There does not need to be a reason. It is his nature."

"You speak as if you're familiar with him." Apaay studied the bones of his face, looking for a change. She knew little about his past. Masuk did not speak of himself when she came to him. He listened. That was all.

"We knew each other as boys. Once, we were even friends." There was an unstable quality to his tone, like the crack of ice underfoot. "But that was a long time ago."

Apaay was unable to conceal her shock. A demon and a prisoner? Friends? That couldn't be true.

Except, what had the Face Stealer told her back in the cave? Before he had become this dark figure, he'd been wolf Unua. If he and Masuk had been friends as boys, then that most likely made Masuk wolf Unua, too.

She wanted to press him for more information. The Face Stealer had betrayed his friend. Why? And for what?

"You know you can talk to me if you need to," she whispered, "right?"

"Can I?" He made a sound that was not quite a laugh. Apaay was suddenly aware that, no matter how grateful she was for Masuk's company, she did not know him very well at all. "I don't know if I can do that."

"You could try."

Masuk sounded like he was having difficulty breathing. "You know what trust gets you?" he whispered. "A knife in the back."

The way Apaay saw it, the only thing left after that was to be alone. It sounded so sad.

"The girl you loved," Apaay said, waiting until Masuk lifted his face, a tepid breeze tugging at her hair. "What happened to her?"

"I don't know. I don't think I'll ever get closure until I have her face in my hands and know it won't be trapped here, kept by *him*." The word cracked, said like the foulest of things.

This was why Apaay turned to him and no one else. Their hatred and self-loathing—it was the same.

"I know her face is here. I can feel it." Masuk tore both hands through his hair, the whites of his eyes flashing as he glanced around the wooded area. "It's killing me that he has her. Please," he begged, a man driven to the edge. "Will you help me look for her?"

The tension radiating from Masuk's form snapped against her body, as if trying to wake her up. "How?" she wondered. "I'm sure wherever it's hidden, it's hidden well."

"That doesn't matter," he retorted.

Apaay frowned in surprise. There wasn't any need for him to be pushy about it.

As if realizing his misstep, Masuk mumbled, "Sorry. That was rude." After another exhalation, he said, "The Face Stealer doesn't trust me. We . . . didn't part on good terms. I won't be able to search the spaces he uses, but you might."

Essentially, she'd be doing him this favor, plus searching for whatever it was Yuki had stolen from the Face Stealer. It was a lot to ask of someone. "And if you get her face back?"

"Then I'm going to return it to her, if she's even still alive. She deserves that much." His chest rose and fell. His hands pulled free from his hair, the strands brushing his cheeks and ears. "I'll leave this place. Disappear. Start a new life."

"Where?"

For a time, he was quiet. "Have you heard of the Banished Lands?"

She shook her head.

"People go there when they want to disappear. With conflict brewing, I figure it's as safe a place as any. Yuki wouldn't be able to find you or your people. Neither would the Face Stealer. Supposedly, those on the island cannot be tracked. You would be free of him."

It's what Apaay wanted: to cast off the demon's power. She'd promised herself as much after finding her village in ruin, watching the Face Stealer through the blurred snow and wind. She had returned Eska's face and found her family. So why was she still here?

If she helped Masuk find the face, he could lead her to a safe place for her people. The Banished Lands might not be their home, but they could begin again. At the very least, it was a new start in a protected area, one where hopefully war could not touch them. Anything was better than the Wood, where every movement of theirs was scrutinized.

That feeling trying to wake her—Apaay finally grabbed it, and the world tilted upright, sharpening into focus. For as long as she was touching this purpose, she could see. Her grip tightened. She would not let go.

"I'll help you," she promised Masuk, eyes burning with newfound purpose. "I will."

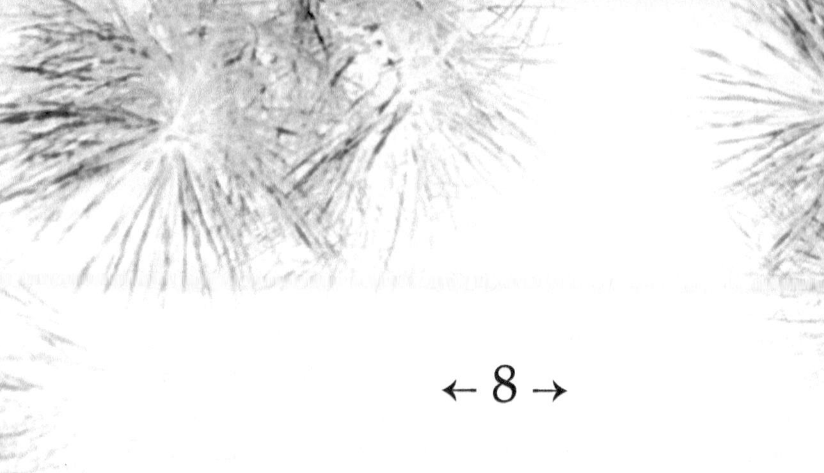

← 8 →

"Lovely evening," came a sleek voice from out of the dark. "Is it not?"

Apaay stiffened and whirled around, spotting the Face Stealer's silhouette off-trail after having parted ways with Masuk ten minutes before. Night veiled his face, though his eyes were piercing. A cool, calculating aquamarine. Light layers sewn of silvery-gray sealskin—both his trousers, which were tucked into his boots, and the short-sleeved maq for his torso—had replaced the heaviness of his caribou parka.

She asked hoarsely, "Here to finally collect on your debt?"

In the weeks since her arrival, she had seen the demon only once, and it had been brief. Apaay had watched him with hollowed eyes as he returned from somewhere beyond the Wood, dressed in winter garb damp from snow, a reminder that not all was warm and alive, that outside the Wood's barrier, the world was encased in ice, and would be for many months to come. She'd wondered when he would send for her.

Pushing away from the tree he leaned against, he sauntered toward her. Now that his wolf Unua heritage had been revealed, it was impossible to overlook the fluid movements. "You know," he said thoughtfully, "one might think you were hiding from your family."

Apaay hissed out a breath. "That's none of your business."

"Isn't it? As this is my home, it is absolutely my business." He stepped in front of her, blocking her view of the moss and shadowy green. "Your mother came to me. She's worried about you."

That surprised her. "You stay away from my mother," Apaay snarled.

"Or what? You'll kill me?" Pointed laughter. "You've already proven you won't."

She was beginning to regret that decision.

"Apaay."

"Don't," she snapped, bristling from the sound of her name in his mouth. "You have no right to address me. I'm fine, and I definitely don't need your pity. Or did you forget? *You* put me in this situation. *You* are the one to blame." Fire fanned her lungs and limbs, demanding that coiled, slumbering fury waken.

His focus dipped to where the heat singed her cheeks. She felt flayed open. "There are larger forces at work here. Forces you do not yet understand. I had to make difficult decisions. Going forward, it will be the same. What Yuki did to your village is only the beginning, and unless you help me find what she stole from me, it will become so much worse, for you *and* your people." A muscle slid in his jaw as he came to a decision. "You will come with me to find what it is I seek," he said, the words thrumming with power.

A rush of heat swept through her blood. Shoving down the gorge rising in her throat, she looked into his perfectly symmetrical face, those multicolored eyes. The blood oath ensured she would carry out her promise, and she could not slight its calling.

"Come." He headed down the path. "It's time to work."

← →

He took her to a tree.

And in that tree, a door.

And through that door, a staircase ascending through the hollow of the trunk, an elongated spiraling against the wood's smooth grain, which had been polished to a gleam. With her hand sliding along the curved banister, Apaay followed the demon up the narrow space, their footsteps ringing.

At the very top, he unlocked a rounded door, which led to a cozy lamplit room smelling of sap and paper, and stuffed with rows upon rows of shelves. Apaay braced herself against the wall from a sudden wave of dizziness.

"Books," he stated slowly.

Apaay nodded. That made sense. Books, not faces.

She pressed a shaky hand to her forehead.

Though the Analak's history was oral, sometimes Papa would return from his travels with a tightly bound scroll that had been traded on the Island of Kir. The written languages were not ones she had understood, of course, but it was a comfort to know similarities existed despite the differences in culture. That underlying need to preserve histories and things that were.

Moving to the nearest shelf, she pulled one of the books free, the cover falling open in her hands. She stroked a hand across the page. The books were lovely, wrapped in gold and brown skins or colored cloth, symbols stamped on the spines. Spaced between the shelves near the walls were alcoves carved out for a desk or large cushioned chair.

"What is this place?" she asked, replacing the slender volume and moving to peer out one of the windows. They were high in the trees, lost among the leaves. In the distance, water cascaded down the side of a rock face, silvery in the moonlight. The clouds made unusual shapes, like those the Analak might carve out of soapstone.

"My personal library."

Right. As if the Face Stealer had any interest in light reading. He probably used this material to gather information on his enemies. At least, that's what she would do. What she planned to do.

Masuk didn't have access to this room, but she did. If this was indeed the Face Stealer's personal library, she might be able to glean information about him, his motives, the secrets he wanted to keep. Such as where he hid the faces he'd taken from the labyrinth.

Wandering back to the shelves, Apaay asked, "This object Yuki stole from you. Where is it?"

He didn't answer, and with her back to him, she could not gauge his reaction. How he stood. If he had moved position without her noticing, perhaps melting into a clot of darkness somewhere in the corner.

Her fingers fluttered against a spine, then lay still. She stopped at the end of one of the rows and turned to find him watching her. The low ceiling gave the illusion of greater height. A stream of shadow settled across the breadth of his shoulders, having not been present a moment ago.

"Look," she snapped, "you're the one who wants me to find whatever it is you want me to find. So if that's the case, why don't you give me a hint so I know I'm heading in the right direction."

"I thought I made it clear I'm unable to do that."

"You said you weren't allowed to tell me anything about what led to its disappearance or what it is, but what about clues on how to find it?"

"I can't tell you that, either."

"So I'm supposed to scour the library without any idea of what I'm looking for?" Her incredulity soared. "What game are you playing here?"

He went to one of the shelves and selected a fat tome. "It's not a game." He dropped it in her arms, and she nearly tipped over from its weight. "I suggest you start here."

If she didn't know any better, she might think he sounded frustrated.

Apaay glanced at the book. The cover was animal skin, soft and pale. Someone had stitched the image of a polar bear on the front with darker sinew. "I can't read."

"Don't worry about that."

He was nearly to the door when she whirled around. "Where are you going?"

He stilled with one hand on the knob, as if surprised by the question. "I have a meeting."

"With who?"

Apaay didn't know exactly how to explain it, but when he answered her, it was from someone else, someone different. He had shed one skin and slipped on another, though his appearance did not change. His eyes were far older, and weary. "Yuki has a lot of enemies. It's imperative we figure out her next move to warn those she might harm."

The words slipped out without thought, so fierce was the desire to know. "And are you her enemy?"

His irises paled to the gray-green of algae clinging to the rocks in summer. "That would depend on what your definition of an enemy is."

"Someone who weakens you, harms you. Someone who manipulates you for their own gain. Someone who does not feel remorse."

The Face Stealer was her enemy.

He hadn't moved. "Then yes," he said. "I guess that would make me her enemy."

She couldn't decide if he was telling the truth. He was always so difficult to read. The sea was exactly the same. Quiet and lulling one moment, then ravenous the next.

Performing one good deed did not make one a hero, just as one poor choice did not make one a villain. But what about a multitude of horrible things? What about a lifetime? Maybe the Face Stealer had freed her from the labyrinth, but she could not forget it was he who had brought her there.

"Is she still at the labyrinth, do you think?" Apaay asked.

"Oh, I imagine," he said, slipping his hands into his pockets and rocking back on his heels. "Once she recovered, I also imagine she had a bit of a tantrum." He smirked. "I'm only sorry I missed that."

"And there's no way she can find this place?" she asked, watching his expression for facial tics that would allude to the lie.

Again, nothing. "I assure you, she will never be able to find it."

"Why?"

Pushing off from the door, he approached and stopped a few feet away. His power brushed along her arms, as if curious about the sudden interest. "So many questions today."

Apaay smoothed her features into blandness. She didn't want to give him reason for suspicion. She would take her family far away from this place, these people, this disquieting brewing of something she didn't understand. "I want to be sure my family is safe, that's all." It wasn't entirely a lie, but one wrapped in a truth would go much further in laying the groundwork for his trust. "I don't want Yuki to find them again."

"She won't. The Wood's barrier contains the most powerful of enchantments, which have been strengthened over the years. Imagine an onion, if you will. Layers upon layers of protections, each more powerful than the last."

That would make complete sense to Apaay, if she even knew what an onion was. Some type of fish, maybe.

"The effectiveness of the barrier lies in its obscurity. Yuki cannot find it if she does not know what to look for."

"So you're telling me there's no weakness to the Wood. That Yuki will never be able to breach it. That, theoretically, I will live out the remainder of my days without ever having to worry about war or death or pain." Her scathing tone revealed exactly what she thought of his claim. "Nothing is without flaws."

A slow, albeit reluctant, nod. "You're right. Yuki would not notice anyone entering the Wood, as I've manipulated the barrier to blend in with the surrounding environment, but she would sense anyone leaving the Wood, as my protection does not extend beyond it. That's why it's important to remain inside the barrier unless I can shield you separately."

A sudden thought made her heart thump in an erratic beat. For weeks, she'd been exposed on the tundra and taiga, prey to a predator she had not seen. "Did you shield me from Yuki?"

Removing a book from the shelf, he flipped through the pages. "I couldn't risk you ruining all of my carefully laid plans, could I?"

Apaay, still hefting the massive tome, curled her fingers around its edges, feeling the flutter of her pulse in her fingertips. Instead of answering him, she set the book on one of the desks. Her arms ached. "Do you think Yuki will join Nanuq if he reinstates the alliance?" The Face Stealer had warned the girl against it back in the labyrinth.

His eyes narrowed further, and she fought the urge to take a step back. She wondered, not for the first time, if he truly understood the intensity of his gaze. "What do you know about Nanuq?"

"My people worship him. The hunters, especially. Some say he is a god. Others believe him to be nothing more than myth."

"Yes," murmured the demon. "They say he is almost a man."

Apaay sent him an unreadable look. Since Nanuq was polar bear Unua, he could shift between his human and animal shapes at will. Perhaps that was what the Face Stealer meant by it.

"A few weeks ago," he said, "I got word from one of my men. Nanuq and Yuki have indeed been in contact. I fear that if they combine forces, they will be unstoppable."

The possibility sent a prickle of ice down her spine. "Did you know Nanuq during the war?"

"I've never met him. He hid behind the gates of his empire while his people fought and died for a world they would never be a part of." The Face Stealer tapped the book she had placed on the desk. "The thing is, he was not born into power. He was born poor, sickly. His parents passed on when he was very young. He was taken in by a neighbor until the age of twelve, when he then disappeared."

It was an unexpected turn.

"No one knew where he went," he responded, in anticipation of her question. "There were rumors, of course, but nothing is certain. Ten years later, he returned to the Polar Bear Empire, joined the army. Clawed and connived his way to the position of Master General, right hand to the king. Soon after that, civil war broke out." He stared out one of the windows. "Now, imagine, after a long year of fighting, you learn of an object that would bring you unrestrained power, thus ending the war between your people." Caught in the spell of his low voice, Apaay found herself unable to move as he stepped closer. "Do you think you would turn away from such a thing, knowing it would make you even stronger than the king?"

If she had been someone tempted by power, then no, she wouldn't turn from such an object. "Did he ever find the object?"

"He tried. With his promise to end the fighting, the war turned in his favor. The king's assassination followed not long after, and Nanuq took the throne. But he never found it." He was looking at her again. That strange light in his eyes she couldn't hope to read. "Would you like to attend the meeting? If you're curious about Nanuq, we'll be discussing him."

The question startled her, for she hadn't realized how engrossed she had become in this conversation. Apaay took a mental step backward. Sit in a room with people she did not know, listen to them drone on about the state of the North for hours? It sounded exhausting.

"No. War does not interest me."

This time, she let him leave.

Once the door closed behind him, she sat at the desk and opened the book he had been touching. The first page depicted a map of the North, the land sectioned off into the five territories. According to the map, the Polar Bear Empire—the Southern Territory—had expanded north following the signing of the treaty. Such was war. Such was greed.

With a frown, Apaay turned the pages. It was mostly writing, but there were images on occasion. Not that it mattered. She couldn't interpret any of it.

She flipped to a sketch of a man drawn in charcoal. The opposite page showed a rough rendition of a polar bear, the lines a touch frantic, giving the illusion of motion.

The polar bear Unua, a voice began, *are ambitious and enduring.*

Stiffening, Apaay whipped around at the demon's voice, yet found the library empty.

It came to her then. She couldn't read whatever language this was written in, so he would tell her the information orally.

Apaay bared her teeth. "Seriously?" she said to the empty room. "Despite what you think, not everyone enjoys hearing your voice."

His laughter only served to heighten her irritation. She wondered if he could see her, somehow, in this room.

Muttering a few choice insults beneath her breath, Apaay yanked the book closer and returned to research.

After a time, she forgot it was the demon's voice she listened to and fell into the lull of his narrative, the fall of one empire and the rise of another. After what felt like close to an hour of listening, Apaay set the book aside and chose another, this one about the Caribou Nomads. Their history was not nearly as compelling. They were isolationist and had not partaken in the war. She thrust that volume aside after ten minutes.

Apaay leaned forward to peer out the window. The canopy was an unending expanse of night-green and silver rippling beneath the wind. She thought of the things she was certain of in regard to this unfeasible task. Whatever Yuki had stolen from the Face Stealer, it was valuable. In addition, he was forbidden to speak of what it was, where it was hidden, or the events surrounding its capture. If Apaay had learned anything of him, it was this: He craved power. He thrived on acting as the guiding hand, shifting the pieces of a game to his benefit. Whatever object Yuki held, did it diminish the Face Stealer's power? And was it the same object Nanuq sought?

That would be too obvious, though she supposed it was possible. But if that were the case and Yuki sided with Nanuq, why not give Nanuq the object? Unless she had her own plans for it? Apaay hadn't found any mention of the object Nanuq had wanted to pillage for power, but there were thousands of books in the library. Who knew how long it would take her to go through them all?

Apaay returned to the stacks. This time, she wandered down a different row, the shelves stuffed with loose parchment, their edges yellowed and curled. She was reaching for a scroll when pain seared the back of her skull and migrated to her face. Gasping, she dropped to her knees. The scroll fell open.

With shaking hands, she brought the document into the light. The pain in her head lessened as she traced a finger over the inked illustration. There was a painted image of each of the five Unua nations in a circle: seal, polar bear, owl, caribou, wolf. Beneath that circle was a human silhouette in rough charcoal, the lines blurred.

Centered at the bottom of the page, she spotted two words she had nearly missed. The Face Stealer's voice crooned in her ear.

The Creator.

She had never heard of such a thing. The placement of the man beneath the five Unua nations was an interesting perspective, as if they were in some way connected. Creator of what? Or who? She could not begin to unravel its meaning.

Apaay didn't know how long she crouched there, studying the scroll, willing it to reveal its secrets. In the end, she stood and returned the document to its shelf. She would return to this impossible quest another time.

As she turned, however, the throbbing in her head crashed into her at full force. She approached the nearest window in a daze. Moonlight and tranquility awaited beyond. Yet when she reached out to touch the pane of glass, she found wood beneath her fingers instead, ravenous darkness.

Apaay stumbled back, staring at a door wreathed in shadow that had not been present a moment ago. Darkness licked at the air, stretching toward her as if it might curl around her limbs. *Open,* hissed a voice.

Squeezing her eyes shut, Apaay plunged her hand into the writhing mass and gripped the handle. When she opened her eyes, she found the shadows had retreated, the pain in her skull gone. Apaay tugged on the handle. Locked.

But somewhere in the Wood, the Face Stealer had a key.

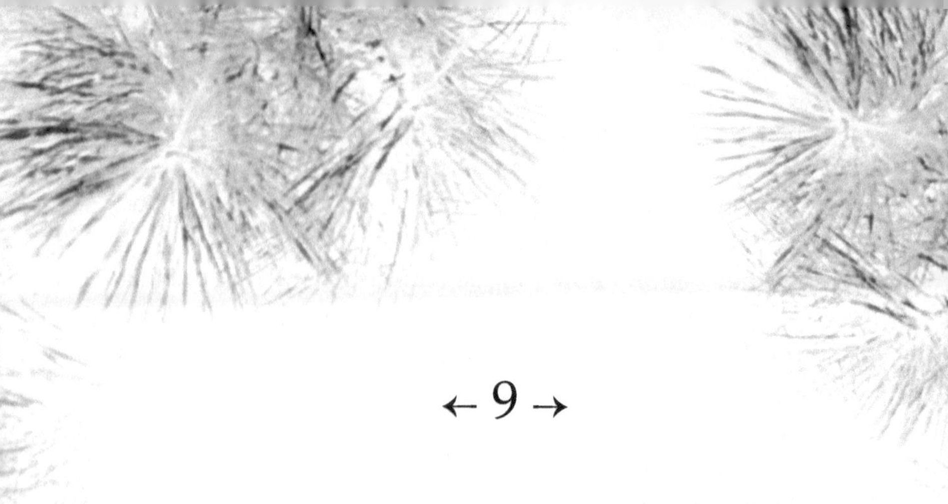

← 9 →

With a hiss of frustration, Ila tossed aside the stick she had been practicing with and kicked at one of the bushes. Her lack of skill was embarrassing, disheartening, frustrating, and made her want to stab something. Or a very specific someone.

Was it entitlement Tulimaq felt? Arrogance? The combat master had been nothing but rude since her arrival, and she didn't know why. His refusal to train her forced Ila into watching him from afar. Then she'd take her pathetic stick and move out of sight so he wouldn't see her clumsy attempts at copying his movements. What Tulimaq did was a dance. What Ila did was more of . . . hopping around and trying not to impale herself. Bruises swelled atop her muscles and bones, and scratches dotted her arms, but that did not stop her from trying.

Today, however, had been long enough. She could only make so many mistakes before doubt reared its hideous head. As time went on, she found the lack of certainty overshadowing her drive. It was a test to her resolve that she'd stuck with it this long. Ila would return tomorrow after a much-needed respite. Maybe the Keepers had left out some fruit to snack on.

As Ila turned toward the trail leading to the breakfast chamber, she stopped. A woman she had never seen before stood there, watching her.

Her stature reminded Ila of a flowering plant. She was tall, a slim brown stalk with a crown of white hair that had been cut against the sharp angle of her chin. Ila guessed her to be seven or eight years her senior. She wore something that resembled a parka in length, but it was sleeveless and had a slit running halfway up the front. Thin gray cloth had been wrapped around her arms, wrists to shoulders, and her calves were covered as well. Her most arresting feature, however, was her eyes. Amber gold and slightly uptilted in a heart-shaped face. Ila felt like a vole spotted by a bird of prey.

The woman's gaze roved Ila's face for some time. Hands clenched at her sides, Ila forced her chin to lift, her eyes to meet those of the woman. No one in the Wood would bring her harm. The Face Stealer had promised as much. Ila, however, was not used to the attention.

"Your weight is shifted too far forward," said the woman. "That's why you keep stumbling. I've been watching you for weeks now. You have horrible feet placement. Your handhold is pathetic. Your elbow keeps collapsing, and your frame will buckle at the first gust of wind."

If the words were intended to deter her, they didn't succeed. The woman had said nothing Ila didn't already know.

"Come with me." Turning, the woman vanished into the brush.

Ila's first instinct was to stay put. That was who she was. Her second instinct was to follow. That was who she wanted to be. It took a little coaxing on her part, but she hurried after the stranger to a cave with cool, bone-dry air. Blue light flickered in small glass globes attached to the glistening walls. The passage eventually opened into a large atrium with tables covered in tools, supplies—bones, glass, teeth, antlers, shells, feathers, rocks, sinew—and weapons in various states of completion. Stalactites made teeth of the ceiling, and small pools of water captured the blue lights in their dark centers.

Ila stood in the middle of the space awkwardly, wondering who this woman was and why she was here, as the woman in question sat at one of the tables and examined a splintered staff. Close to twenty minutes passed of this. It felt as if the woman had forgotten about her.

Ila approached the table, hovering a few feet away as the woman ran her fingers over the cracks in the wood. It was fascinating to watch someone work in complete concentration.

Then her hands stilled. She lifted her head, met Ila's confusion with a probing gaze. "Yes?"

Ila leaned her weight into her heels to put space between them. She almost didn't answer. It wasn't so much a question as a challenge. There was a force to the woman that was borderline frightening. *What am I supposed to be doing?*

A blink in response. "Watching me," she said, as if daring Ila to do otherwise.

The back of Ila's neck warmed. Reading body language and social cues, especially the subtleties, was hard enough for someone with little human interaction. The only thing Ila knew was to ask if she didn't understand something, whether or not the woman wanted her input. *Watch you do what?*

Those gold, unwavering eyes took her in. She muttered something Ila couldn't make out, but the girl guessed it wasn't anything positive. The woman gestured to the staff on the table. "What do you see?"

Ila looked to the weapon in question. *A broken staff.*

"Obviously," the woman said, baring her teeth in a ferocious grin. "Look closer."

Ila did as she was told. The only problem was, she didn't know what she was looking for. She didn't reply, afraid she'd give a wrong answer.

The woman stood with an outward huff of irritation. "Sit." She shoved Ila into the seat she had vacated. "I need to speak with Numiak about something. Study the staff until I return. Don't touch anything else, understand? I'll know if you do."

As the woman brushed past, Ila caught her arm. *Who are you? What is this about?* Had the Face Stealer put this woman up to the task? Was it because Tulimaq wouldn't train her?

"Study," the woman snapped, then melted into the dark tunnel.

Turning back to the staff, Ila pushed one of the pieces across the table. It had split right down the center. The edges of the wood were rough and fibrous. She pressed a finger to one of the points, wondering what it was the woman had dissected from the touch.

Two hours passed before the woman returned, her slender hands slipping into Ila's line of vision and pointing to the break. "See how the wood is darker here?" Ila nodded. "It's rotten. That's what caused the wood to snap. I was fond of this staff, too." She held up both pieces to the blue light before tossing them into a corner.

Hands planted on her hips, the woman regarded Ila with impatience, as if the younger woman was an inconvenience, even though Ila hadn't volunteered for this task. "My name is Kaan. I'm the weapons master here. Before you can competently utilize a weapon, you must first understand it. If you don't have the care for discipline or the drive to work hard, then leave now." The blunt ends of her white hair stirred as she crossed her arms. "I'm not interested in having my time wasted."

Ila didn't move.

"Good." Her smile was too sharp to be anything but downright terrifying. "Come back tomorrow. And this time, bring an appetite."

← →

Ila indeed returned the next day with an appetite.

She found the weapons master inspecting what appeared to be either arm or leg bones. She rapped a hammer against each one, her ear tilted downward. Then she placed them in one of two piles. The blue orbs flickered their pale light against the dark stone, and Kaan sat within the cave's heart, her white hair a beacon.

Turning to Ila, she asked, "Do you know what this is?"

Ila studied the weapon in Kaan's hand. It had a wooden handle as long as her forearm. Attached to the end was one caribou antler, the tines sharpened to points. She shook her head. Whatever it was, it looked deadly.

"This is a nigana." She flipped it into the air, caught it one-handed. "They are carved by the caribou Unua, a nomadic people and masters of weaponry. You will find no better craftsmen in the

North. Sometimes there are two antlers attached to the handle if they're small enough. This is the favored weapon of their people."

Ila accepted the offered weapon. It was quite heavy in the handle.

"Historically, these were agricultural tools used to aerate the soil of their food plots. The males' antlers are collected following the rut in the fall, the females' in the spring after they calf. As a tool, the antler is sought after for its lightness, strength, and diversity in shape. It must be dried at a specific temperature. They have forges in their winter capital, Nigun. It must also be filed down to an exact thickness, otherwise it will crack." Taking back the nigana, she set it on the table.

"Here is the talq." This weapon was shorter, more slender in the handle, with a curved piece of antler protruding from the end that had been shaved into the shape of a sickle. Ila flinched as Kaan slashed out with it. "Their women favor these because of their lighter weight. Are you following?"

Ila nodded, not wanting to miss a single thing.

"You will notice the weapons differ between the Unua nations based on the resources found in their environments. My people, the owl Unua, prefer our avian shape most of the time, so we have spikes that wrap around our legs in flight. On land, we use archery as a form of defense." She handed over a deadly looking arrow.

Ila ran a finger over one of the feathers. It was a light gray-brown color. *Do you use your own feathers for these?*

"Not typically, no. I much prefer goose primaries, which is what these are." Taking the arrow back, she continued, "The seal Unua utilize coral, barnacles, and sea urchins. The wolf Unua prefer bone, and the polar bear Unua tend to favor stone, as much of the Southern Territory is canyon. Although the stone is plentiful, their weapons lack the artistry you see in caribou Unua weaponry."

How do you know all of this? Ila wondered.

Kaan set down an enormous club she'd been holding as if it weighed no more than a pile of sticks. "I studied as an apprentice with the Caribou Nomads for over a decade. This was before the war. You spend your first year measuring the exact weight needed for a talq blade, your second learning how to sharpen an antler so its edge will sever a single hair, but no more. As such, there are only two with the highest mastery rank.

"Unfortunately, I had only reached the second rank before the treaty was drawn and the territory boundaries set in place. Make no mistake, though. You will learn more from me than anyone outside of the Northern Territory. The fact that I'm both beautiful and ambitious only serves as a bonus to you." Her nostrils flared in delicate amusement.

Beautiful and ambitious she may be, but Kaan was scarier than any woman she had encountered.

What about Tulimaq's weapon? Ila asked, thinking of the staff. She didn't see one like it in the cavern. *Where does that come from?*

"I don't know." Then the woman realized what she'd said. "Pretend I didn't say that," Kaan added with her nose lifted. "The bladed staff isn't one I've seen anywhere, at least not his. The seal Unua often wield staffs, but the use of bones is a wolf Unua preference. It's hard to say. Don't bother asking him. I've known Tulimaq for years and I don't know anything other than his name and fondness for tea. I've given up that mystery."

Ila had no desire to talk to Tulimaq. He'd shamed her enough that she had decided to avoid him. It wouldn't be too difficult, as he was currently off on a mission for the Face Stealer, or so she had heard. She sensed the Face Stealer's reach was far greater than it appeared.

"Now." The weapons master pressed her palms together. "You're here because you want to learn, and I'm here because I'm tired of watching you fail. I want you to choose one of these weapons for your training. I'm not nearly as good as Tulimaq in combat, but since he has the personality of a damp fire, you'll work with me and be grateful for it." She indicated the fifteen or twenty weapons on the table. "Take your time examining the weapons. Test their weights. You want to pick one that feels natural in your hand."

Under Kaan's watchful eye, Ila went down the line of weapons, lifting each one. She gave a few awkward passes before setting them back down. Kaan was offering this to her, no questions asked. A gift, though the weapons master couldn't know Ila viewed it as such. The entire process took less than ten minutes. None of the weapons felt right.

"Don't pay any attention to me," Kaan said, as if sensing Ila's nervousness. "I know that's a hard thing to do, but pretend I'm elsewhere and you're by yourself. Which one would you choose if you did not think I would judge you for it?"

Ila took a breath and started from the beginning. The seal Unua weapons weren't a good fit. The staffs were too unwieldly. When she picked up the talq, however, a feeling of rightness washed over her. It was the perfect fit for her hand, not too heavy. She swung the blade and felt the air split beneath the curve of the antler.

She turned to the weapons master and signed single-handedly, *This one.* She was certain.

Kaan stared. For a while, she didn't speak. The gold of her eyes was luminous with what Ila thought to be surprise. "An interesting choice."

What is?

"The talq in your hand? That was your mother's."

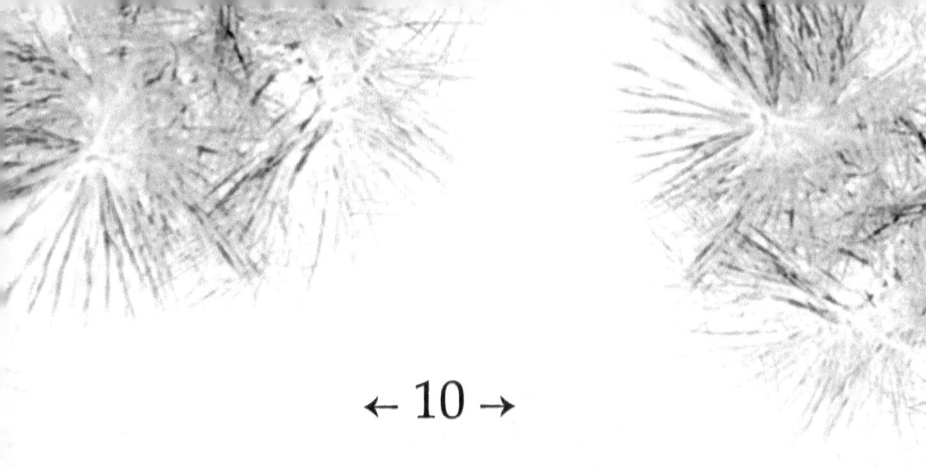

← 10 →

The weapon slipped from Ila's grip.

Slowly, Kaan bent to pick up the talq. "I imagine you have questions."

Blood throbbed in her ears. *Mother.* The word was foreign to her. What kind of place had she been born into, Ila wondered, that would leave this scar on the side of her skull? A violent place? A tortured one? Was she Unua, Analak, something else? Who were her parents? Where were they now? Did they wonder about her? And above all, why had they abandoned her?

Ila looked at the weapon, its tip sharp, slender, but not brittle, never that.

If she had been like this weapon, would her parents have kept her?

"Ila." Kaan was almost too gentle as she gripped Ila's shoulders. "I'm sorry. I didn't mean to upset you."

I'm not upset. Obstinate.

Reaching out, Kaan wiped a tear from Ila's cheek. The teardrop sat like a point of dew on Kaan's fingertip. It was lovely. Lonely. "I will tell you what I know." Though Ila could not hear it, she suspected the words were soft. "Would you like that?"

Ila's teeth sank into her bottom lip, and somehow her legs folded beneath her and she was sobbing into her hands. It was everything she had ever wanted given to her, no questions, no nothing, and yet the offer dragged up a lifetime of pain, bitterness, fury, and even, at times, hatred. Sleepless nights in the cold. Hours of weeping, her body wrung dry. That insidious whisper claiming she was nothing special and never would be. It was not her fault she harbored this deep insecurity. It was theirs.

Yes, she said, still crying. *Yes, please.*

Kaan's shoulders lifted and fell in a sigh. "To be honest, I'm not supposed to be telling you these things." When the woman smiled, it had none of the earlier severity Ila had come to expect. Her face had softened considerably. "But I never knew my mother, and I wish someone had told me about her."

Ila shook her head, staring at the weapon Kaan held in her hand. Made by the caribou Unua. *Why do you have my mother's talq?*

Kaan shifted to sit on her bottom. "It was given to Numiak for safekeeping following the war."

Ila expected Kaan to elaborate, but that was it. Still, it was more than she had ever received before, so she would take it and be grateful.

Yet Kaan surprised her. "I knew your mother growing up. This talq was made for her when she was around your age. She and I would often spar together." Turning the weapon in her hands, she held it up to the light, twisted it this way and that. "It's a fine weapon for a warrior."

When Kaan passed it back to her, Ila gripped the weapon, held it close. *What's her name?* She signed one-handed.

"Qumiq."

And my father?

"Urumak." A small groove appeared in the center of her brow, right above her nose. "Following the war, they settled in a small village, Niuktuk."

Are they still there?

Ila was so focused on the answer that she did not notice Kaan's hesitation. "They are."

It was too much. If they were alive, why hadn't they come for her? *Why did my parents give me up? Did something happen? Was I in danger, or were they? Or—*

Kaan looked into her eyes. "What?"

Ila shrugged to mask her pain. *Did they not want me?*

The weapons master appeared deeply saddened by Ila's assumption. "I don't think it was that, Ila. The war was hard on everyone. It forced people to make difficult decisions."

So they were forced to give me up? If that had been the case, then Ila had been wrong. Giving her up hadn't been a choice.

Movement drew Ila's attention to the mouth of the cavern, where Tulimaq stood, staff in hand, gaze assessing as he took in the echoing space.

Kaan arched a white eyebrow with admirable elegance. "To what do we owe this pleasure?"

He stepped into the blue flickering light, which allowed Ila to better read his lips. "You're needed in the infirmary. Fractured collarbone."

Kaan rolled her eyes. "Of course." Then, in answer to Ila's confusion, she explained, "I'm a healer. Tulimaq trains the refugees when he's not doing Numiak's dirty work." She squeezed Ila's shoulder. "I'll be back. Don't let him intimidate you."

Then she and Tulimaq were alone.

"So Kaan is to train you."

Due to his usual stoicism, she could not read Tulimaq's intention. *Yes.*

He considered her for another moment before saying, "I need to speak with Kaan. Don't touch my staff." He set it on the table. Then he was gone, and she was left in the cavern, the blue light washing over the dark rock, the space above her vast and disquieting.

Ila's focus drifted to the slender weapon. Tulimaq was never without it.

She went to investigate his staff because she couldn't help herself. The weapon was covered in strange carvings. When she passed her hand within a few inches of the wood, the space around it began to hum.

Ila glanced over her shoulder. Tulimaq hadn't returned. He'd told her not to touch the staff, but he wasn't here. He'd never know.

She was reaching out when a large, curved blade descended toward her with frightening speed, almost as if having appeared out of thin air. Ila snatched her hand back as the blade embedded itself into the table where her fingers had been seconds before.

The delayed adrenaline rush sent her scrambling backward. A chair crashed to the floor. *What was that for? You could have cut off my hand!*

Tulimaq merely stared at her. Ila wondered if he hadn't, in fact, left the cavern and had hidden to see if she would follow his order. "Do not touch my staff."

This was because of his *staff?*

Ila snatched up her talq and swung, hard. She didn't realize she had moved. He sidestepped lightly, and the rush of air swept past him. She swung again.

The flat of his boot punched into her stomach, sent her flying backward. Ila landed hard, elbows and knees knocking against stone, then rolled, rolled, before coming to a stop.

When Ila opened her eyes, Tulimaq stood over her, looking down. She glared back in defiance.

"Maybe there is hope for you yet."

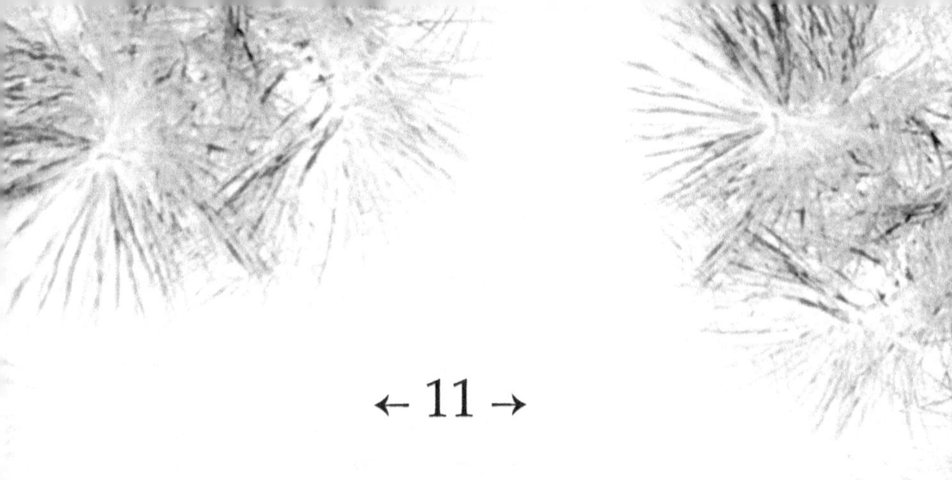

← 11 →

"Eska said you left the tent last night." Chena scraped her dagger along the femur resting atop her thigh. "Where did you go?"

Selecting a bone from the bowl at their feet, Apaay followed Chena's example and began carving. "I went for a walk." She pitched her voice to carry over the festivities currently underway, people drifting around the small islands of fire in the refugee camp. The storytelling would begin shortly. "I was restless."

"Really." Chena peeked at her friend before returning to carving. "Because Eska said you go for a lot of walks these days. She thinks you're not yourself."

A steady scrape, scrape. Apaay focused on tapering the point. It would be a fine dagger, sharp enough to draw blood. "And what do you think?"

Chena's voice softened. "I think maybe she's right." Her look of concern was almost too much, the firelight bringing the emotion to greater clarity. "Apaay—"

"And how are you?" she interrupted, taking in her friend's swollen belly. A fullness touched her face, the inquisitive eyes affectionate but heavy, still, from the tragedies that had befallen their community.

Her friend shrugged and set aside the now-finished tool, choosing another bone resting on the pile. "I'm starting to waddle. I try to look graceful doing it, but I think it's impossible to waddle gracefully."

"You're probably right. I don't know anyone who can waddle gracefully."

Chena scoffed. "You're supposed to tell me I'm the most graceful pregnant woman you've ever seen." When Apaay didn't answer, she continued in an upbeat tone, "Your parents have been so good to me." Her smile was a fraction too wide. "It's not so bad anymore."

Apaay rested a hand on her friend's arm, wishing she could give Chena more of herself. Despite them sharing a tent, they hardly saw one another. Apaay had taken to wandering these days. "I don't believe you," she said, not unkindly.

"Then we are both liars."

Apaay looked to the massive caribou roasting over the central fire. In the forested areas edging the grassy clearing, fireflies glowed an unexpected violet against the night backdrop. "I'm trying the best I can." Even now, a part of her felt so separate from Chena. The laughs they'd once shared seemed far away now.

"Your parents worry. I don't think they know how to help you."

What if she could not be helped? What if she was to suffer from the violence she had inflicted in the labyrinth? What then? She didn't know how to find her way back to herself, find her way home.

"I never got a chance to tell you," Chena said, shifting on the log so their knees touched, "but were it not for you, I would still be in that horrible place. Thank you," she said, near tears, "for saving my life."

Apaay stared at her dagger blade, unaware that she had gone still. "I don't want you to think about it anymore. What's done is done."

"The Face Stealer told me what happened to Nakaluq. I'm so sorry."

Apaay tensed in vague shock. "He did?"

Chena returned the unaltered bone to the bowl and squeezed Apaay's hand, looking saddened when Apaay did not squeeze back.

"I would never have wanted you to make that choice. I know you loved him."

For the first time in many weeks, Nakaluq's memory sent a wave of breathless pain through her. In silence, the refugees began to congregate for the storytelling. An Analak woman moved in front of the central fire, her silhouette flamed at the edges: the storyteller.

Chena whispered, "There's something I need to tell you." She wrapped her arm around her friend's shoulders and tucked Apaay against her side, her large belly pressing into Apaay's ribs. "I've asked the Face Stealer to return me to Muktuk's village."

The shock did not immediately hit. Apaay watched the drummer take his place at the storyteller's side. The instrument was round and flat, caribou calf skin stretched over a ring of wood with a protruding handle that allowed the drum to swing freely during a performance. "I thought you were going to stay here."

"I was," she said, "but I'm close to my due date and I want to be with my brother and his wife." Chena tucked something small and hard into Apaay's palm. "The Face Stealer gave me this to give to you, in case you want to be there during the birth."

Apaay looked down at the rock. It was smooth and gave off a steady heat.

"He said that when I go into labor, the rock will burn hot. So you will know when to come, if you choose."

Apaay curled her fingers around the stone. "I'll try," she said.

"Please don't be mad."

"I'm not." She tried to remain brave for her friend. "Muktuk will be happy to have you back. He's worried about you."

"I know," Chena whispered.

With the first drumbeat, all noise ceased.

The drummer, knees bent, swayed from side to side as he hit the rim of the swinging drum, a beautiful grace to his movements. Beating the bottom section of the rim sent it swinging one way, while beating the top sent it swinging the other way.

In a soft singing voice, the woman began, "On a night much like this one, a man asked a hunter for his daughter's hand in marriage."

Boom, sounded the drum. *Boom*.

Apaay's skin tingled with foreboding. The Sea Mother's story had frightened her as a girl. On the coldest nights, her village would gather in one of the meeting halls to pass the long, dark hours, Apaay's hand clutched in Papa's larger one.

"The girl was on the cusp of womanhood, and lovely. She lived with her father on the coast and spent her days tending their home. It had been a particularly harsh long night. Though the girl tried not to worry, weeks of failed hunts had depleted their food stores. It was for this reason the father accepted the man's offer."

Boom.

"When the girl learned what her father had done, she was furious. She refused to marry this stranger. Refused to leave home. In his desire to calm the brewing tension, the father promised his daughter need not marry the man if she did not desire it. And things were good."

The audience shifted, then stilled. The Unua did not dare blink.

"But that night, while the girl slept, her father stole her away onto his umiak, for the man she would marry lived on a distant island. When the girl awoke in the middle of the sea, she knew her father had betrayed her."

The drumbeats quickened their pace. Apaay didn't notice it at first. It was a subtle thing. The crack of the fire reminded her of snapping bones. The drum sounded too similar to a heartbeat.

"Soon, a storm surrounded them, and the air hummed with a thousand wings. The girl screamed, begging her father to take her back. The storm grew impossibly strong, and waves lashed the boat."

Boom.

Boom.

A build in tempo.

Not one person looked away. The storyteller's movements, and the drummer's, loosened, as if their bodies were the sea waves threatening to drag down the fragile umiak.

The woman's eyes fluttered shut. A stamp of her foot joined the drum. Her face contorted with the fear the Sea Mother must have felt.

"Water began filling the umiak." She made a motion of rain. "The birds surrounded the sinking vessel in a chorus of shrieks.

The girl sobbed, her tears mixing with the salt of the open sea. The father knew he must make a decision, and soon."

Faster and faster, the drum beat a rhythm in her blood. Apaay felt sweat pooling beneath her arms. She couldn't look away as the storyteller's voice pitched high—

"So he tossed his daughter overboard."

—and broke off, a ringing silence.

Apaay's pulse beat erratically. The storyteller had frozen with her arms reaching upward, her fingers like claws over the side of the imaginary umiak.

The woman's arms swung in slow motion, side to side, but did not lower. She sang, "Somehow, the girl had managed to catch herself before hitting the water. The black sea sucked at her legs."

Boom.

"Fearing the umiak would tip, the father swung down his knife and severed his daughter's fingers at the first joint."

Boom.

"The first of the girl's bones sank beneath the waves. They became the seals. Still she sobbed to her father, 'Please.'"

Boom.

Boom, boom.

The drum launched into a low, mournful tone. Blink, and one missed the subtle nuances of the swaying dance, the footstep that was a little more solid than those previous.

"When she did not let go, he took off the second joint. Those joined the first, becoming the whales."

The woman's hands went to her throat, her long braids swinging as her body rocked. "The girl had screamed herself hoarse, but she would not let go. Only the nubs of her fingers remained. Then the man cut those, too, and his daughter slipped beneath the sea."

The drum ceased. Slowly, people began turning their attention beyond the fire, to the lone figure descending the nearest hill.

An eerie quiet fell. The Face Stealer never visited their camp. Apaay had not seen him since the library, and she was content with that arrangement, having spent the majority of her time doing research. Aside from learning more about the Unua nations, she had found nothing of interest, no unusual remark or detail that might point to whatever it was Yuki had stolen. Wasted time, all of it.

The Face Stealer's gaze swept the area, his attention briefly resting on Apaay before seeking out her parents, who he then approached. They exchanged a brief conversation. His arrival sent her thoughts into a helpless spin.

Mama nodded at something he said, then gestured to the far edge of camp. The Face Stealer strode back up the hill and returned with at least twenty bedraggled refugees. Apaay gasped. Torn clothes, bloodied faces, limps and broken bones.

"Naajaluk." Apaay ran to her mother's side and helped lower a middle-aged man onto one of the logs. "What happened?"

"There was another village attack." She accepted a clean cloth and water from one of their own and began cleaning the man's arm wound. The skin looked pulped, as if it had caught on a patch of barnacles. "What did you say the girl's name was?"

Her hands started to shake. She whispered, "Yuki."

"She's hitting more coastal villages. Refugee camps, too." Mama tipped her chin at two women with similar wounds. "Wolf and polar bear Unua who fled during the war."

Apaay looked around. Each of the refugees was being tended to, given water and blankets.

The Face Stealer, she noticed, was gone.

"Please." The man latched onto her arm, his eyes hollowed out. "Have you seen my wife?"

"N-no." She stumbled back, knocking into someone bandaging a head wound. Apaay dragged in a lungful of air and said to Mama, "This is why we should leave. The Face Stealer was in Yuki's confidence. Any connection to him could possibly lead her to us."

"Apaay." She looked sharply at her daughter. "The Face Stealer has opened his home to us, given us anything we need. Do not spurn his generosity."

"But he's—"

"A demon. Yes, I'm aware of that. But circumstances change. This is what's good for our people now. Let that be enough."

It would never be enough. "You don't know about the things he's done, all the faces he's stolen. I've *seen* them. Were it not for him, we wouldn't be in this situation."

Mouth hard, Mama turned from the injured man. "The other refugees?" she said, gesturing to those helping the newly wounded. "They have been here for many years. This haven has been in place long before you knew of it. He is not forcing us to stay. We chose to follow him when Yuki attacked our village. We are free to leave any time we wish."

"Then why not leave now?"

Mama sighed. "Unless you're here to help, please stand back and let the others work."

Swallowing down the hurt, Apaay turned, accidentally knocking into Eska, who grabbed her arm. "Naajatik, wait."

But Apaay shook off her sister and bolted from camp. Her guilt crawled out of the ground and grabbed at her ankles as she fled across the grass, into the trees, past the grove. The Wood brought her to a rock quarry with narrow steps descending to a deep basin, the roar of its waterfall filling Apaay's head and misting her skin. Ila had said the Wood would take her to people and locations with but a thought. She needed to learn more of the attacks on her people, even if it meant interacting with the Face Stealer.

A door was set into the wall behind the sheet of falling water. Apaay lifted her fist to knock when she heard muffled conversation from inside. After a moment of hesitation, she pressed her ear against the door.

"This is our chance. There's no telling when or if another one might occur."

"And if you're wrong?" The Face Stealer's voice was soft, dangerously so.

There was a pause. "I don't think I am, but sometimes the greater good is worth the risk."

Judging from the lack of response, it was the wrong answer. "And Kimmir's death is the greater good? Without him, we know nothing."

"He has not sent us any worthwhile information in almost a year."

"Because nothing has changed. You came to me weeks ago, Tulimaq, and I gave you my answer." Apaay strained to hear the demon's reply over the roaring water. "If Nanuq is indeed moving his troops to Nur, then that is something we need an inside man for. I won't risk Kimmir's safety for information without context."

"And if we learn of Nanuq's movements? Isn't that our goal?"

"Wait."

The conversation cut off. Apaay frowned in confusion before the door opened.

The Face Stealer's black hair was tied back, a pair of glasses perched on his nose. He stared. Apaay figured she must look quite the sight. As it was deep summer, thorns had drawn blood from the delicate skin of her hands, wrists, and face. Leaves and twigs clung to her hair.

"I need to talk to you," she whispered.

No quick or clever remark, no banter or wit. Indeed, Apaay didn't think she had ever encountered the Face Stealer at a time when he did not have something cruel or provocative rolling off his tongue. As he scanned her face, the obvious scratches, his lips thinned.

He removed his glasses. Gestured to the seat across from his desk.

Flicking a glance in Tulimaq's direction, she sat.

He tossed her a clean cloth. "Wipe your face." Quiet.

Apaay clutched the cloth in her hand, where it remained. His office was much smaller than the library. The outer wall was all glass, allowing a view of the waterfall, but there must have been an enchantment on it, because from the outside, it appeared to be stone. The room contained a desk, a bookcase, a small hearth, and a pair of chairs in the corner, cozy and warm. The ceiling was a dark hole above.

The demon turned to Tulimaq, who hovered at the corner of his desk. "Tell Kimmir he is not to interfere."

"I ask that you reconsider."

"My decision stands." The statement rang with command, causing Apaay to straighten in her seat. Shadows fluttered around his powerful form, restless, displeased. "The Wood's safety comes first. I won't budge on this."

Tulimaq lifted his chin, and Apaay swore rage flickered and died in his eyes.

"Very well." The man gave a subtle nod in her direction before closing the door on his way out.

Face creasing, the Face Stealer rubbed his eyes with his thumb and forefinger.

The action was out of place. Human, she realized. "What was that about?" Apaay asked. The question surprised her, but it was too late to call it back. Though her pulse still thumped erratically, it had slowed, somewhat.

"Tulimaq keeps pushing for infiltration. I have a sleeper in Nanuq's army. A spy. He's not the first, but he's lasted the longest."

"What happened to the others?"

He settled back in his chair. More ridges folded the span of his forehead. "To gain acceptance as a kirn of Nanuq's army, you must pass a series of tests that demonstrate your intelligence, adaptability, and cunning. Nanuq is only interested in the elite.

"My first sleeper survived a year in the army before word spread of a traitor in their midst. He was executed as one of the suspects. I never learned why they suspected him. My second man perished during the tests. After that, I swore not to risk another life until there was a guaranteed acceptance.

"My third man has been there for nine years. He lives as a traitor among Nanuq's army. He trains with them, fights with them. Last year, he was promoted to captain. It is my hope that he will soon be promoted to commander, which is the highest post one can obtain outside of general. He's been feeding us information on Nanuq's movements for nearly a decade."

Apaay said, "Can't they tell he's not polar bear Unua? I assume their sense of smell allows them to differentiate between races, even if someone isn't in their animal form."

His chin dipped in affirmation. "You're correct, but I gave him the face of a polar bear Unua. Taking the face of another not only alters your facial features, but your smell. It is the strongest protection I can give someone."

That made sense. She crossed her arms and watched the waterfall through the windows. "And Tulimaq wants . . . what?"

The Face Stealer tapped a finger on the desk, his expression clouded. "Nanuq plans on moving his army from their current base at Kaal to the Southern Territory capital, though we do not know when or why. Kimmir wants to read the general's messages for a timeline and possible intention." He pushed aside a few official-looking documents. "Right now, he's our only inside man. I can't throw away nine years of work on the chance that whatever information those documents contain will help us. The risk is too great." After a moment of thought, his gaze sharpened. "But I assume you didn't come here to discuss war."

Apaay took a breath. Her stomach clenched. "The Analak. Did Yuki . . . ?"

He nodded.

A cold lack of feeling drew the remaining warmth from her face and hands. "These are my people," she intoned. "Innocents."

"I am aware of this."

"So what are you going to do?"

"For now, we will ensure the refugees are comfortable. I've reached out to some old contacts for information. Yuki remains elusive."

Apaay waited for more, but she realized that was it. That was all he intended to do. "What if there are others, people who are hurt or stranded?"

"There are none." Level, cold.

She gripped the arms of the chair and swore the wood groaned under her hands. "How do you know? Did you even look?"

He growled, "How do I know? Because I dug through the rubble of both the Analak village and the refugee camp for survivors. I scoured the surrounding area for any sign of life."

Apaay gritted her teeth. He couldn't understand the helpless feeling in knowing her sister villages were under attack. "And yet you sit here, waiting for Yuki to wreak havoc, and do nothing."

His eyes, a crystallized green, promised much violence. Apaay held her ground. "I'd hardly call what we're doing *nothing*."

"Chena told me she's returning to her brother's community. They're vulnerable." What did it say of her that, deep down, she *did* see the Wood as safe, even though she wanted to leave? She did not have a problem with the Wood itself. She merely hated knowing it was a product of the Face Stealer's power. "You have to place your protection on them. I know you can. You're powerful enough."

The exact limits of his power remained a mystery to her. She knew, for instance, he used the shadows to appear and disappear at will and could most likely travel to any location where shadows existed. She knew they were a part of him, and he of them. And lastly, that the source of his power was so vast so as to seem bottomless. Everything in the world was connected to something else. Did that not mean the connection to his power source could be severed?

"I have already done so. She will be as safe as if she were in the Wood."

Apaay paused, having not expected the generosity from him, then went on. "If you really wanted to help people, why not open the Wood as a refuge for all?"

"Why do you think I created it in the first place? The Wood will always be a sanctuary to those in need, but we haven't the resources to sustain a large population. We take what the land gives, nothing more. The laws of nature surpass even *my* power. Do I wish things were different? Of course I do." Low and even, his argument lashed out. "But I will not risk twenty years' worth of work. You cannot save them all. That is nature."

"No," she hissed. "That is a *choice*. The choice of a human heart." She forced herself to sit back in the chair. "But I should not be surprised. How much is a demon's heart worth, after all?"

He smiled mockingly. "How much indeed."

Apaay bit off a retort, fuming.

He said, with frightening calm, "You do not like it here. I understand. You wish to leave, and for your people to leave with you. You feel trapped, helpless. You do not trust me, and believe I will again betray you. Where will you go, once the blood oath is severed? Despite your hatred of me, the Wood is the safest place for them, and for you. You will have to come to terms with it eventually."

She would not come to terms with it—ever. She and Masuk would be free of him soon, on their way to the Banished Lands.

A knock on the door interrupted them. "Numiak." A woman's voice, somehow more powerful than the waterfall, demanded his attention. The knob jiggled uselessly. "Whatever's urgent enough to interrupt my dessert, it better be good. Now open up." The woman banged on the door harder, causing the windows to rattle.

He sighed, though his eyes lightened. Apaay's positioning didn't allow her to see who stood on the other side.

The Face Stealer said to Apaay, "I'll be a few minutes." He slipped out the door, closing it behind him.

Apaay considered eavesdropping but didn't want to give the impression that she cared about the conversation. Instead, she rifled through the papers and documents on his desk, looking for a potential clue that might lead her to the hidden faces. She and Masuk had yet to discuss what would happen once she found them. She assumed he would wait until she completed the blood oath. After all, he knew how to reach the Banished Lands, not she.

Moving to the bookshelf, she began pulling down books, thinking he might have possibly hidden them between the pages. Moments later, the door opened.

She froze.

"Doing a bit of light reading?" It sounded like a warning.

Slowly, Apaay started putting the books back onto the shelves. "Who was that?" she asked, hoping the question would give her enough time to think of an appropriate response.

The Face Stealer came around to her side. She spotted his long legs in her peripheral vision. "That was Kaan and Ro. Council members, and my oldest friends."

"I didn't know you had friends."

A corner of his mouth ticked up. "Hard to believe with all the enemies I have, I know."

"What is this council for, exactly? Some form of government?"

"It is not quite as official as that," he said. "Kaan and Ro are members of my personal council, which I formed some time ago. My most powerful allies working together to stand against Nanuq."

"I see." She regarded him carefully. "Are there other council members?"

The Face Stealer pushed back his braid, and the smaller braid with the blue beads. "Just the two, plus Tulimaq, my combat master. He trains the refugees. Kaan is the weapons master, as well as a healer. Ro advises me on warfare. They work with me to keep track of Nanuq's comings and goings, any changes or threats to the North. They have been looking forward to meeting you."

"They know of me?" she asked in surprise.

He inclined his head. "They know everything that goes on in the Wood. When I am gone, they protect it in my absence."

She tucked that piece of information away to share with Masuk for later.

With the books returned to the bookcase, Apaay stood awkwardly and crossed her arms. "As much as I would *love* to meet your friends, I'll pass."

That smile, the one that promised terrible things, made an appearance. "It wasn't a request."

"But—"

Something perilous flashed in his eyes. Apaay promptly shut her mouth. "This is your world, too. It's time you start being a part of it." He headed for the exit. "Ten minutes, Apaay, or I come find you."

The door slammed shut.

← 12 →

Apaay found the Face Stealer seated in a room that resembled a sunny glen, all soft grass and wildflowers. Cushioned chairs and couches surrounded a low wooden table. On one couch sat Ila and Tulimaq, the latter of whom she had seen once or twice wandering the halls, looking stoic and out of place. There was a woman with glowing white hair shorn at the chin. A man in a wheelchair with the same white hair and tawny skin. Then there was the Face Stealer. Apaay swore she hadn't made a sound, but he lifted his eyes to her almost immediately.

"I didn't mean to interrupt," Apaay said, hovering in the doorway.

The chatter died, leaving absolute silence. The strangers' curiosity was palpable.

"Nonsense!" The woman, as slender as a stalk of grass, rose from her seat and approached. Her eyes were a beautifully glazed and unblemished gold. "We were wondering if Numiak was ever going to share. He can be so greedy, you know."

"Kaan." The Face Stealer's voice held a note of warning.

Apaay shot the demon a cool glare before turning back to the woman. So this was Kaan, the weapons master. "I am not an object to be kept and shared."

A slow, gleeful smile overtook her face. "So bloodthirsty. Can we keep her?"

The man in the wheelchair rolled forward, distracting Apaay from saying something she might regret. "You'll have to excuse my sister. She's harmless. Mostly." His warm, callused hands clasped her own. "It's nice to finally meet you, Apaay. I'm Ro."

As the warmth from his hands lessened the chill in her fingers, some of the tension bled away. Ro and his sister, while obviously opposite in demeanor, shared a likeness to their features. Both wore lighter, sleeveless parkas that fell to their thighs with a shallow slit up the middle, and dark cloth wrapped around their arms and legs. Kaan's cloth was gray. Ro's was black.

It was then a young girl with two messy braids and an adorable upturned nose poked her head around the couch. She was all elbows and scraped knees. A smudge of dirt coated one rounded cheek.

Unhurriedly, the Face Stealer stood, his attention locked on Apaay in studious observation, as if searching for a reaction. "This is Mika," he said in a voice of utter calm, one large hand cupping the side of the girl's face. She looked to be no older than seven. "Say hello, Mika."

Ducking her head, the girl clung to one of the Face Stealer's legs and whispered, "Hello." She stuck out her hand blindly, face pressed against his thigh.

Apaay clasped the tiny fingers in confusion. She supposed the Face Stealer was old enough to be a father.

"Mika is my niece," he clarified.

Oh. She blinked at the girl. Wide eyes of rich brown stared back. Hadn't the Face Stealer's family died? She supposed that made the girl an orphan.

"It's very nice to meet you, Mika" was her grave response.

With one arm still wrapped around her uncle's leg, Mika whispered, "Do you want to see my doll?"

Apaay looked to the Face Stealer, who was gazing down at his niece, face softened by tenderness. She turned away. "Um." Tulimaq watched Ila, who watched Kaan, who studied Apaay. "All right."

Letting go of her uncle, Mika grabbed Apaay's hand. "You can sit next to me." Apaay let the girl lead her to a chair.

Apaay met Ila's gaze across the table as she sat. They hadn't spoken in weeks. On occasion, she spotted Ila coming and going from an unknown location in the Wood, her palms blistered and her arms bruised. She missed Ila, their shared laughter and gentle teasing. The problem was, she didn't know how to reach across this new divide.

"So." She tried not to hunch her shoulders beneath the six pairs of eyes in the room.

The Face Stealer gestured to the stones arranged on the table. "Would you like to play Taltak?"

"I'll watch." She didn't know how to play anyway.

"Fair enough." He passed a pile of stones to each person at the table while Mika distracted Apaay with her doll. The girl whispered in her doll's ear, adjusted the tiny fur parka lovingly. Her smile charmed. She really was adorable.

Each person checked under their stones, Ila included. It was clear her friend had already met these people, felt comfortable around them, though she avoided looking at Tulimaq, Apaay noticed.

"Keep an eye on him," Kaan said to Apaay, pointing at the Face Stealer. "He likes to cheat."

His chuckle drifted through the room like a creeping fog. "I assure you, my cheatings were but those of a boy in desperation." He nodded at Ro. "You go first."

Kaan snorted. Tulimaq said nothing. It didn't appear as if he was paying attention to the conversation.

For a time, Apaay was content to watch the game. There was a lot of trading involved. Picking stones up and putting them down. The ease between Kaan, Ro, and the Face Stealer was evident in their banter.

"So." Lacing her fingers in her lap, Apaay asked, "Do you all work for Yuki, too?"

Surprise rippled through the small group. Kaan and Ro exchanged a questioning glance while Tulimaq stared at the table.

The Face Stealer's heavy gaze rested on the side of her neck, though Apaay pretended she was not affected by it. The quiet stretched for so long it grew uncomfortable.

In the end, Ro spoke, with his patient tone and warm eyes. The wheels of his chair creaked as he leaned back, his stones stacked neatly on the table. "None of us," he said, "has ever worked for Yuki."

It was such a blatant lie that she scoffed. "*He* did." She didn't need to point for them to know who. The contempt in her voice was enough.

"That was circumstantial," murmured the Face Stealer.

Really? she wanted to shout, scream, rage. Her suffering was circumstantial? The suffering of her people? Did they have any idea what the Face Stealer had put her through?

As quickly as the rage had risen, it deflated. She sat back in the chair and didn't fight the creeping numbness. What was the point? Of any of it?

An undercurrent of tension flickered in the room. The air was dead, as if the Wood sensed the fragility of the conversation. "I understand where you're coming from," Ro said with so much kindness Apaay bit the inside of her cheek to keep the tears at bay. "I understand your hurt. We've all lost people to this conflict."

Across the table, Ila sent her an encouraging smile. Apaay couldn't find it in her heart to smile back.

"We do not support Nanuq or Yuki in any way, shape, or form. Even now, there has been movement to the south. It is concerning," Ro said, passing a stone to Kaan and taking one of hers. "We have learned Nanuq again seeks the object of power, and Yuki seeks to help him find it."

Apaay recalled what the Face Stealer had told her in the library. Unrestrained power. The potential for complete ruination was frightening. What heights would Nanuq reach with such power at hand?

Concerning how? asked Ila.

Ro answered, "You have to understand, the North is a place of convergence. Land and sea. Animal and man. Moon and sun. Winter and summer. An object of power would skew the already precarious balance." He said to Apaay, "I don't know if your people have noticed, but the sea life is not as plentiful as it once was."

Actually, Apaay had noticed. The Analak lived in fear of the Sea Mother's wrath, which was why her people always followed the old rules to maintain her favor.

As for what Ro had said, she believed him. A difficult thing to accept. These people were not her enemies, but a dark cloud hovered where the Face Stealer was concerned. She could never fully trust him.

"Kaan and Ro are my closest friends," the Face Stealer said to Apaay. "As such, you are safe with them."

It was Kaan who made a disturbed sound, halfway between a scoff and a snort. "Let me make one thing clear. These two"— she pointed between Ro and the Face Stealer—"should consider themselves lucky I have not disposed of their bodies at the bottom of a ravine somewhere."

"You love us," the demon crooned.

"I love my brother," she corrected with an air of unconcern. "You, I tolerate."

His features took on an otherness that made Ila pause in the middle of switching out one of her stones. "Kaan." His power stretched long fingers across the table. Kaan scowled as it reached her. "You mean to tell me that over one hundred and fifty years of friendship and you only *tolerate* me?"

One hundred and fifty years? How old was the demon anyway?

Kaan leaned back with one quirked eyebrow. The movement managed to be effortlessly threatening. "Do you not remember when you and Ro trapped me in a bear's den?"

A devilish twinkle in the Face Stealer's eyes, and even Ro smiled as he traded a stone with Tulimaq, the combat master's mouth pinched in what Apaay had decided was perpetual anger. "I'm quite certain I don't know what you're talking about."

Ila, like Apaay, was fixated on the conversation more than the game. Thus, she didn't notice when two of her stones went missing into Kaan's deft fingers, but a glare from Tulimaq had the woman rolling her eyes and putting them back.

"You don't remember? Sita and Kenai—"

The demon went stiff beside her. Kaan stuttered, fell quiet.

The Face Stealer may have been dead, for all he was frozen as a cairn. He said, the words muted, "Sita and Kenai were my sister and brother." The Face Stealer's eyes softened, and he brushed a strand of black hair from his niece's cheek. "Mika is my sister's daughter."

Apaay felt a strand of unease worm through her at the gentleness he displayed. She hadn't asked and didn't care to know. Anyway, he couldn't possibly know anything of family. What was it Yuki had once said?

Power is living your life alone.

Kaan's face strained with guilt. "Numiak—"

"It is done." Final. "Let us return to the game."

They did, for a time.

"Wait." Kaan shot to her feet. "Where did my pieces go?"

Three stones, which had been present a moment ago on the right corner of the table, were missing.

Ro sat to the left of Kaan, Tulimaq on the right. The Face Stealer sat at the far end of the table, more relaxed than he had been a second ago. Mika was too busy playing with her doll to notice the shift.

"They were right here," she said, pointing to the empty space.

The Face Stealer, fingers clasped across his stomach, suggested, "Perhaps they flew away?"

Those amber eyes narrowed at his casual pose, which was all but an elegant slouch. "Is that what we're calling it?" Calm as could be, she padded to his side. Then, much to Apaay's shock, the woman snatched at his collar and hauled him close, their noses inches apart. "Where are they?"

Apaay could not be sure, but she thought she heard Ro mutter, "Here we go."

The Face Stealer's laughter spilled out, deep and overflowing with delight. Apaay's attention locked onto his face. She had never heard that sound from him before. His palms lifted in surrender. "I have no idea what you're talking about."

"You're such a liar." She threw him back into the seat. "Turn out your pockets."

Crossing his arms, he leaned onto the back legs of his chair. "When will you realize I simply can't be beat? How long have we been playing this game? Decades?"

Kaan rested her foot against one of the chair's front legs and pushed.

The Face Stealer swore as the chair tipped back and dumped him onto the ground, small stones spilling from his pockets into the grass.

Mika burst into giggles, and the sound was so buoyant with joy that Apaay felt her mouth softening. Admittedly, she enjoyed watching the Face Stealer flail about in an attempt to right himself.

"So predictable," Kaan quipped, pivoting on her heel. She had only taken a step when a rush of black power swept through the room like a cold wind, and her clothes whipped upward. Stones fell from what Apaay guessed were hidden pockets sewn into the inside of her parka, joining those of the Face Stealer.

Ro sighed, pinching the bridge of his nose between two fingers.

Kaan closed her open mouth with a snap. Chin lifted, she sniffed haughtily. "I have no idea where those came from."

A small bird arrowed into the room to land on the demon's arm. It was a sudden, startling movement that made everyone go still. The Face Stealer shared a look with Ro before removing the small piece of parchment attached to the bird's leg.

"What is it?" Kaan asked lowly, her earlier amusement gone.

He looked from the message to Apaay. "There's been another attack."

And suddenly, she knew. "Survivors?"

"Eleven of them. They've taken refuge at a neighboring village, but a body was found a few miles south of it." A pause as he searched her face. "The villagers say it's not one of their people. I thought . . . it might be possible it's one of yours."

Her heart gave a sluggish thud before picking up speed. One of hers, as in someone who had managed to escape her village's massacre? She saw that day clearly in her mind. An ashen earth under a clouded sky. "You want me to identify it." She released a tight breath.

"If it's not too much to ask."

Of course it was too much to ask. But that did not mean she wouldn't do it for her people. "Fine."

"Which Analak village?" asked Kaan. "It's not Niuktuk, is it?"

The Face Stealer made a vicious cutting motion with his hand.

Silence fell. Apaay glanced between the demon and the weapons master.

Ila blinked in shock. She was already pushing back her chair and rising to her feet. *I want to come.*

Tulimaq stood as well. "They already have enough people for the trip. You would only get in the way."

I don't believe I asked for your opinion, she said, hands snapping. A flush singed her cheeks.

"It's dangerous."

Maybe if someone trained me to defend myself this wouldn't be a problem. Tulimaq opened his mouth to reply, but Ila had already turned away. The behavior surprised Apaay. Ila was usually so gentle. *I'm going with you.*

With what may have been a soft curse, Tulimaq returned to his seat, glaring at the proud line of Ila's back. The Face Stealer glanced between them, curious and somewhat amused. "Well," he drawled. "If that's resolved, we leave immediately. Apaay, you will go with the others to the village. I'll be there shortly."

One by one, everyone filed out of the room. Apaay was the last to leave. As she crossed the threshold into the hall, she looked back, her hand on the doorframe. The Face Stealer, who did not notice she lingered, crouched at Mika's side and lifted her as if she were made of glass. The girl had fallen asleep.

The child began to stir as he reached over and grabbed her doll from the table. "Numi?" Sleepy, sleepy voice.

"I'm here." He brushed the hair from her face. "I have to go, but I'll be back later tonight to check on you. Kaan will be here if you need anything."

"Promise?" A slurred word, half aware.

"I promise. Goodnight, sweetheart."

"Goodnight, Numi."

← 13 →

With Ro in his avian form acting as their guide, Apaay, Ila, and the Face Stealer trekked the ten miles from the cairn they had arrived at through the northern Aatu. Judging by the snow's soft texture and the midnight hue of the sky, it was the month of seal pups, in its final stages: a taste of early spring. Had they been on the coast instead, they would have been able to spot pups on the ice. But Apaay was far from the sea. Without having realized it, she had been pulled into the Face Stealer's scheming world. A search for a man dead.

They reached the village soon enough. From the number of snow houses present, Apaay estimated it held a few hundred people.

Apaay turned to Ila, who wrung her hands together as her gaze skipped from person to person and house to house. "Do you want me to come with you?" She did not understand why Ila had been so quick to volunteer for this journey. When pressed, she'd refused to speak of it.

The young woman shook her head. *I'll be all right. It's past time I explored the world, don't you think?*

Apaay understood the sentiment. With one last smile for good luck, she followed the Face Stealer beyond the village. Ro glided down to settle on the Face Stealer's shoulder. He had built a lightweight contraption that allowed his body to rest in a small bowl, since his legs could not hold his weight. There he perched, blinking those piercing yellow eyes, and nipped at the demon's ear. The Face Stealer swore and flicked the bird's beak. Ro flapped his wings with a screech. Apaay suspected it was his version of laughter.

Less than two miles later, they reached the site. The snow was otherwise pristine save for a pile of rocks that covered the body. It was how the Analak laid their dead to rest.

As the Face Stealer began removing the stones, Apaay braced herself for the very real possibility that he might uncover someone from her village, having escaped the massacre and traveled all this way only to die mere miles from safety. Once the stones were removed, Apaay observed the body. It was indeed a man. It was difficult to make out his face beyond the frostbitten skin, but the red of his furs could not be missed. An unusual color. Her heart slowed. Her shoulders loosened as tension unspooled.

She said, "This man is not Analak."

The words steadied her. The relief was brief, but bright. Then it faded, masked beneath the unfeeling fog that had crept over her heart.

Ro flapped his wings and settled. The Face Stealer asked, "Are you certain?"

Just as she knew it was time to move from an ice house to a tent when the first of the sun's rays appeared, so she knew whether someone shared in her culture. The way of the Analak was not the way of anyone else. She looked, and she knew. Simply.

"Yes." Apaay indicated his clothing. "This man's parka—I'm not sure what it is." It was rough beneath her fingers, which suggested it wasn't fur, but fabric, tightly woven, yet inadequate for the tundra. "His boots are strange, too." Studying them more closely, she noticed they were not waterproof. That wasn't good. She guessed his feet had been the first to fall, and when he had not been able to walk, he had perished. It would have happened slowly. Death in the cold always began with sleep.

Apaay moved toward his head—bypassing the gruesome, flaking black skin—and peeled back his stiffened eyelids. His irises were the blue of glacial ice, lashes like pale fronds. Tugging back the man's hood, she then chipped at the ice until the fur pulled free of his skin. Apaay sucked in a breath. The man's hair was the pale yellow of watery sunlight.

He was like the men she had seen with her father as a girl. They'd butchered the trees and gouged the earth and built walls—high wooden ones.

"He's not from the North." She stared at the ice-encrusted man. "Why would he come all the way from Across the Sea?" And was it in relation to the approaching conflict?

"Why does anyone leave the place where they were born?" The Face Stealer moved to the other side of the body and crouched down. "There is a world out there, and some wish to understand it better."

She supposed that made sense, though Apaay didn't entirely understand. The North was her land. It was a place of fear and awe, loss and brutality, but also a beauty so lovely it made one weep. She would not give it up for anything.

With the demon's help, Apaay brushed snow from the body. She noticed a difference in the red coloring of his fur. The darker, patchy quality looked like dried blood.

"He was wounded," she said. "Can you help me remove the parka?"

They did so in silence. Frost hissed and crumbled as they struggled to undress the man's torso. Underneath the layers of cloth was a wound deep enough for his organs to have spilled out. She grimaced.

"Attacked." The Face Stealer spoke thoughtfully. Ro cried out an agreement. "But by what?"

Something large enough to take a bite out of this man's abdomen. Gouged skin on his chest and shoulders suggested a struggle. It was a gruesome sight. She pressed her splayed palm over an area where the claw marks were most prominent. It was twice as large as her hand. As far as she knew, only one animal in the North had paws that size.

"But was the polar bear an animal," said the Face Stealer, "or Unua?"

If the polar bear had been an animal, why not attack the man's jugular? That was instinct. The bite along his abdomen had been a choice. The choice of man.

"Check his pockets."

She checked. Empty. He didn't seem to have carried anything with him, no food or supplies. Another oddity.

Ro fluttered down and started pecking at the man's mittened hand. Something was poking out from his fist.

Uncurling the man's fingers with small pops from the cracking ice, Apaay removed a crumpled piece of paper, which had been oiled to repel moisture. There was writing on the inside, so she passed it to the Face Stealer. "What does it say?"

Shaking his head, he stuffed the message into his pocket. "I can't read the language."

Apaay stared at him. She was slowly learning the subtleties of his facial tics. Her first instinct, always, was to assume he lied.

Irritation shaved his words to fine points. "That is the truth. I have a few scrolls with information on Across the Sea, but no written record of their people's language. We will need to find a translator for this." He studied the corpse. "I might be able to find one on the Island of Kir. Or the Banished Lands. You can find anyone there."

Or lose anyone, she thought, remembering her and Masuk's plan of escape.

The Face Stealer stood and looked back the way they had come. "We need to get back. I want to speak with the survivors."

The man lay at her feet. In life, he would have been large and muscular, yet death made men so small. "We can't leave him here."

"Yes," he quipped in a tone that said there would be no argument, "we can." Ro flapped his magnificent wings and took to the air. "Judging by his mauling, someone wanted him dead. If that's the case, it's safest not to be associated with his death."

Though this man was not her people, was he not a person? Was there not dignity to life that they should respect and honor in some way? It didn't seem right.

Ro circled overhead, probably wondering why they hadn't moved. The Face Stealer was right. The man's death was too odd. That didn't mean she agreed with the treatment of the body.

"Let's at least cover him with the rocks," Apaay said. After all, it was cold out, and the wind was cruel at this time of year.

← →

Ila felt moments away from retching as she headed down a path of trampled snow branching off from the village. Was it possible to choke on your heart, to pass out from how intensely your pulse beat with hope? Her legs alternated between sprinting and walking. An elder had pointed her in this direction when she'd asked where to find Qumiq and Urumak, her parents. Ila was so nervous she hadn't noticed the woman's confusion. Blood was an uneven pulse in her temples.

For years, she had dreamed of family. *Her* family. She didn't know what they would look like, but she imagined them to be kind, quiet, gentle, and most of all, compassionate. There must be a reason her parents had given her up. They weren't cruel. They couldn't be.

The path ended at a clearing. Ila scanned the area in puzzlement. She had assumed there would be another portion of the village here, a cluster of homes, but it was empty land bordered by pine. Maybe there were more houses on the other side of the clearing? A likely explanation. She stepped forward and promptly stubbed her toe on something hard buried beneath the snow.

Ila brushed away the powder and uncovered a small mound of stone. She looked around. Spotted more mounds peeking out of the white.

The clearing was full of graves.

Ila had only ever known silence, but now it felt as if she was inside it, or it was inside her, and they could not be distinguished.

She walked, stumbled, fell. Stood and brushed herself off. Then Ila was running, her chest tight and the breaths exploding from her mouth. The snow was thick and powdery. Soft. She stamped it into slush.

Ila thought it had to be a lie, but she knew it was not. Branches thwacked her in the face. The fresh sting of split skin brought clarity to what she had seen.

Her parents were dead.

In some ways, it felt as if they had never been alive, not really. They'd been formless, faceless shrouds in her dreams.

Yet Kaan had given her a dangerous hope. For a moment, Ila had thought it might be possible to rejoin her family. Lies, all of it. Why would Kaan lie to her? She didn't think it was to intentionally hurt Ila. Kaan was a lot of things, but she wasn't cruel.

Ila burst into another clearing and slowed. Her skin prickled with suffused blood against the frigid air. The land was blanketed white, and the trees, too. She didn't understand how there could be peace here when, inside, something was caving and crumbling away. Ila couldn't be strong, not about this.

She reached for her talq with a shaking hand and drew it forth, held it up against the dark sky. Then she swung. The air parted beneath the sharp antler blade. She swung again, putting her entire body into the motion. Her swings took the shape of the patterns Kaan had taught her thus far, but there was no smoothness to them, no grace. It was a furious, sloppy madness, swing after swing after swing, the frozen air sawing through her chest as grief swept through her, hot as spilled blood. Above all, there was this: Ila was alone.

Her knees buckled.

She wept.

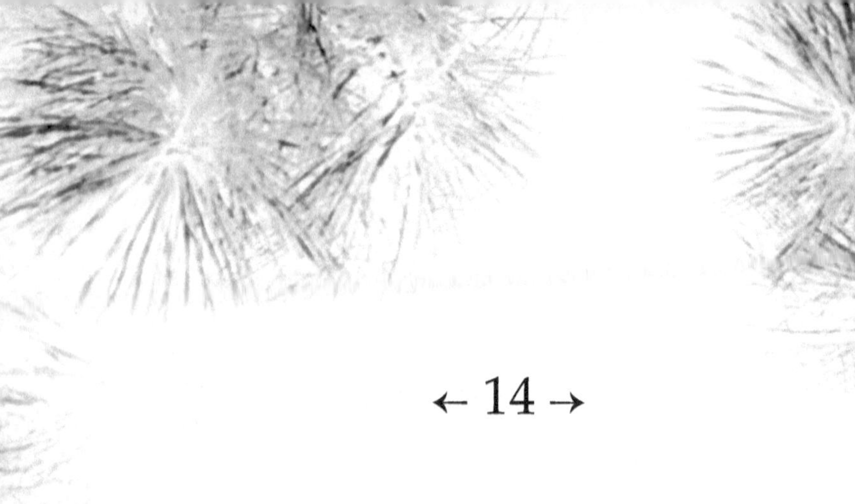

← 14 →

The bound leather book was all but falling apart in Apaay's hands. A map of the Atakana had been inked inside its pages. As Apaay listened to a brief account of a man who would one day turn completely to stone, she flipped through the volume, then set it aside and scrubbed her hands down her face as if she could scour away the weariness. She had pored over books and maps and tomes and scrolls all throughout the night. Hours earlier, Eska, woken by Apaay's nightmares, had begged her not to leave the tent. Apaay told her the same thing she always did: She couldn't stay.

It would be the next one, she decided. The next book would give her a clue as to what Yuki had stolen from the Face Stealer. A step toward severing this blood oath.

The library door opened. Apaay glanced up from her desk as the Face Stealer stepped over the threshold, pausing as he caught sight of her. He wore those black glasses, his hair pulled into a messy knot, arms laden with documents. After a moment of staring at her, he nudged the door shut behind him.

Apaay got to her feet.

"No need to leave on my account," he said, the documents drifting from his hands to their respective places on the shelves.

His gaze touched upon her face, taking in the bloodshot eyes, the discolored skin beneath. "Couldn't sleep?"

After a hesitation, Apaay slowly lowered herself back into the chair, shaking her head. Too many nightmares. Too many questions concerning the man from Across the Sea. Four days had passed since they'd discovered the body. "Thought I might be able to find a connection with the blood oath." She had also attempted to enter the strange shadow door in hope of it leading her to Masuk's beloved's face, but it remained locked.

"And?"

She flipped the book in front of her closed. "Nothing."

He came closer. "When's the last time you ate?"

"I'm not hungry."

"That's not an answer."

His statement put her back up. "It was an answer," she said, an edge to the words. "Just not the one you wanted."

"Be that as it may, it cannot possibly be true."

She stared at the dark grain of the desk, willing him to disappear.

Tension made sparks of the air, singeing her from how near he stood. "Your body is starving, Apaay. You need to feed yourself." He gripped her arm, as if sensing her desire to run, even though she was fully ensnared by the hypnotic quality of his voice.

This was what Apaay hated most. Even despising him, a part of her was drawn to the madness and the cruelty, the sinister nature. She didn't see that side of him now, though. Instead, there was this: worry.

Apaay didn't know how to process the change. Didn't know the Face Stealer was even capable of such an emotion.

She jerked her arm from his grasp, and they stared at one another in wariness.

With a long-suffering look, he hauled another chair over to where she sat, then sent the books in her hands scattering back to their respective slots on the shelves. "We'll eat now. You won't even have to leave the room." Papers rustled and rebound themselves. The desk was empty for only a moment before a spread of food appeared.

Apaay blinked at the various dishes. "How unbelievably thoughtful of you."

"You're just noticing this now?"

"No, I mean it's really unbelievable. Is it poisoned?"

He chuckled, but she swore irritation flared before a cool mask slid into place. "Why don't you try it and find out?" He offered her one of the plates. Blood pooled beneath the slab of raw meat.

Apaay moved on instinct, slapping his hand aside and sending the plate flying. Blood spattered on the floor, and the seal meat slapped wetly against the floorboards.

A roaring silence settled in the wake of her actions, the sudden violence to them. Without taking his eyes from her, the Face Stealer flicked a hand and cleaned the mess, sent the objects into the shadows. He tapped one finger against the arm of his chair. Stopped. "What was that about?" Too quiet.

Her mouth burned with the taste of copper. "I don't do well with blood."

He scanned the food. A moment later, the dishes holding raspberries and cherries vanished. "Have you talked to your family about this? About how you can't sleep through the night?"

Heat scorched her cheeks. She wondered how he knew that. "Have you been following me?"

"No, but I know everything that goes on in the Wood. So I know when you leave your tent after you think your family is asleep."

"It's none of your—"

"Business. I know. But let's pretend it *is* my business. I realize this is not your home. I understand you are dealing with a lot of trauma. But I won't know how to help you if you don't tell me what you need."

Apaay hated that, in this moment, he seemed to care, when in the labyrinth he had shown anything but caring. "Take back all of this. Take back the moment you stole Eska's face. Take back the destruction of my home, the death of my people." Anger and helplessness were puncturing holes into her heart. "But you can't do that. You can't take back time. You can't take back who you are. You can't do a damn thing. You want to help me?" she hissed. "Then leave."

The gray of his irises shifted like smoke under glass.

Two cups of steaming liquid appeared on the desk. He offered her one. "Truce?"

Apaay slumped back in the chair, exhausted by the display of temper. These days, it was easier not to fight. She accepted the tea and took a sip. The liquid warmed her chest and settled in her belly. "I've been trying to figure out what was so important to you that Yuki wanted to steal it. I know you can't tell me," she said. "Obviously it holds power over you." They studied each other in silence, and for once, it was not a silence meant to harm. It was simply lack of sound.

Apaay thought back to her time in the labyrinth, hoping to glean a clue or possible motive. "Did you and Yuki ever . . ."

The Face Stealer choked on his tea and spewed it all over the desk, coughing fitfully. The reaction reassured her. It sickened Apaay to consider, because the girl was physically a child, but with the way they had interacted in familiarity, she had wondered.

"No," he croaked, setting down his cup. "Most definitely not."

Well, that was settled. Taking another sip of tea, she said, out of curiosity about the documents he'd had earlier, "Were you doing research as well?"

The Face Stealer turned toward her in his seat, and a strip of moonlight caught in the long tail of his hair. "There is a myth of an underground hot spring in Nigun, one of the capitals of the Northern Territory. The water is said to contain incredible healing powers." A pause, as if considering whether to go on. "I reached out to an old contact. If it exists, they would know."

"Why do you need it?"

He sighed, stretching out his legs so the toe of one boot touched her calf. "The future is unclear. Any and all advantages when it comes to Nanuq need to be exploited. Death does not interest me just yet."

"I thought you were hard to kill," she countered.

"I am." A flash of teeth. "But that is not the same as impossible."

Her eyelids, which had begun to droop, snapped open. The tea. He'd put something in the tea.

The glass slipped from her fingers, yet the shatter never came. Apaay was cursing his name as sleep dragged her down into the dark.

← →

"Is she sleeping?" A child's voice.

"Hush, Mika. Hold this while I carry her."

More time passed. Apaay drifted and only managed to open her eyes when something heavy was laid across her chest.

It took a moment for the room to come into focus. Beyond the windows, night draped the Wood. There was no moon, but a few oil lamps cast the wood and parchment in a soft glow, the many volumes and scrolls sitting undisturbed on their shelves. Here, the world remained soft and untouched.

The Face Stealer was currently adjusting a blanket over her legs. Apaay, no longer seated at the desk, had been moved to one of the large, plush chairs.

Then she remembered the tea.

"You—"

"Bastard. I know." He regarded her warily while tucking the blanket around her shoulders, as if anticipating the moment when she would lash out. Lamplight wavered in the dark wells of his eyes.

The moment never came.

"You tricked me," she said, voice hoarse from sleep.

His hands stilled against the fur. The shadows of his power were absent, or had quieted somehow, retreating beneath his skin. "You needed rest. I won't apologize for it."

Huddled beneath the pelt of white fox fur, Apaay saw the demon's actions for what they were: another deceiving. But a kindness, too, in his own way. Those few hours of peace had been a balm to her fraught and weary soul.

"Thank you," she whispered.

Apaay assumed he would step back once he finished adjusting the blanket. Instead, he curled his hands over the arms of the chair, settling his weight into his forearms. "What do you dream about?"

She narrowed her eyes at him. "That's none of your business."

And there was the gleam, back from wherever it had disappeared to. "Afraid?" The timbre of his voice was a touch in the dark, silken as it found hot skin.

Apaay looked away. Flinched, thinking she saw a ghost through the window. Never had she seen anything so eaten at the edges. The eyes were deep bruises, large in a narrowed face. The jaw, chin, and cheeks were like chips of rock.

The ghost was her.

She was glad of the blankets, as they could not reveal how she dug her fingertips into her thighs. "Are you going to use this information against me?"

Slowly, he straightened, the angles of his face softening in what might have been compassion. And perhaps the need to understand. "No."

Her gaze met his in the window's reflection. The Face Stealer had poured out his lies like water rushing out to sea, but here was a single truth. An island. One word, murmured and exposed, as she was.

"It's been almost twenty years since the war ended," he said, "and I still dream of all the people I killed."

It was easier to have this conversation through the glass. It offered a layer of separation Apaay needed.

He went on in a softer tone. "One of them was my childhood friend. Before Nanuq rose to power, it was not uncommon to visit the other nations or pass within their territories. The lines had not yet been drawn. My friend was polar bear Unua, but he visited Unana during the summers with his family. Indeed, many visited the Wolf Kingdom's capital. Then Nanuq called his people to fight. My friend could not refuse. It was the last I saw of him until the day of the invasion."

"What did you do?" she whispered, curling into a smaller ball on the chair, not sure she wanted to know, but too engaged in his haunting to fight it.

Again, he focused on her face through the glass. "He would have killed me, killed my people." His right hand twitched against the arm of the chair, which he still leaned against. "So I killed him first."

The Face Stealer dropped his head forward. "I made sure he did not suffer. When it was over, I had to inform his mother that her only son was dead." His throat dipped. "I will never forget her scream."

Shadows began to writhe along his form, and he went on. "It's never easy ending a life. Whether consciously or not, you decide that what you are killing for is more important than life. I can stand by my decision to have killed in order to protect my people, but I can regret that decision, too."

As Apaay knew, no life was a single entity. It was a web, a thread between father and son and daughter and sister and mother and niece and grandparent and cousin.

She turned from the window to find him looking at her. A strand of hair had pulled free of his braid.

"In my dreams," she began, "I'm back in the arena. The woman I killed is staring up at me, except sometimes it's not the woman. Sometimes it's Eska or someone from my village. And I've killed them. I've killed them all." She pressed her lips together to halt their quavering. Sometimes she thought she might be moving past this torment, but the truth was, she only found better ways to avoid it. "H-how do you manage it?"

"The guilt?"

She nodded.

He didn't speak right away. Apaay sensed he was thinking deeply on the matter. "It's not an easy road." Moving to the window, he sat on the ledge, his back hunched. "I've come to terms with what I've done, and still there are days when I wonder what could have come of my life had things turned out differently. I think of who I am now and how different that person is from who I was thirty, forty, fifty years ago."

She recalled his comment from the meeting the other day. One hundred and fifty years of shared friendship with Ro and Kaan. "How old are you, exactly?" Because he looked to be a man in his prime, no older than thirty.

"Chronologically, I am nearly two hundred years of age." At her shock, he surprised her again with a lighthearted smile, a teasing spark in his blue-green eyes. The ring around the pupils was a crushing blue that shattered outward. "You can tell me, you know."

"Tell you what?"

"That I've aged well."

It wasn't enough to make her smile, but she felt a lightness that hadn't been there previously. "Is it because you're a demon?"

He leaned back against the windowpane. "The Unua age far more slowly than humans, with a lifespan of up to five hundred years. There is variation depending on the race, of course." His expression turned thoughtful. "In answer to your previous question, the stain of my actions did not ease for me until I forgave myself for what I had done."

She was not quite there yet. Some days she thought she would never get there. "I thought I heard Mika before. That wasn't a dream, was it?"

"No." With that, he began moving to the door. One by one, he blew out the lamps, not offering to elaborate. No longer was the dark kept at bay beyond the windows. It encroached within the walls and matted in the corners. Her spine locked up. She was being smothered by stone and the dark, and there was water dripping nearby.

"Wait." Apaay clawed at the blankets. "Keep the lights on."

The waver in her voice drew his attention, and he paused near one of the bookshelves. For a moment, all was quiet. Then he nodded, and light returned. Apaay didn't know if she felt greater relief for the light or for his lack of questions.

His long stride brought him to the door, which opened noiselessly. "Sleep, Apaay."

She did.

← 15 →

Someone slunk through the now-open door to the library. A shadow, a shade. It was not a dream.

Apaay was awake.

The figure slipped along the far wall, having not noticed her curled up in the cushioned chair, and for a moment, it was almost as if Apaay's body remembered. The stillness on a hunt. The waiting. A few lamps still burned, enough to illuminate her immediate surroundings. Shelves of books at her back. Windows to her left. There was a bone dagger displayed on the wall, within reach. Anything beyond the large rug warming the floorboards was cast in shadow.

As if sensing her gaze, the person stilled. Apaay lunged for the dagger as the masked figure moved, a blur of motion that ended with a knife at Apaay's throat.

"Ah ah," the figure said.

Apaay froze, her skin tingling with sensation. A dulled, clouded piece of her took notice as she pressed her back into the chair, staring up at the intruder.

The eyes were blue, and so pale they were nearly gray. It was all she saw of the person's face, for it was concealed by a painted mask carved into the shape of a fox head. White, blue, and silver for the fur, the nose black in its protruding snout. The mask curved all the way around the person's jaw, leaving only the neck exposed, the brown skin further darkened by shadow.

"Who are you?" Apaay demanded. Her pulse thundered along her damp temples.

The figure shifted an inch closer, studying her with acute focus. The edges of the painted bone were fired red from the light, the angles narrow and cruel. "Why are you in the Face Stealer's library?"

"He gave me access." But what Apaay didn't understand was how *this* person had gotten in. "How did you get in here?"

A wash of glittering darkness engulfed the room. When it lifted, Apaay found herself staring at the Face Stealer's back, as he had positioned himself between her and the masked figure. The knife now pushed into his chest.

"Haven't you heard of knocking?" the demon drawled, seemingly unconcerned with the weapon pointed at his heart.

Pale eyes blinked behind the mask, thin as crescent moons.

"Are you hurt?"

Apaay startled. He was talking to her. "No."

Satisfied, the Face Stealer settled in the chair beside her and stretched out his legs, crossing them at the ankles. "I realize it's been a while," he went on, "so let me remind you that the Wood is my home, and anyone present here is my guest. And you do not, under any circumstances, threaten my guests." His tone had hardened. He could probably hold court while lying down and it would still hold the promise of pain.

Apaay did not try to pretend his defense of her was anything special. He would likely do the same for anyone to bolster his reputation.

"I did not know if she was trustworthy."

Apaay gasped as the intruder's face was ripped away, mask and all, leaving behind a lack of features to provide context.

The Face Stealer lounged in the chair, head tilted, fingering a small bundle in his hand as he studied his handiwork with a faint air of fascination. As if it had not been he who had done this, but someone else. "You did not know if she was trustworthy, and yet you entered my home, broke into my library, threatened my guest." A cold rage killed the light in his eyes. "Let this be a warning to you. Your services I may need, but should you cross my boundaries, I will make sure you are never seen or heard from again. Nod if you understand."

The figure gave a stiff nod. The mask and face were returned.

The Face Stealer laced his fingers together. "Now, then."

The masked figure jumped as the dagger vanished. "That's mine."

"And now it's mine." The Face Stealer tucked it into his boot. "I'm glad you got my message."

"It was a little difficult to ignore."

The Face Stealer bared his teeth in what might have been a smile. "Yes, well, time is of the essence." He stood, his legs braced, steady and sure against the ground. "Did you find it?"

"First, my payment."

He held up a small bundle wrapped in cloth. "You'll receive this when you've proven you're good on your word."

The masked stranger glanced from Apaay to the clothed bundle, the chill of those washed-out eyes sending an odd current through her. There was something unnatural about the color. "The spring remains. However, it isn't easy to access."

Judging by the Face Stealer's momentary surprise, he hadn't expected this information. He rested a hand on the back of Apaay's chair. "I'm not concerned with the level of protection. Only its location." He peered out the window. "The moon will reach its zenith soon. We should be on our way."

As they moved toward the door, Apaay scrambled off the chair to follow. The Face Stealer glanced at her, then paused, his head tilted in a silent question.

Apaay looked at the masked figure in curiosity. Bared arms. No hint of muscle definition. Lanky built. A sleeveless maq had been layered over thin leggings. Who was this person behind the mask? Why work for the North's most notorious demon? It had been some time since she'd felt anything other than the fog, and she wasn't quite ready to let it go.

"I want to come with you," she told the Face Stealer.

His eyebrows lifted, and the lamplight curved along his jaw. "I thought you said you weren't interested in war."

"I'm not." And she stood by the statement. War, violence—that wasn't her world. "But I need to get out of this library. I need a break."

"A break, is it?" the figure said, voice mimicking one that Apaay knew quite well: her own. Its flat, exhausted timbre sent Apaay back a step. She hadn't realized she sounded so . . . frail.

Turning back to the Face Stealer, she found eyes of deepest blue, the shade of dusk melting into night. No gray. Perhaps there were no secrets to hide. Apaay wasn't sure whether to be relieved or concerned.

"Give us a minute," the Face Stealer said to the intruder.

The masked vigilante slipped out the door. The Face Stealer regarded Apaay until she said, "What?"

Whatever aloofness he had painted on in the intruder's presence fell away. Cautious, sober, precise—this was him now. "I need your word that whatever we discover about the spring, you will keep it to yourself. You don't tell Ila. You don't tell Masuk. Don't give me that look. I know you've been spending time with him. It's all right. I will overlook your poor taste in friends."

Apaay rolled her eyes. He was right to be worried about Masuk. As for Ila, it was more awkward to make an effort at conversation than not.

"The steps unfolding are years in the making, and while I wish there was more time to explain everything, there isn't and we have to make do. I'm almost positive Nanuq does not know of the spring's existence, otherwise he would have invaded the Northern Territory years ago. He cannot, under any circumstances, learn of it. Can I trust you to keep your word?"

Apaay thought of what he'd said. More death, should Nanuq discover the spring. Then she thought of how, for the first time in months, she had slept through the night without having nightmares, and that had been his doing. For that, she was grateful. "You have my word."

← →

Which was how Apaay found herself hiking through the forest in the dead of night, struggling to keep up as they ascended what felt like a small mountain. The switchback trail was extremely overgrown, barely discernable among the brush. Birch trees grew sparsely. The intruder with the pale eyes led the way.

Another person from his past. Despite herself, she was too intrigued to keep quiet as the stranger disappeared around the bend ahead. "Who is that?" she asked in low tones.

A branch snapped beneath his boot. "They call themselves the Pale One."

Her focus slanted to where the Face Stealer walked beside her, his stride long-legged and limber. "Does the Pale One have a name?"

"If they do, they've never told me."

Apaay tracked the masked figure's light-footed gait and was immediately impressed. The soil was barely disturbed. "When they spoke earlier, it sounded like my voice."

The skin around the Face Stealer's eyes crinkled faintly. "Within the art of invisibility, there is the art of blending in. The Pale One has exceptional mimicry skills."

"Is it some type of power?"

"I don't believe so. I imagine it's a skill they picked up from observing others."

"How do you know this—" Thief? Spy? Vigilante? "Person?"

"The same way I come to know most people," he said. "I was in need of information. They could acquire such information. I hired their services."

The sad thing was, Apaay didn't think he was joking. Aside from Ro and Kaan, she wondered if he had any true friends.

Catching Apaay's elbow to help her over a fallen tree, the Face Stealer asked, "How was your sleep?" Once she reached the other side, he released her.

"I didn't dream, if that's what you're wondering," she said, feeling the difference in her body, the lack of tension. A release she hadn't realized she'd needed.

"I'm glad." The trail narrowed, forcing him to walk behind her. "If you felt the tea helped you sleep, I'm happy to provide you with more."

Apaay had needed the silence as she had needed the pain—and the cold sweats, and the nausea—to disappear, and he had given it to her. "What was in the tea?"

"Moonflower. It blooms in the summer. The Keepers collect and dry the leaves."

"The who?"

"The Keepers of the Wood. You haven't seen them? They look like tiny people with leaf hats. They care for the Wood in my absence."

She hadn't, actually. "What do they get in return?"

"They have my protection, as do all who make the Wood their home."

Except the Wood wasn't her home, not really. "The tea did help. I'd like more, if it's not too much trouble."

The trees parted. The Wood stretched and spread before them, the sky bleeding into the trees. They stood on a bald, rocky mound curving above the canopy. The moon, round and full-bodied, looked near enough to touch.

The Pale One stood at the edge of a shallow pool with unnatural stillness. The Face Stealer knelt at the Pale One's side, dipping a finger into the water. Ripples spread from the point of contact. "Elements of the same origin retain their connection to one another," he explained to Apaay. "Because the water cycles through the earth, there is no one origin. It is a single thread binding it to other pools, rivers, streams. The water therefore acts as a mirror, allowing us to see onto the other side so long as there is water present." Gradually, the ripples transformed into something else. "Take a look."

Apaay gazed into the pool. It no longer reflected the star-flecked sky, but massive gates hewn into the mountainside. "This is the Northern Territory?"

"Yes," said the Pale One. They crouched, touching a finger to the water's surface, and it changed once more, offering a closer view: a grassy plain lying at the base of the gates. "These are the gates of Nigun."

This was the entrance to the Caribou Nomads' winter capital. Come summer, they would migrate to Nalwa for the season.

The Face Stealer said, "The Caribou Nomads have not been heard from since the war. Either my messages did not get through, or they were ignored."

Apaay stared hard at the scene. For whatever reason, the caribou Unua had closed their gates. Permanently.

"What are you thinking, wolfling?" His posture was loose, though his face was edged and cruel.

Her gaze narrowed. "I'm thinking you need to stop calling me that."

"Say please and I will."

They both knew she wouldn't.

"Something must have changed," she said, earning a curious look from the Pale One.

The Face Stealer nodded. "I thought as much, too." He turned to the Pale One. "Did you notice anything unusual while you were there?"

"No, but then I do not have anything to compare my experience to." Another image gave the three of them a distant, wider view of the area surrounding the gates. "You cannot enter the capital through the gates. They remain shut at all times, and visitors are killed on sight."

"I'm assuming you found another way in," said the demon reasonably.

"West of the gates is an underground river. It is the only access into the city." Another touch, another altering of the reflection: a smooth underground passage ending in twin blue doors. "The spring is located behind these doors. It is heavily guarded at all times." The Pale One bent one of their legs at the knee and rested their long arm atop, the wrist dangling. A quiet one, they were. "The path will eventually diverge. Take the route on the left." The pool's surface flashed shadow and streaks of light. The doors. The long, winding tunnel. More doors. "You will find the spring behind a glass wall."

The Face Stealer no doubt tucked away those details for a later time. "Guarded?"

The Pale One nodded. The rest of their body didn't move.

"How many guards would you say there were?"

"Between two and three hundred."

"Couldn't you materialize inside?" Apaay asked the Face Stealer. It had never stopped him before.

"An astute assumption, but no. The hot spring's power is touched by their god. I do not believe I would be able to enter the city by that approach. I doubt I would be welcome anyway." He sighed. "At the very least, I know more than I did. I'm not sure when I'll have the time to visit the spring, but soon, hopefully." He passed the Pale One the small bundle from earlier, along with their dagger. "Your payment."

The Pale One tucked both out of sight.

Apaay glanced between the two of them. She wondered how long the Face Stealer had been planning this, but didn't want to ask in case the Pale One wasn't privy to that information. The demon had connections in the most unlikely places. The North was vast, after all, and the Face Stealer almost two hundred years of age. It was plenty of time and opportunity to extend his influence.

"What do you want with the spring?" she asked.

He glanced at the Pale One as if deciding what to reveal, and how much.

The Pale One said, "Do you think I do not know everything you do?"

The demon narrowed his eyes. He said to Apaay, "Having access to its healing powers would go far when war arrives. And . . ." He shook his head and trailed off.

"And?" she said.

He turned back to her, his smile faint and assessing. "And that's it."

Another one of his lies. Another piece of a puzzle whose completed form was unknown to her. At some point in the future, the Face Stealer would infiltrate the Northern Territory in search of this precious spring. The only question was, what lengths would he go to reach it, and who would suffer as a result?

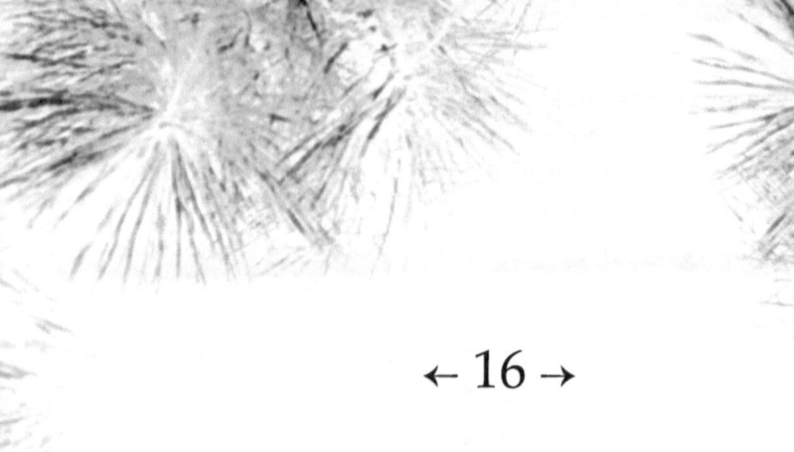

← 16 →

Someone shook Ila awake. Groggily, she rolled over in bed. Another shake, more insistent. Ila grumbled, swatting at the hand. The dream was too good to leave. When she received a third shake, she finally opened her eyes.

Apaay stared down at her, gaze wide and frightened. "I heard something." Fingers like claws on Ila's shoulder. "A scream."

The last of her confusion cleared, but Apaay was already out the door. Ila scrambled after her. She hurried past the bedrooms to a vined hallway with its carpet of grass, moonlight blazing a clear path, and nearly collided with the back of Ro's wheelchair as she turned the corner.

Ila gasped. Kaan knelt in a crimson pool beside a man who was more blood than flesh, more corpse than alive. His clothing was in tatters, the parka completely split across his back to showcase skin as ruined as chewed meat. He wore one boot. The exposed foot was blue-black with frostbite, as was his nose.

"I need a knife," Kaan said, lips white.

Tulimaq, who stood a few feet away with Apaay and Masuk, passed her a knife wordlessly. She began sawing through the man's parka. "Help me get his clothes off."

Ila hesitated to step forward, unsure if it was her place, yet no one else made any move to help. Did they not see the man was dying? Ro's face was startlingly pale. The vines swayed in an eerie, nonexistent breeze, heightening the shock of the situation. The others looked like they had been pulled from bed by the commotion, too.

Kaan turned, and her gold eyes caught the light just so, showcasing them as white orbs as she snarled, "So help me, if this man dies, I will make everyone's lives *hell*."

That settled it. Spurred into action, Ila dropped to her knees at the man's side, plucking the knife from Kaan's fingers so the woman could focus on stopping the bleeding. Only hours before, she and Kaan had been practicing a simple parry. But there had been a shift between them since Ila had discovered her parents were dead. She hadn't brought it up, as it was too painful a thing to discuss, but she sensed Kaan knew something was wrong. Ila thought of it constantly.

Peeling away the cloth from the man's stomach, Ila flinched and fought to hold in her rising gorge. A tree branch protruded from the left side of his abdomen, the weapon about as wide as her hand and as long as her forearm. Fat thorns covered the wood.

The Face Stealer materialized, already striding toward them, dark tendrils trailing in his wake. "What happened? I felt someone enter the Wood." He stumbled then, the color draining from his face as he took in the scene: Kaan's disheveled state, a man half dead, Ila's red-coated hands. "Kimmir?"

The man's eyes fluttered open. "Position . . . compromised." He stiffened as a convulsion gripped him. "Nanuq."

"Keep him talking," Kaan said, fumbling for the bandages that dropped into her lap from out of the void. She tried folding them, but her hands were too shaky, so she gave up and crumpled them into a ball, pressing the wad against the wound. Ila tried blotting a separate, smaller wound. The blood wasn't clotting. It seeped red and furious from his body. The thorns made it impossible to stop the bleeding without inflicting more damage and potentially pushing the thorns deeper into vital organs.

"Kimmir." The Face Stealer knelt on the man's other side, his lips so tight they peeled back from his teeth. "What happened?"

The man opened his mouth, closed it. "I—I was—"

"Shh." Ila imagined the Face Stealer gentling his tone. "Slowly."

"I did what you said." Dark spittle dribbled from the corner of his mouth. "Found the general's messages. Soldier caught m-me before . . . read them all." The man's teeth began to chatter. "Traveled all night. Knew you were counting on me."

The vines had stopped swaying. The Face Stealer's expression chilled Ila's blood. "Who told you that? I never gave you those orders."

Kaan's hands wrapped around the tree branch. The front of her clothes was soaked so deep a red so as to be almost black. "I'm removing the branch."

"Kaan, wait," said the Face Stealer.

"The thorns are poisoned!" she snapped.

Ila sucked in a sharp breath. She didn't know this man or his purpose, what role he played, his connection to the Face Stealer, but every word out of the demon's mouth seeped the room into further darkness. She knew enough of the impending conflict to understand the man's injuries would result in dire consequences down the line.

The man gasped as his eyelids fluttered, as his body grew cold and unfeeling from blood loss, as death reached for him, offering passage from this world to the next. "Am I going to die?"

"No." The Face Stealer's answer was the only certain thing, and he pressed his hands to the sides of Kimmir's face. "I won't let you die, Kimmir. Please. Who gave you those orders?"

The man relaxed somewhat. "Tulimaq told me—you said—"

The temperature in the room plummeted. Ila's spine snapped straight, her eyes tracking the demon warily. Behind him, Apaay covered her mouth with her hands for a reason Ila didn't understand.

"Hold him steady," Kaan said.

The weapons master pulled the branch free of his body, and Kimmir screamed as the thorns tore into him, before falling unconscious. Ila passed fresh cloth to Kaan, wishing there was something more she could do. Kaan kept pressure on the wound, a sheen to her eyes, and shook her head as if to clear it.

The Face Stealer turned his attention to where Tulimaq stood with his arms hanging at his sides, dark eyes shadowed. A rage so cold it appeared inhuman shuttered his face. "Tell me it's not true." When Tulimaq didn't answer, the Face Stealer barked, "Tell me!"

Suddenly, Kaan stiffened. Wrenching her hands away, she fell over backward, blood gushing down the man's torso.

"What are you doing?" The Face Stealer reached for the bloody cloth.

"Don't touch him!" She snatched at his hand.

"What are you talking about?" he snarled, yanking free of her hold. "He's bleeding out!"

He again reached for Kimmir, but Kaan tackled him to the ground. "It's a trap," she said. "The poison doesn't just affect the body. I can feel my power diminishing when I touch him."

The Face Stealer grew more alarmed with each passing moment. He pushed Kaan off of him, sitting upright. "Then how do we save him if we can't touch him, if you can't heal him?"

"We don't."

Ila sucked in a breath through her nose. So they were going to let this man die?

There had to be something they could do, something they hadn't thought of.

A snap of the demon's power, mounting as his rage did. Everything was happening as if in slow motion as the Face Stealer shifted his attention back to Tulimaq and unfurled to his feet. The young man, while muscled, was so slender in comparison to the Face Stealer, and far shorter. Tulimaq straightened with resolve, as if bracing himself for a blow.

The Face Stealer stopped a few inches away, looking down. Empires had risen and died in those eyes, ancient beyond anything she could conceive. "If he dies," he said, "you can be sure that you will pay for what you've done." He glanced at Ro, who was quiet, but the other man had no answers, either. "We need to get that wound shut."

And there it was.

I will do it, Ila said from her position on the ground, except no one was looking at her.

Apaay took a step forward. "What if I do it?"

"No." The Face Stealer didn't lift his eyes from the broken man. "It's too dangerous."

"How is it dangerous? I have no power, so the poison wouldn't affect me."

"You could still injure him further. Have you ever healed someone with this severe an injury before?"

"You don't trust me."

"Frankly, no. Your hands aren't steady enough for the job."

From the corner of her eye, Ila saw Apaay glance down at her palms. She shoved them into her pockets with a glare in the Face Stealer's direction, which he either didn't notice or chose to ignore.

Kaan, Ro, and the Face Stealer argued over the best course of action. There was nothing they could do about the poison until Kimmir's wounds were shut, and they couldn't touch him to do so. Ro couldn't comfortably reach from his wheelchair, and Masuk didn't offer to help. She suspected the Face Stealer wouldn't let him anyway. Meanwhile, Kimmir continued to lose more blood.

Ila pushed to her feet. She was sick of fading into the background. Her hands were steady. She could follow instructions. If they didn't listen to her, she would make them listen to her. *I said I will do it!* Ila repeated, shoving into the center of their circle.

Kaan's mouth opened, then snapped shut. She took in her apprentice, the assurance snapping in Ila's brown eyes. "She has a steady hand."

The three friends exchanged looks. Tulimaq stood apart, watching them carefully.

"We don't have a choice," said the Face Stealer. "Kaan, you guide her through the steps. Hurry."

← →

They had moved Kimmir to a room with walls of draping greenery. In the time it took a handful of refugees to carry him to the cot, Ila keeping pressure on the wound all the while, the room had been stocked with healing supplies by the Keepers. Except for Kaan, Ila, and Ro, everyone had been ordered out. Ro stared at the bloodied man with unusual intensity, his jaw locked, tendons straining in his neck. The coppery scent of the man's blood was starting to invade the space.

"Ro." Kaan stared down at the patient. Kimmir was unconscious, sedated with a sleeping draught. "Can you please open the window?"

As he did so, Ila studied the man's body. Bare torso, wet blood over warm-toned skin, his flesh brutalized. Gouges ran parallel on his shoulders and chest. His pulse flickered shallowly in his neck. Ila's task stretched before her, impossible and overwhelming.

She must save this man.

Kaan asked, "Are you ready?"

The weapons master had gone over the steps to the surgery. One of the thorns had broken off from the branch when Kaan had removed it and was still stuck in his body. Ila's first task was to remove the poisoned thorn. The second task was to stop the bleeding long enough to stitch the wound.

This man might very well die by Ila's hand. But if she did nothing, he would die either way. The information he knew concerning Nanuq's movements was too vital to be lost.

I'm ready.

Moonlight streamed through the now-open window. Resting her hands on the edge of the table, Ila examined the tools. All were carved of bone, with fine points or edges. There were five needles of varying sizes, and sinew she would use to sew the wound closed.

Ila didn't miss the uncertain glance Kaan sent her brother. It hadn't been easy for the woman to hand control over to someone else, especially when Kaan was a healer herself.

"When you remove the thorn," she said, ensuring she had Ila's full attention, "he will start bleeding more heavily than before. You must put as much pressure on the wound as you can. He cannot afford to lose any more blood."

Wrapping one hand around the thorn, Ila closed her eyes. Breathed. The wood was cold to the touch. Her hands, she was surprised to note, were steady.

The thorn slid free. Blood gushed as she applied pressure, her fingers slipping against the drenched cloth. Her mouth was dry, her stomach churning. It was a lot of blood.

"Steady," Kaan said.

A shudder ran through Ila at the give of flesh beneath her fingers. Blood strained like water against a dam. She pressed harder, elbows locked and arms straight, and maintained contact. Both Ro and Kaan were quiet.

Ila assumed that once the blood began to clot, she would be able to clean the wound enough to sew it closed. But as minutes passed, the blood flow did not alleviate. Kimmir's face was infinitely paler, droplets of sweat dotting his temples and upper lip. The blue of his veins ran like streams beneath the sagging skin under his eyes.

She must not have been applying enough pressure. Ila pressed harder until she felt bone slip across her fingers—one of his ribs. Blood leaked from the infinitesimal space under her fingers, sliding through the thinnest of open seams.

Moments later, a tremble ran through her hands. The man began to shake, and Ila's head snapped up, her panicked gaze seeking Kaan, then Ro. Her mentor's hands curled in her lap, the bones of her knuckles shoving against her skin so hard she thought they might puncture through. Ila couldn't speak to them, as her hands were the only things keeping the blood at bay. She asked a question with her eyes: *What do I do?*

Grabbing his sister's arm, Ro shook Kaan hard, once. "Tell Ila what to do. She's waiting for your instruction."

Kaan shook her head. "He's dying, Ro. Ila isn't experienced enough to save him."

"No." His easy manner quickly darkened in anger. "You're not giving her a chance." Then his face softened, and he squeezed his sister's hand, sharing something Ila wasn't privy to. "This is out of your control, Kaan. Accept that. And accept that Ila will do what she can to help." His attention shifted to Ila. He attempted a smile, and Ila, though tired, smiled back.

When Kaan turned to Ila, her eyes were clear. "You'll need to close the wound. Feel for where the tear begins. That's where you will sew it closed. Use small stitches."

With one hand, Ila accepted the needle and sinew Kaan passed her. With her other, she felt for the split in his skin, her fingers sliding through to grip the two flaps of his muscle where the worst of the blood leaked. She pierced the needle through and began the excruciatingly slow process of sewing this man back together.

The world as Ila knew it became flesh and blood and sinew and bone. Dimly, she was aware of Ro leaving. She blinked sweat from her eyes, but her hands didn't falter. The excess of blood made it difficult to see what she was doing. Kaan gave aid by pouring water onto the wound to flush it out.

Years spent carving animals from rock had honed the precision and dexterity of Ila's hands. She sewed up the wound, tied it off, before moving to the claw marks. Kaan added more water. The tight, crisscrossing seams were like the ridges of the Atakana. It wouldn't be a neat line, and he would have a scar, but what was a scar compared to breath in his body?

When the final stitches were complete, Ila dropped the tools and stepped away from the table. According to the moon's location, over two hours had passed.

Moving to Ila's side, Kaan squeezed her shoulder. Everything about the woman's expression drooped with haggardness. But there—a spark of pride. It was still too soon to know if Kimmir would wake. He was alive. For now.

"You should rest," said Kaan.

Ila nodded, not really paying attention. Standing in this death-filled room made her think of other deaths, of a quieter version. She said, *Why didn't you tell me my parents were dead?*

Kaan, startled, opened her mouth, then closed it.

You made me think there could be a chance. The heaviness she'd carried since the Analak village, the one of privation, took hold.

She was too close to tears with someone else's blood drying on her hands. The words needed to come out. *You really hurt me, Kaan.*

"I'm sorry, Ila." Eyes closed, she signed, *I'm sorry.* When she looked at Ila again, the woman was open in her regret. *It was never my intention to hurt you. I should never have said anything about them. I wanted you to know of your mother, and I got carried away. I didn't want to see you hurt.*

She had felt the hurt though, bitterly, which meant they hadn't been figments of her imagination. Was it wrong to feel angry over a thing while also feeling grateful? A tear slipped down her cheek, which she dashed away.

"Come on." Kaan put her arm around the younger woman. "Let's get you cleaned up."

"That will have to wait." Ro had returned. "We're needed in the meeting chamber. All of us."

← 17 →

Hours later, the frantic upheaval of the evening had lulled, though it had not completely dissipated. In the aftermath of Kimmir's attack, there was a sense of trepidation, a fragility to the air, as if one had planted the seed of a poisonous flower and now waited for it to sprout.

The meeting chamber contained a long table and high-backed chairs and was occupied by Apaay and Ila, Ro and Kaan, and the Face Stealer. It was a room of fatigue and shadowed eyes, of having aged years in the span of hours. The vined walls were too close, and the ebb of adrenaline left Apaay drained. The Face Stealer had insisted on her attendance.

This is your world, too. It's time you start being a part of it.

So here she sat, nauseated and shaky, with the beginnings of a headache stirring.

"What of Kimmir?" asked the Face Stealer. Cradling his teacup in his hands, he watched a curl of steam disperse.

Out of everyone, Kaan appeared the most run-down. The Keepers of the Wood had come earlier, bringing out tea and cakes made from sweet grain and pouring cups of steaming liquid for all, their tiny bodies working together to lift the heavy teapot. Apaay nibbled on a cake absently after slipping a bit of moonflower into her tea to calm herself.

"Kimmir is barely alive," Kaan said, staring into her drink with faraway eyes. She hadn't had time to wash. Neither had Ila. As such, blood flaked off their hands and faces and necks. "I don't know if he will survive the night."

Ro studied his sister with an unreadable expression, the skin under his eyes bruised. In his body, still, that simmering tension.

The Face Stealer tightened his grip on the teacup. "Kimmir wouldn't be in this state," he finally said, "if Tulimaq had not sent him to certain death." Like everyone in the room, he still wore his bedclothes, which, for him, consisted of a thin, long-sleeved garment that reached mid-thigh and leggings. Apaay, aware that she was staring at his less-intimidating attire, looked elsewhere. "I do not care what excuse he has for his actions. I told him weeks ago to *not* give Kimmir the go-ahead. Apaay can attest to that."

It was true. Tulimaq had done the complete opposite of what the Face Stealer had ordered. What had been the combat master's reasoning? She did not know much about Tulimaq. Maybe it was time to start paying attention.

"The question," said Apaay, "is why he would go against your orders."

Everyone looked at her in surprise. She tamped down her irritation. It wasn't that she didn't want to contribute. A small part of her did. A larger part wondered if anything she said was useful. Meeting the Pale One over a week ago and learning about the hot spring had opened her eyes a little more.

"What?" she snapped at their continued staring.

"The question," countered the Face Stealer after a moment, "is whether this was a deliberate act or a grave error."

The tension in the room ratcheted higher. A bold insinuation, yet not without evidence.

He was only trying to help, Ila said.

Apaay winced at what she knew was coming. The smoothing of the demon's voice, a cruelly edged croon that whispered *peril*. Apaay almost took Ila's hand to show her support, then thought better of it. They had grown apart these past weeks, and Apaay wasn't sure how to bridge the distance.

"So," he said, locking those swiftly changing eyes onto Ila. "The rabbit finally grows a spine. Why is it that you jump to his defense, I wonder? I was under the impression that Tulimaq went out of his way to avoid you, if I'm not mistaken."

Ila trembled where she sat. It felt as if Apaay were watching a much larger animal tear the wings off a small bird.

"You do not have an answer. Tell me, what evidence do you have that Tulimaq was trying to help, as you claim? Harboring feelings for a man who has the emotional capacity of a rock doesn't count, I'm afraid."

Apaay pushed to her feet. "That's enough," she said, vibrating with fury and sickness. Apaay knew how little effort it took the Face Stealer to rip someone apart. Ila did not deserve that treatment.

A deadly light flared in his black gaze. Night pressed upon the room, threatening to extinguish the lamps on the table.

"Numiak," Ro warned.

The demon was still looking at Apaay when he barked, "Send him in."

All five of them tracked Tulimaq as he entered the room and stopped a few feet beyond the threshold.

The Face Stealer's body was relaxed, though his eyes were feral. The bedclothes, she realized, did not matter. It was his eyes you must always pay attention to. "If it were up to me," he began pleasantly enough, one ankle tossed over his thigh, "I'd have your tongue ripped out and your carcass tossed to the wolves."

One by one, the crickets in the room halted their song. It was so quiet Apaay could hear herself swallow.

"Nine years," he said, pushing to his feet and circling the table. The air crackled tumultuously, reaching down her throat and grabbing hold of her heart and lungs. Apaay caught Kaan and Ro's shared look. *Do something,* it said. She wondered if anyone was brave enough to come between the Face Stealer and his prey.

"Nine years!" he roared. "Gone, because of a *fool.*" He stopped in front of Tulimaq, who had backed into the wall. Their noses were a hair's breadth apart. "Give me one good reason why I shouldn't mark you as a traitor and cut you down where you stand."

Tulimaq, to his credit, did not quail under the demon's wrath, and Apaay did not know if that made him brave or a fool like the Face Stealer had claimed. "Kimmir was the one who approached me with the request. I denied him, but he was insistent. You told me to pass on the message that he not move forward in his plan. That is what I told him." Through it all, Tulimaq's voice was even, detached.

"A week later, I got word from Kimmir. The general had received a message from an unspecified army base located in the Western Territory."

The Face Stealer took a step back from Tulimaq. "An army base of polar bear Unua?"

"Yes."

It was Kaan who spoke. "Have you returned home at all, Numiak?"

Slowly, he slid his hands through his hair. "No." Soft. "There's nothing to return to."

Worry touched Ro's eyes. He drummed his fingers on the wheels of his chair. "I'm assuming they're there to search the grounds for the object? Isn't that where Nanuq believes it to be hidden?"

"The object of power?" Apaay clarified.

Again, surprise on the demon's features at her input. "Yes." A pause. "Why?"

If the object was believed to be in the Western Territory, then maybe it was different from whatever Yuki had stolen from the Face Stealer. She had thought they might be the same. "No reason," she mumbled.

The Face Stealer didn't look convinced, but then Tulimaq said, "That was the point I gave Kimmir the go-ahead. The fact that he had never heard of the base was unusual, and I thought the message might prove informative."

Ila gripped her tea in both hands, pale, still shaken by the way the Face Stealer had carved her open with that silver tongue. Apaay empathized with her, she did, but she was more concerned with this newfound information.

Kaan snapped, "Well?"

Tulimaq glanced at each of them. "The message mentioned wolf Unua as prisoners."

The Face Stealer's face leeched of color. A flicker of emotions—shock, pain, dread—as he grappled for control. It was a strange thing, a very strange thing. Apaay thought she would have been glad of this, his turmoil, but what she experienced felt a lot like pity. "Are you certain?"

"Yes."

Shadows manifested around his form. "That *bastard*."

Tulimaq flinched. "There's something else." He held out an official-looking document.

The Face Stealer read through it, then went still, the only movement the flamelight flickering against his bone structure. "Yuki and Nanuq have reinstated the alliance."

A deathly quiet settled over the room.

Ro blinked, his mouth open. Kaan swore. Apaay and Ila shared a look of uncertainty. The Face Stealer had warned Yuki against the alliance, back in the labyrinth. What did this mean that it had been dug up from its grave? What purpose did it serve, and how would it affect the future of the North?

He set the document on the table. "I have to go to them."

"Sit down, Numiak." It was Ro's even manner.

"There's no time."

"No." Ro caught his wrist as he strode for the door, yanking him to a halt. "You're not leaving until we figure this out. *Together.* Look." Though he lowered his voice, Apaay heard every word. "I know this must be hard for you, but acting alone . . . that's not how we solve problems, and you know it."

The silence yawned. "My people are suffering."

"Who is to say it's not a trap?" He gentled his tone. "They have survived this long. They can survive a few more months until we lay the groundwork for a rescue mission."

"A few more months? Ro, if what Tulimaq says is true, they've been imprisoned for almost *twenty years*."

"And yet they are still alive." He didn't waver. "If Nanuq gets word that we know of this, he might kill them before we have a chance to save them. At the moment, their anonymity is their greatest protection."

The Face Stealer lowered himself back into his chair as Tulimaq said, "I think we need to act."

"*We?*" The demon appeared darkly amused. Ila glanced between them in increasing trepidation. "No, Tulimaq. Were it not for you, Kimmir wouldn't be hanging onto life as we speak. As such, there is no *we*. There is *you*, and there is *us*."

It was one of the few times Apaay had seen any true expression cross Tulimaq's features. She thought it might be shock.

"At least," he amended, "for now. We will speak later of the mission I have for you. You're dismissed."

The door shut with a quiet click. Apaay winced at the pounding in her head. She still didn't know what to make of Tulimaq. He had made a mistake, and a grave one at that.

"Mission?" Kaan asked. "You didn't say anything about a mission."

"That's because I made it up. Although now that I think of it, I might have a task for him."

"What are we going to do?" Generally, the weapons master was bold, assertive, unwavering in her opinions. Tonight, her sense of security had been rocked, her manner demure. "Without Kimmir, we have no way of tracking Nanuq's movements."

The leaves from the overarching trees stamped shadows onto the demon's face. It was unearthly how well he fit into the places of little to no light. "That's why I need your father's aid."

"Numiak." Kaan sighed in a way that made Apaay suspect they'd had this conversation before. "Our father's word is law. Without his consent, we can do nothing. The Flock is under his command, not ours. I've said it before and I'll say it again: Go to him. Explain your position."

"You know he despises me."

"And he will continue to do so unless you come forward with the truth."

"I have an idea." The Face Stealer turned to Ro. "You are next in line for Avi, are you not? Why can't you speak to your father in my stead?"

Ro was quiet for so long Apaay didn't think he would answer. Thanks to her research, she knew the Avi was leader of all the owl Unua. "You know where I stand on the matter of my father."

"Perhaps it is time to have that conversation with him."

Whatever conversation the Face Stealer was referring to, it was obvious Ro did not share the same sentiment. He ignored his friend.

"You know," Kaan murmured, "there's always the Raven."

The Face Stealer's head swiveled in the weapons master's direction. Ro also watched her as if she had suggested they throw themselves off the nearest cliff. Which, Apaay admitted, she sort of had.

"Are you mad?" said the Face Stealer in bewilderment. "Actually, never mind. I already know you're mad."

"What do you want me to say? You refuse to approach our father with a possible alliance. At the moment, we don't know what Nanuq's intentions are save finding an object of power that may or may not be hidden in the Western Territory, that may or may not even exist! With Kimmir injured, we have no eyes on the inside. Nanuq grows stronger with each passing day, and we have no means to build a force that might stop him from crushing us a second time. If you have another suggestion, I'd *love* to hear it."

"I don't know," growled the Face Stealer. "I don't know!"

"Then why are we even having this discussion?" she snapped with a wave of her hand. "I thought you told us you had a plan. What's your plan, Numiak? What is your plan?"

Conversation ceased, the silence so abrupt Apaay's ears rang. Or perhaps that was the pressure throbbing behind her eyes, which continued to build as this meeting dragged on. She rubbed her temples with a wince before dropping her hand.

Darkness sputtered, swelling as the Face Stealer's pupils pooled to the whites of his eyes. Ila was pushed so far back into the seat cushion she may as well have disappeared. Ro shook his head in weariness, dropped his shoulders. Power crackled on Apaay's tongue, and still that pressure demanded her attention in the back of her mind. Its strength dictated she couldn't give her full attention to the discussion.

Ila signed, her hands trembling, *Who's the Raven?*

The Face Stealer canted his head. His eyes were all pupil. "The Raven," he said, his voice not quite a whisper, a skating of ice and wind, "is a dark god who dwells in Taggak."

"The Shadow Realm," Apaay elaborated at Ila's confusion. "The Analak know him as the Messenger. He ferries the newly dead across the Sky Bridge to the spirit world."

"He has immense power," said the Face Stealer. "But he is not of this world."

"And you are?" Apaay said.

Slim rings of violet emerged around his pupils. They were shrinking back to their normal size. The shadows, too, settled into the bumps and hollows in the rooted ground, the lamps relighting. "Not entirely." That ageless power rumbled in the air. "I may have been made from Taggak, but the Raven *is* Taggak. Far older, far more powerful than I. As such, I do not think it would be in our best interest to ask for his aid. He would be unlikely to give it anyway."

"What choice do we have?" Kaan said. The weapons master wouldn't let the demon push aside her suggestion so easily. "With the alliance reinstated, we face a far more powerful adversary. The seal Unua will join with Nanuq. Your people are, for the most part, dead, imprisoned, or scattered. The caribou Unua might ally with us, but it's not a guarantee. That leaves my people, should you ever approach our father. The Raven would act as a powerful ally."

The Face Stealer splayed his hands on the table. "I understand where you're coming from, Kaan, I do, but even if we did approach him with the idea, you forget he is imprisoned."

She shrugged, unconcerned with the obstacle. "Free him from his imprisonment."

Ro choked on his tea, spewing liquid across the table. It vanished with a wave of the Face Stealer's hand. "I knew you were mad, but I didn't know you were *this* mad. There's enough chaos in this world, don't you think?"

Kaan ignored her brother. "Do you remember what happened the last time Nanuq came into power?"

"I will never forget." So many emotions were wrapped around that one statement. Guilt and turmoil and shattered hope.

"Then you know it will happen again, and soon. At some point down the line, Nanuq will release his armies on the North, and he will not stop at one territory. He will take the Central Territory, the Northern, the Eastern. When that time comes, we must choose: Join him, or go to war." Planting her hands on the table, she leaned her weight into her forearms, looking at each of them in turn. Kaan was fierce in the moonlight. "I know what my answer will be. I will fight to keep my home and people safe. But if we want to give ourselves that chance, we need power on our side. Give the Raven what he wants. Make a deal to free him from his imprisonment. Have him join his strength with ours."

Ro said, "I still think we should consider other options."

The Face Stealer turned to Apaay, considering. "What do you think, wolfling?"

Surprise shimmered through her. "What do I think?" Hands curved around her teacup, she stared into the amber liquid. "I think I don't care."

"Really? You're not interested in the state of the world? What about the lives of your people?" The force of his stare bored into the side of her head, and she swore the pounding increased. "Did you not see what happened to Kimmir? This is bigger than you know. Now tell me: Do you still wish to do nothing?"

Her eyes were as cold as his voice, as cold as she imagined his heart to be. She uttered, simply, "Yes."

He turned away without another word.

Discussion turned toward timelines, strategy, warfare. The throbbing in her head worsened, spearing into an acute pain. Whatever force was trying to get her attention, it wasn't lifting its power.

Shakily, she stood, and Ila stood with her. The voices cut off.

Using the chairs for balance, Apaay shuffled to the doorway as the Face Stealer materialized directly in her path. "Where are you going?"

Her hand dropped from her forehead, but she didn't lift her eyes. "I'm leaving." It was impossible to dredge up emotion through the pain.

"Oh, let her go," said Kaan.

Apaay could have kissed her.

With a chilly glare, he stepped aside, allowing her and Ila to pass. The door closed with a snap on their way out.

Silently, Apaay strode down the short hallway and turned a corner, slumping against the wall when she was out of sight. She pressed her palms to her eyes, trying to quell the swelling pressure, a force she was helpless to block out.

Ila's hands came to rest on her shoulders. Always so light, her hands.

The pain began to migrate from her temples to her cheeks, then to her chin and jawline, until her entire face seared with agonizing heat. Apaay gasped, unable to see. Her knees hit the earth and sank in.

"Water," Apaay croaked, hoping Ila would be able to read her lips even though they were partially shielded by her hands.

Pulling Apaay to her feet, Ila ushered her to a nearby creek. Kneeling on the damp bank, Apaay lowered her face into the water. A chilly, bracing relief spread across her skin, sweet enough to drink, soft enough to soothe, as it engulfed the fire in her face and snuffed it out.

Once the rash-like burn subsided, Apaay pulled back. Ila watched her with concern.

What was that? her friend asked.

I don't know. But it had been horrible. Another few minutes trickled by before the dizziness subsided and she could stand. With a pained breath, Apaay signed, *I feel something. A tugging sensation, like when I heard the faces in the labyrinth.* It could be the face she'd been looking for—Masuk's beloved.

Is it painful for you?

Not so much anymore. With a start, Apaay realized this was the first time they had conversed in weeks. Ila was different to her. The girl was coming to know her own strength, and Apaay was glad of it. One of them needed to heal. *It might lessen if I find where it's coming from.*

"Apaay?"

Startled, she looked over. Masuk hovered on the opposite side of the creek, his face folded in agitation.

She said to Ila, *Can you give us a minute?*

Ila didn't look happy about the interruption, but she moved away to give them privacy.

"What is it?" she said when Masuk hopped the creek.

"I wanted to see if you had any updates for me."

"No." She shot Ila a look. Her friend glared at Masuk, arms folded across her chest. He didn't notice, as his attention was on Apaay. "I'm not sure if the faces are in his office." There was also the strange shadow door in the library. That seemed a more likely possibility. "It's too risky to search at the moment."

Masuk's eyes darkened with an unreadable emotion. "He would know."

She studied him in uncertainty. Was it anger she felt tightening the air? Whatever it was, she didn't like it.

"I'm doing the best I can," Apaay explained, feeling strangely guilty at not having more information for him. She would have thought he'd be more understanding, considering she was looking for two different objects for two different people. "I'm going to need more time."

"You're right. You're absolutely right. But, Apaay—" Serious eyes fell heavy against her. "We don't have forever."

"I know that." The more he pressured her, however, the more reluctant she was to press forward. She fought against her frustration. Toward him? Herself? She didn't know. "Do you have any more information for me? Something that might give me an idea as to where the Face Stealer would keep the faces?"

He squinted through the sunlit trees, and stared for a drawn-out period of time. "I wish I did, but I don't."

"When you were trapped in the labyrinth, did you learn of anything related to Yuki? Something she might have taken that wasn't hers?"

He frowned, though didn't look at her. "No. Why do you ask?"

She had thought Masuk might know something, a clue to help her discover what, exactly, Yuki had stolen from the Face Stealer. It was disappointing. "No reason." This was too exposed a place to discuss it. Ila could read their lips.

He shifted his weight onto his heels. "If you find anything, let me know." And as quickly as he had appeared, he hopped the creek and vanished into the brush.

Apaay stared after him, perplexed. How odd. How very, very odd.

Is everything all right? Ila asked once Masuk was gone.

Apaay shook her head. She couldn't talk to Ila about this, though she wanted to. Her frown deepened the more she thought of Masuk's behavior. She still felt the pull in her mind. *This way.*

When they reached the tree leading to the library, Apaay knew where the thrum of power was coming from. Gesturing Ila up the spiral staircase, she pushed open the door to the room where she had spent so much of her waking and sleeping hours. As usual, it was empty, since only she and the Face Stealer had access to the space. Apaay hastened them to the secret door engulfed in shadow.

Ila's fear was palpable, but Apaay didn't flinch from the coiled mass pulsating around the door's frame. She reached forward, and the shadows parted to allow her hand to pass through. The handle warmed at her touch.

"Open," she demanded.

A lock thunked out of place, and the door swung inward.

An oily sensation ran through her. She hadn't thought it would actually work.

The curtain of shadow shifted like a cloth nudged by a breeze. Cold air whooshed outward to touch her face, and suddenly, the pressure in her head vanished. Apaay stared into the void. If the doorway led to Masuk's beloved's face, might it be an answer to easing her grief, knowing she was not a failure? She tried to fight the feeling of water creeping up her neck.

Ila latched onto her arm as she stepped forward.

Apaay paused. "You can't stop me, Ila. I'm going in there whether you like it or not."

I'm not here to stop you. I'm coming with you.

She swallowed, turning back to the door. "Don't let go."

Together, hands clutched tight, they stepped into the cold, deep dark.

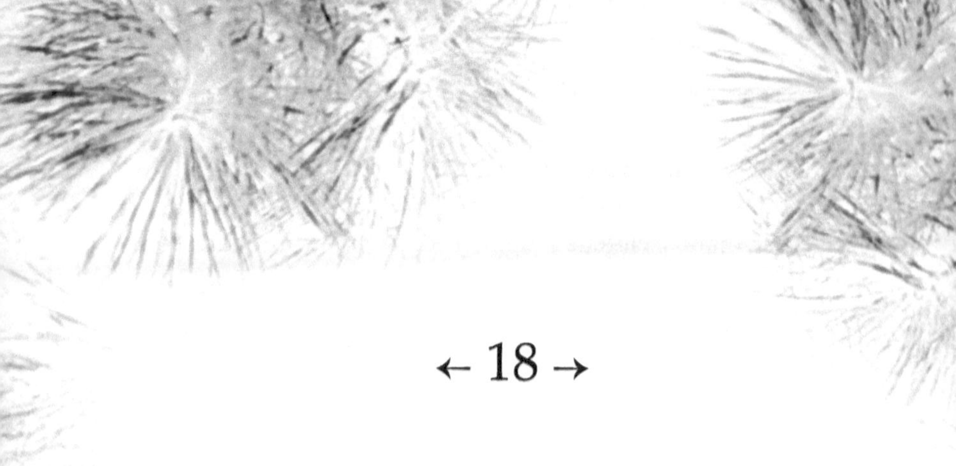

← 18 →

It was an ageless dark. A place of such abysmal fathoms Apaay knew it was not of this world. It grasped at her skin, stroked along her mind, utterly engulfing. The world was an opaque shutter. She could see nothing beyond it.

The ground began to slide out from under Apaay's feet. A flash of heat licked at her body as the darkness grew, grew, *grew*. Here were iron bars, a pail of water, a blanket smelling of musk, the rust of old blood. Beyond the cell were doors and hallways and ever-changing rooms.

Clutching Ila's hand so hard her bones creaked, Apaay dropped to her knees. "I can't," she choked out, though Ila could not hear her. It was too heavy, too much, too soon.

Light from the library streamed through the doorway but went no farther than the first few feet. Apaay realized she had not heard herself speak, had only felt her mouth changing shape. No voice. It, too, was lost in the void.

This was what happened when she found herself in dark, enclosed spaces. It was why she could not sleep in Ila's room, or her family's tent. Why she found herself, night after night, returning to the open meadow, the secluded grove where moonlight dappled the water's surface. Even if she wanted to, she did not have the ability to scream, for it was contained within her mind.

Vaguely, Apaay felt Ila kneel in front of her. Apaay blinked, yet saw nothing.

Ila fumbled for Apaay's hand and signed into her palm, *Do you want to go back?*

Back into the library, back into the light.

But something had called her into the dark.

Lifting her head, Apaay looked over her shoulder, but she no longer saw the library door. The shadows, it seemed, had answered for her.

With growing dread, Apaay allowed Ila to pull her upright and lead her forward in measured steps.

The emptiness was eternity. She had no idea where they were stepping. If they might suddenly find themselves plunging through a crevasse that had ripped open the earth. Whatever this place was, the Face Stealer doubtless had no issue maneuvering, for those who were made from darkness had nothing to fear.

There was nothing to be afraid of. This was not a cell, not the labyrinth, not her death bound in iron. Apaay had chosen to walk through that door. She needed to find out if the face Masuk sought was indeed tangled in these depths. By finding this face, his past would no longer haunt him, chase him, chew at his insides. If Apaay could fix Masuk's circumstances, there might be hope for her, too.

It was becoming increasingly difficult to breathe. The hollow beneath her breastbone pained her, as though a pick of ice was lodged between her ribs, yet heat crawled through her chest, closing her airway in the process. Apaay gasped, a hand flying to her throat.

In a surge of desperation, Apaay lunged, dragging Ila behind her. She was in the dark water beneath the ice. She was clutching that bone knife and stabbing it into the polar bear Unua's throat, driving it into Nakaluq's heart. She was standing at the edge of her village, looking down at the smear of ash.

Yuki's high-pitched laughter echoed in her head as she fell into the boiling water. Again, as she was thrust into a blizzard, naked to the blistering chill. Two months in hell and she had escaped alive, but she wasn't living, not anymore.

No matter how fast she ran, Apaay could not reach a place of reprieve. Ila's hand began to slip, and Apaay did not realize how sweaty her palm had become until Ila's fingers slid free.

And Apaay knew this was one more shame she must face, because Apaay . . .

Apaay kept running.

← →

Ila's hand, now empty, dropped to her side, curling around the fur of one trouser leg. No more than a few minutes had passed since Apaay's disappearance, but it was already too much time.

She left you.

Ila denied it as soon as the thought surfaced. Apaay wouldn't have done this. Apaay, who had fought for Ila, who was willing to *die* for her sister, would never do something like this.

These recent months, however, painted a different picture. Apaay had withdrawn into herself, a ghost of a girl Ila had glimpsed but a handful of times. Ila would lie in bed staring at the canopy, wanting so badly for *her* door to open, for Apaay to seek *her* support in this trying time. But she was afraid. What if Apaay turned from her? What if she was, in fact, disposable?

Saddened by the thought, Ila continued onward. Soon, the black basin above her head shifted hues. The coolness in the air began to warm, and an acrid scent singed the hairs in her nostrils, her skin tightening, itching beneath her arms and the space behind her knees where sweat gathered.

Somewhere beyond, something was burning.

Tears welled from the sting in the air, and as she crossed the threshold of an open doorway, a wall of desiccating heat plowed into her, sending her two steps back.

White tongues lashed at the charred walls of what appeared to be a bedroom, the smoke so thick she could barely make out the windows, or what was left of them. The air rippled with orange light, ash swirling as fiercely as a tempest rising. If she were to move any closer, the fire would melt the skin from her hands, yet there was an otherness to it all. Distance. Whatever this was, Ila was an observer.

Heat gathered beneath the soles of her boots, and Ila had no warning before light and heat rammed together like two boulders colliding, a portion of the nearest wall exploding with blistering, glittering force.

Ila's skull rammed against the wood. Pain ripped down her neck and spine. She cried out, clutching her head in both hands and curling into a ball. The world was spinning, rippling, burning before her eyes.

She climbed to her feet and was stumbling toward the doorway when a tiny form rolled from the bed nearest to her, pulling the blankets with it. Shoving them aside, Ila gasped at the child huddling beneath the fur. The girl looked to be only three or four years old. Long dark hair streaked her shiny, sweaty skin, and she clapped her hands over her ears before looking around, eyes like whole moons, face collapsing in a petrified sob. Ila, her hand outstretched, couldn't find the power to move.

A door to her left burst open, wood chips splintering the air. A tall figure approached, distorted by the thickening smoke. Ila stiffened in surprise, dimly aware of how the embers flickered from the sudden wash of shadow trailing in the Face Stealer's wake. He was dressed in clothes befitting a warrior, a spear slung across his back, a bone mask dangling around his neck, skin spattered with mud and gore. He didn't give any indication she was there.

He couldn't see her, Ila realized. Neither could the girl, whose face crumpled with relief at seeing another person in the smoke. Ila choked on an inhalation as, on the far side of the room, a wooden beam plummeted to the floor, sparks raining down. The flames gorging on the walls climbed upward, blackening everything they touched.

The Face Stealer cradled the girl against his chest. They had barely moved two feet when a second, larger beam buckled from the ceiling and struck the Face Stealer's shoulder.

They went down. Caught beneath the flaming beam, the Face Stealer struggled to right himself. It was clear he was not at full power.

Another portion of the wall blew out. The Face Stealer extinguished the ravaging inferno with a wave of darkness and took the girl into his arms. A gash on the girl's head dripped blood from where the beam had struck her. Another collapse of flaming wood descended, blocking their path to the door. The mass of air pressed upon Ila's chest. Vibrations shuddered through the soles of her feet and traveled up her legs.

The building lurched to the side.

Get out, she thought. *Leave this place.*

A blink, and they were gone, having enfolded themselves into a pocket of shadow.

Knowing they had escaped alive, Ila stumbled back through the doorway. She had seen that girl before. Her eyes, or was it something else?

She finally realized what it was as, with a sense of ill dread, Ila reached up and traced the scar curving along her skull.

← →

She needed to go back.

Apaay had run as fast and as far as she could, tearing through the endless dark. That initial moment as she'd fled, Apaay had touched some unknowable piece of herself, one that remembered doing this long ago. A sense of freedom, a spirited life. Apaay didn't understand, but she had *felt.* The vibrations in the earth. The coiling of her muscles, feeble though they were. It was but a glimpse into a heart she no longer recognized, so she pushed it from her mind and ran until her legs folded. Then she'd rolled onto her back, gasping for air.

The darkness remained, and shame.

She had left Ila behind.

It hadn't been intentional. The fear had slipped into her blood so easily. Apaay couldn't separate then from now. It was, always, now. How many times would she abandon those she loved before she stopped?

Feeling wearier than she ever had, Apaay pushed to her feet and forced her legs to move, each one lifted and set down, heavy as boulders, shuffling in the direction she believed she came from. Though her heart still raced, the tightening around her throat had eased. The shadows wouldn't smother her. She had gotten out.

Then: the muffled slap of shoe on stone. It was the first sound she had heard in hours.

Stone gave way to frosted white grass. The sky was a sweep of simmering violet where the sun settled below. Wherever she was, the long night had already begun closing in. She stood on a single strip of untouched grass in a vast clearing. The remaining earth was trampled and scarred, as if a herd of caribou had cut a swath through it.

Despite the landscape's unfamiliarity, Apaay had the strangest sense she had been here before. Which was silly. She could not recall there ever being a time when she had seen this place. She'd spent her life near the sea, and there was no salt in the air, no burning brine leading her to shore.

That presence pushing at her mind urged her to follow the tracks in the half-frozen mud. A walk hurried into a slow jog. Yes, she knew this place. Home. It did not make sense, for this was not *her* home. Suddenly she was afraid. A searing pain ripped open her side as fatigue pooled in her limbs, the last of her power guttering. It had been so long since she'd experienced a burnout. She hardly had the energy to stand, much less run, but she needed to reach the den. Three hours had passed since the breach.

Apaay came to an open meadow. She skidded to a halt, breathing hard, the air searing. Smoke, rising from above the canopy.

She was too late.

Apaay bowed over her knees, confused as to why she felt this anguished when she did not know what was going on. Her entire body ached as if she had run twenty miles without stopping, and she fell to the ground with a gasp. What was happening to her?

Footsteps on the edge of the clearing.

Apaay stiffened, panic sinking its teeth into her as two pointy black slippers came into view.

"The almighty Face Stealer having fallen. A pity."

Apaay physically recoiled from the sound of Yuki's voice. She could only lie there, in agony, waiting for it to end. The frozen ground soothed the swelling on her face. She had not noticed it before, but there was blood mixed with the mud, fresh, and shards of bone.

"You." The voice spat from her mouth, so deep it reverberated in her chest. "You did this." She jerked, yet hadn't the energy to sit up. She couldn't even shift into her wolf form. "You killed these people."

"No, Numiak." Black threads swept back from her childlike face, damp from the ocean's spray, which still clung to her. "*You* killed them."

Apaay experienced another wave of confusion. Numiak, Yuki had said. This body wasn't hers. Neither were the thoughts.

"You had a choice," Yuki went on. "You always had a choice. I told you if you chose the future, you could one day become someone great. Now look at you. Bleeding out, no better than the carnage soiling your home."

Yuki had come from Tor, infiltrating the Wolf Kingdom while he had been fighting with the Owl Clan to keep Nanuq's forces from taking Nannek. He had done all he could to protect them, but it hadn't been enough. He had trusted the wrong people.

"I didn't believe it when Kenai told me," he managed through his pain, teeth coated in blood from a gash on the inside of his cheek, a blow to the face he had been unable to stop. "I still can't believe it."

"Why?" The tips of Yuki's slippers nudged his forehead, and she crouched down, gloved hands coming to rest beneath her chin. "Am I that unlovable?" Her mouth was hard, though her eyes were wide, exposed.

The Face Stealer growled, "You are so selfish you have no love for anyone but yourself."

Her lips thinned. "That's not true."

"Your own father didn't even love you."

Her face contorted into something fierce and utterly inhuman. She snapped to her feet, breathing hard. "Don't say that."

"He didn't love you," the Face Stealer repeated. The words were cold. "He never will. The invasion changes nothing."

"I said that's not true!" She whirled around, hands clasping her elbows. Then she lunged and aimed a vicious kick at his side where the open wound bled. He momentarily blacked out. "I should kill you," she snarled in his face.

The Face Stealer laughed. He laughed because if he did not, he might break. He hadn't the strength to stand, to save his home, to prevent the death of a great and powerful people. He couldn't believe he had misread the signs. Now he had no brother to turn to.

"You know what the worst part is?" Yuki whispered, crossing her arms as her fury softened. "I wanted so badly for us to be a family, you and Kenai and me. I wanted that more than I wanted this." She gestured to his prone form. "You don't know what it's like not to have a family. I sacrificed, too, you know." Her chin dimpled. "I would have let you go free, had you not stabbed me in the back."

"I warned you, Yuki, of what would happen if you joined Nanuq. Do you expect your father to come for you? The day he abandoned you was the day he decided he no longer had any need of you."

The sheen in her eyes brightened. She had never looked more like a child, with the dirt smudged on her face. "See, that's where you're wrong. Nanuq has promised to help me."

"Nanuq has no interest in helping you." He thought of the Owl Clan, back at Nannek. They had been overrun. "He's using you for his own gain."

"Wrong again. He does, and he will." Yuki tilted her head. "And Kenai will stand by my side through the process."

Pain had eroded the last of his strength. The smoke was so thick he could no longer see the sky. "Why don't you just kill me?"

Yuki laughed, a trilling little sound. "Now that, Numiak—that would be entirely too easy." Her white teeth flashed, as sharp and even as a shark's. He had forgotten how black her eyes were. All pupil. Dark moons. "I'm going to make the rest of your life darker than you could have ever dreamed."

The girl lunged, and the Face Stealer did not have time to scream before explosive agony ripped apart his chest.

← →

Apaay awoke splayed across the warm floorboards of the library, teeth chattering. Light from the many windows spilled onto the rugs. Morning. She was back within her own mind and body, yet an ache lingered in her chest from where Yuki had struck her. Or rather, the Face Stealer.

As her pulse slowed, Apaay reflected on what she had witnessed behind the door. Not the hidden faces, as she had expected, but rather shrouds of the Face Stealer's memories. A haunting. She had felt his fear, endured the pain of a broken body and heart. The latter she knew quite well.

With a soft groan, she pressed the heels of her palms to her eyes. Yuki had betrayed him. And the other name—Kenai. His brother, it seemed, had betrayed him, too.

Apaay understood the turmoil of wanting to save those you loved but being unable to do so, and that introduced another problem. She didn't want to see him as anything more than what he was: a stain on the cloak of the world.

But she did. Impossibly, she did.

"So glad you could finally join me."

Apaay jerked at the sound of his voice and turned to find him sitting on the floor across the aisle. Leaning against one of the bookshelves, one leg outstretched, he razed her with a glacial gaze, as unreadable as the shadows currently wreathing his form. In a strange way, the coldness of his stare grounded her. Here was the demon, the nightmare, the thief. That broken spirit ground into the mud had been a stranger.

Pushing to her feet, she glanced at the shut door. Ila was nowhere to be found.

"How did you get inside that door?" Soft.

Apaay felt the first nudge of fear. "I don't know. I wanted it to open, and it opened."

He didn't challenge her claim. "So you thought it within your right to . . . walk right in?"

She didn't answer. Couldn't answer.

"What did you see?"

She swallowed, her throat crammed with lies but unable to voice them. If those had been his memories, then she had absolutely invaded his privacy. She thought to gentle his temper by skirting the question. "Nothing."

Uncoiling to his feet, he closed the space separating them in two strides, his words a cold hiss as he said in punctuated beats, "Don't *lie* to me, wolfling."

And what of all the lies you've told me? she wanted to say, yet hadn't the nerve to. In a halting voice, Apaay began, "I was in a forest." She stared at a spot on the floor, unnerved by his nearness and power and heat. "There was smoke. I was— You were wounded." It probably wouldn't help her situation if she admitted to having seen everything through his eyes.

"Was anyone with me?" A careful question.

She whispered, "Yuki."

He flinched. If it had been his memory, then he already knew what Yuki had done. From the excruciating agony in his chest, she guessed the wound had been fatal, and she wondered if the Face Stealer had died and come back to life. Yuki had moved so quickly Apaay hadn't seen the weapon in her hand.

"What else?"

Apaay hesitated. When he had fought Yuki back in the labyrinth, his mood had been equally unpredictable.

"What else?" he barked.

"You mentioned your home. Yuki betrayed you." Pressing her hands to her thighs, she added, "Your brother did, too."

With dead eyes, the Face Stealer turned away, his back a snarl of locked muscles. Apaay didn't know why panic fluttered in her chest, so she tried to explain. "I'm sorry, but I couldn't stay in that meeting." Sitting there, feeling as if she hadn't control over the matter, had choked her. "It was too overwhelming."

"Stop," he growled as he whirled around. "Do you think I have time to focus on your personal problems when Nanuq is plotting war? You have no idea how important this meeting was, do you? You've been so wrapped up in feeling sorry for yourself that you're blind to everything else. You don't get it, Apaay. It's not about you. It's never been about you. It's about something far greater than you."

The ugly feeling intensified. He was right. It *wasn't* about her. It was about doing something good for a change. Her life was too broken to bother with anymore, but there was hope for Masuk. Grace could still be given to him.

The Face Stealer tore a hand through his hair. "Kaan and Ro were only able to get away from their father for a few hours today. He doesn't know they've been meeting with me, did you know that? Otherwise, he might claim a breach of the treaty and incite war against *me*, which is the last thing I want. But since you chose to stick your nose in something that was none of your damn business, I had to end the meeting early, with absolutely nothing resolved, and I can't risk them coming here again on short notice."

"I'm sorry," she whispered, trying to think of how to repair the damage she had wrought. "I didn't mean to overstep."

"I don't care," he spat. "I don't give a *shit* that you're sorry. I don't care about what you have to say, or what you think, or how you feel. I don't care," he repeated, he seethed, "about *you*."

Apaay swallowed, the numbness creeping through her chest to fully blanket her heart. Hadn't she known he didn't care about her? Yet the Face Stealer went on. Because there was no god, Apaay thought, to help her. There was no mercy for her pain and never would be.

"Because honestly?" he said. "Why should I care? Ever since you arrived, you've done nothing but mope around. You don't eat. You don't sleep. You push everyone who tries to help you away." He flung out his arms. "I have tried over and over to reach you, but it's obviously not working. Tell me what to do. Tell me how to help you."

Apaay felt herself crumbling as his words flayed her with vicious intent. It was almost a relief to let go.

"You don't know, do you?" He shook his head in disgust. "You look like you haven't slept in a year. Don't you think there's something wrong with that? Would you have preferred I leave you in that cell? Is that it? Is that what you want?" A long pause stretched and stretched. "Say something," he demanded.

The look she sent him was just that—a look. There was no emotion behind it. It was a window with no light burning.

"You can't, can you? You're free from the labyrinth, your family is protected, yet you do nothing to move forward with your life." And Apaay thought that was all, but he went on with a furiously whispered, "If you can't climb out of this dark place, then maybe you deserve it. What have you done for your people except fail them? You have taken their homes from them, their livelihoods. You," he said coldly, "are nothing."

The last word rang in the air with horrible finality. When it seemed as though the Face Stealer was done speaking, Apaay finally lifted her head. It took a great effort to look him in the eye. A greater effort to not break in front of him.

"You think I don't know that?" she said, so softly she feared her voice might disappear, *she* might disappear. "You think I don't already know how worthless I am?" A harsh laugh splintered in her throat. It was pain, but it was deeper than pain. It was truth.

Keep it together, she thought, fighting tears. *Say what you need to say, and then you can break apart in private.*

"I know I'm worthless," she hissed, teeth bared and eyes snarling and hands curled into fists. "I know I'm nothing, less than nothing. I am a horrible person." The numbness had reached the tips of her fingers. "My village was slaughtered because of me. That woman, the polar bear Unua, a *mother*—" Her throat strained as the confession snagged. "I killed her. And I killed her children, too. Because now they will live without hope in their hearts."

There went another crack, right down the center of her chest. "And I killed Nakaluq." Her heaviest guilt. He was in the spirit world now, too young to have left this life. She hadn't wanted him to go.

"So if you think for one second," she said, strength failing, "that your words mean anything to me—" She swallowed. Choked on her own shame. "They don't. But thank you. Thank you for reminding me of who—what—I am." A piece of refuse not even worth the trouble to pick up. "I am sorry for ruining your meeting. I'm sorry for wasting your time. But I assure you it won't happen again."

Without waiting for a response, Apaay left the library and closed the door behind her. She did not know where she would go, but she was not welcome here anymore.

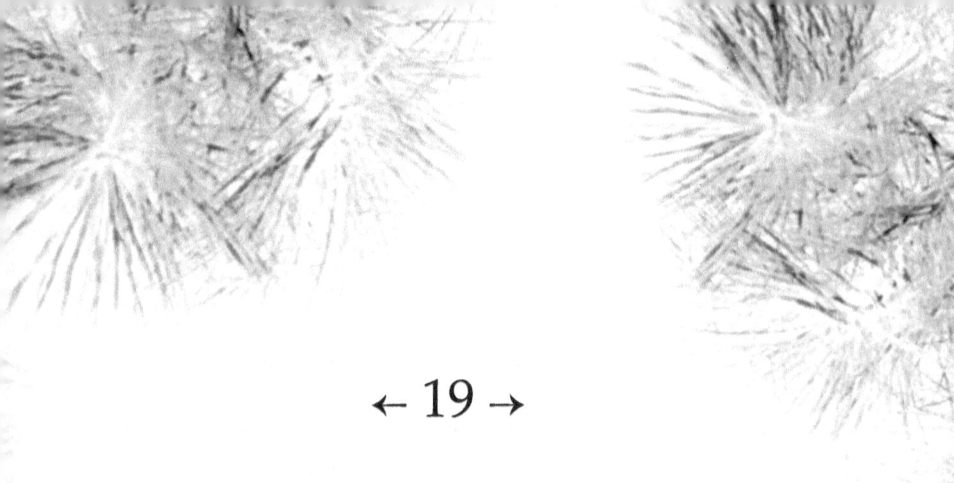

← 19 →

The door to the Face Stealer's study exploded open and slammed against the wall. Ila stepped over the threshold, the waterfall pouring at her back, a fine mist clinging to the threads of her hair. The Face Stealer sat at his desk and peered at her over the top of his black-framed glasses, an expression of mild curiosity pinching the skin around his eyes. Tulimaq sat in the other chair. She ignored him.

Feeling as though she had the strength to rip the Face Stealer's body in half with her bare hands, Ila slapped aside the document he was reading. It fluttered to the floor. *What did you do?* she demanded, hands a blur. *Tell me!*

He regarded her for an incredibly drawn-out period of time, his mien unchanged. Then, calm as could be, the Face Stealer picked up the piece of parchment and smoothed it atop his desk. "You're going to have to be a little more specific, as there are hundreds of things I do in any given day. For example, only five minutes ago, I ate a snack."

She stepped closer, breathing hard, eyes wet from frustration and helplessness, because whatever it was this demon had done to her friend, it might be the last thing he ever did. *You know what I'm talking about.*

Only hours ago, after fleeing the smoke and flame of that strange shadow land, she had managed to find an exit, which had deposited her in the breakfast chamber. There, she had sat on one of the overly large mushrooms and thought of all that she'd seen.

She was the girl in the fire. It explained the pull Ila had felt, the scar on her skull, the shock of recognition at seeing the child's face. *Her* face, younger and soot stained. The Face Stealer knew her past. He must.

So why had he never told her? Why did he let her continue believing she was no one? Ila had expressed these vulnerabilities to Irnik in the labyrinth. He had always listened, but he'd never responded with any reassurance. Why would he unless he had something to hide?

Afterward, Ila had gone in search of the Face Stealer and found Apaay around the corner. She'd looked empty. Ila had seen that blankness only once before: after the Face Stealer had shorn Apaay's hair.

Setting aside the document, the Face Stealer removed his glasses, as if wanting a better look at her. He watched her the way someone did when realizing the person standing before them had been misjudged. Tulimaq, as well, observed the situation with keenness, a crack in his façade. "She stuck her nose in a place where it did not belong. Whatever consequence Apaay received, she brought it upon herself."

The door, she realized. He was talking about the door. *And me?* she asked. *I went through the door, too.*

His surprise flared, his head tilting in consideration. "And yet you did not show up outside the door with her. Why was that?" Fingers linked, he studied her with such intensity Ila had the urge to cover herself with her hands. "Oh, wait." A mocking twist to his mouth. "I know." He leaned forward. Eyes of pale gray, like fine ash, gave a quick perusal, then dismissed what he saw as unimportant. "She abandoned you, didn't she? And yet *you* are angry with *me*? Why is that, I wonder?" His mouth cut a cruel line, and he rose to his full height, a long unwinding of his well-muscled form. "I was not the one who brought you into that dark place, and I was not the one who left you there."

The heat coalescing in Ila's sternum fanned outward. No matter what he implied, she wasn't disposable. She had value, contributions to give the world. Kaan had told her only a few days ago how quickly she was improving. At times, the talq even felt like an extension of herself. The Face Stealer was wrong about Apaay, and especially about Ila. She was here, out in the open, and she would not be afraid, not ever again.

Stop trying to turn this argument around, Ila signed. *This isn't about me. This is about Apaay. This is about whatever horrible thing you did or said to her.*

"I didn't tell her anything she didn't already know."

And what was that?

"That she is nothing."

Oh no.

Why would you do that? Ila demanded. *Why would you say such a horrible thing?*

Suddenly his face changed. Ila was so furious, so distraught over the thought of Apaay isolating herself further, she hardly noticed the deadly quiet settling over him. "Do you think I have time to play her little games, to dwell on her emotions, the minutiae of her life? What has she done for the past two months but brush aside every offer of help I've given her?"

Ila hardened her heart against his words. Why would her friend's apathy frustrate him unless he cared? *I understand,* she said. *You're angry about what happened with Tulimaq.*

His mouth went flat. Tulimaq shifted in his seat. "Do not think to assume anything of me. You know nothing."

Instinct told Ila to back down. It wasn't true, what he said. She *did* know, even if he convinced himself otherwise. Even if he chose to believe a lie.

"Do you think Nanuq or Yuki care about her woes?" he went on. "Do you think what she feels matters in comparison to what war will bring? I'm doing all I can to ensure we remain safe. By refusing to cooperate, she puts everyone at risk."

The pressure behind her eyes was too great. Tears welled and spilled over—a relief. *You don't understand. She needs help.*

"And I'm supposed to care? It was her choice. She chose to step through that door. She chose her friend over her dog. She chose to ignore me when I told her to stay in the cell."

Ila crowded his personal space, since he seemed so willing to do the same to her. *It was her choice? Really?* She might have laughed if it wasn't so terrible a belief. *It was never a choice. You, who have always had the power, and she, who has none.*

A muscle feathered in his jaw. He looked very close to slamming his fist through the desk. "It's not the same."

Ila scrubbed her face in frustration. He had no idea what he was talking about. Compassion must be too foreign a concept to him if he had never before witnessed its healing properties. Ila wondered what would have happened to her had Irnik—Numiak— never shown her kindness. She might have lost hope a long time ago. *You mean to tell me you've never lost someone you cared about or had something precious taken from you? You've never had to start over? Ever?*

His gaze slipped away to look elsewhere.

Ila dared to rest a hand on his arm. He was not so scary, she decided. He was exactly like her. *You need to do something.*

The Face Stealer pinched the bridge of his nose, and she felt the warring in him, of wanting to stay on course, and of wanting to change, too. "Why can't you help her, or the prisoner?"

She won't come to me. The thought of being tossed aside as if she didn't matter had stopped Ila from trying. One could only take so many blows before something fractured. *As for Masuk, I don't think she'll go to him for this.* Apaay's low self-worth might be too personal a thing to discuss with anyone.

Please, she pleaded, the very word causing her knees to quake, her heart to come completely undone. *We're losing her.*

But Ila feared it was already too late.

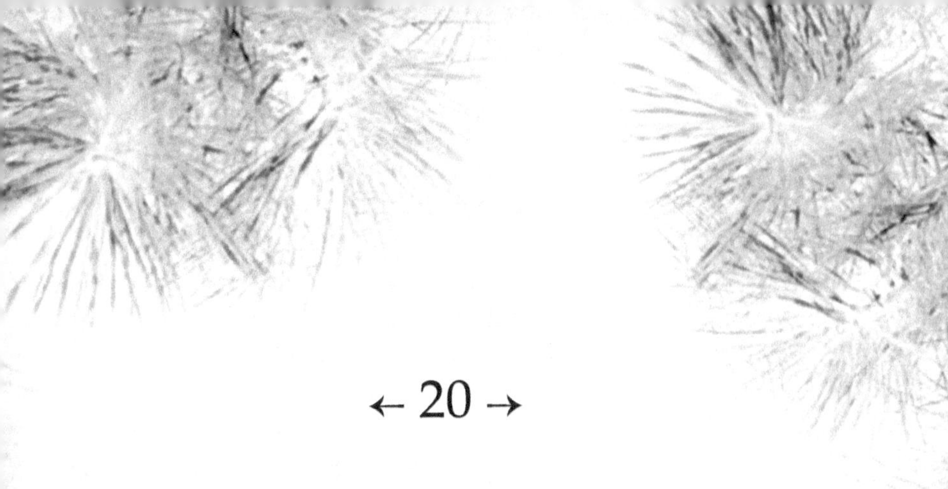

← 20 →

Alone, Apaay walked the path she had taken nearly every day now, that familiar paving of sun-warmed rocks, the grass so vibrant it hurt her eyes. The path would take her to the shallow pool, the steady tree with its gnarled old branches, a presence that had seen this world change a thousand times over.

When she entered the grove, she dropped to her knees beside the water. Ripples extended from where she touched its surface, distorting her reflection. Apaay bit down on her lip. Maybe it was supposed to be this way. Maybe this was how she would always see herself: clouded and unclear.

"Who are you?" she whispered to that wavering girl.

The emotion gripped her so intensely she choked. Tremors traveled upward from her toes—legs, arms, torso. The whole of her, shaking uncontrollably, as the first cry cracked against the back of her teeth. She didn't want to hide anymore. Didn't know how. Didn't care.

Her whimper dissolved into a high keening that lifted the hair on the back of her neck, a horrible stretch of sound, sharp as a hawk's cry. Curling her arms around her stomach, Apaay bent over her knees and pressed her face into the grass as sobs broke her body into smaller and smaller pieces.

"Why?" she sobbed. "Why me?"

She didn't have an answer. Apaay had thought it would help to speak this question aloud, but it only made her feel more alone. Once, she had been a hunter. And she had burned so fiercely and so bright. But that fire, which had carried her miles and miles through the storm, had flickered and fluttered and died.

And now she was left to darkness. Crippling, quelling darkness. She had fallen so deeply into this pit she knew she would never see light again. Because she did not deserve the light. She did not deserve gentleness, laughter, *good*. She, who had caused so much pain for her people.

For a moment, she thought it could have been different. After seeing the Face Stealer suffer at Yuki's hands, Apaay had thought maybe there was more to the demon than she had first believed. It had taken a lot to admit the meeting had overwhelmed her, and in her time of need, he had shut her down.

You are nothing.

Nothing.

She mouthed the word, tasted salt.

Closing her eyes, Apaay eased her body's tightening, her face smoothing as tension ebbed. The trickling water soothed, as did the breeze. She had begun to doze when the Face Stealer spoke from behind her, his voice softer than new-fallen snow. "Apaay."

"Don't," she said, fluid leaking from her nose and smearing across her cheek as she turned her head to watch the water through blurred vision. "I don't want to hear your voice." Low, melodic, with the power to destroy her. It was destroying her now.

"I need to talk to you."

Didn't he understand? She didn't want to talk to him, or anyone. She wanted to be alone.

"Please go away," she wept. She was nothing but frayed seams. *"Please."*

Rather than give her space, he came closer. Apaay should have known he wouldn't listen. She heard him kneel beside her on the grass.

Her eyes snapped open as, with unexpectedly gentle hands, he brushed aside the strands of hair sticking to her face, his expression so uncharacteristically grave it looked out of place. Apaay wondered if she imagined his touch. It should have filled her with revulsion, yet her body cried out at the contact, this display of much-needed compassion.

Apaay watched as he sat a few feet away. Knees bent, elbows resting atop his knees, he stared into the tranquil pool, subdued. The sun threw his profile into sharp relief.

"I used to come to this place," he finally said. "A long time ago." His voice was like the trickling creek, low and unhurried. "There was a grove like this one in the Western Territory a few miles from my home. I used to play there as a boy."

The thought of the Face Stealer as a child was so alien to her Apaay didn't know how to respond. She imagined him as this tortured little creature, confused by his dark nature.

"Over the years, my world changed, but the grove never did. Then Nanuq came and . . . well, you know the rest."

Apaay's gaze never strayed from his face, the way his unrest sat out in the open, with the barest shift of his mouth or eyes, and the memories not far off.

"After Nanuq invaded my home, I needed to rebuild in some way. When I created the Wood, free of war, this was the first thing I made." His eyes went out of focus, shifting like moons behind the clouds. "It was a dark time. I came here nearly every day those first few years, taking comfort in the seclusion." His shoulders pushed against the neat seams of his maq as he inhaled, the sinew pale against the darker hide of the caribou. "This was—is—a place of healing for me."

It wasn't that she believed he felt nothing. Apaay had seen him differently when he spent time with Ro and Kaan. This, however, felt like vulnerability. "Did you know that I was here? Can you feel when I enter this place?" She hadn't known this was his haven first, his haven, too.

He shook his head. "I don't know where people wander off to in the Wood if they desire to be left alone. Wherever people go, it's in the privacy of their own thoughts."

Apaay breathed a sigh of relief and wiped the tears from her face, her skin tight from where the salt had dried. She was glad he did not know of all the times she had come here seeking forgiveness. Those moments were private. They did not belong to him.

She thought the Face Stealer was done, but then he said, "The first few years following the invasion, I would visit the grove and stare into the water, wondering what had gone wrong. For years, the anger ate at me. I somehow convinced myself that the only way to be strong was to be hard, cold, indifferent. I suppose I should not be surprised. The way I grew up, it's a miracle I have not given in to the darkness completely."

Apaay didn't know what to say. He had never spoken about his past so openly before. She sat upright, guarded, waiting.

"I shouldn't have taken my frustration with Tulimaq out on you," he said, trapping her in the frost of his gaze. "It was cruel and hurtful, and I was an absolute bastard. For that, I am sorry." He ran a hand over his hair, lowered it with a self-deprecating laugh. Apaay had always felt as if a barrier existed between him and the rest of the world, but now it was gone, and she glimpsed someone quite different than before. "The truth is, I wasn't saying those things to you. I was saying them to me."

The dying light warmed his cheeks and mouth. He was waiting for her answer, she realized.

"I do not forgive you," Apaay whispered, a shred of anger flickering inside her. Did he expect her forgiveness? Did he think a few choice words would make her forget everything that had come before? And yet intertwined with the resentment was a thread of confusion, because she felt, in all the time she had known him, that this was one bright spot of truth. Honestly, his apology *did* help. That he felt remorse, that he recognized his words as unacceptable and cruel, helped.

"I know you don't." Quiet. "I'm not asking for your forgiveness, and I don't expect it. I have done"—deep breath—"horrible things. But I wanted you to know I'm sorry for what I said. It was out of line, and I regretted it as soon as I said it."

He turned back to the water, and it was silent for a time as Apaay considered his apology. The Face Stealer broke the silence first. "I thought we had more time to prepare. At the very least, I thought it would take months before the alliance was finalized." Dropping his head into his hands, he sighed. "Kaan and Ro returned to the Central Territory. They couldn't stay. At this point, I've run out of options."

"What did you do," Apaay asked, remembering the discussion following Kimmir's attack, "to make the Avi so angry?"

"It's a long story."

When he left it at that, she asked, "Do we not have the time?"

"We do." He lifted his head. "I didn't think it was something you wanted to hear."

"I'm asking, aren't I?"

"Such a sharp tongue you have." His gaze dropped to her mouth before he stared through the trees. "It's quite simple, really. I promised the Owl Clan my allegiance, and I abandoned them in their time of need."

"What happened?"

Their eyes met, and Apaay startled at the sense of familiarity. They had been in this position before, staring at each other's reflection in the dark window of the library, except now it was he who was giving up a piece of himself, and Apaay who was listening.

"We knew Nanuq was going to invade the Western Territory," he began, "but we didn't have an inside man at the time. As such, we could never fully trust any intercepted messages. We knew, however, that Nanuq believed the object to be in our possession. So we started to prepare."

The cadence of the Face Stealer's voice reminded her of the many nights spent poring over books, his narration the only sound.

Then, there had been a distance to his words. Now the story was too close.

"I had recently been promoted to commander. My unit was to guard Talguk, a port city on the coast. My second-in-command," he said, "was my brother. Early on, we ruled out the possibility of Nanuq passing through the Atakana. It was winter. A high risk of avalanches." His throat worked. "Many weeks passed, and communication went silent. I was sent to complete a mission on Naga's coast."

"Why would they send you there if they knew the invasion was going to occur?"

"I was a member of an elite special operations group. We were sworn to secrecy when accepting a mission and weren't allowed to discuss it, not even with the other members of our unit. My mission was in relation to the invasion. And no," he said as Apaay opened her mouth, "I'm not authorized to speak of it."

She muttered a few choice words under her breath.

"It was during my mission that I got word from my brother. Nanuq was heading for Unana. I told Kenai to move my men to Kesikan Pass. Then I received a distress signal from Kaan. Nanuq's forces had reached Nannek, their southernmost city." The words came slower with the memory. "I went to offer aid."

Leaning forward, he dropped his head into his hands, curving his fingers around the back of his skull. "It was five days of hard fighting. On the sixth day, we received a distress call from the west. I thought at first it was from Kesikan Pass, asking for reinforcements, but it was a third force. Seal Unua had invaded Talguk by way of Tor and now made for Unana." A tremor ran through his body. "When I heard what had happened, I didn't think. I *couldn't* think. We had prepared for an eastern invasion, not a western. And I had pulled my unit from Talguk, essentially leaving the coast exposed." His eyes shut. "I left the Avi and his people to fend for themselves so that I could try to slow down the seal Unua."

What Apaay had witnessed beyond the doorway in his library must have been the day of the invasion.

"Unana fell that day, along with the head family. In my absence, the owl Unua were never able to recover." He lifted his head, his eyes clouded. Apaay, caught within the tatters of his memory, did not notice how her fingers dug into her thighs.

"The Avi doesn't believe me, but I regret what happened that day. I regret the pain I caused, and I regret that I did not reach out sooner to try and mend our broken trust." His irises, a dark, troubled garnet, were indistinguishable from his pupils. "But I do not regret putting my people first."

Apaay fought to swallow the sudden stone in her throat. If their positions had been switched, she suspected she would have done the same. The Analak, whether of land or sea, were her people. There was nothing she would not do for them, nothing too dark or too disturbing.

"Your brother betrayed you," Apaay stated, "didn't he."

The Face Stealer's past was in the grove with them, fresh as spilled blood. "He was aligned with Nanuq's cause, though I did not know it at the time. The invasion at Kesikan Pass was merely a distraction for the true invasion to the west. Because of Kenai's manipulations, Nanuq knew we had left the coast exposed." He stared hard at his feet. "My family is dead. I will never get my brother back."

Apaay considered all that he had said, and asked, "Why not go to the owl Unua, explain what happened all those years ago? Why not try?"

"Did you not hear what I said?"

"That's never stopped you before."

He lifted his head to take her in. Apaay wondered what he saw and if it was the same thing she did: someone who wasn't ready to give up yet, but who didn't know how to step away from the edge. "Come with me?"

Her shock broke across her face in what was probably a hilarious combination of revulsion and incredulity. "Are you asking me or telling me?"

"Asking."

She thought of his apology. She thought of him broken and bloodied at Yuki's feet, and the smoke rising up, and how each passing day brought them a little closer to war. But above all, she thought of how tired she was of hiding, her lack of agency, the need to feel like she was doing something—anything—to move forward with her life.

She said yes.

← 21 →

Outside the warm haven of summer, the long night was fully in bloom.

The branches bowed with the weight of late-season snow, the trunks frosted with ice. White eddied in the spaces between the trees as Apaay and the Face Stealer trudged onward through the night, their boots punching holes in the crust. Apaay's teeth were so cold they ached. How could she have forgotten what it was like to be crushed in winter's grip, fragile as an autumn leaf?

The Face Stealer set a ruthless pace. Every breath was to choke on a mouthful of knives. The Central Territory lay east of the Atakana, its capital, Sinika, some five hundred miles away. If the Face Stealer could request a private audience with the Avi, he might be able to sway the sovereign to join in a united front against Nanuq. But light, the Face Stealer had told her, did not shine favorably upon him. The Avi had not forgotten, would not forgive.

Apaay wondered if they were walking toward their deaths.

"We're nearly there," said the Face Stealer. Pushing aside a branch, he waited for Apaay to pass before releasing it.

Apaay was going to ask where *there* was when a silhouette caught her eye: a cairn.

The Face Stealer circled the landmark. Generally, the markers were built of flattened stones stacked atop one another in the shape of a man, but this was something else. Not arms, but wings. A bird taking flight.

"This will take us to the edge of their territory," he said, pressing one mittened hand to the bird's sloped shoulder while reaching toward her with the other. Moonlight puddled on the ground at their feet, pale on white.

Apaay stared at his palm without moving. The last time she had taken the demon's hand, they had materialized at the edge of her village, she unaware of its destruction. Apaay hadn't known it then, but that had been a moment of great change. The truth was, she didn't know how to start the long path to forgiveness. Did she even deserve forgiveness? Did she deserve . . . anything?

"Sometimes," came the Face Stealer's muted voice, "there are moments in our lives when the darkness blankets everything that is good. We find ourselves in this tunnel, unsure of how we got there, but unable to escape it. Each day we walk it, yet we are no closer to reaching the end. Most days, we don't even know if there *is* an end."

When Apaay lifted her head, her eyes were wet. The Face Stealer stared back, unafraid of her anguish. She didn't know where the strength came from to go on. She had walked through life and death, it seemed, and here she was, still breathing. "H-how did you go on after the war?"

The faintest line formed between his eyebrows. "For a long time, I didn't. I became this shell of a person who didn't see the point in fighting a battle I had already lost." His breath misted out in a wispy cloud. "And yet the days passed. Eventually, I did reach some semblance of life again. The darkness was not as great. Some days, there were even moments of happiness." Absently, he skimmed a palm over the bird's wing. "It gets better. You might not feel like it ever will, but it does. Little by little, day by day, it will get better."

Apaay didn't bother wiping the tears from her cheeks as they spilled over, hot against her frozen skin. She didn't care who he was in this moment, who she was. Right now, she needed someone to tell her it would get better, and she was desperate enough not to care that these words came from him.

When Apaay clasped his hand, she was thrown down a deep well, pressure squeezing on all sides. She collapsed, smaller and smaller and smaller, the burn of her lungs migrating to her throat and face as she fought to drag in air until, at last, they were spit forward.

Apaay pushed to her feet and glanced around another snowy clearing. The trees were thicker, dense with amassing shadows, and the air was not as cold, not chilled from the mountains they had traveled from.

"From this point forward, we'll be traversing the Central Territory." He pointed beyond the cairn, twin to the one they had started from. "Stay close, and stay alert."

They made haste, or as much haste as they could manage. Even with the Face Stealer breaking a path, Apaay struggled to keep her footing in the loose snow tumbling in his wake. The sense of being watched trailed them. She could not see beyond their immediate surroundings where the light did not penetrate.

When Apaay started falling behind, the Face Stealer had them rest. Trying not to feel too grateful, she sat down, blood pulsing hard in her fingers and toes, a curl of steam slipping past her lips as the demon prowled the perimeter, pausing every so often to listen. She saw the wolf in him at these times. Could imagine those yellow eyes cutting through the dark.

He suddenly snapped to attention, peering into a space beyond the brush.

Apaay froze as well. "Is someone out there?" she whispered, slowly rising and brushing powder from her legs. Without conscious thought, Apaay stepped toward him. She did not know these woods. She did not know the dangers they bred.

A moment passed before he answered. "I thought I heard something." He gestured her nearer, and Apaay sprang to his side. "I don't want to give the Owl Clan reason to strike before I have the chance to explain. They might view me as a threat."

"You do seem to attract a lot of hatred."

A wry twist to his mouth. "When you've been around for as long as I have, you're bound to make a few enemies."

Apaay would not quite call it *a few*. More like the world.

"Are they close?" she whispered. Pine needles rustled as the wind buffeted them. His posture was oddly loose. Shouldn't he be more alert?

Dipping his head, he murmured into her ear, "Close enough."

Apaay stiffened, suddenly aware of their proximity. His breath fluttered against her neck, gentle as moth wings.

With a gasp, Apaay shoved him back so hard she fell into a nearby snowbank. His deep laughter floated into the trees.

"You're despicable!" she spat, face aflame. And to think she had been concerned for their safety. To think *he* had been concerned for *her* safety.

That only made him laugh harder, a deep, full-throated hoot with none of the conniving demon present, only pleasure and a touch of affection. "Wolfling, you wound me." His fingers alighted on his chest. "You know I only ever have your best interests at heart." A strange irony she didn't understand filled his voice. "Besides, it's well known—"

A roar of pain shattered the silent wood. The Face Stealer dropped as the air filled with the hiss of arrows. Apaay didn't have time to seek cover before one punctured her right shoulder, agony shredding open her upper arm. She screamed.

A wave of dark power boomed, and the arrows careened to the side, toppling from the air and clattering in a messy heap some yards away. Apaay fell to her knees in the snow, teeth gritted, blind to anything but the pain. She couldn't move her arm. More hissing, more clattering, yet it was quickly drowned out by the throb of blood in her ears, the beat of her heart, a warning that death had come calling. Apaay bit her lip against another swell of agony.

"Apaay, look at me," the Face Stealer demanded. *"Apaay."*

Cracking open her eyes, she found him on the ground as well, staring at her across the clearing. Strain tightened his features, his skin pulled tight against bone.

"Where were you hit?"

The world slowed. Sound cut off. She tried her best not to move or breathe too deeply. An arrow shaft jutted from her arm. On the next wave of pain, she heaved bile into the snow, and the sound of deafening battle came crashing through the silent barrier, and a fear-stink along with it.

"Don't close your eyes," he said. "Nod if you can hear me."

She nodded.

His tone was steady, firm and strong, something she could hold on to, and she grasped it like a physical thing. "Tell me where you were hit."

Apaay shivered, feeling hot and cold all at once. An arrow sliced through the snow not two feet away from her. "Shoulder," she gasped.

He bit off a curse as a second arrow embedded itself into his thigh. Never removing his gaze from hers, he yanked it out. "Can you make it to the tree?"

It was difficult to follow his questions. A cold sweat coated her skin. Looking up, Apaay watched the arrowheads catch the moonlight, bright as falling stars. She didn't understand how something so deadly could be so beautiful.

"Apaay, you have to move!"

That woke her up.

Using her knees and one arm to brace herself, she crawled to the nearest tree. She no longer heard the cutting of weapons, only her heaving chest, the rasp of air against her throat, and the Face Stealer's voice leading her to safety. The snow broke around her as she pushed through the pain until she couldn't anymore. The agony was too great.

More arrows. The Face Stealer slapped them aside with his power, and the earth trembled, a great force rising and falling, gathering in strength. The vibrations were so intense they tunneled into her teeth, a ringing filling the inside of her skull. The Face Stealer cursed as he sliced a swath of darkness through the trees, and then he was hurtling toward her, fast as the wind.

An explosive *boom* splintered the trees, needles clouding the air. The Face Stealer was four steps away when he dove and landed atop her, a domed barrier materializing around them as glittering red power burst through the forest, ravaging the land like wildfire. Apaay squeezed her eyes shut, her face pressed against his chest, but the light flared behind her eyelids, red like fury, like revenge.

The red wave slammed against the semi-transparent shield with a crack. The barrier shuddered, but held.

The Face Stealer's arms trembled. Apaay glanced at his upper torso, where an arrow shaft protruded from the left side of his chest. She reached toward it before catching herself. "The arrow."

"It's fine." Sweat slicked his face and dripped onto her cheeks, his head swiveling in various directions. The arrows had stopped firing, but Apaay suspected he didn't care about the weapons. What were they compared to his might but kindling? No, he was looking for the source of power.

Glittering red lashed the barrier again. Uprooted trees lay on their sides, one having snapped in half after it slammed against their blockade.

Apaay bit back a gasp as the Face Stealer accidentally jostled her shoulder. "Who is it?" Adrenaline clung to the edges of her skin. She hadn't felt this awake in months. "Another one of your *friends*?"

"Not exactly." Pressing a hand against her collarbone, he said, "Stay down."

A swift uncoiling to his feet. The barrier remained surrounding her as the Face Stealer stepped through it, exposing himself to further danger. Apaay almost told him to stay put before she realized how ridiculous that sounded. She must be delirious with pain to even consider his safety.

As soon as he was free of the shield, the world exploded.

Snow melted. Flames gorged the birch and pine. Apaay thought her eyes would shrivel if she looked too closely for too long.

And then a man stepped from the woods, or what she first thought to be a man. His eyes were two red coals, burning.

Not a man. Not even human. A naaluet, one of the lesser demons of the North, but no less dangerous for it. When spirits crossed the Sky Bridge to reach the spirit world, not everyone made the full journey. Only those who possessed a light heart passed on. Those with tarnished souls burned in fire, and so became flame.

Sparks showered like exploding glass. Another lesser demon came into view, then another. The naaluet may have been hurling flame in his direction, but the Face Stealer was never in one place long enough for it to touch him. There was smoke and there was fire, and Apaay focused on the bright and the dark to distract herself from the infiltrating wooziness.

The naaluet's power slammed against the barrier. It pressed in, hot and intense, and slowly began to melt away the surface layer. Apaay scanned the ground and grabbed the nearest weapon—one of the arrows. White spots blotted against the semi-dark shield, accompanied by a low whine, and then a scream as a crack ran through the barrier, the sight tracked by the lesser demon's dull red gaze. As far as she knew, naaluet could be killed. She would aim for the neck.

The heat intensified, filling the dome with hot, sticky air. Fractures crawled across the barrier like shattering glass. Apaay's hand tightened around the arrow as the light seared her eyes, drawing tears. She didn't let them shut.

A scream rent the air. The weight of the fire was too great. In the time it took to blink, the demon's power was already rushing toward her from all sides. Apaay covered her head and waited for the burn.

It never came.

For long minutes, all was silent. Apaay breathed in the dark, her heart pounding in her chest. Then moonlight slipped through the shadowy blanket, and the Face Stealer appeared at her side before she realized he had left. "Let me see," he said.

"Is he dead?" She looked around, but there was no sign of the naaluet. Her shoulder throbbed. "I'm fine."

"I took care of them, and no, you're not." He was furious, though his hands were gentle as he pushed aside the shredded pieces of her parka. The arrowhead was deeply embedded, the shaft colored with black-and-white speckled feathers. "I should have been paying more attention to our surroundings."

"You mean instead of poorly attempting to charm me?"

"Look what it got you," he said in disgust. "An arrow in the arm."

The beginnings of hysteria tickled her throat, and Apaay bit down on panicked laughter. "You have an arrow sticking out of your chest. I think that wound is a little more fatal than mine." Even though her arm *really* hurt. She felt faint.

"Don't worry about me," he snapped. Carefully, he examined her wound, having pulled her into a sitting position so she could lean against his side. Apaay was grateful for the support. "The arrow hasn't gone through," he said, brushing hair that had come loose from his braid out of his face, "but I don't want to aggravate the wound by trying to remove it."

"Can't you make it disappear?" She waved her hand like he usually did when pulling things from the void.

The Face Stealer raised an eyebrow at her imitation of him. "In this case, no. I can only control objects I've called into existence. Since someone else made the arrow, it has no tether to my power."

"So what you're saying," Apaay managed, "is that you're useless."

His head snapped up from where he'd been studying the wound. A bit of amusement warred with his surprise. "I guess I am," he said, mouth tilted in a half smile. "Can you stand? We're not far from Sinika."

"Unfortunately, Numiak," came a cold voice through the trees, "I'm afraid your journey ends here."

Apaay froze as two figures stepped into the moonlight. She recognized the first as Kaan, who she had last seen at the meeting hours ago. The second woman was of short stature, thick in the shoulders and thighs. A streak of black broke the white waves of her hair. The resemblance between the two was clear in the shape of their noses, their stubborn chins, same as Ro. The wrappings around this woman's arms were gray like Kaan's, unlike the black that Ro wore.

"What a surprise," said the woman.

"Umiq." The Face Stealer dipped into an awkward bow from his kneeled position. "It's good to see you, too."

Her yellow eyes narrowed to sharp points. "I didn't say it was a good one," she hissed. "We should have let you die."

"I am somewhat hard to kill, I assure you."

"Yes." Her sneer was fierce. "You are a bit like a cockroach." She took in the wrecked clearing, the small fires dying out. The trees looked old enough to have lived hundreds of years. Wood burned so easily. "It wasn't enough to abandon us, was it? You had to call the naaluet to finish your dirty work."

He held up a hand, his gaze cooling. "I did no such thing. On the contrary, I was starting to believe you had sent them to kill *us*. You failed, in case it wasn't obvious."

"A likely story." A murmur, one of anger touched by confusion. "We did not send the demons. One of our scouts spotted the naaluet weeks ago on the southern border, but this is the first time they have been so near."

"Then why do their arrows have your feathers as fletching?"

"I don't know," Umiq snapped. At her back, Kaan studied one of the arrows in closer detail. A prickly sensation rolled across Apaay's skin. It was a strange coincidence.

The Face Stealer looked to Kaan. "Can you look at her wound?" No distrust in his gaze. Apaay relaxed somewhat.

Umiq grabbed Kaan's arm, holding her back. "What do you think you're doing?"

Kaan yanked her arm free. It wasn't difficult, as she was an entire head taller than the woman. "You may be my elder sister," she said coolly, "but you don't control me."

The tension between the siblings was palpable as Kaan knelt at Apaay's side to examine the wound. Umiq stood a few yards away, simmering. "It's deep, but it doesn't look like it's hit bone yet." Another moment passed before she sat back on her heels. "While I would normally see to this, my power is still recovering from a recent procedure. Our healer can tend Apaay when we return."

From Umiq's repulsed expression, Apaay knew the woman would rather chew off her own arm than allow a human girl and a demon to enter Owl Clan territory. "And when Father finds out they're here? Healing her wound won't matter if he kills them on sight."

Apaay's stomach lurched in unease. So she had been right. They *were* walking to their deaths.

"Don't worry about Father," said Kaan. "Leave him to me."

Gradual awareness crept across Umiq's hostile expression. "Did you know the Face Stealer was planning on coming here?" she demanded of her sister. Then she stilled. "Wait a minute. Have you been meeting with him?"

Kaan crossed her arms, stood her ground. The Face Stealer lifted his eyebrows at Apaay, as if to say, *Prepare yourself.* "We met with Numiak today, Ro and I. No, *listen* to me." Kaan clamped down on her sister's arm before she could jerk away. "It's time, Umiq. It's time to move forward and repair relations between our peoples."

Umiq swung, but Kaan's reflexes were faster. She caught Umiq's wrist before the woman's palm made contact with her cheek.

The siblings froze, staring at each other. The Face Stealer's countenance was grave.

Apaay had never heard anything so frightening as Kaan's voice in that moment. "Do not," she said, "raise your hand against me. Ever. This is your warning. Next time, I will cut it off."

Umiq fought her sister's grip, face splotchy with rising temper. "Traitor," she hissed. "Have you forgotten history? Do you remember Nannek? Do you remember the days before the River Iniak ran red with blood, before the great Whitewoods fell? Were it not for this demon"—she stabbed a finger at the Face Stealer, baring her teeth—"Nannek might still be under our rule."

"You don't know that," Kaan replied, calm despite the wrath thrown her way. "Nannek would have fallen eventually, whether or not Numiak was present. Nanuq's forces were too strong. It is *because* I have not forgotten that we are here." She exhaled through her nose. "War is coming, Umiq. We need to prepare."

The older woman's eyes glittered as she looked between Kaan and the Face Stealer. Apaay, thankfully, was not the object of her venomous gaze. "It is obvious you've made up your mind. Who am I to stop you?" Her smile was a terrible thing. "It will be my pleasure watching Father rip this traitor apart."

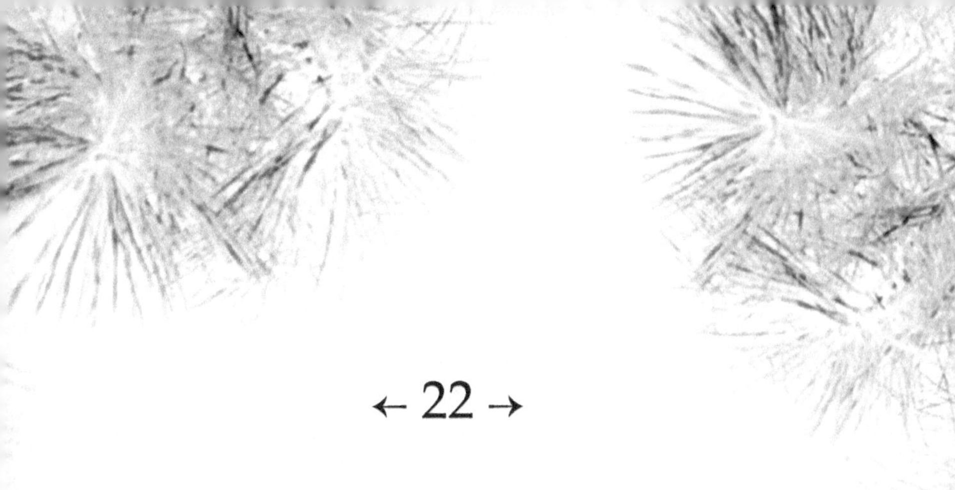

← 22 →

Ila swung her talq with enough force to sever a man's arm. Again, again. Seconds later, Tulimaq entered the clearing, his staff in hand and his wiry arms coated in a sheen of sweat. He took one look at her and said, "Your grip is wrong."

Ila lowered the weapon with a hard swallow and fought the unwelcome voice telling her she had no place playing with weapons. She wouldn't let Tulimaq shame her anymore. If she made a mistake, it was only because she worked hard to improve.

If you're here to criticize me, she said, chin lifted, *you can leave.*

He said nothing, of course.

His silence always made her feel like he was judging her. *Too slow, too weak,* she imagined he thought. Most days, Ila could ignore the belittling voice in her head, but she possessed a heart prone to sensitivity, and that came with its own struggles.

Turning her back, Ila resumed her exercises. Tulimaq's opinion no longer mattered. Kaan supported her, believed in her. Kaan, her mentor and friend.

As for Tulimaq, she didn't know what he was to her. He thought her heart weak, but what did he know? Ila was doing everything in her power to prove she was worthy of the light. If she could wield this talq with intent, could she not live her life the same?

From the corner of her eye, she noticed him approach. Would he watch her train? Pick out more errors? She cursed her fumbling hands. Ila considered going elsewhere, but she didn't want to run. This was her training spot, and she would not let him drive her out.

Dropping her arm, she faced him with a look of irritation. His default expression was indifference, anger, the two often intertwined. Did he ever laugh, smile, cry? The likelihood of the sun and moon trading places was a far greater possibility. *Why did you go against Numiak's word? Kimmir could have died because of you.* As it was, he would live, but how deep the trauma ran, no one knew. Until he made a full recovery, he was bound to the Wood.

Tulimaq thumped the end of his staff against the dirt, considering her. "When given the opportunity to strike, you don't hesitate. The information was too valuable to ignore."

Ila shook her head. She knew nothing of warfare, but even she knew you didn't go against your leader's word. *It wasn't your decision to make.*

"It was more of my decision than it was yours."

She let the sting of his words slide off her back. Said wearily, *Why are you here, Tulimaq?* He had never sought her out before. Something must have changed.

His usual stoicism smoothed into tenuous curiosity. "You stood up to Numiak in his office. You were angry, but you were unafraid."

Unsure of what direction this conversation was headed toward, Ila waited.

"You will meet me at the heart-tree each sunrise. The work will be long and brutal. There will be no shortcuts. There will be no coddling." His gaze raked her form. "You will work hard. You will constantly second-guess yourself. You will sometimes feel as if you can't go on. But in these ways, you will become strong."

The set to her shoulders broke and reformed. She straightened. He was talking about training. About training *her*. *You agree to train me?*

"You will complete five hundred crunches daily," he answered, unmoved. "One hundred push-ups. Two hundred squats. Starting now."

Now? As in right now?

The smile looked completely out of place on his mouth. Ila blinked in surprise, her gaze lingering a moment too long.

"Begin."

← 23 →

The next four miles were the longest Apaay had ever endured. The pain radiating through her shoulder, arm, and chest was pointed and undying. Kaan had bound her arm to minimize movement, but Apaay felt the arrowhead sawing deeper with each step, the small imperfections along the edges catching flesh.

With gritted teeth, she pressed forward through the pine-scented shadows.

The silence between Umiq and the Face Stealer was coiled, venomous. Such was the legacy of war. Nanuq's rise to power and subsequent invasion of the Western Territory had wiped an entire nation from the North, while the resulting treaty had drawn lines between friend and foe. An end to fighting. Or so the people had believed.

It was clear that matters had never been resolved. The attacks on her people, the influx of refugees, the man from Across the Sea, Kimmir's attack . . . So had the war really come to an end all those years ago, or had it been squatting in the background as people rebuilt and returned to their lives, seeking to shed the red coats they had worn, the friends they had buried, the security they had lost? Seeking to move on?

Apaay was so deep in thought she didn't notice they had stopped until she rammed into the Face Stealer's back. "Why are we stopping?"

He lifted his eyebrows. "We're here."

She glanced around. Snow and conifer, and far above, shielded behind the boughs of dense iced needles, the stars. "I don't see anything."

"You didn't think Sinika would be on the ground, did you?"

She didn't know what to think. About him. About the shield he had cast over her, protection from the arrows and the naaluet's power. She was not naive enough to believe he had done it out of caring. In order to find whatever Yuki had stolen from him, he needed her alive. She was a means to an end. Nothing more.

"Don't drop her," the Face Stealer warned.

A tug on the back of her parka, and she was airborne.

Apaay choked off a cry. Kaan, talons curled into the fur of Apaay's collar, lifted them high into the trees on silent wings. Moments later, she deposited Apaay on a branch next to the Face Stealer, and it was like standing on the shoulders of a great king.

This high in the canopy, the shadows were thick as puddled ink, but there was so much light Apaay did not feel stifled by them. Spheres spun of the thinnest glass swayed from braided twine, which hung from the branches at various heights, as clear and round as beads of water, blue flame flickering from within. Some were as small as the berries she harvested following the thaw. Others were larger than her fists, all perfectly, impossibly round. A pleasant tinkling sound skipped across the dark like a stone on water as the globes tapped against one another in the breeze.

Apaay didn't know where to look first. White streaks painted the air as owls fluttered from branch to branch and tree to tree. Wooden walkways encircled the trunks four, five, six levels above, bare of snow and leading to larger platforms that Apaay suspected allowed their people to land and take flight. The owl Unua in their human forms moved between the platforms by taking the stairs or crossing the arched bridges, which acted as the arteries and veins connecting the larger parts of this thriving city.

Above, the canopy provided a ceiling of interlocking leaves curved atop their heads. Lights burned within additional globes tucked into the round windows of the trees. Open doorways—some tall and curved, others small and compact—offered glimpses into the nooks: hanging fabrics, piles of grasses and rocks and miscellaneous objects, as if having been gathered for nesting. In some places, huge glass domes perched on the ends of particularly sturdy branches, stuffed full of pillows in vibrant textiles, which she suspected had come from Across the Sea, and warm bodies burrowing in. There were walls, but Apaay did not think it would be so bad to sleep in a place with the whole of the world beyond the glass, near enough to touch.

Sinika. The City of Trees.

It had not been created by the trees. It *was* the trees, and the leaves, and the bark, and the roots, and the sweet air strumming against the boughs. It was a city of wood and glass, of pine, of light burning. A civilization that was seamlessly the forest, the very essence of the wood.

A clench in her chest. Her heart was trying to tell her something. But there had been such disconnect between her body, mind, and heart for so long that Apaay couldn't identify the feeling. Sadness? No, she didn't think it was that. It did not carry the same weight.

If it was not sadness she felt toward the city, then it must be awe.

Because it was beautiful. And because it was free.

Within seconds of their arrival, every owl Unua, whether human or animal, swiveled their heads and blinked luminous yellow eyes at them.

"They don't look pleased to see you," Apaay muttered to the Face Stealer. The stares were borderline hostile.

"No. They shouldn't be."

She saw men hiding in the trees. Some type of fighting force, she guessed. They wore beige arm wrappings, their white hair tied into topknots. With their bowstrings pulled taut, they aimed arrows at the Face Stealer's chest. Although, he already had an arrow sticking out of it, so Apaay wasn't sure how much more damage they could do.

It was half a breath before the largest raptor she had seen yet dove from the platform above and landed before them as human.

The man's face was like a blade. Few wrinkles lined his skin, though Apaay suspected he was many hundreds of years old. The great feathered collar he wore rustled as he stepped forward. The slit in the front of his parka, a design she noticed was unique to this culture, parted to reveal slender legs wrapped in cloth and elegant slippered feet. The cloth wrapped around his arms was white. It was the only one of its color.

One by one, the owl Unua bowed, including Kaan and her sister. Apaay considered doing the same, but the Face Stealer's grip on her arm prevented her from doing so. The man's eyes were enchanting: deepest amber encircled by a thin ring of gold.

"I thought I made it clear," came the man's tempered lilt, "that if you set foot in my territory again, I would not hesitate to rip out your throat." He did not speak above the barest whisper.

For once, the Face Stealer did not respond with his honey-drenched tone. Indeed, he did not respond at all.

Apaay thought he might have tightened his grip on her arm but couldn't be sure, as the pain in her shoulder provided a terrible distraction. The Avi, in all his command, did not frighten Apaay. But the Face Stealer's silence did.

"Kaan, Umiq." The man inclined his head, and the beads attached to his multitude of skinny braids clacked with the movement. "I'm disappointed to find you in such poor company."

"Father." Umiq hurried to his side like the most loyal of dogs. "Kaan and Ro have been in contact with the Face Stealer. He wants us to ally with him against Nanuq."

Kaan went to his other side. "Father—"

"Silence."

Her nostrils flared, yet she didn't argue, glowering at her older sister. Apaay bit her tongue and wondered where Ro was in all this. She assumed he was watching over the Wood.

The Face Stealer dared to step forward. Some of the owl Unua, watching from the platforms, shrank back, the white of their hair lost to the dim. "Pak—"

A coil of power lashed through the trees, startling many birds into flight. "Do *not*," the Avi intoned, "address me so informally." He looked down his nose, his eyes slitting in feral rage. "You are a smear on all that is good in the world. You are a virus, a plague."

Umiq bore an ugly, self-satisfied smirk that Apaay would have slapped off if she wasn't so certain she would die for the act. Kaan watched it all unfold, unable to interfere. No matter how great her desire was, she would not speak for her friend. Kaan's loyalty was to her people. And the Avi *was* her people.

"I'm here to make amends," said the Face Stealer.

At the same time, Apaay said, "Won't you listen to what he has to say?"

The man's attention slid to Apaay, as if only now noticing her. He canted his head. "What is this?" His nostrils flared. "A *human*?"

Apaay lifted her chin.

The Face Stealer slipped his hands into his pockets. "She's no one." Flippant.

"If she's no one," the Avi replied, "then she's disposable, is she not?"

The tree shuddered with a groan, shaking the bridge and sending the remainder of the birds into flight. A massive branch dropped with startling speed and rammed into Apaay's stomach, forcing her to grab hold as it launched her backward, the platform dropping out from under her. There she dangled, hundreds of feet above the ground.

The Face Stealer lunged.

"Stand down!" the Avi thundered.

The Face Stealer went immediately still. Pain seared from Apaay's injured arm all the way to her skull, where it burst behind her eyes, forcing her into a far greater darkness. She blinked and tried to get her bearings, or at least get her heartbeat under control. Turning her head as much as she could, she saw the Face Stealer look at her and nowhere else.

The Avi approached his adversary with measured steps. Apaay had never seen the Face Stealer bend to another's power. Though he had followed Yuki's command in the labyrinth, she had always sensed he could choose to do otherwise, but hadn't cared enough to bother. Now he clenched his hands at his sides, vibrating with the need to move.

"Is this not what you did to my people in the war? Turned your back and left them to slaughter?" Avian screams broke over and over with their remembrance. "I counted on your support, and when we needed you most, you fled. Your cowardice killed my people, left us with scorched earth, the Dead Plains, our land no longer. Tell me, Numiak." He hissed the words into the Face Stealer's ear. "Why shouldn't I do the same?"

The fur of Apaay's sleeve slipped against the bark as the weight of her body pulled her down to the crook of her elbow. She tried to swing one of her legs over the branch but didn't have the strength. She had lost too much blood.

A wheeze squeezed past the tightness in her throat. The freezing air was cold enough for frostbite, though she was sweating heavily enough to burn with fever. There were eyes, so many eyes, glowing like fevered moons. Apaay didn't dare shift her gaze from where her arm touched the tree as she tried digging the fingers of one hand into the plates of the bark, but the mitten slipped, and darkness grasped at her legs.

"You have to understand the position I was in," said the Face Stealer, his form strained, ready to spring the moment she let go. "It was either my people or yours. I chose mine. You would have done the same." His chest rose and fell shallowly. "You know me. I grew up here, right alongside Kaan, Ro, and Umiq."

Umiq bristled at that, and her father answered with a cold, "I knew the boy you were, not the demon you've become."

A small cry cracked in Apaay's chest as the arrow sawed deeper, hitting bone. The burn migrated to her back from the agony of holding up her body, and in her desperation, she let slip the name she vowed to never touch her lips. "Numiak!" She had maybe a few more moments before her strength gave out.

The Face Stealer whipped his head toward her again, showcasing a gaze of crystalline violet. White outlined his lips from how ruthlessly they pressed together.

Lifting both hands in surrender, he sank to his knees, darting repeated glances at her hanging form. Their audience was a sweep of bated breath, waiting for the Avi's punishment, Apaay's surrender. Waiting for the last leaf to fall.

Apaay blinked tears from her eyes. She slipped another inch as her muscles screamed, and something inside her, locked and impenetrable, began to uncoil.

Apaay would have thought, after everything, that she wouldn't fight this inevitability. Would have thought she'd welcome the darkness, that cold, persistent ache in her chest, an old friend she couldn't bear to leave. She had awaited death for months. She had *wanted* to die.

Yet she clung to the branch so fiercely. That terrified her even more, that there might be something to live for, even though she didn't know what it was. She had fought to breathe all these months, fighting a current dragging her down, and now that she hadn't a choice as to whether she lived or died, Apaay couldn't find it in her heart to let go.

"War forces us to make impossible choices," said the Face Stealer with another glance at Apaay. "I was going to come back, but Yuki—" His throat worked. The curse prevented him from divulging information. "I was detained."

"Father." Kaan stepped forward. "Nanuq and Yuki have allied. They are too powerful to fight alone. You know this."

"No. What I know is the trust between our peoples was broken." Many of the birds shrieked in response.

"It can be repaired," she argued.

Apaay slipped another two inches. She squeezed the branch tighter, knowing she didn't have much longer.

"The world is already divided," Kaan continued. "How will we ever move forward if we're always clinging to the past?"

Apaay blinked away a new wave of tears. The question brought pain to her heart, and a softness. Something she hadn't let herself feel in a long time.

It was the sun rising after the longest, coldest, darkest night, and it was right on the threshold of touch, if only she had the courage to reach for it.

Kaan stepped closer to her father. "Think about our people. Think about what kind of legacy you want to leave behind. Do you want to be known as someone who turned his back on humanity?" A hand on her father's arm. "Or do you want to be known as a leader who ushered his people into a new era of unity and peace?"

Absolute quiet. The kind of stillness Apaay had not experienced since leaving home.

The branch jerked across the platform. As soon as solid ground was beneath her, Apaay let go and slammed onto her back.

Shock rippled through the masses. The Face Stealer remained kneeling, not daring to push his luck in helping Apaay to her feet.

"No," hissed Umiq, shoving forward. "Father, you forget yourself. Remember what you told me: Forgiveness is weakness."

"Umiq." A quiet but firm reprimand.

The woman's nostrils flared. "Maybe time has dulled your sense of betrayal," she said, sneering at the Face Stealer, "but it has not dulled mine." A muscle feathered in her jaw. "I challenge you, Numiak of the Wolf Kingdom, to the Nayinkai."

A hush fell over the canopy.

His smile: cold. His eyes: flint. His face: stone.

"I accept."

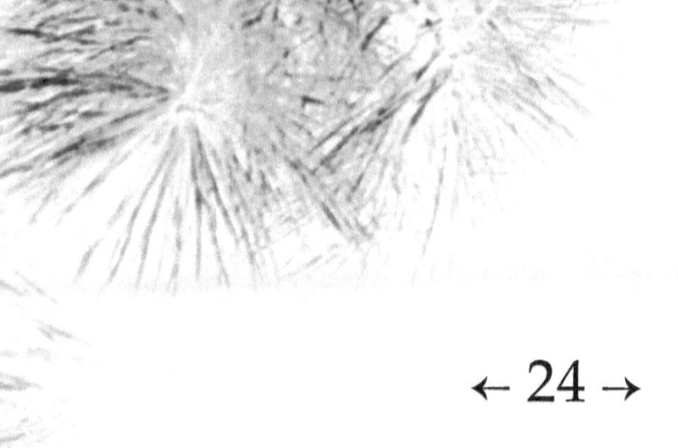

← 24 →

"The Nayinkai," said the healer as she prepared a pot of tea, "came from the time when the people of the North still lived in their animal skins. Then, there were no men, only the bears and caribou and voles and whales. Our people call it Taguranaq: Before."

Steam hissed as the water boiled over. The woman removed the pot, handing a cup to Apaay with steeped moonflower at the girl's request. Cupping her palms around the wooden base, Apaay brought the cup to her nose and inhaled the floral scent. "When was that, exactly? Were the Analak here?"

"No. This was long before your people arrived. Even before the Iskra."

The Analak had migrated to the North from across Tor, but they had not been the first to do so. There were stories of people who had come thousands of years before, their civilization and way of life abandoned. They were called the Iskra: the first of the Analak.

The healer sat cross-legged beside her, watching as Apaay did from a recess in the glass dome overhanging the platform where the Nayinkai would occur. Spectators, both in their avian and human forms, perched on the branches, benches, and bridges as the Avi, seated on a throne of thatched pine needles, observed the gathering spectacle.

Kaan had brought Apaay to the healing wing an hour before. The healer, identified by her necklace of lemming bones, had removed the arrowhead, stitched her wound, and given her a draught to numb the pain. Clean bandages now wrapped Apaay's shoulder and upper arm. The warm air smelled of salt and herbs and soothed the cold stiffness in her face.

"That time did not last," the healer continued, her amber eyes clear among the heavy folds of bronzed skin. "When the Iskra came, they plundered this land as if it were their own. The caribou were targeted first for their antlers, which were sold to the highest bidder. My own ancestors fell to the arrows, their feathers plucked for their beautiful white plumes."

The hypnotizing quality of the woman's voice painted a very different version of the North. "What happened?" Apaay wondered.

"They pushed us out, forced us to search across greater distances for resources. The Iskra were like giants, too strong to fight against, with strange powers. The Nayinkai arose from necessity, a way for the animal species to claim resources. Those who lost were forced to migrate elsewhere." She sipped her tea, lowered it into her lap. "It worked. For a time."

A roar boomed against the glass, howls and shrieks clawing its surface. A snowy owl darted past and touched down on one side of the arena: Umiq. Spheres of blue flame spaced around the platform illuminated its center.

Umiq flapped her wings with a piercing cry as a smudged shape prowled across the stage. A wolf, painted in sweeping darkness, with eyes like suns. He paced back and forth, studying his opponent.

Apaay thought of the Face Stealer's eyes the moment she'd screamed his name, seconds away from tumbling to her death. Months spent in his company had solidified her knowledge of the colors and emotions he harbored. Gray for aloofness, distance. Blue-green for when he was feeling playful.

She did not know what violet meant.

"Eventually, animal and man clashed. Our god, Inirlaq, tried to find a solution where both species could live in harmony. In the process, he fell in love with a human woman. Their son was the first of the owl Unua."

As Apaay knew from stories passed down, by the time the Analak had settled, the Unua nations were already established. The Iskra had gone extinct.

Pressing her face to the frosted glass, she peered below. Condensation collected from the heat of her breath. As the cries trailed off, the opponents stepped into the center of the arena, facing each other. They were animals, honed by instinct. On this night, they were enemies.

The Avi stood. Apaay tasted a sharpness on her tongue and was more on edge because of it.

He spoke, the sound warped beyond the glass, and the audience answered with a fervent "To the death!"

Apaay gave a jolt. She hadn't realized this was a fight to the *death*.

The Face Stealer prowled the outer ring of the platform, not making any move to strike. Umiq hopped awkwardly before taking flight and circling overhead.

There was no better or stronger form, only different. Wings gave Umiq grace where her awkward legs stumbled on land. The Face Stealer's build lent him strength, a steady, grounded form, but as he could not take to the skies, he did not have the advantage of escape from the sheer drop on all sides of the platform. Any sign of his usual power was absent. No shadows trailing, no tendrils fluttering in his wake. They became what they were in the beginning. They became the sky and the earth and wings and claws and two hearts beating.

A swift dive sent Umiq plummeting as her cry ripped through the canopy. Apaay gasped at how quickly she moved, how her wings flared out and her tail tucked inward as she went in for the kill.

Apaay pressed both of her palms to the glass, her skin prickling from the chill. The Face Stealer ducked to avoid the talons and whirled around, lifting onto his hind legs to swipe a paw in a diagonal cut, but Umiq was already gone, circling high overhead. A well-aimed swipe from those talons meant a severed artery, blindness, a torn throat.

Another dive came not a moment later. They clashed and broke apart, the Face Stealer hopping a few feet backward. He turned before she could drive him any closer to the edge. She was at his flank. Now his blind spot. Yet instead of striking and retreating, she landed between his shoulder blades where he couldn't reach. Skin scrunched between her talons, and Umiq jerked backward in a flap of wings, pulling hard, twisting. Apaay gasped as his skin ripped. In the blue light, dark liquid poured onto the wood and iced over.

First blood.

Baring his teeth, the Face Stealer tossed his body to the side in an attempt to dislodge her. Umiq flapped her wings for balance. The audience cheered, and higher up, with the pine needle throne at his back, the Avi let slip a faint pleased smile.

More ripping flesh, blood dribbling out. The Face Stealer finally managed to toss Umiq away. Apaay, who had much to learn about this violent world, was learning more every day. She didn't necessarily see it as a good thing.

As she watched the Nayinkai from above, Apaay could not ignore the similarities between it and her duel in the labyrinth. She remembered how strong she had felt, high on the rush of power as the icicle gouged into the bear's gullet. In her bear form, the Unua woman had been immense. So strong she could crush Apaay's windpipe with one sweep of her massive paw.

Apaay had not been more powerful, in the end, to walk away. She had just been lucky.

Cool fingers alighted on her brow, a thumb drawing downward to smooth the folds that had gathered. "It will be over soon," said the woman kindly.

But the Nayinkai raged. Blood pooled onto the platform and slicked over. The Face Stealer favored his left foreleg, perhaps from an old wound. They grappled for control, snapping and lashing at the other, unaware that they moved closer to the ledge, and Apaay's stomach clenched as Umiq attempted to recover from a failed strike and the Face Stealer clamped onto her wing.

Apaay went cold. The healer, she thought, had stopped breathing.

A piercing shriek erupted, Umiq's other wing flailing in an attempt to dislodge his grip. The Face Stealer only had to snap his jaws together and Umiq's wing would be ruined. Apaay didn't know how that would translate into her human form. Ro, for instance, was still able to fly, for it was not his arms that had been injured.

Apaay saw Kaan biting her lip, the Avi squeezing the arms of his chair and his face full of the knowledge that one of his children might be permanently grounded, should she live.

The Face Stealer tossed the raptor onto the ground, the wing untouched save for saliva. Apaay released a shaky breath. Crushing Umiq's wing would have all but guaranteed a win, but she was glad he hadn't.

Umiq began to attack more aggressively, as if provoked by that near-crippling blow. Her attacks forced the Face Stealer nearer to the edge of the platform. He ducked his head to save his eyes from a gouging. Another step backward.

"What happens if he goes over?" Apaay asked the healer, briefly pulling her attention away from the fight.

"Assuming he had enough energy, he could use his power to save himself before hitting the ground, but his win would be forfeit."

"What would that mean for us?"

"I do not know. It would depend on how merciful the Avi is feeling."

Umiq rammed into his side, sending him back another few feet. Apaay did not have time to cry out before his hind legs slipped over the ledge.

The trees filled with cacophonous screams, beating wings.

Apaay leaned forward as her pulse spiked, but she could go no farther than the glass. Smeared shadows and dusky light clouded her view. What would happen to her, she wondered, if he died? If he did not? There were lives at stake, and not just their own.

The Face Stealer dangled there, his upper torso clinging to the platform, nails digging into the wood while Umiq ripped out chunks of his skin from his shoulders and back, occasionally diving for his eyes. His hind legs wheeled. The Face Stealer managed to tug himself a few inches forward before the raptor snagged at his muzzle. A flash of teeth, sprayed blood. A snarl ripped through the sleeping wood.

"He's going to fall," Apaay murmured.

He dropped another inch.

Apaay felt strangely numb to it all. The Face Stealer, as much as he liked people to think otherwise, was not invincible. He was an animal subject to the laws of nature. He was exactly like them.

When Umiq wheeled away, preparing for the next dive, the Face Stealer crawled forward by his forelegs. He gained a few inches before her return. This time, she ripped into his side.

She was making him suffer, Apaay realized. Instead of ending him, she was drawing out his pain as long as possible. Revenge for what had befallen her people. Apaay thought she would have enjoyed the torment, but it made her want to vomit. Through it all, he managed to pull himself to safety. Umiq's shriek of outrage followed. She dove, and he swiped at her with deadly force.

She hit the platform. The Face Stealer pressed a paw to her chest, against the thin bird bones, and halted her struggles. He lowered his muzzle to her neck, teeth bared.

It was done.

From somewhere in the trees, the Avi's disembodied voice rang out. "You may take her life, if you wish. It is your right to do so."

A cold horror trickled through Apaay. He would allow his own daughter to die? She sought Kaan in the crowd. The woman looked physically ill.

The Face Stealer returned to his human form. His clothes were torn, his face bloodied. The skin around his nose was gouged. "She needs a healer," he managed, spitting out a mouthful of blood.

Apaay's exhalation clouded the glass.

When no one made any move to help, he snapped, "Now!"

He was not the Avi, but there was such command in his tone that immediately three people hurried forward to carry the woman off the platform. From his throne, the Avi inclined his head. "This is your choice?"

"I think," said the Face Stealer, slowly and in pain, "there has been enough death for your people, has there not?" His gaze was cool. "Umiq may despise me, but she fought valiantly. She is a strong warrior who loves her people. If we're to face Nanuq, we need every person who can fight, and she is one of the best."

The Avi rose to his feet, the feathered collar streaked blue under the lamps. One look from that ancient, prevailing gaze and the owl Unua knelt, palms resting on their knees.

"Numiak of the Wolf Kingdom has spared my daughter's life. If this does not demonstrate his willingness to make amends, then I do not know what will. Tonight, we celebrate the alliance between the Wolf Kingdom and Owl Clan for the first time in twenty years."

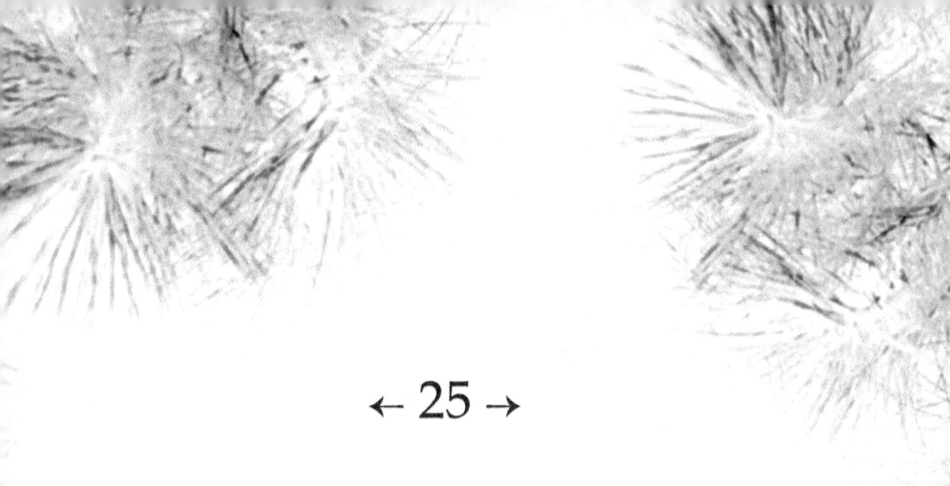

← 25 →

On this night, the Aatu Forest had come alive. The air was vibrant, thick with herbs and spice, as the people gathered to celebrate the newfound alliance, and for many, the healing of a decades-old wound. Though Apaay sat by herself in one of the tree's hollows, the shift of bodies traveling from platform to platform and bridge to bridge pulled her in as swiftly as the tide, and she did not feel so alone.

Drawing her knees to her chest, Apaay watched the celebration unfold, the loosening of limbs and lowering of inhibitions as a pale alcoholic drink was passed from hand to hand and mouth to mouth, the white of the owl Unua's hair so bright it hurt her eyes. Three glittering bridges led to the central platform, where the majority of the dancing took place. On a different platform sat a large, curved piece of glass, twice the height of a man. Only when the owls fluttered past, directing the wind beneath their wings, and a mournful, full-bodied melody flowed, did she realize it was an instrument.

And so the night went. The people gorged themselves on food and drink, and lost themselves to the carnality of living in a world that killed without thought, the current pulsing through Sinika's veins, both old and young and new all at once. And there was laughter. So much laughter Apaay was swimming in it. There was no room for anything else.

"How are you feeling?"

Apaay jumped at Kaan's voice, glancing up. Black ceremonial paint rimmed the woman's eyes, and white dots stamped down her nose. Like her father, she wore a feathered collar that Apaay had learned symbolized her place in the family hierarchy. A few people glanced at them in curiosity, some going out of their way to witness the second daughter speaking with the human girl.

Apaay touched the bandage beneath her parka. Warm skin, but no longer hot to the touch. Clean stitches extended beneath her trailing finger. "Better." The healing draught had numbed the ache, and now it was all but a faded memory. "Thank you," she said, "for standing up to your sister for me."

Kaan leaned against the tree, arms folded. The ends of her hair brushed her jaw. "Umiq has a hard time letting go. She's a lot like our father in that way."

"But you went against your father's wishes."

Folding her legs beneath her, Kaan sat beside Apaay, their shoulders touching, and listened to the drums join with the melodic croon. "You were hurting," she said simply.

Apaay bit the inside of her cheek. It was everything—the journey, her injury, the ostracization she felt among the owl Unua, even among her own people—that brought her emotions closer to the surface. She felt . . . something. That Kaan had recognized her pain and wanted to do something to alleviate it was nice.

"Do you know what I thought when I first met you?" Kaan asked.

With her head resting against the bark, Apaay was almost afraid to ask. She said softly, "What?" That she was weak? Someone undeserving of grace?

The woman touched Apaay's shoulder, easing the tension before it had the chance to gather. "I thought you were someone I would very much like to know. I saw myself in you." Though her mouth curved, the rest of her face remained impassive. "I knew you were a survivor. Like me."

The admission took her by surprise. Admittedly, she was curious. Kaan, for all her brazenness, seemed like someone who'd lived a privileged life. Her father was a king.

Looping one long arm around her knee, Kaan drew it to her chest. "Love, they say, is often blind." The woman's voice lacked inflection, and a shadow passed over her features. "I remember the first time he hit me."

Apaay tensed. The laughter in the air no longer sounded welcoming. "Who?"

"A boy I once loved. It was a long time ago."

Cautiously, Apaay touched the woman's arm, if only to make sure she was still breathing. "He should not have done that to you," she whispered. To think anyone would want to hurt this powerful woman made Apaay want to weep.

Kaan's throat bobbed, and she skimmed her fingers across her cheek, red from the cold, as if it might be a handprint still lingering after all this time. "You're right, of course." She wouldn't look Apaay in the face. "We were arguing. I can't even remember what we were arguing about. Isn't that funny? It was probably something that wasn't important."

The revelers screamed in delight as two women, locked in a passionate embrace, decided it was the perfect time to start removing their clothes. The couple was ushered off the platform, and the space they'd occupied closed like a seam stitching up.

"I hope you hit him back," Apaay said.

Kaan sighed. "I was much younger then. At the time, I kept thinking it was my fault. *I* was the one who had hurt *him*."

And that, Apaay thought, was how the dark cycle began.

"Six years, and I never told anyone about the abuse." The flush along Kaan's face darkened. She shoved the hair from her eyes in a sloppy gesture. "He never again hit my face. It was always the parts I could cover up."

A dull fury spread through Apaay. "Did Ro notice, or Umiq?"

"He was busy fighting on the border. As for Umiq, we've never been close. She had her life. I had mine."

"What about your friends?"

"Honestly, I've never had very many friends." At Apaay's look of shock, she snorted. "I know. Hard to believe. I usually remembered to cover up, but one day Ro returned home unexpectedly and caught me as I was leaving the river. He didn't believe me when I told him the bruises were from sparring practice." She rubbed her knee absently. "Ro challenged him to the Nayinkai and tore him apart."

Kind, steadfast, quiet Ro, whose love for his sister would bring death to those who did her harm. Apaay saw him in a different light. A deadly one.

"I still think about it," Kaan went on. "How I was too weak to walk away. How if Ro hadn't intervened, I would probably be dead by now."

"That's not true." If there was one thing Kaan needed to hear, it was this. It made her sick to think that things might have ended differently. "You *are* strong. It's not your fault. It was never your fault. That man made a choice, every day, as to whether he would love you or hurt you." After a time, she said, "I'm sorry you went through that."

Kaan's throat bobbed. "Me too," she whispered.

Together, they watched the dancers as the beat increased in tempo and flung into a blood-pounding rhythm. Apaay followed Kaan's gaze to an area of shimmering, writhing, undulating bodies. The Face Stealer had joined the celebration and was dressed in clean clothes. She had not seen him since the duel, though she knew he had been reviewing the alliance contract with the Avi and his advisors. Bandages covered his shoulders, chest, and face.

"What was he like?" she wondered, watching him twirl an elder around the dance floor, laughing as she laughed. "Before?" It was such a strange concept, the idea that he may have been someone else once and not the wicked, unknowable figure she knew.

"More trusting, I would say." Her next words came low. "War has hardened him."

And it wasn't over. Nanuq's reach would eventually extend beyond his borders, affecting them in far worse and, she feared, permanent ways. Maybe she hadn't cared about what was happening to the North before.

And maybe she should.

"War has hardened all of us, I think," said Apaay.

The Face Stealer's senses were keener than most, yet she hadn't thought he would be able to pull her voice from the crowd. But he lifted his head, searching, and met her gaze in the dark.

Before she could decide how to react, he had already turned around.

Apaay tilted back her head and watched one of the owls flutter overhead. "The Analak fear him," she said.

"You speak as if they are separate from you. Is that not who you are?"

Her dishonesty with herself these past months had swelled like a wave moving toward shore, and it seemed it had finally reached it, foam breaking upon the rocks and driftwood. "I don't think I know who I am anymore," she managed, the whisper pained.

Killer, betrayer, loner, fraud?

Kaan must think her silly. How did one not know who they were? Of course she was Analak. She would always *be* Analak. But it was as if she saw that part of herself from a great distance, and no matter how fast she ran, she did not come any closer to reaching it.

Kaan cast her a sidelong glance full of rumination. "There may be an answer for you, if you're interested."

Apaay pulled her attention away from the revel, the swaying blue lamps. The thunder of oiled hide snaked along her bones. "What do you mean?"

"Have you heard of the First Man?"

She shook her head, intrigued.

"There is a legend my people tell of a man who tricked Inirlaq into giving him immortality. The Keeper of All That Lives and Dies. When it was discovered what he had done, he was cursed to remain a part of the earth. When he turns completely to stone, our world will end. If you truly want to know who you are, well—" She shrugged. "Maybe you'll find the answers you're looking for."

"Flower?"

Apaay's head snapped up, her gaze meeting that of a young man dressed in fitted trousers and a vest plumed with feathers, his arm wrappings beige like the majority of the population. Bent forward at the waist, he offered her a blossom with four scarlet petals.

"Um." She shook her head, unsure as to why this man offered her a flower. "It's lovely."

The skin around his eyes crinkled. "Beauty desires beauty, does it not?" His irises were the pale amber of hardened tree sap.

"He's asking you to dance," murmured Kaan with obvious amusement.

Dance?

Apaay's entire face flooded with heat. Aside from Pana back home, she hadn't had much experience with men. Sure, she had kissed a few here and there. She didn't understand what the excitement was about pressing two pairs of lips together.

But he was handsome. His eyes, despite her fumbling, were mischievous, sincere. Apaay swallowed down a groan. She wasn't a dancer. Harpooning a seal she could do. Moving her feet, swinging her hips? No.

The young man peered at her through long, snowy lashes. "Just one?"

She touched the stem. Acceptance. His hand clasped hers, warm and firm. He lifted Apaay to her feet, where she wobbled awkwardly, clutching the flower to her chest as he led her to the dance floor. Many shot them curious looks, but as most people were flush with drink, Apaay didn't take offense at it. And when the boy swung her into his arms, she forgot all about the stares.

The beat picked up, and Apaay struggled to keep pace. Their bodies brushed, parted, and returned. He twirled her, around and around, and when he dipped her backward, startled laughter burst free. And Apaay did not know his name, but she was never more grateful that he was able to pull from her a sound she had believed to be gone. As she followed him through the feverish steps, Apaay sank into the feeling, breathing hard but unwilling to slow.

Too soon, the dance ended, and the young man pulled her close, his grin wide. He was hardly out of breath. "I thank you for this honor." Then he pressed a kiss to her palm and took his leave.

Her fingers curled inward to hold the warmth of his mouth there. Still feeling a bit unsteady, she returned to the tree, Kaan having disappeared.

Moments later, someone settled beside her. "A night for dancing, I see."

She supposed she should have been used to the Face Stealer's comings and goings. No doubt he took great pleasure in startling her. "I don't believe I asked you to sit here."

"Don't pretend you don't love my company, wolfling."

She opened her mouth to retort, but when her gaze landed on his face, the words died.

A bandage ran across one cheek. There was another across his nose, the cloth dark with blood. One of his eyes was swollen shut. More bruising on the other cheek, the one not covered in bandages. He looked ghastly, and that was being kind. She couldn't imagine what his back looked like.

"The alliance?" she said.

"It is done."

Apaay nodded in a distracted manner. "What does that mean going forward?"

"Oh." He sighed. "A lot of meetings and what-ifs. We'll compare information about Nanuq, discuss strategy. I imagine Umiq will do everything in her power to dispose of me."

"She would have beaten you," Apaay said, only half aware of her thoughts, "had you fallen off the platform."

His fox's smile. "Tell me you weren't worried about me."

This again. "I wasn't worried about you. I was worried about *me*." She poked a finger into her chest. As much as she hated his power over her, she would be a fool to deny that in a situation such as this, his protection ensured her survival. "Why didn't you kill her?" She couldn't quite keep the disbelief from her voice.

The question took the allure out of his smile. "You would have liked that, wouldn't you?"

"No, I thought *you* would have liked that."

"You also thought I was going to crush her wing." A shadowed stare.

"Yes." No point in denying it. Then, softly, "But I'm glad you didn't."

His gaze touched upon her face, the bandages hidden under her clothes. It then followed to where she watched Kaan dance, a circle of admirers surrounding her, all smiles for the Avi's second daughter. The weapons master pulled a shy boy onto the floor, and the crowd cheered, in awe and complete adoration.

"The people really love her," Apaay observed.

The Face Stealer nodded. "It is true. But Kaan is not who they need."

She looked to the demon in question.

"Kaan is one of the strongest people I know," he explained, "and yes, the people do love her. But she is too reckless with her decisions, too fierce in her caring. Above all, a leader decides for the good of the whole. Unfortunately, that requires emotional distance."

Apaay recalled Kaan's suggestion of seeking the Raven for help, her reluctance to listen to other possible solutions.

"Ro," Apaay guessed. "That's who will lead when the Avi steps down."

The Face Stealer dipped his chin in affirmation. Kaan's laughter drew in the children, their parents. "Theoretically, yes. If Ro gave himself a chance, he would be a fine leader for his people, but first he must make peace with his personal demons. We all face our darkness in different ways." For a time, they sat in companionable silence.

"Hungry?" he asked, and thrust a bowl of food in her direction. "It's not meat," he assured her. "They're mushrooms." He popped one into his mouth. "Good flavor." Steam uncurled from the pile of tender, wood-charred fungi, the herbaceous scent making her stomach clench in newfound interest. It had been so long since she'd experienced hunger that she had forgotten what it felt like.

When she did not immediately respond, a seriousness touched his eyes. "You need to eat, Apaay."

She looked him straight in the face. In some ways, the gouges on his cheeks reminded her of Masuk. "How do I know you didn't poison them?"

His mouth curled with wicked intent, and maybe relief, too, that she hadn't denied his statement. "You don't. Just because I'm showing you a little kindness doesn't mean you should trust me." He ate another mushroom, unperturbed and knowing full well how uneasy that made her.

Apaay barely suppressed a grimace. She should probably take his advice. "I ate earlier. The healer brought me berries."

"You mean the ones you tossed off the platform when she wasn't looking?" A bald stare. "Yes, I saw that. Now." He shook the bowl. "Eat."

Her nostrils flared in warning. The absolute arrogance of him. "What is it about you? Do you get some sick thrill from threatening people?"

"This isn't about me," he seethed, his tone laced with all the force of a storm brewing. "This is about you, your health, your healing." His fingers curled around the lip of the bowl, and she suspected he might heave it into the branches. Which would be a shame, as the mushrooms smelled delicious. "When are you going to admit you need help?"

Apaay pressed her lips together to hide their unsteadiness. He was right. She *hated* when he was right. "Why is this even an issue with you? You don't even *care*." The last word was hoarse with strain, and she hated that even more.

He glanced away, light shying from the planes of his face. Apaay felt the Face Stealer gather himself, as if he were preparing to challenge her claim, but the only sounds were the owls' coos and the pulse of blood in her temples, slowing the longer the silence passed. He didn't care. He'd told her, cruelly, how little she meant to him, how worthless was her life. She was angry because he didn't care, and maybe she wished he would.

The fact was, he had never asked her how she'd been coping. The only times he had mentioned her well-being were in connection to the blood oath.

Eat. You need energy to look through all these books.

If you don't sleep, you might miss pertinent information.

Unless the blood oath was a front. A mask to hide the true concern.

Apaay drew her knees to her chest, wincing from the pull of her stitches. "Look, Numiak." The Face Stealer went still beside her. His name was a language she didn't understand. It would be some time, she figured, before it lost its bitterness. "I'm tired. I don't want to argue with you."

The dark hue of his eyes leeched away like dye in water. "What, then? Will you continue to waste away until you no longer have breath in your body?" His calm demeanor shifted into icy rage. "I did not think you were someone to give up so easily."

It didn't escape Apaay's notice that it was perhaps the one true compliment he had given her.

"I know you don't want to die."

"Maybe I do," she snapped, cheeks hot. What would he see when all was revealed? "I deserve it after what happened to my village."

"I know you don't mean that."

"You don't know a thing about me."

His laughter was surprisingly contemptuous. "I know you." He turned toward her, the air stirring with the scent of woodsmoke that was at times so familiar to her it almost felt like a memory. "You're not afraid of dying. You're afraid of *living*."

The accusation slammed into her. *No,* she started to say. *You're wrong.* But it came back and slammed into her again with greater force.

Her chin dimpled. Her eyes filled. She would not allow herself to cry in front of him, not again. She thought she had purged her pain in the grove, but there was still some left, it seemed. This time, though, the pain was not as great. At some point between breaking apart on the grass and now, it had eased.

"You can say whatever it is you want," he said, searching her features with intensity. "But when you were dangling from that branch, barely holding on? That was not someone who wanted to die. That was someone who wanted to live."

He was right. She hadn't been able to let go.

Apaay no longer cared if her voice quavered. "What's the point? Even you said I was nothing. I know you meant it, in that moment."

He looked beyond to where the revelers paired off, arms linked, feet tapping as they sprung into a lighthearted jig. "I was ashamed."

"That's a lie, and I hate you for it."

"Believe me, there is no one on this earth who hates me more than I do."

Force of habit let rise the words that would hurt him, shame him, weaken him, break him. *And why do you think that is?* she'd snap, the answer obvious. As he had done to her, so she would do unto him.

Apaay grappled with the urge before shoving it aside. It was easier to build walls than to bring them down. "What were you ashamed of?"

The edges of his mouth curled, though his eyes didn't lighten. "Myself. The memories you saw inside the library were ones I had locked away a long time ago. No one was ever supposed to see them."

"What was that place?"

"It is part of Taggak. As I have strong ties to it, I can enter the realm at will, though generally I avoid it. At the very least, it allows me to store things for safekeeping." He bit into another mushroom, chewing thoughtfully. Apaay's stomach growled again. "Contrary to what you believe, I do know what it's like to fail your people."

Smoke rising from the trees. Then darkness.

"Why do you lock away your memories," Apaay murmured, "if you still remember them?"

To which he countered with "Are there not some things you would rather forget?"

Many things. It hadn't worked. Maybe it wasn't the right approach. Maybe instead of trying to forget, she could remember. Acknowledge it, then move past it.

"I owe you another apology." He still wouldn't look at her.

"You already apologized."

"No." He spoke in a halting voice. "It's not about what I said to you in the library. It's about . . . everything else."

Apaay felt her back lock up. "Oh."

Shifting position, he faced her fully, and she was hit with the force of his dark gaze. It was an age before he spoke. "I'm sorry. I'm truly, deeply sorry for everything I put you through, now and in the labyrinth. I'm sorry for the pain I've caused you and your people. If

I could go back and change the way I acted toward you, I would in a heartbeat."

He paused, then went on, and each word was like a drop of water after months of drought. "I'm sorry for not being your friend when you needed one. I'm sorry for pushing you down when you needed someone to help you up. I'm sorry about Nakaluq. And your hair—" She had the strangest sense he might reach up and touch one of the locks falling across her forehead. "I'm glad it's growing back."

They stared at each other, her eyes a bit wide, and his. Tension gathered with the knowledge that this was as vulnerable as they had ever been with each other, and they were for once on equal footing, equal ground, with no desire to cut into the other. It was strange. She didn't entirely know what to do with this realization.

Apaay forgot, sometimes, that there was beauty in winter, in the death of the earth. It was not green or colored in reds and pinks and golds. It was not warm. It was not thriving.

It was still. It was one long thought strung out. Life withered, yes, but eventually the earth thawed. The green returned. And so the cycle began anew.

Much had changed in the six months since setting out from her village to save Eska from eternal darkness. For so long, Apaay had clung to her old life, but the painful truth was, it no longer existed. And neither did the girl.

If she left that girl behind, she could become someone new, yet still herself at the core. She could work toward rebuilding herself instead of mourning the person who no longer was. She could choose the future, choose peace. She could, finally, begin that long road toward forgiveness.

Here, amidst the thrumming beat of song and dance, amidst the cold and the snap of pine, amidst the promise of togetherness and a new, greater purpose, Apaay was not thinking about the pull of darkness. She was not drowning in that void, desperate for air. For the first time in months, Apaay's head was above water.

"Just because you brought me food and told me your sob story," she said, tilting back her head to take in the lights' cerulean glow, "doesn't mean I forgive you."

His mouth softened in what may have been relief tinged with affection. "I know."

But when he once again offered her the bowl of mushrooms, she ate them all.

Every. Last. One.

And then she did it again.

PART TWO

DAWN

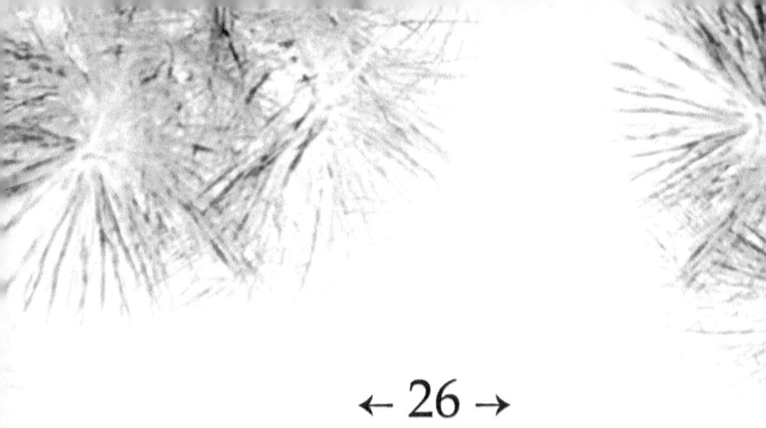

← 26 →

"**A**gain."

Knees bent, Ila swiped at Tulimaq's fur-clad legs with her talq, the frozen earth crunching beneath her boots as she shifted her weight to the balls of her feet, a difficult move when crouched this low to the ground. It was sluggish and messy, all of it, but she gave everything she had. She could not afford to give anything less.

There, in the moonlit dark, with the mountains cradling them and the trees pressing near, she and Tulimaq traded blows in a subtle, choreographed dance. Her mentor pushed her to think of all possibilities: strike or parry, lunge or dodge, attack or retreat. Sometimes she got it. Other times—

Driving the weapon into the space beneath Ila's armpit, Tulimaq leveraged her onto her toes before driving down with impressive force. Ila slammed onto her back.

The combat master stood over her, his face devoid of emotion. As usual, his hair was pulled as tightly against his skull as possible, leaving no room for a wayward strand. "Again," he said.

Grumbling, Ila pushed to her feet. One month into training with Tulimaq, and Ila was growing strong. Tomorrow, her body would showcase the most spectacular bruises.

You wanted this, remember?

Eight weeks ago, a training accident had left her with a broken wrist, Tulimaq gazing down at her without remorse, saying, "I told you to protect your wrist. I told you over and over again. Maybe now you will learn to listen." Then he'd left, leaving her to seek out Kaan for healing.

Except Kaan had been in the Central Territory, along with the Face Stealer and Apaay, negotiating an alliance. So she'd splinted her wrist, wrapped it in cloth, and emerged into the clearing the next morning where they trained, her right arm bound in a sling, her left hand gripping the talq awkwardly.

"Are you healed?" he asked, when the answer was obviously *no*.

Ila set down the weapon to free her left hand and signed, *I won't improve by lying in bed all day. This way, I'll learn how to fight with my left hand as well.*

It was the first time he had looked at her with any shred of respect.

Now, Ila no longer knew the look of her own skin, and she was glad of it. Pain was progress. It was leaving that woman in the cell behind. Sometimes she convinced herself Tulimaq enjoyed beating her into the dirt. Somehow, she didn't think she imagined it.

Ila resumed her starting position, waiting for the signal. Tulimaq reflected her stance with spread feet, bent knees, and his nigana held at center. As always, Ila studied him for an indication of his intention. Tulimaq's greatest advantage was his unreadability.

The key, he'd told her as she ducked beneath his swinging arm, was to keep her center aligned. Balance. Flow. These were the qualities necessary to mastering this particular strike. Crouched, she whipped up her weapon with enough force to snap Tulimaq's arm in half, but her positioning was off. She glanced down to remedy the problem.

Too late, Ila remembered her training. Tulimaq snagged her arm, tugged her the slightest bit off-center, and gravity did the rest. Ila went sprawling in the muddy snow.

I know, she said, climbing to her feet and tossing her weapon aside in frustration. The reprimand was always the same.

He said it anyway. "Never take your eyes off of your opponent. It's a stupid way to die."

I said I know.

"Then why do you continue making the same mistake?"

Because it's hard to focus on multiple things at once! She flung up a hand.

His scowl matched her own. Would it kill him to smile every once in a while? Ila seriously thought it might.

He jerked his chin at her weapon. "Pick it up."

Her frustration with the situation was overshadowed by the guilt at having treated such a magnificent weapon so poorly. Her mother's talq. It was the only thing she had left of her family. Ila felt a stab of sadness at the memory of all those graves and promptly shut it out. She could not afford distractions.

After wiping the mud from the antler blade, she faced Tulimaq and returned to the starting position.

"Again."

← →

They trained an hour longer before Tulimaq called for a break. Ila, dripping sweat, shivered in her furs. The creeping cold reminded her she was no longer in the Wood and hadn't been for weeks now, her tranquil bedroom traded for the Atakana's glacial peaks.

Last month, Tulimaq had received orders to investigate the occupation of the Western Territory rather than join the Face Stealer in negotiating the alliance. Ila saw the order for what it was: a warning. She imagined this was Tulimaq's chance to earn his way back into the Face Stealer's good graces.

Tulimaq was to find the labor camp. He was not to engage. He was to gather as much information in the shortest amount of time possible: arrivals and departures, the number of officers, the number of prisoners, their treatment of the prisoners, where they ate and what they ate and when they ate and where they slept, if they slept, if they were sick or wounded, beaten or whipped, tortured or maimed. Then he was to return, unhurt, alive. He was to go alone.

That had been the plan, at least. Until Ila decided she had no interest in remaining behind.

On the morning of his departure, Ila set out after her mentor with a pack full of provisions and a feeling of expanding horizons. The snow had been good for one thing: tracks. Ten miles in, she'd stumbled upon his deserted campsite. Assuming he had gone to hunt, she'd settled down to wait.

Hours later, Ila woke to the prick of a knife at her throat. His cool, if irritated, gaze. "What are you doing here?"

She returned his unruffled expression, though her pulse skipped a beat. Tulimaq would have to drag her back to the Wood before she went willingly. *Isn't it obvious?*

He scanned her body in a brief assessment. Then: "Help me collect firewood."

That had been three weeks ago. They had yet to find the work camp.

As Ila settled beside Tulimaq, he passed her a cup of tea warmed from the small fire they had built. Ila smiled her thanks and took a sip, closing her eyes as the liquid warmed her chest. There was something in the tea, a portion of the Face Stealer's power, that prevented Yuki from sensing them outside the Wood's barrier. Since the snow wasn't sticky enough for shelter, they huddled beneath a granite outcrop, interlocking branches packed with mud for the walls. Tulimaq chewed on a piece of caribou.

She returned the tea to him. He sipped from the cup, his mouth touching the rim where hers had a moment ago. "I came across tracks while collecting wood. They were human."

He hadn't mentioned this earlier. They had collected wood hours ago.

"I'm going to investigate later tonight."

I'm coming with you.

Tulimaq stared at a point in the distance with an absurd amount of concentration, which Ila knew he did when hearing something he didn't approve of. "It's safer for you here."

She knew he'd say something like that. At this point he understood there was no stopping her, though that didn't prevent him from trying. *I want to be a part of this. I don't want to be left behind.* Not when she could contribute.

He sighed, set down the tea, and said, "Someone needs to stay here and keep the fire going."

So I've been reduced to the fire feeder, is that it?

"It was your choice to come," he reminded her, eyebrows lifted and amber eyes unamused.

Ila's reasons for involvement weren't things Tulimaq would understand. The war was a catalyst to moving her life forward. She could make a difference, make a name for herself. She was Ila, the woman who would be remembered, if not by name, then by her deeds. *I'm not staying here.*

In the end, they went together, Tulimaq acting as her ears. He moved seamlessly with the land, similar to how Apaay moved. He wasn't Analak, though. Apaay had said as much, once.

"He just isn't," she'd said. "The way he walks, the way he eats, the way he speaks . . . I just know."

They picked their way across the softened snow, pieces of root and rock jutting from the ground. According to the wash of gray sky to the east, winter was beginning to ease its oppressive presence. Ila scrambled across a fallen tree in her attempt to keep pace. The terrain grew wilder the higher they climbed. It was more rock than soil, the snow patchy and uneven under the trees. Tulimaq skipped across a few boulders half buried in the snowdrifts and peered over the top of the hill.

Ila stopped, awaiting his instructions. He hopped down a moment later, pulled her into a crouch at the base of a tree, and pointed below.

A large swath of forest had been felled, snow trampled from a network of narrow paths cutting through the clearing. Large square structures constructed of wood were arranged in a half circle, a few smaller buildings clumped in the center. Snow topped their peaked roofs, soiled from ash.

As Ila had never been exposed to war and its effects, she wasn't completely certain of what she was seeing. People, yes, but they were poorly clothed. They wore the thinnest of skins patched over bodies of scrawn. They wore no shoes, only scraps of cloth wrapped around their bleeding, blackened soles. On more than one individual, there were missing appendages. Toes or pieces of a heel taken by frostbite, on occasion a nose. They swung axes and shovels beneath a sky the gray of a rain cloud, digging holes. The ground was pocked with them.

Then there were those who stood off to the side and watched. Their furs were thick. Their cheeks were full, their hair a shiny, healthy black. Their weapons set them apart.

Ila dug her fingernails into her palms. Women and children toiled in the clearing, some no older than six or seven. No men. With every look, she unpeeled another layer, revealing the grime and horror beneath. Some were tied to posts. Ropes made loops around their necks as if they were no better than dogs. In a far corner, someone was being beaten.

Ila thought she would sick herself. Her breaths came in sharp, shallow bursts. She watched the beating until another guard interfered, but by then, Ila knew it was too late.

A hand passed over her eyes, cutting off her view. When she regarded Tulimaq, he said, "This is why I didn't want you to come. The world is not kind."

Ila wanted to look again. It felt like denial, turning away from their suffering. *Why?* she signed.

"Power." He spoke simply.

She leaned against the tree, feeling power*less* and vastly out of her element. *What do you mean?*

"There is the law of the gods. We see this in the animal kingdom: predator and prey. Each creature seeks to fill a role, complete a cycle." He glanced at the clearing, his attention skipping from building to building as if searching for something, though she did not know what. "Then there is the law of man. In the law of man, power is not designated by physicality, and roles are not absolute. Man shapes the world in his favor. The gods have no place in the law of man."

Ila stared at his profile, though he didn't meet her eye. *What do your gods believe?*

"You mean my god?" He had a hard sort of smile, which was to say, not a smile at all. "My god forsook me at my birth. I do not believe in my god."

Then what do you believe in?

"Truth."

The word made her skin prickle in foreboding.

He gestured to the clearing below. "I suspect Nanuq wanted to ensure the surviving wolf Unua would not mutiny."

Ila said, with vicious feeling, *Nanuq is a monster.*

Though Tulimaq's expression didn't change, Ila suspected he was purposefully keeping his reaction in check. "Is it so different from what happens in the animal kingdom?"

Killing another animal for food is survival. This is a waste.

"Is power not survival?"

Ila glared at him. *We're not animals anymore. We are of a higher intelligence. We're blessed and cursed with our morality. We feel.*

"And animals don't?"

She gestured to where one of the guards slammed the butt of his staff into a woman's back. Her knees buckled, sending her into the hole she had been digging. *How can you justify this?*

"For Unua, the curse of our existence is the inability to separate our human nature from our animal nature. The human side seeks power. The animal side seeks survival. But evolution has taught us that power *is* survival. That is how one continues to live."

Somehow, his explanation threw water onto her simmering fury. Moments later, she calmed down enough to process what Tulimaq had said.

You're Unua? she asked in shock. Because to defend someone such as Nanuq, he must understand what it was to have one heart in two separate worlds. She wondered if there was a little tear in his chest from the forces pulling against each other.

Lifting his head, he stared at a spot over her shoulder before giving her what she wanted: his undivided attention. "What if I don't want that label? Or what if I want it but have never been able to claim it?"

Ila had no idea what he was talking about. She pushed him to elaborate, but he would say no more on the matter.

She said bitterly, *At least you know who you are and where you come from. I do not even know that much.*

Tulimaq appraised her for a long moment before he stood. "Stay here. If I'm not back within the hour or if something happens, return to camp."

She stood as well. *What if you get hurt?*

"Worrying will only expend energy," he told her. "It would be a waste to do so."

Of course, Tulimaq could fend for himself. Whether he wielded a weapon or not, there was something untouchable about him. She didn't want to admit she only asked that question because she cared. Then he'd probably glare at her and she'd feel silly for caring when she could hardly consider them acquaintances.

In the end, he left without saying goodbye, which she had expected. With her back to the tree, Ila passed the time by scanning the woods, occasionally searching the camp for a sign of her mentor. The most important task was to acquire a headcount of the prisoners and guards. From what she could see, there were not very many of the latter.

Ila pondered what Unua nation Tulimaq could be from. Polar bear, the very force that would split the world beneath its hammer? But he had known Numiak for so long, and the Face Stealer did not favor Nanuq's people. Although, a few of the refugees were polar bear Unua. It wasn't impossible. Wolf Unua, then? He could have survived the war, fled. She didn't know much about the other nations.

The wind whipped across her face, and Ila grew stiff with cold. Briefly, her thoughts drifted to Apaay. She and the Face Stealer would have returned to the Wood by now, hopefully with the alliance secured. Would Apaay have made peace with herself, or would she still struggle with day-to-day living?

Ila almost missed the presence at her back. She turned as someone rammed her from behind, throwing her against the tree roots. Two hands clawed at her neck, and Ila tried to roll sideways so she could free her right arm, which was caught beneath her body. She saw rope. Felt its abrasion against her wrists. Panic surged and seared her vision.

She finally managed to tip onto her back, kicking the man in the stomach as hard as she could, then his knees, and finally, as her desperation reached its peak, between his legs.

The man fell back and the rope slipped from his hands. Ila scrambled to untangle her legs and arms and fled, crashing through the brush. Return to camp, Tulimaq had told her, but she ran in the opposite direction, not wanting to lead the scout there. Ila plunged through a particularly dense patch of undergrowth. Branches lashed at her face. One snapped across her nose. She didn't dare look over her shoulder for fear of tripping over a root.

An uprooted tree blocked her path, but the place where the base had pulled away created a hollow. Clambering down, she huddled among the roots. There, she waited.

And agonized.

And breathed.

Ila held her breath until her lungs seized, then slowly released the air through her nose. She couldn't stop the trembling in her limbs. She didn't know whether the man had chased her, if she should flee deeper into the woods, if she should remain.

Gradually, her eyes adjusted to the thicker dark. She saw what she had not seen before, in her haste to flee. Clumps of white and gray fur. Bones, thin and fragmented, and tracks in the dirt.

Then she lifted her head and froze.

A gray wolf stood at the mouth of the den, watching her.

Ila thought she might actually pass out from fear. It was alone, which did nothing to comfort her, considering she was an intruder in its home.

Ila squeezed her eyes shut. A huff of air warmed her face and neck. She stiffened, bit her lip to hold in the wail. A wet nose touched her cheek.

The minutes crawled by. It was scenting her, a vague part of her realized. Then the heat and musk radiating from its body disappeared.

When Ila opened her eyes, it was gone.

Another hour crawled by, and during that time, Ila did not dare move. Logic told her to run, but her mind had frozen the moment she'd stared into the animal's intelligent gaze. She began to worry that Tulimaq had returned to camp without her. The thought forced her out of the den, Ila searching for the wolf all the while.

Stealth over speed, she decided. Stealth over speed.

The path of snapped branches and overturned rocks guided her. A harsh wind rattled the boughs of the trees and tossed snow into the dirt. Ila paused every so often to press her fingers to the trunks. No vibrations. That was good.

When she reached her lookout spot, she dropped to her knees and peered over the edge, pushing back her white hood so her hair and skin would blend in with the darkness.

Movement drew her eye. Two men surrounded by a loose circle of onlookers traded blows. The circle parted, allowing Ila a better view, and she forgot all about staying silent as her gasp rang free for anyone in the vicinity to hear.

A guard's fist slammed against Tulimaq's nose. Blood sprayed. Ila clapped her hands over her mouth. The crowd was growing hostile, some shaking their fists, others shoving Tulimaq back onto the ground when he tried to stand. He wasn't a large man by any means. His weapon was nowhere to be seen.

Another strike to the face sent his head snapping to the side. A kick to the stomach followed. Curled into the fetal position, Tulimaq tried to protect his head from the worst of the blows. Ila couldn't watch. She couldn't *not* watch. It ended when another guard, the largest she had seen yet, snagged the back of Tulimaq's parka and dragged him out of sight.

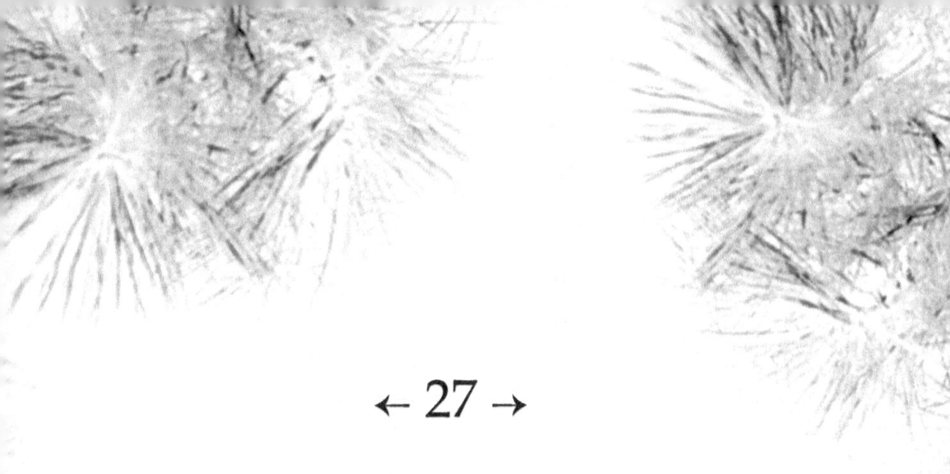

← 27 →

They had taken him. Bloodied and beaten him. Carted him off like the corpse of a freshly slain deer.

Near an hour of trembling and Ila had yet to move. She didn't know how to get back to the cairn, back to the Wood, back to safety. Without Tulimaq, she would not find their way home.

Home. When had she begun to see the Wood as such?

The problem was Ila didn't trust her own judgment. When the opportunity arose to make a decision, she reverted to her chained self. How did someone with so little lived experience know the decision was right, or that it was necessary, or how to choose?

She mentally slapped herself. Distressing over a choice she hadn't even made would get her nowhere. Great leaders made choices. They cleared the fog of indecision and chose a path, and she would do the same. Ila would not abandon Tulimaq.

She thought back to the last few weeks of training. *Your excitement is making you careless,* Tulimaq would say. *You need to wait.*

So Ila waited. She watched the comings and goings of the guards, seeking patterns in their routes. There were seven of them. The first completed a two-minute loop around the camp. Judging by the man's languorous pace, not much happened in his day-to-day routine. After all, the world believed these prisoners to be dead.

Three of the guards remained at their posts outside the buildings, while the fifth and sixth kept watch over the prisoners. The seventh was a rogue. He never took the same path twice, and his rounds were sporadic. Sometimes, when she believed he had entered one of the buildings, he appeared at the far edge of the trees. These likely weren't the only guards present, just those within sight. Another two had carried Tulimaq off to who knew where.

The next hour trickled by. She had sat still long enough for the cold to infiltrate her clothes, and it was time to move. With the first guard starting his loop around the camp, and with the rogue guard screaming obscenities at one of the child workers, drawing the attention of everyone in the vicinity, Ila scrambled down the snowy mountainside. Now that she had decided to act, she experienced a strange lack of fear.

As she reached the bottom of the slope, the first guard rounded the corner. Ila dove into a bush.

The man paused, his attention falling to the trampled snow, which had been untouched prior to his round. Brow furrowed, he scanned the area with suspicion. Through the bare branches, Ila could see the tips of his boots, the chapped skin of his cheeks.

The man turned his head, as if someone was speaking to him. Another guard approached. "Did you spot something?"

The first guard slowly shook his head. He looked around again. "Thought I did, but I think it was an animal."

Eventually, the guards moved on. With their focus turned elsewhere, she studied the buildings in closer detail. Tulimaq had been dragged to one of the structures in the back. Darting to the nearest building, she crouched low and peeked around the corner.

The rogue guard and a second guard walked toward her, deep in conversation, but she must have made a noise—her feet squelching in the mud, or a loud breath—because the men suddenly looked up, their shock evident.

Ila stepped back so quickly she slipped in the mud and fell onto her back. Vibrations raced up her spine, of pounding feet. Her heart wrenched in uneven jerks. She glanced at the wall, noticed where the wood differed in grain. A door.

Yanking it open, Ila darted inside a large, rectangular room crammed with statues of various animals, like behemoth versions of her carvings. A large fire emitted light at the end of it. Ila managed to climb over the back of a large raptor with outstretched wings and drop into a crouch before the door flew open behind her.

From her position, she spotted two pairs of legs weaving through the statues, the guards' mud-encrusted boots leaving tracks on the wooden floor. The fire beat waves of heat against her back.

Only one door led in or out.

Ila crawled as quietly as possible toward the back corner, hoping to circle around them. She imagined the statues as trees. The men beasts. The open door her cool, safe rabbit's burrow. If she could not be quieter than them, or stronger, or faster, then she would be clever.

Shadows cast by the imposing statues blanketed most of the room save the area near the hearth. She lost sight of the first man. The second guard moved along the wall, then to the center of the room, while Ila slipped behind the statue of a towering porpoise. Leaning her shoulder against its back, she *shoved*.

A great crash shuddered through the bones of the building, stone splintering and spraying dust, the men fighting to get out of the way as the porpoise's momentum tipped the next statue, and the next, and the next. Ila scrambled to safety as the first guard reached her. She ducked his blow, then plowed her fist into his face.

The man's kick sent her against the polar bear statue behind her. Ila braced herself for another strike, but it never came. The man's eyes widened at something beyond her shoulder. Ila barely had time to move before the statue toppled forward, pinning the man's body beneath it. Ila couldn't help but think, as she fled, that it looked as if the bear had *jumped* on him.

Outside, Ila ducked into the forest. There she remained, watching the open door to the building until the men limped outside. It drew the attention of two nearby guards, and then another, and now five men huddled around as the children continued their backbreaking work, and the women, too.

The camp slowly pulled away from the hibernation-like lethargy she and Tulimaq had arrived to. A girl who had been digging holes scanned the trees. One of the guards overseeing the labor snapped his whip. The prisoners returned to their tasks, but not without the occasional backward glance. It wouldn't be long before the area was overrun with guards.

Using the shadows for cover, Ila crept to the building Tulimaq had been dragged to. Smoke belched from its rooftop. She barreled through the door, talq raised.

The room: small and cramped and windowless. A table littered in maps. Tulimaq on his knees in the middle of the room, hands unbound. Five men surrounding him.

Tulimaq's eyes widened, and Ila was moving, already lunging to meet the largest of his captors, a man with a wide, solid chest, hair pulled into a knot. Ila didn't feel fear, but something stronger. A fury and a need. To best them, and in the process, show something of herself. She had wanted to see the world, and now she would meet it in all its blood-soaked glory.

The man's shoulders were enormous, like boulders shifting under rippling skin as he swung his club with enough strength to bludgeon her. Ila stumbled out of striking range. His club hit the floor hard enough to splinter the wooden handle. The rock attached to the end rolled across the ground.

He swung the broken handle at her skull. The table went flying as she darted out of reach, the maps tossed in the air. Before he could strike again, Tulimaq rammed him from the side and sent him tumbling across the floor.

"There!" Tulimaq cried, pointing.

Ila wheeled. One of the guards dove. His knife caught the lamplight, brief as a star snuffed out, before it plunged into her thigh. Ila screamed and dropped her talq, her body jerking as the man yanked his weapon free.

Tulimaq exploded into her line of vision with a whirlwind of kicks and strikes. One man went down from a blow to the head, a second from a strike to the neck. The third and fourth backed away in surprise as he hit hard and with deadly precision.

Ila pressed her hand to the wound, blood seeping through her mittens. It *hurt*.

Tulimaq fought three men at once. He was slender as a blade of grass, bowing to the wind but not breaking. She searched the floor, the pool of blood, and saw her talq lying a few feet away.

Gritting her teeth, Ila pushed aside the pain and snatched up her weapon.

"Eyes on your man," Tulimaq reminded her.

She turned and found herself face-to-face with a much larger opponent.

The man's weapon descended, and the motion was familiar. This was the pattern she and Tulimaq had practiced these past weeks, in the snow and in the rain, cold mud clinging to her teeth. The man's arm swung toward her unprotected side. Instead of leaning too far forward and upsetting her center of gravity, she planted her weight into her heels, then, as his arm passed by, launched her weapon upward, right into the center of his forearm. Bone fractured. His mouth opened in a soundless bellow.

He dropped, and Ila suddenly understood what Tulimaq had said before about survival. Her talq was level with the man's neck. Blood sprayed as the sharpened antler bit into flesh. It gouged a deep line across his throat before hitting the vertebrae of his spine. Then he fell.

Ila couldn't stop staring. The red pool spreading outward from his neck lapped at her boots.

She had killed a man.

Tulimaq dug through the man's pockets, shifting to block her view of the body. Then he took her hand and uncurled her fingers from around the weapon. Her knuckles creaked. The talq dropped to the ground.

She lifted her eyes to his, which were furious. His mouth pinched. "I told you to go back to camp," he said, and Ila was glad she couldn't hear the anger in his words. "Why didn't you?"

She thought it had been obvious. *Because you were hurt.*

He paced to where the maps were crumpled on the floor. He stared at them for a time before returning to her side. "You're a fool."

He cupped his hands over the back of his skull. "Did I not tell you before we came here that your safety and the success of the mission depended on following instructions? You do as I say, not as I do."

Ila lifted her chin with dignity. *I don't know why you're so upset.* It was making *her* upset, as if she had done something wrong in caring for his life, or his death. She could never read this man. *Should I have left you here, then? Left you to die?*

"I had it under control," he said, looking far more solemn than someone ought to after having been saved. "I was in the middle of negotiating my release. If you had stayed where I had told you to, if you had *listened* to me—"

How was I supposed to know what had happened to you? All I saw was you being dragged away. Emotion choked her, overwhelming in its unexpectedness. She punched him in the shoulder. There was little force behind it, but the gesture got his attention.

She hit him again, and would have hit him a third time had he not captured her hands in his. His face was a bloody mess. One of his eyes was completely swollen shut. Served him right for scaring her that way.

Tulimaq stared into her upturned face in confusion as she fought to control the tears, but they rose, fast and hard as adrenaline ebbed, spilling over. Did he see a silly girl he wished he'd left behind in the Wood? She had been afraid for them both.

Tulimaq brushed her hand aside to study the thigh injury, his expression veiled. "Did you have any trouble while I was gone?"

A man attacked me.

A blink was his only display of emotion. He began tearing cloth from the dead man's clothes and used it to bind her wound. "What did he look like?"

Ila winced at the flare of pain. She couldn't remember. He had been a man, though, one who had not known his own strength. Or maybe he had. *I don't recall, but I was trapped in one of the buildings with all these statues and—*

They had come alive.

Tulimaq's focus shifted from the wound to her face. They stood quite close. "And?"

But she only laughed a little laugh, exhausted down to her toes. She needed a fire to sit near and warm her feet.

Tulimaq handed over Ila's talq, glanced at the fallen men. All but the one she had killed were unconscious. Ila thought there must be something wrong with her. She felt nothing for the dead man, and yet could remember how torn up Apaay had been after learning she had killed a woman in the labyrinth arena. This was war, after all. "We should leave before they discover us."

What about the prisoners?

"We can't take them with us. You know this."

Logistically, she and Tulimaq would not be able to save the people in this camp. If they were to return to the Wood safely, they had to leave immediately.

It's not right, she told him.

"It's survival."

A part of Ila knew this as truth. Survival was not of the heart, but of the body. They couldn't help these people if they were dead.

As they reached the top of the mountainside though, Ila couldn't help but look back at the toiling prisoners. The threadbare girl, someone's daughter. The children who were less humans and more birds, bent and starved.

There was always someone left behind.

← →

"Keep up," Tulimaq said over his shoulder as he led them through the conifer forest. Ila did her best to keep pace, but after the first day, she started to lag behind. Tulimaq had said he'd overheard the guards discussing a second work camp that held the men. It was a four-day hike, should the weather cooperate. Now that the first camp knew of their presence, the guards would likely send a messenger to the brother camp, and Ila and Tulimaq wanted to arrive there first. After, they would return to the Wood with their gathered information.

Ila was exerting so much energy she didn't notice the cold clogging her head and chest in the following days. They hiked long miles without stopping for rest. Perhaps six or seven hours after setting out on the third day, she slowed, feeling too worn out to continue. Her watery eyes ached. When she coughed, it was wet. Liquid in her lungs.

The sound drew Tulimaq to a stop in front of her. He turned, saw her using a tree for support. His eyes dropped to her feet.

"Take off your boots."

Ila blinked slowly. *Stay awake.* She tried crouching down to do as he said but ended up falling onto her backside. Brushing aside her hands, Tulimaq untied her boots, yanking them from her feet in rough pulls, both the inner and outer layers.

Her feet, when he revealed them, were damp, the skin soft and wrinkled like cloth. There must have been a tear in the waterproof casing. It was the only explanation. His expression blanked. The stronger the emotion, the thicker his shield. Anger, true anger, was never more evident than when he divulged nothing at all. "How long?"

She hacked up phlegm and spat it on the ground. Fell back against the trunk, shivering, though she sweated beneath her furs.

He looked utterly terrifying staring down at her. The only thing Tulimaq hated more than poor fighting form was stupidity, and Ila thought she may have already crossed that line. In her defense, she hadn't known. Her feet would be cold whether they were wet or dry.

Tulimaq wasn't strong enough to carry her, but his added support allowed her to hobble along for another mile until they reached a cave. By that point, Ila shook so violently she wasn't much use in setting up camp. Tulimaq left to gather firewood. When he returned, he slipped off his parka and pulled it over her head. Her skin was like ice.

He began yanking tufts of hair from his parka hood and piling it near her feet, stacking small twigs atop. Using flint and a piece of metal, he got the fire going. A thin tendril of smoke coiled up.

What about the camp? she signed after he removed her wet mittens and set them by the fire. She was afraid the smoke would attract unwanted attention.

"Forget the camp."

She settled down, knowing well enough not to argue. Ila fell asleep watching him pace the mouth of the cave, his hands behind his back.

← →

They were supposed to have reached the men's work camp the next morning, but Ila worsened overnight. Her bones ached. Her muscles ached. Even her teeth ached. Tulimaq spent most of the morning pacing, glancing out at the snowy landscape, where moonlight dripped onto the black branches and pooled silver in the shallow depressions between the hills. At least her feet had dried from the flames' warmth.

"I'm going to the men's work camp," Tulimaq said later in the day. "I'll be back."

Her muscles cramped as she struggled into a sitting position.

"Stay here," he repeated. The curl of his mouth was borderline animalistic.

Ila flopped back against the wall, eyebrows raised all the way to her hairline. Taking care of someone required a degree of compassion. Was that what made the combat master uncomfortable? Indeed, Tulimaq was about as compassionate as a thorn bush.

He left without another word, leaving her to the empty cave. She must have dozed, because when she next awoke, Tulimaq had returned. He sat near the fire, skinning a hare.

How long were you gone for?

"Go to sleep." He sliced at the hind legs.

The motion of the skinning drew her attention to his callused fingers, the bony knuckles. She'd never had a chance to talk to Tulimaq about anything other than her training. This was as good a time as any. *Was the camp far? Did you find out anything?*

"Sleep," he snapped.

Ila rolled her eyes and tugged his parka tighter around her. It was to be expected. He was who he was. She couldn't change him. The parka smelled like him, like salt and herbs from all the tea he drank. Though her body was tired, her mind would not stand still long enough for her to sleep. Selfishly, Ila wanted to stay in his company a while longer.

How do you know so much about survival?

He set the rabbit's skewered body at the perfect height over the flames. There was a meticulousness to everything he did. "If I answer your question, will you go to sleep?"

She flapped a hand at him. *Yes, yes, all right.* Whatever he wanted to hear.

Tulimaq leaned against the cave wall where the shadows danced, elbows propped on his bent knees. He wore his angry face. In other words, his normal face. There was a different shade to it though. Shadowed by reluctance.

You don't have to talk about it. I know I'm being obnoxious. If it's too difficult to discuss—

"It's not."

Ila disagreed, but she wouldn't argue with him. He would open up in his own time, or he wouldn't.

He sighed. "When I was born," he said, "it was with the promise that I would never rise above my station."

What a strange thing to say. *And what was your station?*

"A place where one sent another to be forgotten."

Vague enough to pique her interest, but without any substance. Frustrating, but not unexpected. Since this was the most he had ever spoken about himself, Ila didn't interrupt. She doubted he'd reveal this much ever again.

"Nanuq had begun to move his forces north. With his power growing, it wasn't safe. My mother fled to a small village in the Atakana, living among the Analak for some time before settling at a refugee camp. I was seven.

"I spent the next ten years of my life living at a camp no larger than seventy people. There was a refugee who had defected from Nanuq's army. He trained me in the art of the staff, and I worked tirelessly at it." He picked up his staff, running a finger along the wood. "The strength in my body became my motivation. I sought to be the best in my ability. To this day, no one has ever beaten me."

Yet, Ila said, only half aware of what she was saying.

He studied her. "You think you will be the one? Grown men have tried and failed."

What does being a man have anything to do with it?

Tulimaq shook his head, said nothing.

Fat droplets rolled down the crisping meat and dropped into the flames. It smelled delicious. *How did you come to work for Numiak?*

He gazed into the fire, which crumbled and coughed ash into the air, sent sparks along the ceiling like newborn stars. "A few years following the invasion, Nanuq sent out a decree across the North. Anyone who brought him a surviving wolf Unua would be compensated, no matter your nation. I was poor. I had nothing. The idea of glory drew me to the hunt. For years, I searched, and during that time I came across a woman in the forest, badly wounded. It was Kaan."

Ila's lips formed a small O of surprise.

"The closest healer was one day's hike away. I carried her there so she could be healed. A week later, Numiak came to pay me a visit. I'm guessing Kaan told him what had happened. He wanted to know of my skill with the staff. I had trained for over fifteen years at that point. He invited me to the Wood and gave me the task of training the refugees."

Ila watched as he pulled the rabbit from the fire. *What about your mother?* She accepted a strip of meat he tore from the body. It was hot and smoky in flavor.

"Years later, I returned to the camp and found it gone, the place in ruin. I never saw her again."

I'm sorry, she said.

"Don't be. It had nothing to do with you." He devoured his own rabbit meat.

Ila tilted her head. The bluntness of the words didn't sit well. *Do you ever let anyone in?*

He stared at her in confusion. "Why would I do a stupid thing like that?"

Yes, why *would* he do a stupid thing like that? It truly baffled Ila that he was not even remotely curious as to what it was like to open himself up to another person. In a way, she understood. Look at what had happened to her and Apaay these past months. But for Tulimaq to never let anyone in *ever*? She imagined him as this lonely little boy, all alone save his mother and the trees.

Curling into a tighter ball, Ila tucked her arm beneath her head. *Will you find her, do you think?*

He fingered the end of his braid. "I know now that I won't."

What do you mean?

"My mother? She's dead."

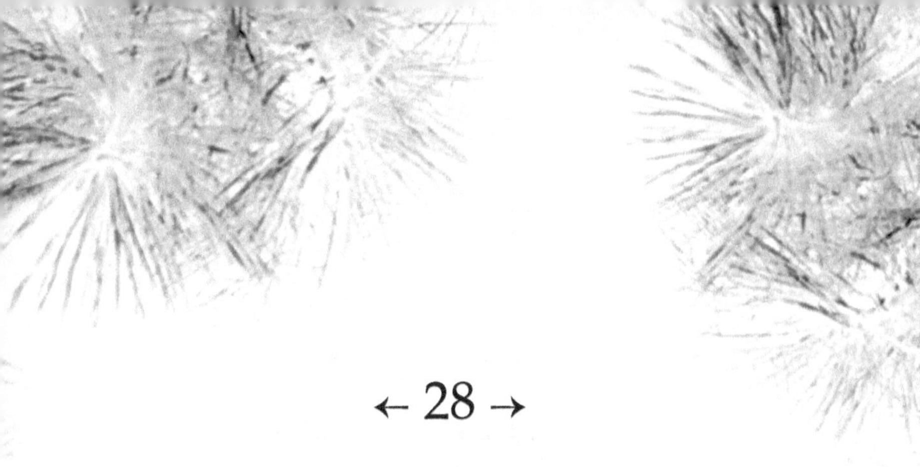

← 28 →

Tulimaq revealed nothing more of his past that night, or the night after. Once Ila was well enough to travel, it was as if the conversation between them had never occurred. She was back to wearing her boots, the seam repaired. Tulimaq had demanded she wear his during recovery. When she had tried to argue, he glowered at her until she put them on. As luck would have it, they were the same size.

Ten days later, the Wood at last came into view. Tulimaq pulled her to a stop at the barrier and said, "I'd like to keep what happened in the labor camp between us."

She looked at him in confusion. Ila assumed he wasn't speaking of the men's labor camp, as he hadn't told her anything about his trip there. *Numiak has a right to know.*

"I will tell him the information he requested, but I was going to leave out the part about our near capture. I've already angered him with my previous miscommunication. Should he find out, he might refuse to send me on any future missions."

Ila supposed he was right. They'd gathered the necessary information, and no one had gotten hurt. At least not permanently. Her thigh wound was well on its way to healing. She nodded her agreement.

"I'll see you tomorrow," he said, backing away.

Tomorrow?

Eyebrows raised, he let slip a shade of a smile. Ila thought she might have imagined it. "You've recovered, have you not? Training begins at dawn."

As if he would let her forget. If she was not so certain Tulimaq didn't care, she might presume he enjoyed beating her with an overly large stick.

Once inside, they parted ways, Tulimaq disappearing down the tunnel of ivy she assumed led to his chambers and Ila moving toward her own bedroom. It was late morning. Bright after weeks spent in the dark. Pushing open her door, she faltered in the doorway.

Seated on Apaay's bed, knees drawn to her chest, was Apaay herself. She gave a small wave.

Ila glanced around the room. She took a hesitant step forward, shutting the door behind her. *What are you doing here?*

Apaay swung her legs over the side of the bed. In the month since she had seen Apaay, Ila noticed her friend had put on a little weight. Her collarbones weren't as noticeable, her face as gaunt.

How was your trip? Apaay asked.

It was fine. Ila folded her arms, then felt silly for doing so and dropped them. This was technically Apaay's room, too, but she hadn't slept here in weeks. Ila supposed that made it *her* room now.

Apaay fiddled with a hangnail. *You were supposed to return last week.*

The weather set us back. She didn't mention her illness.

Apaay nodded, the movement stiff. Ila shifted from foot to foot, which Tulimaq always snapped at her for doing. Time and distance had not soothed the betrayal of Apaay's abandonment in the shadowy place beyond the library door. Seeing Apaay sitting on her bed as if she had a right to be there . . .

I need to talk to you about something.

Apaay opened her mouth, then closed it. She swallowed. "Ila—"

No. Lip curled, she cut a most fearsome glare to her friend, who looked more like a stranger with each passing day. Why did her hands have to tremble? Why couldn't she be cold and unfeeling? Life had to be easier that way. *I'm still mad at you for what you did.*

The heaviest, hardest stone heaved up her throat and lodged there, all the things she might say if she had the ability to speak with her mouth instead of her hands. But maybe there was a blessing in this. Her hands could not crack with emotion as she imagined a voice did. *You left me.*

Apaay slipped off the bed and came forward tentatively. She stopped a few feet away, as if sensing that was the limit of Ila's boundary. *I'm sorry, Ila. I am so, so sorry. I thought I could overcome the darkness, but I wasn't ready.*

You didn't come back for me.

"I did!" she cried, looking all the more awful about it. She switched back to signing. *I went back, but I couldn't find you. I thought maybe you had found your way out. I kept looking, but then I came to a different place. You weren't there.* She shuddered. *The land was burning.*

They weren't talking about the land, Ila wanted to snap. They were talking about how Apaay had left her. Her fingers itched to say as much. She curled them into her palms.

Please, said Apaay. *You have to believe me.*

Even if Apaay hadn't intended to hurt Ila, what about impact? Didn't that matter?

Ila decided to let it go for now. She had to believe they could overcome this trial, and it wouldn't happen if she held tight to resentment. *What did you think of the girl?* The girl whose scar was exactly like hers.

Apaay sat back down, this time on Ila's bed. Ila remained standing. *You mean Yuki?*

As far as she knew, Yuki hadn't been present. *Didn't you see the fire?*

I smelled a fire from where I was, but it was a long way off.

That made her pause. *Where were you?*

One of the stone animals on Ila's pillow rolled into the dip Apaay's thigh made against the mattress, and she held it up to the light in examination. *Somewhere in the forest. Isn't that where you were?*

Ila frowned as a thought came to mind. Was it possible they had witnessed two separate events? If that were so, Apaay had not seen the Face Stealer saving Ila as a child. Years before she and Apaay had ever met, Ila would often trace her scar as she laid in the cell, weaving stories of its origin. A gouge from a blade. A surgery gone wrong. Something fierce and dangerous and more than Ila had been. As it was, a burning beam had split open her scalp. A battle wound. She would take it.

Ila answered, *I was in a burning building. There was a little girl there. She couldn't see me.*

Apaay lowered the carving, curiosity sparking across her face. *She wouldn't have been able to. Those were the Face Stealer's memories behind the door.*

Which made her wonder. If the Face Stealer had been present in Apaay's memory, how could he have been in Ila's, too? They were either two separate memories, or they were the same memory at different points in time.

Apaay had seen smoke from a distance. Ila had been inside the inferno, the walls blackening like skins. If it was indeed the same memory, which had come first? Saving Ila, or Apaay's encounter in the forest?

In the memory, Apaay said, *I saw everything through the Face Stealer's eyes. The journey had weakened his powers.* Apaay frowned as her fingers alighted on her chest. *I think Yuki may have killed him, or hurt him badly.*

They looked at each other, perplexed. How strange that Apaay had seen his memory through his eyes, while Ila had not. The silence stretched. There used to be so much ease to it.

Ila asked, *How was visiting the Owl Clan?*

Something good must have come of the visitation, because for the first time in a long while, Apaay's sadness seemed less acute. *The alliance is sealed. Their capital is very beautiful. Did you know the owl Unua invented their own light source? They light flames in these glass orbs they blow in their underground forges.*

I didn't, she responded with a half-smile. It was a beautifully pristine summer morning. It seemed a shame to waste it. *Do you want to take a walk?*

Apaay curled her legs to the side. Her throat worked. *Actually, I came to ask you for a favor.*

Ila drew herself up, feeling like she needed to shield herself, which was ridiculous. *What kind of favor?*

Apaay fingered the carving before setting it on Ila's pillow. She looked mournful, staring at it. It wasn't the wolf Ila had carved for her. She wondered what had happened to it. *It's about Masuk.*

At the mention of Masuk, Ila stiffened. She didn't think she would ever be able to forgive him for stealing away her friend. *Go on,* she answered, lips thin.

A long time ago, the Face Stealer stole the face of a woman he loved. I've been helping him search for this face, but we haven't been able to find it. When I was in the Central Territory, Kaan told me about a man formed of stone who will answer any question asked. If Masuk found the First Man, he could find the face's location. He would finally be able to move on.

Ila was long past showing patience when it came to Masuk. *Why is this relevant to me?* she gestured curtly.

Apaay didn't seem to notice Ila's agitation, which only angered the young woman more. When had Apaay stopped *seeing* her? *When doing research for the Face Stealer, I recalled seeing a map in one of the books, a mention of the First Man. The problem is, he's located outside of the Wood.*

We're not allowed outside of the Wood. Not without the Face Stealer's protection.

You were.

Because the Face Stealer sent Tulimaq and me on a mission. It was only half a lie. *He gave us something to put into our tea that shielded us from Yuki.*

Apaay fisted her hands atop her thighs. "The Face Stealer won't let me leave. He won't let Masuk leave, either." Resolve hardened her mouth. "I came to ask if you'll distract the Face Stealer while I go into his office. The book with the map was in the library, but he must have taken it, because it's no longer on the shelf."

Ila didn't know what was more repulsive: that Apaay would do something so incredibly dangerous, or that she wanted Ila to help. *So you're sorry because you need a favor, but if you didn't need something from me, you wouldn't be sorry? Is that what you're telling me?*

Her mouth snapped shut. *No. I am* sorry *for what I did, truly.*

But you also need a favor. All the tentative hope she'd felt at seeing Apaay in their room snapped into pieces. *I won't do it.*

Please. It's important.

So important that you would risk the safety of everyone here, even your own family? Saying what she did next might have been cruel, but Ila had spent months wondering what she had done to be ignored. Ila had never given up on Apaay, but it felt as if Apaay had given up on her. *That doesn't sound like the Apaay I knew.*

Apaay dropped her hands. "And who would that girl be, exactly?"

Someone who didn't let the needs of a man she barely knew overshadow the needs of her family and friends. Someone who didn't shut people out.

Her expression was quietly tormented. *Ila.* Gentle. But also sad and lonely and confused. *I've tried to find that person again, believe me. And Masuk—*

Masuk what? She felt like hitting something. A tree. The mattress. At some point during the argument, clouds had drifted and curled their arms around the sun.

Nothing, Apaay said. *Never mind.*

But Ila wasn't done. *You seek out Masuk, but not me or anyone else. Have you gone to visit Chena since she left? Do you even spend time with your family anymore, or have you abandoned them, too?*

"Stop it." Apaay lurched to her feet. "Stop shaming me. You have no idea what I've gone through the last six months. If I have to lean on someone else to get through the day, I won't apologize for it." She blinked rapidly. "Helping Masuk gives me purpose I lost in the labyrinth. Why are you so angry with me for trying to help myself?"

Crossing her arms, hands fisted, Ila glared at a spot across the room.

Apaay watched her for a moment. *So you won't help me?* she asked with obvious distress. *After everything I did to help you? Tell me. Where would you be if I hadn't shown up at the labyrinth?*

Ila lifted her chin, inch by slow inch. Her anger stirred and slithered through her with fangs wide open. *Careful, Apaay, or you might say something you'll regret.*

No. If Apaay had spoken the word aloud, Ila imagined she might have spat it. *The only thing I regret is thinking you were a friend.*

Shoving past her, Apaay bolted from the room.

The hurt Ila experienced fueled her training the following days. She felt used. Bent and crumpled and discarded. Her emotions churned as the soil did beneath her bare feet, the grass damp with dew, her talq hacking against an imaginary opponent. It was silly, but when Ila had seen Apaay in her room, she thought her friend had finally come to apologize for her neglect. It turned out Ila was the fool, because what had she wanted? Help. For *Masuk.*

Why was Apaay so ready to help him? And why was she so eager to make their friendship disappear? Instead of Masuk, Apaay could have asked Ila to go with her. Ila desired to open the door on her past, present, and future. The First Man, whatever or whoever he was, might be the answer to a question that had haunted her for far too long.

Who am I?

With a particularly brutal undercut, she brushed the thought from her mind. She would not think of this man, this myth. She was her body and her blood and her muscles as she lunged, dropped, rolled. And she was the thump of her braid against her back, the placement of her hands along the antler. Her mind was a river, carrying her worries downstream.

Ila transitioned into another pattern she had yet to master: a back-handed strike. In one sweeping motion, she raised the weapon above her head when someone suddenly grabbed it, stopping her downward swing.

Pulse elevated, she whirled, her cold expression reflecting exactly what she thought of the interruption.

Tulimaq's gaze roved over her face in a quick, impersonal assessment. "How long have you been training?"

It was late afternoon. She had started before sunrise. He always told her she wouldn't improve if she didn't make time to practice. Well, she was making time.

Ila tugged on her talq, but he jerked it from her hands, spinning the slender weapon lazily. It came so easily for him. *Give that back,* she said.

"Not until you answer my question."

Ila shook her head, not in any mood to play into this power struggle. *Keep it, then.* She started heading toward one of the trails when he caught her arm.

She spun, slapping aside his hand. *So it's fine when you refuse to answer my questions, but I'm not allowed the same courtesy?*

He tossed the weapon aside. "Distracted training is ineffective training."

Of course. It always came back to training. *Yes,* she said, more tired than she'd felt in a long time. *You've told me before.*

"So why do you keep doing it?"

Ila glared. *I wasn't training,* she might say. Or, *It's none of your business what I do with my time.* But he wouldn't understand. He had never cared to. And if he didn't, then who was left? Everything seemed to be slipping through her fingers: Apaay, her future, the possibility of family. She could not clear the image of that large white field full of graves from her head no matter how hard she tried to distract herself. She had nothing and no one, and the scream was rising like gorge up her stomach, soon to fill her lungs and throat and mouth.

Ila burst into tears.

Suddenly, Tulimaq was right in front of her, standing like an awkward pillar. Ila might have found it amusing if her heart didn't hurt so much. She had wanted to prove herself to Tulimaq for so long and didn't want him viewing her as weak. What was her friendship with Apaay but a menial concern compared to the mounting unrest between the Unua nations? He cared little about her personal life. Strong in heart, he'd once said. How strong could her heart be if it was breaking?

He lifted a hand as if to touch her shoulder, then dropped it. He shoved a piece of cloth at her. "Here."

Shaky laughter eased the tightening in her chest. She accepted the offered cloth and wiped her face, too embarrassed to look at him. He must think her silly. People were suffering in that labor camp. The children were all eyes. The men were gone.

She offered the cloth back to him.

He didn't take it. "What's that?" He gestured to the skinny braid she'd brushed aside, its ornamentation. Then he did something that shocked her to the core and reached for it himself, his slender fingers turning the stone this way and that. His nails were oval-shaped, short, and clean.

Tulimaq had never voluntarily touched her outside of training before. Even when he adjusted her stance or corrected her grip, the touches were impersonal and brief. Maybe even too brief.

Ila accepted the stone when he passed it back to her. *Apaay gave it to me. Her people tie objects to their hair to represent particularly special occasions or accomplishments. This stone was supposed to represent our friendship.* But she had put too much faith in it, having forgotten that a single drop of water could, over time, erode the strongest of stone.

His gaze was deep, penetrating. Ila felt her heart pound the longer he considered her. *I thought you and Apaay were friends.*

For the first time ever, he'd communicated with gestures rather than words.

We were. She looked through the breaks in the trees to where the ground sloped, the glitter of a stream drawing her eye. *I don't know what we are now.*

Ila knew she was ignorant in many ways. She didn't have the life experience of those around her. But what about the human experience? Surely it wasn't naive to think that a shared experience gave way to a deeper bond.

"Things change," Tulimaq said. "People change. You find you might not need them as you once did."

Ila felt ill. Was he saying Apaay didn't need her, or that she didn't need Apaay? She was too afraid to ask. *I don't know what to do. I feel like she's gone down this path and doesn't want me with her.*

He rubbed a hand across his mouth and jaw, the skin smooth and unblemished and the color of pine cones in the sun. "Maybe that's your problem. Maybe you're not meant to go down that road. Maybe you're not meant to follow her."

You know, you're really not making me feel better.

Would you rather I lie?

She looked away. *No.* But why couldn't she follow Apaay? Why couldn't they travel hand in hand, two instead of one?

"I know it's not what you want to hear," Tulimaq went on, "but sometimes, keeping someone close is how you move forward. And sometimes, in order to move forward, you have to let go. You have to ask yourself how much longer you're willing to wait for something that might never come to pass. If this friendship brings you pain, maybe letting go is the better option."

Ila clutched the stone tighter. *But I don't want it to end.*

He shook his head and turned away, as if looking for some distant shore. "We never do."

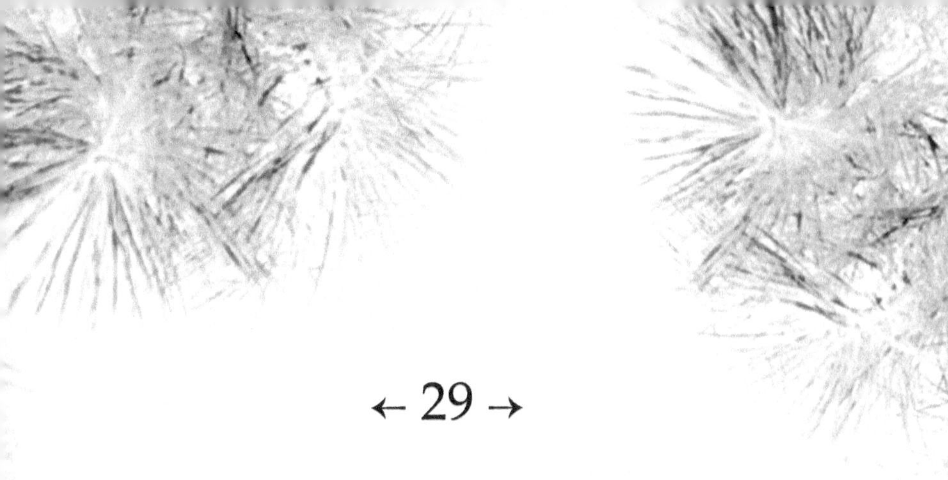

← 29 →

The leaves of the moonflower plant grew damp in Apaay's palm as she stood on the drenched gray rocks outside the Face Stealer's office, the waterfall roaring at her back. The Face Stealer was away. He had left thirty minutes ago to meet with the Avi concerning recent movements to the south. As this was an urgent matter, Apaay suspected she had some time.

Slipping inside his office, she closed the door behind her.

Silence descended like a hammer's head. Apaay half expected something to happen. There was a wrongness to being here, a distinct feeling of betrayal. Yet here she stood.

In the weeks following their return from Sinika, she and the Face Stealer had settled into a weird sort of truce. Sometimes they even shared breakfast together, now that her appetite was returning.

The truth was, it didn't sit well with her. Apaay thought of sharing mushrooms with him high in Sinika's trees. She hadn't liked the way he'd looked at her, as if he *knew* her. That frightened Apaay. The Face Stealer didn't know her. He couldn't. He was a demon and she was the young woman who had suffered at his hands. The world made sense that way.

So let this be a reminder to him. He had his world and she had hers, and they were not, and never would be, the same.

Apaay refocused on the office. The space was orderly and warm. His bookcase groaned under the weight of tomes and scrolls. After a few moments, Apaay deemed herself safe and approached his desk. It was cluttered with documents, as well as a large map of the North that showcased the icy, bitten coast, the mountains and forests and seas. Apaay touched a coastal area slightly northeast of the Aatu Forest: home.

She closed her eyes. Turned away from the map without another thought.

Something small and white suddenly arrowed through the room, sending Apaay stumbling back as it swept past her face and landed on a branch jutting from the wall. She caught herself on the edge of the desk. A tiny owl perched, watching her with enormous yellow eyes.

Apaay stared back. She glanced at the floor, the mess of documents, damp from where she had knocked a cup of water onto them.

Biting back a sound of distress, she hurriedly bent to gather the documents. Mist from the waterfall blurred the view outside. She would be able to spot the Face Stealer's approach, unless of course he decided to materialize *inside* his office, but then what was the point of a door?

Apaay felt the bird's eyes on her back as she studied the desk and tried to remember if the papers had been organized in any particular manner, but in the end, she plopped the documents down with a softly uttered curse. By the time the Face Stealer returned, she would be long gone and it wouldn't make a difference.

Apaay began at the bottom shelf of his bookcase and worked her way upward, pulling book after book, flipping through the pages before returning them to the shelves. His collection was small, but varied. Most of the tomes were in written languages, though a few had no writing at all, merely blank pages. An oily sensation slithered through her when she touched those. Apaay shoved them back onto the shelf quickly.

Then her pulse slowed. Her breathing eased. A slender volume in gold called to her, and she pulled it free, the book falling open to an illustration of a man, the lower portion of his body encased in stone. Apaay studied the map on the next page, only dimly aware of the bird's soft *cheep*.

A muted click. The unmistakable sound of a knob turning.

Apaay froze as horror seeped into her limbs. She looked to the tiny owl, who regarded her with its bulbous eyes haughtily.

Tearing the map free and shoving it into her pocket, Apaay jammed the book back onto the shelf and bolted for the desk, squeezing herself into the space beneath as the door opened. Apaay pressed a hand against the wood, breath held, and peeked through the crack between the desk and the floor.

The Face Stealer's boots came into view. Could he sense her presence? Once he saw his desk, he'd know someone had been here. The Face Stealer was a man of details.

The owl chirped.

"Right on time," he said, moving toward the bird.

A rustle of parchment. A message? She received her answer a moment later when his curse rang throughout the room.

He strode to his desk.

Pulled out the chair.

Thrust his filthy, mud-caked boots beneath, forcing Apaay to shrink back and suck in her stomach to avoid touching them. If he moved his feet three inches to the right, he would graze her arm.

Apaay studied the tips of his boots, the dark substance coated on. Animal dung, definitely. She switched to breathing through her mouth, her eyes watering from the noxious fumes. She wouldn't be able to hold this position forever. The question was, had the Face Stealer returned because he knew someone had entered his office, or was it a coincidence?

A cramp began to worm through her right leg from holding it at an awkward angle. She heard the scratching of a pen on paper, the flipped pages of a book. Apaay didn't think it could get any worse, but then he toed off his boots and whipped her across the face with an equally hot, equally vicious stench.

She gagged.

By now, her limbs were trembling so badly she knew she would not be able to hold this contortion for much longer. The heat burrowing into her lower back was agony.

Abruptly, he stood. Through the crack, Apaay watched him move to the bookshelf. He removed a stack of tomes and spread them out on the floor, studying them.

Slowly uncurling her body, she maneuvered around the chair and tip-toed across the rug.

"Leaving so soon?"

Apaay whirled, a hand pressed to her racing heart. His blue-green eyes danced. He knew. He had known the whole time! His boots. His *feet.*

"Is the owl a spy?" she demanded. The tiny raptor puffed its feathers indignantly. "Is that how you knew I was here?"

Fighting a smile, he strode toward her. "I smelled you the moment I opened the door," he said by way of explanation.

She had forgotten his keen animal senses were stronger than any human's.

"At least I smell better than you," she remarked with a pointed look at his feet.

"As a matter of fact," he said, hands behind his back, "you smell—" And he closed the distance, the tip of his nose skimming the curve of her nape where the fine hairs stood at attention. "Delicious."

"You'll step back if you know what's good for you." She managed to speak without strangling herself on the words.

A moment later he pulled back, cold air taking the place of his warm breath. The blue of his eyes grew richer, brilliant and bold and entirely unreal. "I'm afraid that's the problem, wolfling. I *don't* know what's good for me." His eyes twinkled, bright as new stars. "But let's not draw this out. Tell me why you were sneaking around in my office." He wandered over to a small table by the window, as if he didn't truly care about the answer, and reached for a metal teapot resting there. "Tea?"

She watched as he hung the teapot over the fire. "That would defeat the purpose of a secret, wouldn't it?"

He turned, appraising her. The only thing worse than being the object of his gaze was being the only object of his gaze. "I'm intrigued. What could I possibly have in this room that you would need?" He considered this with his arms crossed, one shoulder leaning against the wall, head angled. "Besides my company, that is."

"Vanity. What a surprise."

"Avoidance. How predictable."

You keep telling yourself that.

The teapot began to scream. The Face Stealer stepped toward it, but Apaay said, "Let me," and brushed past him, removing it from the fire. She felt his eyes on her back for a few drawn-out seconds. The offer had been too eager.

"What did the Avi have to say?" she asked, still holding the teapot, her gaze fixed on the crumbling coals. She relaxed her hands with some effort.

After another moment, he returned to his desk, and Apaay began spooning the tea into his cup. "There's been evidence of polar bear Unua in the Central Territory. Scat. We don't know why they were so far north."

She added bits of moonflower to the leaf mixture, then poured the scalding water over it. The tea would mask the subtle sweetness of the moonflower. Once the leaves steeped, she removed them and prepared her own cup. "Were they near Sinika?"

"Farther south. No one in the border towns had been attacked, luckily." A pause as he watched her carry over the tea. "Nanuq grows bolder."

Apaay set both cups on his desk, taking care to place the Face Stealer's cup closer so he would know which one to grab.

Steam drifted in the air. Breathing in the heat, hands curled around the cup's wooden body, Apaay sat in the seat across from his desk and tried to emulate the air of someone who had nothing to hide. Dishonesty did not come easy to her, but the demon would never let her leave voluntarily. After ingesting the moonflower, he would fall asleep for a few hours, allowing her the time to find the First Man with Masuk and return before he discovered where they had gone.

The Face Stealer didn't touch his drink. Apaay allowed herself only a passing glance at it before taking a sip of her own. She would need to coax him into drinking.

"Could they be traveling to the work camp?"

He shook his head. "If that were the case, why were they so far east? I'm worried it's something else we aren't yet aware of."

"You don't think they were the ones targeting my people, do you?"

He dipped his finger into his tea, then sucked a drop from his finger. Apaay waited for a change in expression, yet his features remained neutral. "No. The burnings were the work of the naaluet, who allied with Yuki in the last war. It is my guess that she again commands them." He pondered for a moment. "They could be looking for other refugee camps, though. Many of the polar bear Unua defected from Nanuq's army and went into hiding. If Nanuq found them, their punishment would be severe."

She hoped never to meet the conqueror who had brought so much suffering to the North. "What will the Avi do if he finds any polar bear Unua? Kill them?"

"Technically, he has the right. The polar bear Unua are trespassing on his territory." He ran a finger over the patterns carved into the cup. "I don't think he will, though. At least, not yet. Ro said his father plans to track them. This might be one of the few opportunities we have to learn more of Nanuq's intentions. In the meantime, their archers are being dispatched to the borders."

Finally he took a sip of tea. "As for the work camp, there's too much uncertainty surrounding the situation. What does Nanuq plan to do with the prisoners? Will revealing our knowledge of the location upset something in the future? I don't have the luxury of considering consequences when I'm knee-deep in negotiations."

Apaay shifted in her seat, wishing he would finish his drink already. She was supposed to have met with Masuk by now. "You don't have to make a decision yet. You can take the time to figure out the best solution."

"Wiser words have never been spoken." He reached for his tea, accidentally knocking a book off the desk in the process. Apaay bent down to pick it up before grabbing her drink. He lifted his cup as she lifted hers and said, "To new beginnings."

Apaay dipped her chin, unable to explain the spike of panic she felt. He wouldn't know she'd put the moonflower in his cup until it was too late. So why did she feel as if something had changed? "To new beginnings," she whispered.

Never taking his eyes off her, he drained his tea in a single gulp.

Apaay did the same and set her cup on the desk. His stare was making her uncomfortable. "What?"

"I underestimated you, wolfling."

She looked at the empty cups, then back at his face. The quiet was telling her to pay attention.

"A drugging attempt?" Dark lashes swept down, feathered like the outstretched wings of a raven against his cheekbones. "How unexpectedly dark of you." His gaze lifted. "I'm impressed."

The tightness of her throat prevented her from swallowing. He would be impressed that she had drugged him. If he had known about the tea though, why did he drink it?

Then she realized what he had said. "Drugging *attempt*?"

A slow smile, as if pleased with her understanding. "I didn't drink from my cup," he said.

"What are you talking about?" The question snapped out. "I watched you."

"Yes, but it wasn't *my* cup." Calm, so calm.

"You mean—"

The skin around his eyes pinched with rising glee. "I switched them."

Apaay's only reaction was to blink. "H-how?"

With an infuriating grin, he pushed his cup off the desk, where it rolled to a stop a few feet away. "Oops." Apaay was still staring at the cup when he said, "You think I don't know what moonflower smells like? Let me remind you I was the one who introduced you to it."

Apaay hadn't considered what type of fragrance the leaves would release when steeped. She supposed she had become used to it over the months.

Shaking his head, he rose to his feet in an elegant motion. "No one has ever tried to drug me before. I suppose I should be flattered." His tone, which had retained its lightness, dropped threateningly. "Why were you trying to drug me, Apaay?"

Apaay's cheeks warmed from impending drowsiness. From the amount of leaves she had put in the tea, it would take two minutes before the full effects set in. She could hold out for that long.

He had nearly reached the window when his step faltered. As those powerful shoulders swelled with a sudden inhalation, he whirled around. It was perhaps the most delicious sound Apaay had ever heard, that stunned and quavering "How?"

Slowly, Apaay rose from her chair and approached. She had taken power back and found she liked it. "Did I forget to mention?" she said with false sweetness. "I didn't drug just *your* tea." He had been so sure of himself, of her, of them both. "I drugged mine, too."

No, Apaay decided, there *was* something more satisfying than the quaver, and that was his look of absolute shock. She tried not to laugh at how good it felt to have finally outsmarted him.

Oh, hell. She deserved a bit of a laugh.

"I guess I should thank you for drugging me all those weeks ago. Really, you did me a favor." Her smile was as sharp as his eyes, though judging from the potency of the drug taking hold of him, they wouldn't be sharp for much longer. "All I had to do was wait for the opportune moment."

It had presented itself in Sinika beneath the swaying blue lights as Kaan informed her of a myth, a man of stone. Apaay had started preparing for this moment weeks ago. Daily, she had stewed the leaves and ingested the sleeping draught until the effects did not overpower her. Now the only side effect she experienced was ten to fifteen minutes of drowsiness.

As the Face Stealer's legs folded, he lunged unsuccessfully for his desk chair and collapsed onto the rug, the chair toppling with a heavy thump. He managed to roll onto his back, peering up at her in bewilderment. "You tricked me," he said, and if she didn't know any better, she could have sworn admiration flickered in his gaze.

Apaay dropped to her knees beside him, leaning close enough for their noses to touch. His heavy-lidded eyes widened a fraction, two pools of the water's deep. "Sweet dreams," she whispered.

Then he was out.

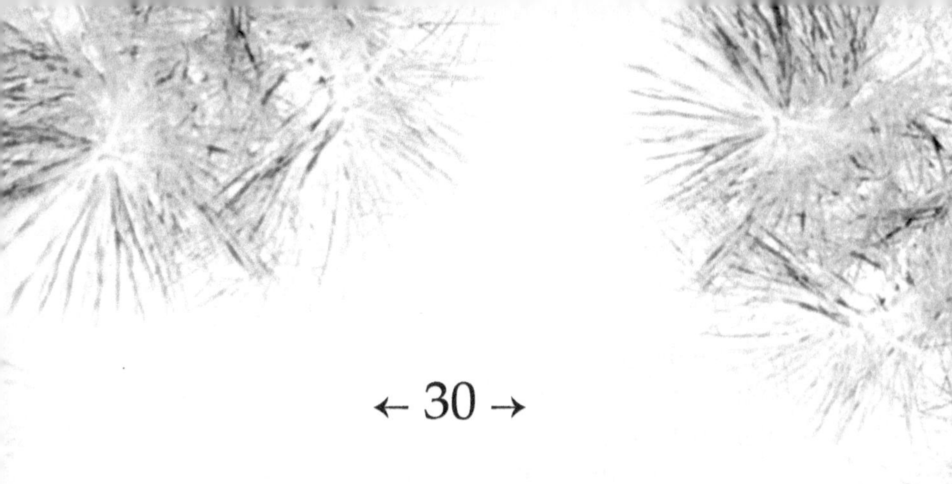

← 30 →

Masuk was waiting near the heart-tree when Apaay stumbled into view. Her foot snagged on one of the twisty roots, and she would have careened into him had he not caught her arm. The lingering effects of the moonflower made her head swim.

"It's done?" he asked with thinly veiled urgency.

Apaay leaned against his side with a tired nod. "He returned earlier than I expected." Her voice was not quite smooth. Drugging the Face Stealer had been a risk, but a necessary one. Did she regret it? Maybe a little, deep down. Maybe more, if she hadn't been so intent on fighting her changing perception of him. This—she and the Face Stealer at odds with each other, her seeing him as a dark thing with no light places—was too familiar of a feeling to let go. "I drugged him."

Masuk's expression took on a startled quality, and beneath that, something more brutal, so fleeting Apaay convinced herself she had imagined it.

Perhaps she had, because Masuk's eyes were clear when he faced her again. She said, "Did you get the draught?" While she had searched for the map, Masuk had stolen the protective draught from Tulimaq's room. Unless they found a way to ensure Yuki couldn't track them, Apaay would not have agreed to this. Luckily,

Ila had mentioned the draught to her after having returned from her mission with Tulimaq. She wouldn't risk the Wood's safety.

He pulled it from his pocket with a stiff nod. They each took a sip of the liquid, which tasted like water, and maybe mint. The protection should last long enough for them to find the First Man and return.

Tugging the map from her own pocket, Apaay smoothed it against the trunk. "I'm not sure where we're located, exactly." Trees cloaked the Atakana. They grew denser south of Kesikan Pass, but she thought they were farther north than that, nearer to Unana. She had no evidence to support this belief, only a feeling.

"Here." He pointed to a not-quite-perfect oval. It looked to be a lake formed from a volcanic crater. "Ila and I passed by this lake when we first arrived from the labyrinth, so we must be east of it." She followed the path he drew against the parchment. "We're probably somewhere in this vicinity," he said, circling the area with his finger.

"There's the First Man." The illustration depicted a figure sprouting from the earth.

With a nod, Masuk folded the map and slipped it into his parka before Apaay could object. Not that she would. They were going to the same place anyway.

As they were already dressed warmly for the excursion, Apaay and Masuk wasted no time. They passed casually through a few of the larger chambers so as to not draw attention to themselves. The pathway eventually split. Apaay went right as Masuk turned left. She stopped. "It's this way." Apaay pointed in the direction she and the Face Stealer had gone to reach the Owl Clan.

"I found a different way out."

"Oh." The right path was soft grass, no trees to clutter their view of the sky. The left path led to a grove with heavy white blossoms that dripped sweetness, the air cloying. They had nothing but time here, so of course Masuk may have found another exit during his explorations. She shrugged and followed his lead.

The grove stretched high with green walls, the leaves deeply saturated against the huddle of gray clouds. Water sang across a creek bed somewhere in the distance, and the sound was as lovely as it was eerie. After some time, they came to the base of a cliff, vines clambering up its face. Apaay tilted her head back and said, with thinly veiled skepticism, "We have to climb this?"

"Look closer."

In the middle of the rock was a glass door. If he hadn't drawn her attention to it, she would never have noticed it. Gripping the handle, Apaay tugged it open.

Her body seized from the plunge in temperature, her lungs locking as she fought to pull in the freezing air through her nose. As soon as the door shut behind them, they were left in near darkness, the gray of the mountains a shade lighter than the swath of backdrop, with trees all around.

They walked, or rather, trudged, for the snow was waist-high, and fresh. Masuk led, referring to the map every so often. Wind boomed against the mammoth peaks and sent the air around them shuddering.

"Can I ask you something?" she said, pitching her voice so it carried over the wind.

"What is it?" He referred to the map. Pointed. They continued the trek.

"Is there a place you call home?" She fought for breath. The air was so cold her teeth seared, and the pain radiated through her jaw, higher, all the way up to her skull, spreading behind her eyes. "Somewhere you can return to?" As she had done since their escape, Apaay wondered about the circumstances surrounding his imprisonment.

He didn't answer. Maybe he hadn't heard her. Yet the set of his posture had changed. Masuk walked like a man determined not to look over his shoulder and see how far back his trail extended.

"Not anymore," he said.

Apaay froze as the earth shook. Snow tumbled free of the great canopies and piled into mounds. Masuk watched the peaks with an awareness that went beyond simple observation.

The trembling ceased. Left behind was the fading echo of a roaring white wave.

"Avalanche," he said, and his focus narrowed to where they stood, deep in the valley between two mountains. "We should keep moving."

With an edgy glance at the snow-topped range, Apaay forged onward, remaining as close to Masuk's back as possible, for he blocked much of the wind. For her own sanity, she did not think about the possibility of an avalanche. The world was old, and there was nothing older than this: a clash between earth and wind.

When she stumbled a third time in five minutes, Masuk helped her up, brushing the pale flakes from her trousers. "You don't have to come with me," he said, voice rough. "If it's too difficult of a journey, I'll take you back."

"I'm not leaving you."

He stared at the tops of his boots, hard. "You should. Everyone else does."

Apaay wasn't sure how to respond to his change in demeanor. The lack of *feeling.* "What do you mean?"

"I didn't think you cared."

"Of course I care. You're my friend."

Masuk turned away, looking extremely uncomfortable.

They were friends, weren't they?

"I don't understand," Apaay whispered.

They stood in an open plain, small and huddled and so young compared to the granite jaws of the Atakana. "You don't want to be friends with me." Finally, he lifted his head. "I am not a kind person, Apaay."

She studied him cautiously. It sounded like a warning, and one she should heed. She didn't waste her breath telling him he wasn't what he claimed to be. It was not what he wanted to hear.

"I hurt people," he said, challenge in the set of his jaw. *Prove me wrong,* his eyes said. *Tell me I am different. Tell me I am someone else.* "I hurt a lot of people before the Face Stealer captured me."

Apaay glanced at his hands, which hung loose at his sides, and denied the fear creeping through her. Apaay had been drawn to him because no one else understood the darkness quite like him. But maybe that had been her mistake, to trust in someone not because of who they were, but because of who you wanted them to be.

He said, "The people tried to keep me away from the woman I loved, so I took their loved ones away from them." Steady, steady gaze. "Permanently."

The words were a dash of cold water splashed across her face. "You killed them," she whispered.

"I did." No change in expression.

"Why?"

His fingers twitched. "Did you not hear what I said?" he snapped.

Apaay forced her attention away from his hands and back to his face. "I don't mean why you killed them." She would get to that later. "I mean why they tried to take her away from you."

Masuk indicated for them to keep walking. Apaay hesitated before falling into step beside him, though she kept her distance. "I have no idea. Jealousy?"

There was something about his voice. A snag she'd never heard before. It sounded as if he wasn't telling the whole truth. "Why won't you tell me?" she asked, forcing the question into a whisper. Sound echoed easily in these valleys.

"Because it's none of your business, that's why!" he burst out, whirling around with a feral gleam in his remaining eye.

Apaay backed away so quickly she fell onto her backside. Her mind reeled. "I'm sorry," she said, and for the first time in all these months, Apaay noticed the weight he had put on, the strength having returned to his body while hers had wasted away. "I shouldn't have pushed you."

"You're right," he agreed. The contortion of his features pulled at his scarring. "You shouldn't have." Turning, he went on ahead.

Apaay brushed herself off and went after him, if only because she wanted to see the task through. Had there always been this instability in him? Apaay had been fairly confident she knew Masuk. It turned out she knew nothing at all.

Two more miles passed before Masuk called for a halt. "This is it." The map fluttered in his hand.

Apaay glanced around. She didn't see anything, and said as much.

Masuk reached for her hand. She flinched, and he paused, staring at her with none of the earlier rage. Then, gently, he took her fingers and tugged her forward.

Apaay stepped from cold into warmth, dimness into light, a dead, dormant land into one that was vibrant, breathing, alive.

Her gasp slipped free, only to be caught within the warm current of air that nudged against them, as if curious about the newest visitors. The wolverine fur of her hood tickled her cheek as she pushed back its heavy weight.

They stood in a ring of trees spaced equidistance apart, having passed through a barrier similar to the Wood's. A smooth paving of rock carved with various symbols took the shape of a perfect circle. In its center was a small, overgrown mound, the upper portion distinctly human in shape, its skin a dark gray, cracked and dry.

This, Apaay thought in wonder, was where gods and man and myth met. "Is he . . . awake?"

Masuk considered the First Man as he passed her the map so she could slip it into her pocket. "I don't think so." Still, he didn't move. "I think we have to wake him up."

Apaay grabbed his arm before he could move. "It might be a trap." Or a test of the god who had put him here. One did not disturb higher beings of power if one wanted a relatively peaceful life.

He looked to where her fingers clutched his sleeve. "It will be all right," he told her, quiet and very close to a lull.

After a moment of indecision, Apaay released him. She didn't believe a word he said.

He crossed the paved stone soundlessly. Apaay folded her arms, watching Masuk eagerly circle the First Man. The ground beneath them didn't feel like the earth. Small currents ran through it and extended outward in all directions. An otherness to the place, felt in the atmosphere, seen in the too-green grass and vines clambering over the rocky base, and tasted in the warm haven they stood in.

Masuk touched the stone mound with the very tip of his finger.

A horrible screeching sound ran claws through the air as ice speared across the ground and the wind invaded the pocket of tranquility. The earth was groaning, and it was so much louder now, and closer, and Apaay wasn't sure if an avalanche approached or if that was her heart trying to bang its way out of her chest. The stone was alive. It shifted and rose up, as tall as a man standing, spilling earth from its sides. Two deep gouges carved into the rock came to rest on Apaay's face as if they were eyes.

"Have you come for answers, then?" A rakish caw, a clawing of nails, a howl tunneling down into her teeth.

Masuk stepped back, never taking his gaze from the man, his face a twisting of hope and despair. Apaay stayed where she was and didn't move. The man might be trapped in rock, but that didn't mean he hadn't any power. After all, he had been touched by a god.

"I've come," Masuk said, "because I'm looking for something lost, and have been for a long time."

Rock cracked as the man twisted his neck. "Many seek something lost." Though he answered Masuk, he was looking at Apaay. She stared into his pitted eyes and fought the need to tremble. He must see everything she was, everything she hoped to be. He must see the tatters of her weary soul. "What is it you seek? Love? Purpose?" The First Man then turned his pupilless gaze onto Masuk. "Redemption?"

"I've come for the location of my beloved's face."

"You seek nothing else?"

He paused for a moment. Apaay realized she, too, could gather information from the First Man, if she desired. Like the name of whatever it was Yuki had stolen from the Face Stealer.

Masuk said, "I do not."

Though the First Man's face did not change, his voice suggested a subtle amusement. "There was another like you, a thousand years before. He had come from Across the Sea, seeking material that would create the strongest, most powerful of weapons. His people were at war, you see, and he demanded victory."

A new awareness washed over her. Centuries had come and gone, yet the memory was enduring. That man from Across the Sea might have returned home. The First Man, however, remained.

"He came to the North, a place he had never been, and expected to be owed this information. As if war was reason enough for me to grant him this wish. I warned him that power always comes with a price. He didn't listen to me. He had spent twenty-five years on this earth while I was but broken rock in the ground."

"What happened to him?" Apaay wondered.

"I gave him the answer he sought. His people won the war. Many decades later, a new conqueror swept the land, having learned of these impossibly strong weapons. The man's people had won, only to find themselves slaughtered for the very answer the man had sought to solve his problem."

And if Masuk learned of the information he sought? Surely the location of a face wasn't the same as a push for power. Though, truthfully, she didn't know the details of his situation, only the large strokes. "Maybe we should reconsider," Apaay said.

Masuk's head snapped around. "I thought you agreed to help me."

"I do want to help you." Apaay lifted her hands in a placating gesture, recalling his earlier anger. "I'm concerned, is all. Have you considered the consequences of receiving this information?"

It was the wrong thing to say. "Do you think I care about the consequences," he hissed, "when I've been living them for the past twenty years? A life without someone you love *is* the consequence." He said to the First Man, "Tell me what I want to know."

"You must know, nothing in this world is given freely."

"What do you want? I have nothing to give you. I have no worldly possessions." He flung out his hands in a fitful gesture. "I have nothing of value."

A sound like two rocks scraping together reached her ears.

Was the First Man *laughing*?

"Do you know, boy, who I am?" The hairs on Apaay's body spiked in response to the thunder of his voice. "I am the eyes and ears of the world. I have met you a thousand times with a thousand different faces. I have listened to your story, again and again and again."

"What do you need?" Color stained high on Masuk's cheeks, though his scarring remained pale as ever. "Tell me and I will bring it to you."

A creaking sound came out of his mouth. Apaay suspected it was a sigh. "I do not trade objects. What would I need of them when I am trapped here, bound until the world dies? No, boy. I trade information. That is how I learn of what has changed, what moves as I stand still. I require," he said, "a secret."

Masuk looked like he had gotten kicked in the stomach. He glanced at Apaay, though he wasn't speaking to her. "But it wouldn't be a secret if she heard, would it?"

"That is the price of the information you seek. And her price, too, should she ask something of me."

How did the First Man know she had a question?

Masuk frowned, as if he hadn't considered the possibility. "You have a question?"

As a matter of fact, she did. "Yes."

"Your secret," said the First Man.

She swallowed. These days, she was made of secrets. She must choose only one.

In a halting voice, Apaay said, "Never have I been surrounded by so many people who want to help me. And never have I felt so alone."

The First Man stared at her. "Pain of the heart is not easily healed. What is your question?"

"What did Yuki steal from the Face Stealer?"

Masuk's nostrils flared. Her heart gave a hollow thud. What was it about the question that upset Masuk?

"Ah." The stone moved a fraction. "Unfortunately, I do not have an answer for you. Due to the nature of the curse, the Face Stealer is unable to speak of the object or pass on that information to someone else. Thus, I do not know. The Face Stealer has come to me before for answers. The answer has never changed."

Apaay's stomach sank. It had been worth a try, at least.

"Now, boy." The First Man turned his attention back to Masuk. "What is your secret?"

He opened his mouth, closed it with a pained expression. "I'm sorry, Apaay."

Cold fingers touched down her spine.

"The Face Stealer—"

"What?" Apaay demanded. She felt the moment build to when he'd say whatever dark secret lay in his heart, bring it out into the open, like a billow of smoke sent to smother her. "The Face Stealer what?"

"He's my brother."

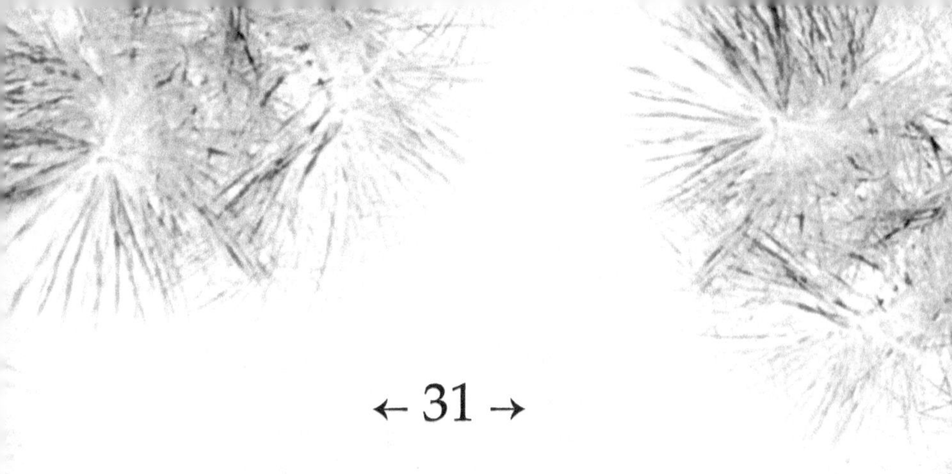

← 31 →

Apaay tried to banish the feeling of finding herself in a sudden storm. "You're lying," she quavered.

"He is not," said the First Man. "I recognize it as truth."

If he was not lying, then he was confused. He was so confused as to who he was that he spoke what he thought was true. He and the Face Stealer didn't look anything alike. She almost said as much before catching herself. How could she truly know what Masuk looked like with the scarring on his face?

Masuk had told her the Face Stealer had locked him up. Left him to rot for twenty long years. She tried to make sense of it. Had they both waited, then, for her to come? Had they planned it so she'd find Masuk's cell and help him escape? Had Masuk known all along that Yuki would seek vengeance?

"Were you working with him?" she demanded, practically vibrating with fury. "Did you know about Chena? Did you know about Nakaluq and my parents and my village?" When he said nothing, she snarled with unmasked ferocity, "Tell me!"

"I didn't," he said. This, how he looked to her right now, was the most anguished she had ever seen him. He looked to be in physical pain. "I swear to you, I didn't."

A wolf howled in the distance. Fists clenched, muscles coiled, Apaay whirled around and stomped away. Pain radiated in her jaw, and the stinging sensation she had experienced all those weeks ago returned to her face. But it was brief this time, and the cold soothed the pain. What if Masuk's secrets had not been protection, but manipulation?

The quiet burrowed inside of her. She thought of the labyrinth. Even then, she had not been able to escape the beating of her heart. It had chased her, and chased her. Deeper into her nightmares and dreams. But that sound was far away now. Apaay wasn't sure what she was looking at anymore. Or who.

"I wasn't working with my brother," he repeated to her back. "I had never even *seen* Yuki until we escaped. I swear to you. Apaay." He stepped toward her.

Tension crawled up her back and sank stiff fingers into her shoulders. Her first instinct was to withdraw, return to the dark. It would welcome her as if she had never left. But she couldn't go back to that place, not when she was trying to climb her way out. A returned appetite might not be reason for celebration, but it was something. It was definitely something.

Apaay closed her eyes and inhaled. The cold air awoke in her chest, soothing her fury.

The Face Stealer had warned her of Masuk. She hadn't listened to him, for obvious reasons. If she hadn't wasted time trying to help Masuk escape the labyrinth, Apaay might have reached her village before Yuki had. Her people might still be alive.

"Masuk isn't even your real name," she whispered, turning to face him. "Kenai. That's your name." This was the Face Stealer's brother. *He* had brought Nanuq to the Wolf Kingdom's borders. "You're supposed to be dead."

"What do you mean *supposed to be*?"

"The Face Stealer told me you were dead."

The tips of his fingers came to rest on the left side of his face and traced the meanest of the scars, following to where it rippled outward and smeared into the deeper brown of his skin. "Yes," said Masuk. "He would say something like that."

"Why would you lie to me about your name?" He couldn't know the significance of names in her culture, though he had somehow known the cultural significance of hair to the Analak after her head had been shaved.

His mouth trembled before he clamped his lips shut. "Maybe I didn't want to be that person anymore. Maybe I wanted to forget that person. Maybe I liked who I was when I was with you." He lifted his arms, let them drop to his sides. "Maybe I thought I could start over, start a new life."

"You can't run away from who you are. You can't hide from the things you've done."

"Why are you so mad at me? How is this any different from you hiding your pain from your family?"

"Because they don't understand me, and this isn't pain. This is deceit."

"Who says it's not my pain?" he roared, tossing up his hands. "You? You know nothing about me."

It took all her willpower to stand her ground. The worst part was, she *didn't* know anything about him, and she wanted to. "I hid nothing from you, but you hid everything from me. That's not how friendship works. Don't you think I would have liked to know that the man who helped torture me is your brother? Don't you think I wouldn't have opened myself up to you if I had known?" Every question released a new wave of fury and shame, that she had given so much to someone who shared blood with the North's most notorious demon. "Don't you think I'm now questioning your motives because of who the Face Stealer is, because of who you are?" She stared at him, shaking, her eyes wet.

Masuk was breathing hard, the sound of someone trying to hold tight to the frayed ends of his control. "This is his fault. Everything is his fault. I *hate* him," he spat, spittle spewing from his mouth. His lips peeled back from his teeth to reveal the tips of his canines. "Every time I *see* him—" He crouched down, curled forward, then snapped to his feet and paced in the opposite direction, as if he could not contain the anger in his body.

Apaay watched him with caution. Her eyes met those of the First Man, who had remained silent thus far. Masuk wasn't acting like himself. Or maybe he was. If so, she might be seeing him clearly for the first time.

"He's a terrible person," Masuk said as he returned, Apaay stepping back to keep space between them. "He did horrible things to you. He's done horrible things to me, to others, and not just stealing their faces. Did he mention that he murdered our sister and father? Our *mother*?"

That stopped her. *My family is dead,* the Face Stealer had said. She didn't know what to think and which brother to believe, if she should believe either of them.

As if sensing Apaay's doubt, Masuk pushed forward with his argument. "He manipulates people into trusting him."

"You mean the way you manipulated me?"

"It was never with ill intent. I never expected to leave that cell. When you showed up, I thought it was another trick. It had been so long since anyone had spoken to me or showed me kindness that I lied. Yes, I pretended I didn't know my name, but that was the only thing I lied to you about."

Apaay did not believe him.

He made a sound of frustration. "He's using you like he used me."

"How do I know you're not using me, too?" she threw back at him. "You said you killed people, but you forgot to tell me they were your *own* people. You turned traitor to your own nation." It didn't matter that they weren't her people. All five Unua nations were necessary for a healthy North. Give one too much power and it skewed the balance. That must be why the Face Stealer had locked up Masuk.

So then why had the Face Stealer allowed Masuk to escape the labyrinth with them? Why let him remain in the Wood?

Masuk didn't argue the claim, which was almost worse. "See, this is why I didn't tell you," he said with a bitter laugh. "You're looking at me as if you have no idea who I am."

"Because I don't! I have no idea who you are!"

The accusation seemed to break something in him. "Yes, you do. You know who I am." But he sounded confused, as if he was trying to convince himself of that, not her. "Maybe I did horrible things to my people, turned traitor like you said, but it would have never happened if the Face Stealer hadn't killed our family. You're not looking at the cause, Apaay. What you are seeing is the effect. The end of a story, not the beginning. Do you think I want to be related to someone without a soul? With no sense of empathy?"

"What about dishonesty? Does that run in the family, too?"

Masuk sent her a wounded glare. "You can despise me all you want, but don't forget he was the one who brought you to the labyrinth. I wasn't the one who stole your sister's face. I wasn't the one who destroyed your village or hurt the people you love. I am not your enemy. I," he managed through trembling breath, "am a victim. Just like you."

He was right and he was wrong. He had killed, but so had the Face Stealer, so had she. Apaay couldn't shake the feeling of something having changed.

"Tell me one thing," she said lowly. "Were you ever my friend, or was this always a motive for finding your beloved's face?"

A few snowflakes drifted down and caught in his hair. "I don't want to lie to you, Apaay. I've enjoyed your company, and that's separate from my need to find my beloved's face." After scrubbing his hands over his chapped cheeks, he added, "I came to the Wood knowing it was temporary. Whether I found the face or not, I was going to leave." He lifted his head, caught her eye. "I had hoped you would come with me to the Banished Lands."

Apaay, who was now questioning every interaction with him, didn't hear the sincerity. "Masuk—Kenai. I . . . don't know." With Nanuq and Yuki having reinstated their alliance, the Wood was most likely the safest place for her family, even more so than the Banished Lands. The Face Stealer had once implied the source of his power was so vast as to be essentially limitless. It would go a long way toward protecting those she loved. "I need some time."

His breath unwound. His shoulders sagged with the new weight of sadness. Apaay took that as acceptance and turned toward the

First Man, who regarded them with the same blank face, but with a stirring of curiosity in the air. "He gave you a secret. You owe him an answer."

The man's smile cracked through the granite that had begun to harden his jaw and chin. "But we were all having so much fun." A grinding laugh warred with the snow crashing down a mountainside in the distance. "What do you want to know?"

Masuk stared out to where the cold awaited them, the copse of trees stretching to an impressive height. His eyes were shadowed when he refocused his attention on the First Man. "Where is the location of my beloved's face?"

"There is a door inside the Face Stealer's office hidden behind his bookcase. There, you will find the face you seek."

So it had been in his office the entire time, not the shadowy library door as Apaay had first believed.

According to the moon's location, about three hours had passed since they'd left the Wood. Apaay said, "We should go."

"Before you do," said the voice, "there is another face with the others. A young woman whose features are drawn with regality. You must promise no harm comes to that face. It is imperative it does not fall into the wrong hands."

"We promise," she said, though truthfully didn't think anything of it. Who was she to deny the Keeper of All That Lives and Dies?

They took their leave. Now that they knew the face's location, there was no time to waste. The hike had taken them hours. With renewed vigor, they sought to cut that time in half.

"I have to ask," Apaay said after some time had passed. She watched him falter, then quicken his pace. "How can you justify wiping out an entire nation? Even if you love someone, is that truly worth the sacrifice of your own kind?"

Snow shushed around their ankles. It was light and powdery, delicate. "I don't expect you to understand," he said. "The relationship between the Face Stealer and me has never been easily explained. Everything that has happened begins and ends with him."

A fierce cry severed the air, and she froze. Not an animal.

Man.

Apaay, in her adrenaline-induced state, found her legs working harder, carrying her faster and farther over the ground than she would have believed possible.

They fled beneath the gray veil. The valley steepened, and momentum sent them to its bottom, where the majority of the snow had collected. The air bit with such chill that her breaths rang in the stillness. Above, the clouds thinned and stretched, like water seeping into cloth. There were the shadows, twitching as if being shaken awake. The dark, too mysterious to read, and frightening, always frightening.

"Why are people chasing us?" she demanded. They couldn't possibly be affiliated with Yuki, could they? She and Masuk had taken the necessary precautions.

Masuk's silence on the matter only heightened her dread.

"Are you sure you got the right draught?"

"There was no draught."

Apaay stumbled. "What?"

"I said," he growled with a flash of teeth, "there was no draught. I couldn't find it in Tulimaq's room. You drank plain water."

The bottom dropped out of her stomach, and a cold horror reached up and wrapped its long fingers around her neck.

"Down!" Masuk cried, tackling her as an arrow screamed past her ear. It embedded itself in a nearby tree, quivering.

He hauled her into a standing position, shoved her forward, and it was to the most painful music, the whine of arrows cutting through the frost, their impacts in the wood a dull promise. Apaay didn't dare look behind them as they wove through the trees to try and throw their pursuers off course. "We're leading them straight to the Wood," she panted.

"It's our only option."

"If you hadn't lied about the draught, it wouldn't even be an option," she snapped. Because of him, Yuki knew of their location. They would bring peril to the Wood's doors, and the Face Stealer couldn't do a thing about it. He was unconscious.

"I'm sorry."

"Stop. I don't want to hear it." The only other option was to fight. It had been too long since she had thought something so dangerous. Fighting was freedom. Fighting was choice.

Pushing her legs faster, she kept pace with him as they cut a hard right, trying to think of a way out of this situation. Another arrow whipped past Masuk's shoulder. The weapons were falling in greater density, forcing them to zigzag and make for more difficult targets. Apaay found herself slowing, unable to ignore the burn in her legs or how her lungs felt as if they were slowly being seared away.

Masuk choked out an anguished curse. Then he went down, blood spilling across the snow.

Apaay reached for him, shaking so hard she thought she'd fall over.

"Don't," he managed through gritted teeth. He took two deep breaths before reaching out to touch the wooden shaft that pierced his side. His body locked up and the tendons pulled in his neck.

Slowly and with much care, he wrapped his fingers around the arrow and ripped it out with a bellow. He caught himself on the ground with one hand as he tipped forward, the arrow slipping from his fingers, the white-and-black fletching spattered in red.

Apaay froze. She'd seen those feathers before. They had decorated the arrow that had struck her on the way to Sinika.

"Get to the Wood," Masuk ordered, having to pitch his voice over the nearing cries. They sounded like animals. Another arrow landed a few inches from her leg.

She tore her attention away from the feathers. "I'm not leaving—"

Her mouth dropped open.

Different eyes, the irises a pale blue, like floes of ice, yet glistening with human intelligence. Masuk had been a man. Now he was a wolf, a magnificent animal with a gray pelt and long legs. Apaay found it difficult to breathe. He reminded her of Nakaluq.

He lurched to his feet, blood oozing from the wound to mat his fur. Together, they bolted for safety, and he was so much faster than she. A free spirit of the world.

They rounded a thicket of trees. Light fluttered through the dusk, beckoning them toward eternal summer.

"Ila!" she screamed, so forcefully it burned the back of her throat. The fear was so overwhelming Apaay forgot Ila wouldn't be able to hear her. "Ila!"

Pain severed her abdomen, and she went down.

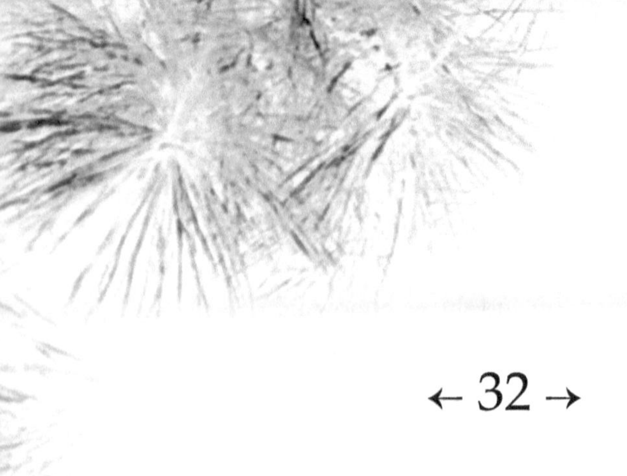

← 32 →

Ila was deep into one of her training sessions when the sudden stillness of Tulimaq's body sent her on high alert. She glanced around the clearing.

"I thought I heard something." Lowering his staff, Tulimaq cocked his head, listening. Ila tightened her grip on her talq. Then came his frown. "It's your friend. I think she's in trouble."

Apaay? She and Apaay hadn't parted on good terms last week, but that didn't stop the concern. *What's wrong?*

He jerked his chin, telling her without words to follow. It had rained recently. The air was muggy and sweet-smelling, and the muck sucked at her ankles as she leapt over exposed roots. Tulimaq was all aggression. A lean figure whose long legs lent him a wider stride compared to Ila, but in the weeks since she'd begun training, her endurance had grown as well, and she sprinted the half mile behind him without tiring.

A break in the trees lay ahead. Then came the meadow, and after, a tunnel of heavy, hanging branches, a pine needle floor. It was green, and then it wasn't. The trees no longer bore leaves, only the sharp points of their branches. A breeze huffed behind them—no, a frozen wind that bit the exposed skin of her arms.

The plants were dying. Something wasn't right.

Abruptly, Tulimaq pulled her down to the base of a spruce tree, one finger pressed to his lips. Crossing her arms, Ila huddled closer to the trunk and clenched her teeth together so they wouldn't chatter, watching him. With his attention flitting from branch to branch, he didn't notice her gaze shift from his eyes to his nose, narrow and unbroken, to the cut of his cheekbones, and lastly, to his mouth. A bead of sweat slid down the side of his neck, a tendon pulled taut there.

Expression grim, he signed, *Seal Unua beyond the trees.*

Her pulse beat a crescendo in response. The seal Unua were quite far from the Eastern Territory. *How can you tell?*

Their boots.

Ila peeked around the tree. A mass of soldiers marched through the grass in intimidatingly straight lines, bearing uniforms in seaweed green, pointy black boots, and weapons constructed of coral. They looked like they had taken the sea with them onto dry land with their large, rounded eyes of jet and oil-slick dark hair. *How did they get in?*

Tulimaq tugged her back around. *The barrier is down. Something must have happened to Numiak.*

She felt tossed among the waves. *What about Apaay? Can you hear her?*

He continued to watch beyond her shoulder. *No.*

Ila's mind was clear, and her heart beat strong, if unevenly. *Her voice came from that direction?* she asked, pointing. In her worry for Apaay, Ila forgot the resentment, the neglect, and the rift dividing them. She thought only of her friend's safety.

Tulimaq yanked her down as Ila stood. *Think,* was his lightning response. *What will we gain by revealing our position? There are at least one hundred and fifty soldiers that I can see.* The tightness around his jaw was the only change Ila noticed in his features. His pupils seemed to dilate the longer she looked at him. *I will look for Ro and Kaan. If the barrier is down, they'll need help protecting the refugees. Find Numiak.*

Ila looked in the direction Apaay's voice had supposedly come from. *But Apaay—*

Stop. Gripping her upper arms, he gave Ila a little shake. *Go to Numiak's office. There's a small mirror in his desk drawer. It will show you his location.*

She nodded, resigned to her task. As soon as she found Numiak, though, she'd search for her friend.

Ila almost did something ridiculous like throw her arms around the combat master. She grabbed Tulimaq's arm instead, holding him there, the ridge of forearm muscles taut beneath her fingers. She finally settled on, *Be safe.*

It was good Ila didn't expect anything more than a curt nod. If she worried about him, that was her own problem, and one she doubted he cared to know. *You too.*

They parted ways, Tulimaq moving toward the meadow, Ila running back through the woods. She leapt over roots and fallen trees, sleek as a doe, and scrambled down the hillside, rocks and leaves sliding against her feet. With winter having overtaken the Wood, the cold air seized her lungs and set fire to her chest, but she didn't have time to change clothes.

This, she realized, was war. It was a cold wind screaming down the mountainside with cutting force. She widened her stride and pushed her body as if she could outrun that wind. But it was already here.

Ila reached the waterfall, which had solidified into a frozen pillar curled over the top of the rock shelf. She hopped the rocks across the basin, then stopped. The office door was ajar.

Ila scanned the area, but it was empty, at least the places she could see. Pulling her talq from its sheath, she aimed the blade outward as she stepped toward the doorway. Shadows had descended with the fallen barrier.

A faint glow cast the room in a golden half-light. Ila took one step into the room and faltered, sucking in a sharp breath.

The Face Stealer had collapsed, his form unmoving. He looked dead. He couldn't be dead. Was he dead? Ashen skin, sprawled limbs. She didn't see any blood.

Crouching beside him, Ila pressed two fingers against the side of his neck. Nothing. She tried the pulse point in both wrists, but no blood flowed.

Ila sat back on her heels. If the Face Stealer was dead, what did that mean for the rest of them?

She needed to find Kaan.

The woman's workshop was nearby. Ila took the fastest route. A mile through the brush in the dark and she reached the mouth of the cave, went deeper and deeper into the void.

Kaan, bent over her workbench and smoothing the tines of an antler, snapped her head up as Ila burst into the chamber. One look at the girl's wild gaze and she was on her feet. "What's wrong?"

Ila heaved, hands braced on her knees. *There's been a breach to the Wood. The barrier is down. I think someone killed Numiak. He's not breathing.*

"Show me."

They returned to his office, having to take the long way around when they spotted soldiers in the distance. With the barrier gone, so was the Wood's ability to manipulate its surroundings. The infiltrating darkness cloaked everything in sight.

Kneeling beside him, Kaan checked the Face Stealer's pulse with a troubled expression. "You were right. There's no pulse." She stood and studied the office in confusion. Tulimaq had drilled this into Ila. Not to look, but to *see*.

She examined Numiak's desk as Kaan did. It was neat. No sign of a struggle. A tea kettle cooled on the far table. The cups were empty.

Kaan plucked one of the cups from the desk. She held it to her nose, and her eyebrows shot skyward. Dipping the tip of her pinkie finger into the remaining liquid, she dabbed it onto her tongue and flinched. "Oof. No, Numiak isn't dead. He was drugged. He'll be out for a couple of hours, I suspect." At Ila's confusion, she explained, "Someone gave him moonflower. I've never heard of it stopping a pulse, but he could react differently than others."

Hands on her hips, the woman peered down at Numiak's unconscious form. "I guess there's not much we can do except leave him here. We'll lock the door. He'll be safe."

A feeling like a bird diving low swept through Ila's belly. She thought of Apaay asking her to distract the Face Stealer while she stole a map from one of his books. Ila had refused.

Apaay, she thought. *What have you done?*

← →

Apaay and Kenai were surrounded. With her back against a tree and blood slowly leaking out, her body was nothing but fear.

In wolf form, Kenai tore into men as they descended on them like a rushing river, their bows having been exchanged for weapons with protruding coral. Apaay could barely keep track of the kills. Men appeared and fell in succession. The snow ran red, the bodies piled higher, dismembered or their throats torn out, and the weak, desperate cries of the wounded became something of a litany.

Soldiers had blocked the way through. Apaay didn't know what was happening to those inside the Wood.

"Apaay." Someone slapped her cheek. She focused on the face in front of her. Kenai, human again. A trickle of blood colored his temple, his hair clumped in matted strands against his sweaty neck. "We need to get to higher ground. There are too many of them." He glanced over his shoulder. Another wave of soldiers dispersed from the far reaches of the forest. "Can you stand?"

She nodded. Bad idea. The world was spinning.

Using the trees for support, Apaay followed Kenai away from the Wood. The fighting sounds had momentarily ceased.

"Faster," he said, pulling ahead.

The snow was wet with the approaching thaw. She slid on an icy patch.

He looked behind them. "They're coming."

"Go, then." She growled the words between her clenched teeth. "I'm not going to make it."

He uttered an oath. Running back to her side, he swung her over one shoulder. Behind them, the men gave chase as Kenai ran for both of their lives. He was impossibly strong. The jarring of his footsteps intensified the pain. Apaay gritted her teeth and pressed her palms against his lower back to support herself, feeling the shift of his muscles beneath her mittens.

"There's a cave up ahead. If we have a wall at our backs, it might give us a chance."

"How much farther?" she managed. The edges of her vision softened, taken over by the black.

"Not far. It's around this bend."

Apaay ducked her head to avoid the thwacking branches. "How do you know about the cave?" she asked, suddenly suspicious.

He didn't answer.

← →

Ila and Kaan had locked the Face Stealer in his office and now headed for the barrier, or where it used to be. They passed bodies on their way, both refugee and animal alike, strewn across the Wood's grounds. It seemed the animals, too, had sensed the threat to their home, and fought back.

The refugee camp was located three miles from the barrier, but that didn't mean the soldiers hadn't reached it. A few of the Unua refugees had combat experience, but Apaay's people were not soldiers. Ila hoped Tulimaq had found Ro, that they did all they could to protect their home.

Suddenly, Kaan skidded to a halt at the creek bank, her feet sinking into the half-frozen mud. All the color drained from her face. "Mika."

Ila went colder than cold. Kaan was already changing direction, their strides longer, their arms pumping faster, and their hearts sick with fear. The seal Unua had already overtaken parts of the Wood, fighting hard and without mercy. Mika was just a girl.

They followed the creek to where it converged with a river that had frozen over. Kaan hopped onto the ice and continued to run along its shimmering surface, Ila right behind, until they came to a massive cave with hanging vines at its entrance. Inside, the darkness was nearly complete. The tunnel plunged deeper into the rock. Ila rammed her shoulder into the wall as they turned a corner. Kaan jerked to a halt ahead.

The room had been destroyed. The bed broken in half. Clothes shredded. There was blood, too, smeared on the wall and flecked on the dark rock, freshly black. Oil lamps had been knocked from their places on the shelves, save one that was close to guttering. A single light in the room.

Kaan's face was pale as seafoam. Her chest rose and fell in a fitful gesture, and her eyes sheened with welling tears. She tore off the blankets on the girl's bed, kicking aside fallen enemy weapons as she went, crying the girl's name. She circled the room thrice as Ila rushed to peer under the bed, in the chest where Mika stored her toys. Empty.

"If they hurt her—" Kaan clutched the back of her skull and began to pace. Her usual level-headedness had gone, caving beneath the stress. "They're here for the Face Stealer, but Mika will be used for leverage unless he hands himself over."

They? Ila signed.

"Yuki's army."

Then they did not have time.

"Come on." Kaan jerked her chin, and they were again running back the way they'd come. They didn't have the luxury of discussing the next step. Ila trusted her mentor to lead her to Mika. Or into battle.

They were passing by the meeting room when something in the grass caught Ila's eye. By the time she lifted her hand to call for Kaan's attention, the woman had already vanished between the trees.

Ila hesitated. Mika was wolf Unua, and these were wolf tracks.

She spotted additional signs beyond the prints—trampled grass, rolled pebbles. The tracks led her to the entrance of Kaan's workshop, which was where she had been not twenty minutes before. Ila ran a few steps into the cave before slowing, her eyes adjusting to the thicker darkness.

A few blue lights remained. Ila lightened her tread. Her attention flitted from corner to hidden alcove, a hand on the wall to guide her.

The earth rumbled then, coming to life beneath her feet. Dust and rock shook loose from the ceiling and rained onto her shoulders, a larger stone hitting the back of her head with a sharp sting. Ila touched the wound, found it wet.

The wall at her back exploded into glittering darkness and ice.

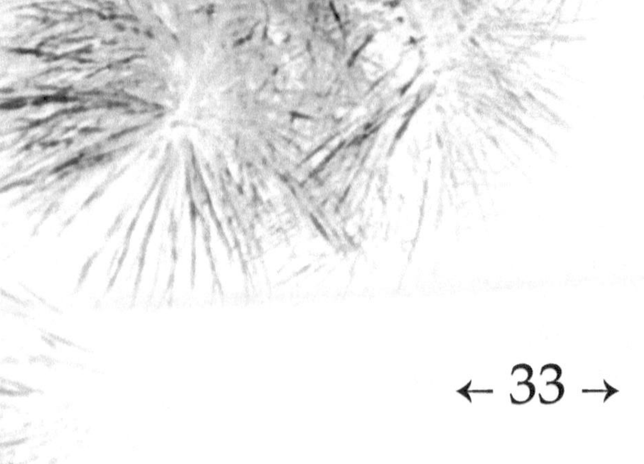

← 33 →

The force of the explosion sent heat lashing through the enclosed space, tossing Ila against the cave wall at her back. The snap of bone ricocheted through her. A sting, then agony. She hit the ground with a cry, blood pulsating around the break in her wrist, and covered her head to protect it from the flinging debris.

Four figures stepped through the gray veil.

Sleek, slippery material clung to their frames. Netting stretched across their shoulders and upper torsos. And then those black boots that looked so much like flippers. Seal Unua. Yes, she could see it now.

They hadn't yet spotted her. The dust was thick as ash. Ila, huddled against the wall, slowly pushed to her feet, crouching low. She'd lost her talq during the explosion. No time to look for it now. Turning, she fled deeper into the cave, in the direction of Kaan's workshop. She needed a weapon.

The flickering blue lights threw spindly shadows against the passage walls. When she reached the cavern, the lamps had been extinguished and a frail light slunk along the ground, casting the area in shades of blue-black and gray, and in the corners, darker. The long table against the wall held weapons in various stages of completion, but none finished. She only had pieces to work with.

The stench of rotting fish descended seconds before the pair of massive hands did, pinching her arms to her sides. Ila dropped. The man's weight shifted onto his toes. In that second, his balance no longer belonged to him. It belonged to *her*.

It was as if Tulimaq's presence guided her through the motions she'd practiced until her hands bled. Turning her body into his, Ila swept a leg behind his knees and shoved him back with her unbroken hand. His arms wheeled. Ila slipped away, using the opportunity to dart up the narrow ramp carved out of the wall, which led to a shelf jutting over the cavern floor. Kaan had stored completed weapons up here to free up table space. There was a nigana with the antler tines sharpened to slivers. A few knives. A staff of spruce wood.

She grabbed the nigana. The four soldiers had congregated at the ramp's base. The blue light of the ice bruised against their skin, turning the hues into cooler tones of raw umber. Ila stood at the point where the incline met the ledge, her weapon raised. The shelf was at least fifty feet high and so narrow that only one person could stand on it abreast. Though Ila was diligent in her training, she was also realistic. She had two months of practice. They had years. Her best chance would be to face them individually.

They came, one after the other. The first man bore a knife. He swung, and Ila lifted her arm to meet him as she had done throughout her practices, but it became immediately clear that the block was all wrong. She was used to exerting a certain amount of force against Tulimaq. This man was heavier in the torso, taller. His blow buckled her knees.

His next strike came before Ila could rise. The blow jarred through her. She gasped in pain and aimed a kick at his kneecap.

He stumbled, and she kicked again. Ila had given herself over to instinct. There was the rising of a girl on the ground, a shoulder rammed against the man's stomach, and pain at the point of impact, and pushing through it. There was his fall, the breaking of his body on the rock below. There was strength in her heart, the knocking of something wanting to be let in. For the first time in her life, Ila understood what it meant to burn as brightly as possible. She was greedy for the feeling.

The next soldier took the place of his fallen comrade, hacking at her neck while the other two waited on the ramp. Ila ducked out of reach, keeping close to the wall.

Now that she no longer held the advantage of higher ground, the man began putting all his weight into his downward swings. The first block, Ila thought her arm would shatter from the force. The second time, she dodged, the club gouging a hole in the wall where her head had been seconds before, grit spraying.

She fought one-handed, her left pressed to her chest. Ila protected herself from his blows to the best of her abilities, but she didn't have an opening herself. He forced her back time and again, giving her no chance to retaliate.

The club arced toward her abdomen. She saw the trajectory in her mind. Ila pivoted her hips to block when the man unexpectedly dropped his club and yanked her forward. She couldn't stop the momentum. Her heart soared to a sickening height and plunged. The mistake had been made. By the time she realized what he intended to do, he had already swung her over the ledge.

Ila screamed. She must have screamed, for her mouth was open, her throat and lungs and belly filling with a terrible pressure. Her hands shot out as she dropped, catching in the tough netting of the man's clothing.

Somehow, the other soldiers had caught their comrade so he wouldn't go over the edge with her. They were the only things keeping her alive. The agony of grinding bones in her broken wrist sent a painful tremor up her arm.

In his startled state, the man had dropped his weapon. He shook her violently, trying to dislodge her grip, and the pain, the pain, the pain . . .

She didn't want to die. The likelihood of surviving such a fall was slim. She thought, *Please*. She thought, *Save me.*

The netting cut off circulation in her fingers. Her hands slipped from the uniform, barely caught on the ledge. Another cry pushed through her tightening throat. Something pulsed in the stone.

A stronger tremor coursed through her, spreading out to the tips of her fingers and toes. She went hot and cold all at once.

The soldier slammed his boot atop her broken wrist. Ila bit off a scream as that hand slipped, leaving only one gripping the rock. Had she come so far in so little time only to die in the first home she had ever known? No. What Ila needed was for the men to disappear. She needed the ledge empty so she could safely pull herself back up. Ila waited for the slam of his boot against her other hand, but it never came.

Delirious with pain, Ila looked up. The men were gone.

She swung up her leg and pulled herself back onto the ledge, peering over it. A shaky confusion took hold. The men lay broken on the ground. As if they had been pushed.

Using the wall for support, Ila descended the ramp and returned for her talq at the cave entrance. She didn't have time to wonder about the how or why of the soldiers' deaths. Taking one of the alternate exits, she found the wolf tracks not long after and followed them to another creek, swollen and lashing, and past it, to a clump of bramble. Mika had the right idea. Run, hide, disappear. Ila parted the branches and looked into Mika's huge gray-brown eyes. A ring of white showed around them.

Kindly, Ila reached out, brushed the child's soft, tear-streaked cheek with her fingertips. The girl was in shock. Her hands were chilled, her lips blue. Mika didn't try to run as Ila pulled her into a one-armed embrace.

The girl's body heaved against her, trembling. Ila squeezed her as if she could infuse warmth into Mika's skin. Small fingers curled into the fur of Ila's maq.

With the girl clutched close to her breast, she glanced around the woods. There wasn't time to take Mika to the Face Stealer's office, but she knew the area. Ila took the quickest path to the heart-tree and set Mika at its trunk, pointing up into the frail leaves, their edges silver in the moonlight. *Climb,* she said, and Mika clambered up to hide in the branches. Only her eyes were visible in the dark.

Stay, she signed.

Then she went to help her friends.

← →

The cave smelled of metal and wet stone. Apaay was overcome with cold. The frost in her chest creaked and groaned as it cloaked her ribs, her breastbone, moving upward to her throat. Then the ice broke all at once. Everything hurt.

She didn't know how long she'd lain there, eyelashes fluttering against her stinging cheeks. There were winter sounds, howling and shrieking, and they roared through the cave, interspersed with snaps and cracks of ice, Kenai's snarls as he fought the enemy. The seal Unua had run out of arrows, yet she and Kenai had all but run out of time.

He and the Face Stealer were brothers.

She still couldn't believe it.

A pebble dug into the back of her neck. *Stay awake.* She had been spoiled in the Wood, with no fear of frostbite or hypothermia. Now that they knew where the Face Stealer housed the faces, she and Kenai could make their move. Then it would be as they had planned.

A high-pitched yelp brought her closer to consciousness. Opening her eyes, Apaay peered past the mouth of the cave where the sodden gray clouds gathered. Where, in one month's time, there would be sun. "Kenai?"

An answering snarl as flesh tore.

She struggled into a sitting position. A man cried out. It sounded closer. Animal screams and human wails. She would have gone to Kenai if she had been able to move.

She hoped Ila was safe.

Ila dashed through a landscape that had turned unrecognizable. Chill, dusk, and shadow had destroyed the tranquility of Ila's home. She came across more than one animal that had perished from exposure. Ila tried not to dwell on it as her arms were bare, her lips chapped, her slippers too thin. She hadn't even a hood to protect her scalp.

Men littered the ground. Some bore bodily wounds. Others had their throats or eyes torn from teeth or talons. The more distance she covered, the forest thorns drawing blood from her arms, the more death she encountered. She needed to find *someone*.

Her answer came moments later when she stumbled upon the fighting. It was, to be precise, chaos.

They were overrun. Their group was shaped in a half dome with Tulimaq covering the front and Ro and Kaan on the flanks. The refugees took up the center, both Unua and Analak. The wave of soldiers broke upon them. They did not slow.

Tulimaq fought three soldiers at once, the blur of his staff drawing Ila's eye. A fourth arrived at his back, then a fifth as he cut two of the men down. A few heartbeats later, one opponent remained, and still Tulimaq appeared unruffled. Ila reminded herself that he was more than capable of handling his opponents alone.

Aside from the few times she and Kaan had sparred, Ila had never seen the weapons master in action. She was a song, fierce and utterly merciless as she felled men with slices to their necks, chests, and abdomens. Ro swooped overhead, whipping the lower part of his body across their opponents' faces, blinding them with the spikes wrapped around his legs. His current victim dropped onto the frosted grass and writhed, hands clamped to his bleeding eyes, or what was left of them, as a fellow soldier stood over the man's prone form and tried to bring the owl down. Ro dove beneath the coral blade and rose to safety, his gold eyes keen.

She didn't see Apaay anywhere.

The thought of her friend wounded or in pain turned her empty stomach. She hardened her heart against the possibility and steadied her shaky grip on the talq. Before courage deserted her, Ila threw herself into battle.

She had killed a man at the labor camp for survival, and this was for survival, too. There was so much death that after her third miraculous kill, Ila grew desensitized to the sights, the feel of flesh giving way beneath her talq, the blood-rust burning her nostrils and hanging like a wet cloud over the field. Ila didn't know what it meant that she no longer flinched at the butchering. Was she heartless? Hungry for power? Proud, even? Unlike Apaay, she hadn't grown up believing that all life and objects possessed a spirit, that this type of killing was both disgusting in its violence and a waste. She killed because if she did not, they would put a blade through her heart.

She and Kaan locked eyes across the way. Ro protected his sister's back by tearing those barbed spikes across the scalps of the approaching men. Skin split and blood sprayed. Kaan quickly cut another man down before giving support to the refugees' right flank where soldiers had broken through. One of the elders was slaughtered before Kaan could reach him. Ila watched it happen in shock and sadness. She wondered how close Apaay had been to him.

A prickle crawled down her spine that had nothing to do with cold. Whirling around, Ila scanned the area, seeking its source. Tulimaq, swamped by the enemy, didn't see one of the soldiers lunging for his back.

Time slowed. Ila couldn't find the strength to lift her weapon. She screamed.

Tulimaq's head snapped toward her, and he twisted, dove, crashing into the man's stomach. They went down, spattering muck and gore and their weapons cast aside. Fists shot out and made contact with the hardest and softest parts of their bodies: nose, jaw, kidney. Another seal Unua broke from the fray and charged toward her, jolting Ila out of her distraction in time to heft the weapon, the force of the blow rolling into her shoulder joint, her broken wrist held to her chest. She broke away, tripping over another body she hadn't seen. The man's blade severed the tip of her braid as she stumbled.

Their weapons clashed once more and held. Her arm trembled.

It became too much to hold. Ila dropped away from his swing. Ro, as if sensing her diminishing strength, dove for her opponent and tore open the man's scalp. Ila then cut him down.

Heaving against the frosty air, Ila startled as a hand clasped her arm. She whirled and would have shoved the antler blade into her captor's neck before realizing it was Tulimaq, his eyebrows raised as the weapon halted a hairsbreadth from his throat.

He touched her wrist, lowered it. They stared at one another long enough for Ila to grow uncomfortable. *What?* she asked, but more so with her expression, since it was too painful to sign. They were some yards away from the worst of the fighting. Still no Apaay.

His attention dropped to her broken wrist. Ila shrugged to say she was fine.

"Here." He slipped off his parka and passed it to her, waiting until she pulled it on before handing back her weapon. "Remember to keep your wrist locked." Then he hopped back into the fray.

Ila watched the combat master for a moment before studying what remained of the fighting. They had done considerably well. The tide had turned in their favor, and the enemy continued to fall. An arrow to the chest knocked a soldier to the ground. One of the refugees had done the deed.

When she looked closer, she realized with surprise it had been Apaay's younger sister, Eska. In terms of facial features, there wasn't much similarity to the siblings, but the stubborn set to Eska's mouth was the same.

The girl swiped the hair from her face, smearing mud in the process as she approached. "Have you seen Apaay?"

Ila shook her head. It was too dangerous a distraction right now, and even though she knew the most important thing was to quell the fighting, her heart lay elsewhere.

A pale flutter drew her eye upward. Ro swooped low and hovered a few feet ahead, looking back over his shoulder. She and Apaay's little sister exchanged a look of confusion.

"I think he wants us to follow him," Eska said.

Together, they leapt over fallen bodies and hurried through the trees, too exhausted to travel faster than a slow jog. Ila wiped the sweat from her cooling brow and tried to keep up with Ro flying ahead.

When they finally reached another group of soldiers beyond the now-defunct barrier, Ila was near collapse. Only five figures remained standing, and all were men save one. A gray wolf had its jaws latched around one of the soldier's arms, its grip so strong she imagined bone crunching between its jaws. Then it went for the man's throat. The body had yet to hit the ground when a second soldier charged. The wolf stumbled off, waiting a moment as its hot breath steamed the air, before taking the man down.

Eventually, the wolf turned toward her. Something unstable flickered in those glowing eyes, like a flame burning too hot for too long. Ila let loose a cry and rushed forward, weapon raised. She had nearly reached the wolf when Ro dove between them, flaring out his wings to bring her to a halt.

She tried again, and again Ro blocked her path.

Eska touched her arm. "I don't think the wolf is an enemy."

Ila peered closer. Three heartbeats passed before the words pierced her adrenaline-induced state. Gore stuck to its shining white fangs, though it made no move to attack them. It was a beautiful creature. The spark of intelligence in its eyes identified it as wolf Unua. Which of the refugees, she wondered, had come to their aid?

Ro directed them to the mouth of the cave. It was there they found Apaay's body.

Eska screamed, dropping to her knees. Ila stared in shock, the breath having stopped cold in her chest. Apaay's head lolled to the side. Blood coated the girl's shoulder and abdomen.

Reaching out with trembling fingers, Ila held them over Apaay's partially open mouth. She heaved a gasp, and it was as if all the bones in her body went liquid and soft as faint heat prickled against her skin.

Apaay was alive.

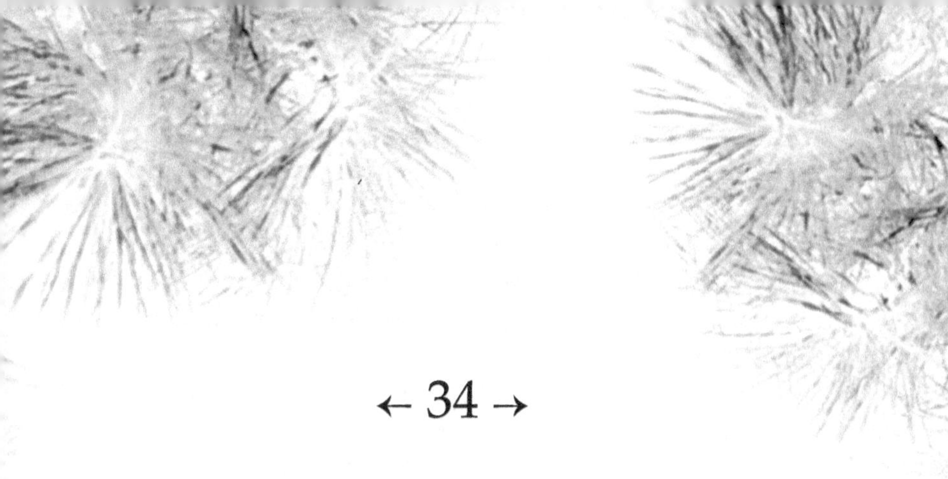

← 34 →

Ila had been to the infirmary once before, after she had sprained her ankle during sparring practice. From the outside, it looked like a squat toadstool, its roof the grassy bulb of the hill. The inside had been carved out, and one long pane of glass curved around its front, tossing sunlight back into her face.

The dead had been many. Near two hundred of the refugees had lost their lives, and too many animals to count. The seal Unua had carried horrible weapons that cleaved limbs from torso, head from neck. In some places, blood had soaked the soil so completely she'd felt the squelch beneath her boots.

With the enemy dead and the protective barrier restored, Ila had come to clear the air. As soon as she'd seen her friend passed out in the cave, her heart had pulled. Apaay had been wearing furs dressed for cold, waterproof boots. Which was to say, she'd been prepared.

Ila was ready to give her any excuse. Apaay had been captured. Taken. Someone had betrayed them and tried to steal her away to that horrible labor camp, and would have had she not fought back. They had told her to dress warmly, for it would be a long journey. They had forced her from the Wood's protection.

Ila paused at the door. Blood and dirt smeared her skin in the adjacent window's reflection. She stared at that girl, at the one who had taken up a weapon in their time of need, and wiped at one of her cheeks. Her hand lingered, the wrist now whole and unbroken, thanks to Kaan. She looked strong. At the right angle, intimidating. Ila didn't care for intimidation. As for strength, she looked strong because she *was* strong. She, Ila, was strong.

Turning away, Ila pushed open the door, unable to avoid this meeting any longer.

A carpet of leaves littered the floor. Warm light the color of boiled fat poured through the glass panes. Cots were arranged in a line against the back wall and attached by thick roots hanging from the ceiling. In total, the wounded occupied sixteen of the twenty-five cots. Apaay, the only person awake, occupied the cot at the end of the room and watched Ila approach. Her eyes were wary, her skin ashen. When did one decide enough was enough? Apparently when it had almost been too late.

Did you leave the Wood after I told you not to? she demanded upon reaching Apaay's bedside.

Apaay looked at her solemnly, a blanket covering her legs. She turned an arrowhead over in her hands.

Well? Ila snapped.

Apaay dipped her chin. "I did."

The constriction in her throat felt foreign. She had never harbored this much anger toward one person before. Ila didn't know what infuriated her more: that Apaay had gone against Ila's word, knowing full well what would happen if she left the Wood unprotected, or that she didn't seem to care.

With a hiss, Ila snatched the arrowhead from Apaay's fingers. *What is wrong with you? Are you trying to get everyone killed?*

Apaay crossed her arms in a jerky motion. "Obviously not."

Then why? What were you trying to prove?

More silence.

The only reason Ila didn't scream in frustration was because she didn't want to wake the other patients. How was it possible to love someone and want to bash their head against the wall at the same time? Ila blamed Kaan. The woman's bloodthirsty tendencies were rubbing off on her. *If I told you leaving the Wood was a bad idea, don't you think I had good reason to say so? Do you even care about the repercussions?*

"Of course I care," Apaay snapped. "Don't you dare assume I don't. I never would have done this if I didn't care."

About who? Your family? Because it seemed like the only person you cared about was yourself. Apaay's gaze flickered. *Maybe you didn't notice because you were unconscious, but the barrier disintegrated. Seal Unua breached the Wood. You led those people right to us!* Her pulse beat hard in her neck as she remembered the reason for Apaay's disappearance. *Where is it? Where's the map?*

Apaay went still. Her hands curled into the blanket. Eventually, she pulled it from her pocket, her mouth drawn. "I thought we were protected outside the Wood, but there was a misunderstanding. I'm sorry—"

Ila snatched it from her. *Stop lying. Stop saying you're sorry when you're not. What you did was selfish, Apaay. You put your own needs above everyone else's, and as consequence, you nearly ruined everything.* She waved the arrowhead in Apaay's face, and Apaay pressed back against the pillow with a guarded look. Well, good. Maybe she liked intimidation after all.

Now that Ila's anger had been set free, she couldn't call it back. It had been simmering long before, deep inside where the hurt lay, the abandonment. Did Ila no longer mean anything to Apaay? That's what it felt like. *I honestly can't believe you drugged the Face Stealer. He's the only one who's keeping us safe from Yuki and Nanuq, and you basically gave away our location.*

Emotion flashed in Apaay's gaze. Guilt? "Ila, no offense, but you know nothing about the Face Stealer. So what, now that he feeds you and gives you a bed to sleep on, suddenly he's innocent of his deeds? Have you forgotten who he is?"

She wouldn't let Apaay pin the consequences of her choices on someone else, especially when Ila saw the demon's underlying motives to be good. *I haven't forgotten. I've just chosen to move past it. Maybe it's time you did as well.*

Apaay blinked rapidly, her eyes shiny. She dropped her gaze and switched to sign language. *You're wrong, saying I put my own needs above everyone else's. I did this for Masuk.*

That was the danger of resentment. *This is the last time,* it crooned. *The very last time.* Until it happened again. The next time, fury was a sharper point. The promises became empty. Everything was full of holes.

The pain felt like she had opened a vein inside herself. *So you'll listen to Masuk,* she said in disbelief, *but not me?* Ila's hands trembled violently. *Is he so much better of a friend than I am?*

Apaay tipped her head back and rubbed her eyes with the heels of her palms. If Ila had been feeling kinder, she may have suggested they finish the conversation at a later time. Unfortunately, she was feeling the opposite of kind. She was feeling downright savage.

Her anger hadn't one source. It went back to the labyrinth, and before that, to the time of her birth. The terror she'd experienced at believing her friend to be dead. How alone she'd felt these past months. Confusion over where she'd come from, who she was. Even though Ila hadn't experienced Apaay's trials, it didn't mean she couldn't feel as deeply. Ila had a heart, a big one, and she had dreams, and her hands knew how to make fists out of anger. After the adrenaline of a life or death situation, Ila was short on understanding.

It has nothing to do with friendship, Apaay said. *This was something he needed, Ila. This was something I needed, too.*

But you don't need me, is that it? Ila stood there, not knowing what to do or how to make sense of this change. It would be easier if she didn't put faith where it clearly didn't belong.

Masuk and I understand each other because we both know what it means to lose everything.

And I don't?

Apaay lifted her chin, her eyes full of sorrow. *How can you lose everything if you had nothing to begin with?*

The words cut swiftly, as did the eruption of pain. Ila sucked in a sharp breath. She could not believe these words were coming out of Apaay's mouth. The girl she knew, the one who had protected her and fought for her, was gone. She could barely steady her hands long enough to sign, *Who are you?* Tears spilled down her cheeks. *What happened to my friend?*

Because she didn't know.

She just didn't know.

← →

Apaay lay curled on her side facing the wall, Ila having slammed the door closed minutes before, when she heard it open again, then click softly shut. She held her breath, listening. These footsteps were decidedly more deadly. Awareness crackled through her limbs.

Leaves rustled beneath the light tread. Apaay tightened her arms against her chest, refusing to turn around as shadowy power drifted over her. She had barely survived Ila's ire. This would be far worse.

"What the *hell*," said the voice, slow and cool in her ear, "were you thinking?"

The sensation was like a knife to the spine, jolting her upright. "Get out of my face," she growled.

The Face Stealer studied her from above in blunt assessment, as if Apaay was still a puzzle he could not solve. Unlike Ila, there was no sign of the battle on him, though his eyes were glassy, a side effect of the moonflower.

"Touchy." A twisted form of pleasure unfolded along his mouth as he leaned a few inches closer. Her heart rate increased, though from spite or his nearness she couldn't say. Abruptly, he leaned back, a glass of water in hand from where he had reached for it on the bedside table. He took a sip, his gaze never leaving her face.

The man was still too close. "If you know what's good for you—"

His smile turned downright feral. "Wolfling." He might have stopped there. He said so much in so few words. "I believe I already told you I *don't* know what's good for me." A vague tilt of his head. She wondered what he saw when he looked at her. "You are, of course, welcome to change my mind." The way his gaze roved over her made the direction of his thoughts perfectly clear.

Apaay bit the inside of her cheek to avoid spitting at him. "Your arrogance has risen to a level I cannot even fathom."

"I'm not here to talk about my arrogance." He set down the glass with a snap and settled on the edge of her mattress. On the other side of the room, the patients snored softly. "I'm here to talk about yours."

He wanted to play this game? Fine.

"You're going to have to be a little more specific," she enunciated. Though having been tended to and dressed in clean clothes, Apaay was tired and sore from the healing. Not in any mood to be flayed by his cunning tongue.

The tightness in his face took on a punishing quality. Apaay prepared herself for retaliation. Whatever the strike, she would not take it on her knees.

He leaned back to look at her. Propped his ankle on his thigh. His arms were bare, shadowed by the hanging roots. "Perhaps in your hazed state of the last four months, you have forgotten what I told you, so I will repeat myself. After all, one of us has to keep track of our comings and goings."

Oh, he was so good at making her feel the fool. She wanted to slap the condescension from his mouth.

"Believe it or not, the rules set in place are not because of you. They are for the protection of all who seek the Wood." Light sliced a line across the bridge of his nose. "Do you know how long it has taken me to ensure this place remains safe? Because of your recklessness, the Wood is now forfeit."

Her throat bobbed in a sign of uncertainty. *It's not my fault,* she wanted to say, but it was. She had trusted Masuk to take the necessary precautions, and his lies combined with her recklessness had resulted in death and a broken haven. Apaay had always been driven by emotion, not logic or rationality. When the emotion became too large to contain, it spilled over, and she acted. It was who she'd always been. This time, the consequences had been too dire.

She had risked a lot to aid Masuk. To look at someone and not flinch away—he had done that for her, and she to him. Even when she had been little more than an animal in Yuki's labyrinth, he'd seen her. It was one of the reasons why she'd trusted him in the first place. For a young woman who had spent her life fighting to be noticed, it was more than loyalty. It was everything. Yet he'd managed to manipulate her into doing him this favor, taken advantage of her vulnerable state. She didn't want the Face Stealer to know how unsure she was about everything. He'd had power over her for far too long. "You're saying a human girl was able to break your defenses so easily? I'm unimpressed." She was happy to note her voice didn't wobble.

"You're unimpressed? That's all you have to say? Not that our refuge was discovered? Not that you're sorry you drew the soldiers here?"

"Were not the soldiers all killed? If there were no survivors, no one can reveal its location."

"I don't know if there were survivors because I was *unconscious.* If I hadn't been, the barrier would not have fallen." His nostrils flared. Light flamed the dead leaves on the floor, turning brown into gold. "Where did you go?" he demanded.

Oh, he was not happy about that. "As if I would tell you." If the demon found out she and Masuk had gone to the First Man, he might make the connection to what she sought. If he moved the faces, they would never find them. And she still wanted to leave, go to the Banished Lands, right?

"Leaving the Wood with Masuk unprotected? You don't know who he is. You know nothing about him."

Apaay couldn't stop the flinch, damn him. "You're just mad because I beat you at your own game." Power. The instant he'd drunk the tea, it had become hers.

The Face Stealer plucked a flower from a vine trailing down the wall, crushing it in his fist. The sweet scent of the blossom permeated the air. "It was a thoughtless decision."

"No," she hissed, because Apaay wanted to make sure there was no misunderstanding between them, that she was, and always had been, absolutely clear in her intentions. "I *was* thinking. I was thinking I would do anything to set things right. I was thinking you locked this poor man away, stole the face of a woman he loved. I was thinking he was alone and had no one, not one person who would help him." She broke off, afraid that he would see the lies interwoven with the truth. Her fury was in part inflamed by the shame of causing such harm, and of this new mistrust she harbored toward the Face Stealer's brother. What did it mean that the Face Stealer's reasoning was beginning to make sense, disrupting these beliefs she had tended for months? It frightened her more than anything. Thus, Apaay returned to what was familiar: loathing him, scorn for his actions and the pain they had caused her. If she focused on these things, it was easier to believe he was all dark, not simply misunderstood as she was coming to learn. "My intention has always been to help Masuk. I told you I did not forgive you. Did you think my mind was changed because you *acted* nice to me?"

In his silence, she saw he had considered the possibility. "My mistake, it would seem."

Apaay sent him a close-lipped smile. She could be cruel, too, when it served her purposes. "Yes. It was."

He lifted his hands to his face. "I need you to tell me where you went," he said, voice muffled behind his fingers. "The battle is over, but without more information from you, we're at a disadvantage if by chance the seal Unua return."

"Here's an idea: Why not *move* the Wood? Then it won't matter if they return because we'll be somewhere else."

He sighed and dropped his hands. The mattress shifted as he turned toward her, the heat of his thigh radiating against her leg. Apaay considered inching away but thought that would bring attention to his nearness. "Once again, you assume my power can *fix* things. It can't. Theoretically, yes, I can move the Wood, but it wouldn't happen anytime soon, and it requires too much power that I don't have right now."

"So you admit you're not all-powerful."

He didn't take the bait. "In order to access the amount of power required to create something as large and complex as the Wood, it's not enough for me to use what I have in reserve. I'd need to go to the source. I'd need to open a doorway to Taggak and it would have to be in the location I want to move the Wood to. Everything in this world is tied to something else. My power is no different."

Startlingly, it paralleled her own beliefs. The collective understanding that names acted as a thread between generations, or how the spirit of a felled animal might be reborn in another. The ways of her people and the North were vast, but there was an intimacy to its parts. Connection.

"Remember when I said I couldn't remove the arrow from your arm with my power? The same principle applies to the Wood. The refugees are not made from my power, so if I were to move the Wood, they would not move with it. They would have to physically travel to the new location." He tapped a finger on his knee. "No more avoidance. Tell me where you went."

"If you want to know," Apaay said, leaning back against her pillow, "why not ask Masuk?" She watched him carefully as she added, "After all, he is your brother."

It was as if Apaay were once again drowning in his memory. Emotion flitted across his face. Pain and fury, resentment and hurt, guilt and loss. It was there, after all this time, and fresh. "How do you know that?" His lips barely moved.

"How do you think?" she said, unaware of her voice dropping to match the level of his. "He told me."

"He told you." Hoarse laughter followed.

"You said he was dead."

"To me, he is." It was spoken simply, without remorse. For some reason, Apaay found that terribly sad.

The Face Stealer was slow to stand. Apaay didn't realize he intended to leave until he was halfway to the door.

"Why did you do it?" she demanded to his back, scrambling out of bed. "He's your brother, and you caged him, left him to die. You took from him the most precious thing he had."

"More precious than loyalty? More precious than family?" He stopped in front of the door, hands in the pockets of his trousers. "He is the reason our people are gone." The planes of his face turned severe and unforgiving. "What did he tell you?"

Too much, but she wasn't fool enough to think it was everything. Apaay didn't want the Face Stealer thinking she and Masuk were anything but loyal, trusting friends, otherwise it would weaken her position. "That's not how this is going to work. You will tell me your side of the story, and I will see if it aligns." If it didn't, one of them was lying. She couldn't trust either of them. Masuk—Kenai—had claimed everything had started and ended with his brother, so she would hear it from the beginning.

The Face Stealer rubbed a hand against his forehead. His eyes were very dark, like puddles of oil. "You want to hear about my childhood? I assure you, it's not important enough to warrant remembering."

Moving to where she could view him in profile, Apaay leaned one shoulder against the glass. "I'll be the judge of that."

With a weary sigh, the Face Stealer said, "Very well," and stared through the window, looking out at the brown earth. "The first thing you should know is this: I killed our mother."

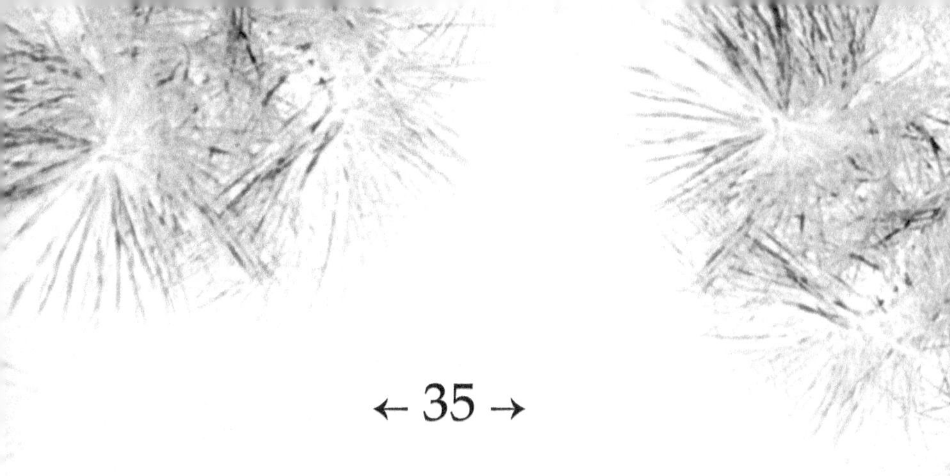

← 35 →

"How did I do it?" he wondered aloud. "Suffocation? Did I slit her throat in sleep? Poison, perhaps?" With a flat expression, he looked into Apaay's face. "She died in childbirth. I never did get a chance to meet her."

Oh. So he hadn't done it on purpose. Hadn't done it at all. His mother must not have recovered from the delivery. It wasn't an uncommon occurrence.

"Go on," he whispered, his eyes like pits. "Tell me how you thought differently. Tell me how you believed I murdered my own mother."

It was probably safer to say nothing, considering his power twitched in agitation. He turned back to the window.

"It was a difficult birth, as I'm sure you can guess. She did not survive the night."

Apaay fought against a surge of compassion. Losing one's mother was a terrible thing. She didn't quite succeed.

"After her passing, my father changed. My mother was the one thing he loved, and I took her from him. In his grief, he withdrew. The times he was home, I made sure to never look him in the eye or touch him in affection. I had learned my lesson after he took a whip to my back."

Apaay didn't want to ask, but she would hate herself if she didn't. "How old?"

"I was seven."

She closed her eyes and said nothing.

The longer the Face Stealer spoke, the more tension wound through him. Apaay wanted to see his hands, whether they were in his pockets or free, clenched or rigid like claws, but that would mean missing the emotion that freely passed over his face.

"I always wondered what kind of man could do that to his own son." It was spoken in a hushed tone, as if he asked the question to himself and had forgotten she stood beside him.

With a deep breath, he continued. "Due to my father's unpredictable nature, the responsibility of raising me fell to my siblings. As I grew older, I began to understand why my father pretended I did not exist. People always said I took after my mother, but since I didn't know what she looked like, I didn't have an opinion on the matter. There weren't paintings of our mother at home. Our father had tossed them into the river. But Sita had kept one hidden, which I found one day. It was true that she and Kenai took after our father, but me . . . I looked like her." Softer: "I looked like her son."

Apaay asked, "Did your siblings ever try to stop your father from hurting you?"

"What could they do? They were children themselves." The press of his hand to the glass left behind an imprint. He stared at the smudge. "The year I turned twelve was a difficult one. Sita went to live with the Owl Clan as an apprentice. During that time, Kenai became my father, my mother. Even now, when I try to remember my father's face, I can't. The only one I see is my brother's."

He trailed off. Apaay tried not to look at him, but she was compelled. His irises were the clear blush of a burgeoning dawn, the outer rims flecked with gold. They held little warmth.

"With the absence of my sister, I grew much closer to my brother. At eighteen, he was granted a spot in the Pack. I remember that day. It ended with our father punching a hole through the wall, a black eye for Kenai, and a broken arm for me."

Apaay was bracing herself for the next phase of the story when one of the patients murmured in his sleep. They both turned, watching him twitch beneath the blankets. A nasty gash had left blood crusted on the side of his skull. The man rolled to the edge of the bed and began to thrash.

The Face Stealer went to the man's side and grabbed his hand so he would stop flailing. He shushed the man under his breath until he settled, and Apaay fought to hold the nausea at bay. This man could have died because of her. Many had. How had everything gone so wrong?

Apaay followed the Face Stealer's movements as he returned to the window. A moment of silence ebbed before he continued. "As the years passed, Kenai and I drifted apart. He never told me directly, but I know it burdened him to care for me on his own." He was still, like the dead trees. "I can't imagine you know what it is like, to love and hate someone in the same breath, to know that whatever they used to feel for you was tainted by obligation." He turned to her in sudden interest. "Do you know what that's like?"

Apaay answered him with a murmured, "No."

He returned his attention to the landscape. "Years later, I joined the Pack in an attempt to reconcile with him, but Kenai wouldn't acknowledge me, even when we were placed in the same unit. He began disappearing for long lengths of time. He was angry, hateful." The Face Stealer shifted back onto his heels, his hands in his pockets. They bulged beneath the material, having gathered into fists. "What I didn't know was that Kenai wanted war. He saw a lack of order, believed the North belonged to man. If I had known, maybe I could have stopped him."

Apaay's earlier ire had subsided with the end of his tale. She tried to process what he'd told her.

"It's quite fitting, isn't it?" he murmured. "My own father thought I was a monster. So I became what he wanted me to be."

The sun glinted beyond the trees. When he turned to her, Apaay continued staring out the window. "That is what my brother told you, is it not?" The twist of his mouth told her he knew Kenai had done no such thing.

Why had he, then? Was it to make her feel for the boy he had been? If so, he had succeeded.

"Why won't you look at me?" he said.

She ignored the twinge in her stomach and kept her eyes on the horizon. "You're not that interesting to look at."

Catching her chin, he tilted her face toward him, and Apaay allowed it. His heavy-lidded gaze searched hers for a long moment. "You're getting better at lying," he said, the low notes of his voice vibrating through his fingertips, "but you'll never be as good as me." He dropped his hand. "Perhaps you are realizing your opinion of me no longer stands as it once did. Does that frighten you?"

He had given her his truths. Apaay supposed she could give him one of hers. "Yes."

Judging by his surprise, he hadn't expected her to admit that. "There are reasons for the things I do, Apaay. I'm fighting for what is good here."

"So am I."

"Are you sure? Are you absolutely certain helping Kenai is for good? Because I would think long and hard on what kind of person he is. What you know is only a fraction of our history, and Kenai has the benefit of your good faith, while I have the disadvantage of your loathing."

She was readying herself to answer when heat seared the pocket of her trousers. With a gasp, Apaay reached for the stone there, dropping it on the floor when the heat grew too intense. The rock glowed red around the edges.

"Chena's in labor." She raced for the door, then stopped, whirled around. "I need to go to her. Kaan can come with me so I'm not alone."

The Face Stealer had every reason to deny her. She had left the Wood without protection, had risked all their lives.

"Kaan is on her way to the Owl Clan," he said. "I will go."

← →

The birthing chamber reeked of body odor and fear. Not even the fire could mask the scent. As Apaay crawled farther into the room, she spotted Chena reclining against a pile of furs, a thin blanket covering her bent knees. The space was large enough to fit four people, a small hearth, and supplies: buckets of boiled water, thinner blankets for cleaning, needles whittled of bone. Kia, Chena's sister-in-law, pressed a cloth to the girl's glistening forehead. The woman's hair was loose, the laces of her boots undone, for any knots or ties could lead to the umbilical cord wrapping around the baby's neck.

The village midwife, her hair loose as well, knelt before Chena and told her to breathe, breathe, that's it, just like that, as another contraction gripped her, an exhalation cracking from her mouth. Her face, red and wrinkled like a berry left too long in the sun, spasmed as the pain ripped her apart, her shriek powerful enough to shatter ice.

"I'm here," Apaay whispered, gripping Chena's hand after settling at her side. She swiped the damp strands from Chena's face as her friend gulped for air, her glazed eyes resting on Apaay in confusion. Apaay did not think the tears were simply from pain. It was the frightened look of a girl whose world was about to change forever.

"Apaay?" Trembling breath. She stiffened and braced for another contraction.

"Don't talk." Apaay kept her tone steady. There was enough terror in the room without adding hers to the mix. "Hold my hand and breathe."

The hours were long and the labor was difficult. The lamps drove away the invading dark. Apaay had assisted in enough births to recognize the signs. There was too much strain in Chena's body, and it didn't look as if the baby had dropped yet. At one point, the midwife helped Chena into a squat, bracing a hand on her back to keep her hips and spine aligned. Close to two hours were spent in the squatting position. When Chena grew too weak to hold herself up, they returned her to lying on her back.

Apaay remained quiet, offering encouragement when she could. The heat of the chamber slowed her thoughts and pressed sticky hands to her skin. She sensed the passing time like a knife point against her throat, for the baby was a month early. If it was breech, they would have to turn it. When the midwife ran out of cloth, Apaay left to gather more, relieved to escape the stifling heat.

The eighth hour came and went, as did the ninth, the tenth. Chena sobbed freely, her only reprieve the brief moments following her contractions when she trembled, on the brink of exhaustion. The contractions had begun to occur in closer increments, fierce waves that did not relent no matter how Chena begged.

"Remember when we were little," Chena gritted out at one point, her face so flushed with blood it looked bruised, "and your mother used to tell us to go outside quickly when we woke up, not to stand in the doorway—" She broke off, her gasp ringing in Apaay's ears. "Because that meant the baby's head would get stuck when we gave birth. We used to laugh about it." Her breathing came more quickly. "What if the baby's head gets stuck?"

"It won't," Apaay vowed. "Don't think like that." It was known that putting stress on expecting mothers would affect the baby negatively. Chena didn't need additional worries. "Everything will be fine."

"I wish Silla was here," she whispered as Kia left to feed her son. "I think about how patient he was, how calm. He would have been a wonderful father." The last word had no more substance than a huff of air.

Apaay dipped a cloth into a bowl of cool water and passed it along the side of Chena's face. She was ashamed to realize she had forgotten what Silla looked like. She remembered his steadfast nature, his complete adoration of her friend, but his features blurred in her mind. All things faded with enough time. "Can you imagine him telling one of those ridiculous stories?"

A wheezing laugh chased the wail as Chena braced for another contraction.

"You're beginning to crown," said the midwife, peering under the blanket.

Chena shook her head, flinging sweat. "No. I'm not ready." She tried closing her legs, but the midwife's shoulders prevented her from doing so. "I can't have this baby without Silla here. He—he promised me we would raise the child together." Her voice broke. Chena's chin sagged against her chest as the fight went out of her. "Please. Put it back."

"The baby needs to come out," said the midwife, not unkindly.

"I need more time."

Apaay touched the woman's shoulder. "Give us a minute."

The woman did not look pleased, and Apaay suspected she only left because Chena was starting to slide into hysterics. Once the midwife had gone, Apaay lifted the brown-black hair streaking her friend's neck and cooled the area with water. "I miss him," whispered Chena. "Sometimes I miss him so much I can't breathe." Tears fell, and she went on, the words garbled. "I don't know what I'm doing. I don't know how I'm going to raise this child without him."

Apaay's throat squeezed, and she wrapped her hand around it, chasing the ghost of that feeling. This is what it meant to be vulnerable, to not turn away in fear. She had not given her friend this grace in all the weeks she'd spent avoiding Chena in the Wood. She was giving it to her now.

"Look at me, Chena." As gently as possible, Apaay wiped the tears and fluid coating Chena's face. "You have every right to be afraid, but you're not alone. Silla will watch over you and keep you both safe. He knows how wonderful of a mother you'll be. How you'll give your child a beautiful life."

The girl sagged deeper into the blankets. "You can't know that, Apaay."

"I do, Chena." Lifting their intertwined fingers, she pressed her friend's hand to her cheek. "I assure you, I do."

Their friendship was their memories and trials, their hopes and secrets and dreams. It was this night, and it was the next night and the next, and it was the morning that would soon come.

The midwife returned to peek beneath the blanket. "I need you to give me one big push. Can you do that?"

With her hand gripped in Apaay's, Chena nodded.

"All right. Push hard."

Chena squeezed Apaay's hand so tightly her fingers bulged purple. Apaay kept her gaze on the midwife for signs of worry. However many healthy babies and mothers there were, there were those who didn't make it, and often the signs were too subtle to notice.

"Good girl. Push again."

Soon, the contractions were so severe they stole Chena's speech. A wild ferociousness overcame her as at last her child entered this world with a fierce cry.

"Oh!" The woman crowed a laugh. "She's a vocal one."

Chena slumped against the pillows, her eyes fluttering. "I have a daughter?" Her face was bloodless.

"How do you feel?" asked Apaay. She didn't like how cool Chena's hands were. "Dizzy?"

She shook her head. "Tired."

The midwife wiped mucus from the child's mouth and spoke to her in a soothing voice, bestowing favorable qualities onto the baby, the skills she would need to grow into an excellent seamstress, a woman of strength. A soft hat of caribou skin went over the child's head to keep it warm. Then the midwife said, "Come meet your daughter," and Chena laughed as the woman settled the tiny, wrinkled girl into her arms. Wisps of black hair poked from under the hat.

With the child nestled safely, Chena gazed down at the bundle of healthy brown skin. "My daughter," she whispered in awe.

Apaay said hoarsely, "Chena, she's beautiful."

"She is, isn't she?" Chena couldn't stop staring. "I love you," she whispered through her tears, rubbing the tip of her nose across her daughter's soft cheek. "I don't know you, but I love you."

The child began to suckle, one hand curled. They watched this in wonder. Suddenly the birthing chamber did not feel so suffocating. It felt close. Womb-like. The baby's mouth pulled free with a wet pop, and a shriek breached the silence. A sound of life, of coming awake. It echoed in Apaay's chest.

"Can I hold her?" Apaay croaked, failing to smooth the quaver in her voice. It was a person. The tiniest, most fragile thing. "Please?"

With a weary smile, Chena passed her daughter into Apaay's arms.

The baby blinked owlish eyes, her mouth small and tender. Apaay traced a finger down the girl's cheek and felt the tears rise, felt a shift deep inside as she stared down at the daughter of her oldest friend. She couldn't fight the emotion, huge and overwhelming, as it broke over her. She'd thought she would never find her way back to herself, never touch what she reached for: proof that she was healing, or a sign, or *something* that told her things would be all right, maybe not now, but somewhere on the horizon. And here, now, with her dear friend, this miracle . . . She wept with the child in her arms. A daughter born in winter, but whose mother was an invincible summer.

The night is long, but the sun will soon greet you.

She had lost hope in her heart. The days had been long, but the nights had been eternity. Yet she saw it now: the sun in the fog of her soul. It felt like grace had finally been given to her. It felt, impossibly, like coming home.

For the longest time, she had seen only endings. But what about beginnings? What if instead of mourning old lives, she could celebrate new ones?

"Apaay." Chena squeezed her fingers in concern. "What is it? What's wrong?"

Apaay shook her head with a watery laugh. "Nothing." She wiped her face. The breath shuddered in her chest. "I think everything's going to be all right." She nearly broke down again and skimmed a finger pad across the child's cheek. "It's going to be all right," she murmured.

Maybe she wasn't the same person she had been, and maybe it had taken time to accept that, but this birth had reminded Apaay that she had so much love to fill her life if she chose to let it in. She would water her life with that love and never allow it to wither again.

With one last kiss, Apaay passed Chena's daughter back. "Make sure her ear is pressed to your skin," she said with affection. "You don't want her getting earaches."

Chena looked down, her face streaked with sweat, but overflowing with complete adoration. In the coming days, she, Muktuk, and his wife would decide the baby's name-soul. "I can feel her heart beating," she whispered, three fingers pressed against her daughter's narrow chest.

A nudge in the back of Apaay's mind gave her pause. "What did you say?"

"Her little heartbeat." Chena drew Apaay's hand to where the flutter thrummed against the delicate skin. "Do you feel it?" She was smiling.

Apaay was quiet in her heart, quiet in her soul. She was watching flint strike, sparks scatter, flames erupt. She stared at the baby's chest, the shallow rise and fall.

Who am I but a heartless demon?

The words, spoken long ago after Apaay had asked the Face Stealer for a favor in the labyrinth. She hadn't thought anything of it at the time, because she had agreed he was cold-blooded and cruel. But the word *heartless* could also mean something else: one without a heart.

What was he always saying? He was very hard to kill. When they'd been attacked in the Central Territory, an arrow had hit the left side of his chest. He hadn't died.

You know I only ever have your best interests at heart. Irony in his voice.

And then:

How much is a demon's heart worth, after all?

How much indeed.

Dazed, Apaay snatched back her hand as if burned. It couldn't possibly be true. "I'll be right back."

Chena was so enamored with her daughter she didn't notice her leave.

Outside, the camp busied itself with daily tasks. Apparently, one of the tree platforms had rotted and was in need of repair. She found the Face Stealer at the site of construction, tying two planks of wood together.

"Come to keep me company, wolfling?" He bent closer to study his handiwork.

Apaay stared at the top of his head. His hood had been pushed back, revealing the simple tail with its single braid of blue beads. "I need to speak with you. Alone."

He peered up at her. The land was shadowed green and blue, yet red flared in the spaces where the fires burned. "Was there a complication with the birth?"

"Chena and the baby are healthy. It's something else."

With vague curiosity, he brushed the snow from his trousers and led her to one of the meeting houses. At the moment, it appeared to be used for food storage. Buckets of roots, nuts, and dried berries had dwindled over the course of the long night. They would have collected these in the summer months.

As there was only one lit lamp, it was quite dim. "Take off your parka," Apaay said.

An eerie stillness passed over him. Apaay realized how that sounded, considering she had drawn him away into an empty snow house without explanation. If even a hint of flush touched her face, she would toss herself off the nearest tree, and she wouldn't be sorry about it.

All at once, his body relaxed. "Really, this is hardly the time—"

"Oh, shut it, will you?" She yanked both layers over his head as if he were no more competent than a three-year-old. He stood half naked before her, and Apaay's mouth went a little dry at the expanse of brown skin.

Well, it had been overly warm in the birthing chamber, and she was dehydrated. Probably.

Apaay searched his gaze. Something about his face was different. A clarity in the bones, maybe, or eyes that were less cruel. Did he know? she wondered. Did he know that *she* knew?

Without taking her eyes from his, she said, "I lied to you about what I saw in your memory. I told you I watched Yuki torture you that day in the forest, but that wasn't entirely true."

An animal instinct sharpened in him, and a small furrow appeared between his black brows. "What do you mean?"

"I mean I *was* you. Everything I saw, everything I felt . . . I was watching everything unfold from your eyes."

The tilt of his chin suggested fascination. "Could you hear my thoughts? Did you know what I was feeling?"

"Yes. There was a moment right before I woke in the library when I felt like I was dying. I thought Yuki had stabbed you. The pain in my—your—chest was the worst pain I had ever felt. For a while, I was confused as to how you were still alive if she had killed you. You may have an abnormally long lifespan, but you can still die, right?"

He nodded, his face unreadable.

"But you didn't die, did you?"

The silence stretched. He was waiting for her to continue.

With only the smallest hesitation, Apaay pressed her palm to the Face Stealer's chest.

He sucked in a startled breath, held it. Apaay recognized what was missing. For though the heat of his skin lit fires beneath her palm, the cavity of his chest was as hollow as the innards of a drum.

"She stole your heart," Apaay whispered in awe and disbelief. "Yuki stole your heart."

It almost felt as if the memory of his heart thudded through her palm in a quickening tempo. The slow burn of amusement warmed his features. His eyes were suddenly all the colors of the world before settling into a new shade: rich earth brown.

"You brave, brilliant, clever girl," Numiak managed through his laughter, briefly cupping her face. The grin was so open, so elated, Apaay didn't know what to do but stare. A dimple winked in his cheek that she swore hadn't been there previously. "You figured it out."

Rolling her eyes, Apaay stepped back, forcing him to drop his hands. "How could I not when you were so *helpful* about it?"

His attention moved to her cheeks, the place where his hands had rested, and the longer he stared at them, the redder they grew. "I know. I'm sorry. I wish it didn't have to be this way. When Yuki stole my heart, she cursed me so I wouldn't be able to tell anyone the details of that day."

"Does that mean the blood oath is broken?" she asked, more than a little hopeful.

He shook his head and slipped on his clothes. "Your task isn't fulfilled until you retrieve it for me."

She thought of the labyrinth, with its many changing rooms and false walls. "Is it in the in-between?" Apaay wasn't sure if she could return to the hell that had broken her.

His features were grave. "I'm afraid, wolfling, the place we'll be going to is far worse."

← 36 →

Hours later, Ila found herself at the blue basin where the creek emptied out. Broad leaves the size of birds pressed shade onto the water. After leaving the infirmary, she had managed to slip away unseen. Death had come to their doors, but they had protected what was theirs.

Ila peered into the pool, at her crisp, clear reflection. Muscle definition curved her biceps and shoulders. Her face was narrow in the chin like Apaay's, but fuller from the nourishing foods she had eaten, the healing of this place. Gray-brown eyes stared back at her.

Me, she thought. *That person is me.*

Reaching up, Ila touched her hard, knotted scar and was again reminded of a past she was a stranger to. After these long months, Ila still had not made peace with it. She didn't want fragments of her early life. She wanted the picture whole and unblemished. Above all, she wanted to *understand.* Which was why she was leaving. Tonight.

At first, Ila had stayed in the Wood because there had been nowhere else to go, and this was where Apaay was, and why would she want to be anywhere else? Then she had stayed because it had become her home.

But Ila finally saw what she had not seen before, in her attempts to save a friendship that did not want to be saved, was not meant to be saved: She and Apaay walked different paths now.

When we first met, Ila began, signing to the water, to the Wood, to anyone who might be watching, *I thought you were a dream.* This memory was soft. It always had been. Though the moments between her and Apaay had grown strained, at least she would always have this one. *You were the first person besides Irnik who treated me like an equal. And maybe it was selfish, but I was so happy you were there. With me.*

She blinked against the sting in her eyes. The anger lived inside her. It was her heart and her lungs and the cavern of her stomach, the newfound hole in her heart. It was too agitated to be quieted, too bruised to heal properly, too hurt to trust again.

Her lashes swept downward, and she stared into the water. It was so clear she could see straight to the pebbled bottom. *I want you to know that I'm sorry. I wish things could have turned out differently.* Ila had done all she could to mend things. In the end, it hadn't been enough. *But wherever you go, even if I'm not with you—* Her chin dimpled as her face collapsed beneath the weight of her sadness. *I hope you find what you are looking for.*

The sob snagged on a piece of her broken heart. She didn't want to leave, didn't want to be apart from Apaay, yet Ila wiped her wet cheeks and untied the small stone from the end of her braid. She had clutched it in sleep all these nights. It had been a comfort then.

Dropping the stone into the pool, Ila watched the ripples carry outward from where it had plummeted through. It was as Tulimaq had said. Sometimes, keeping someone close was how you moved forward.

And sometimes, in order to move forward, you had to let go.

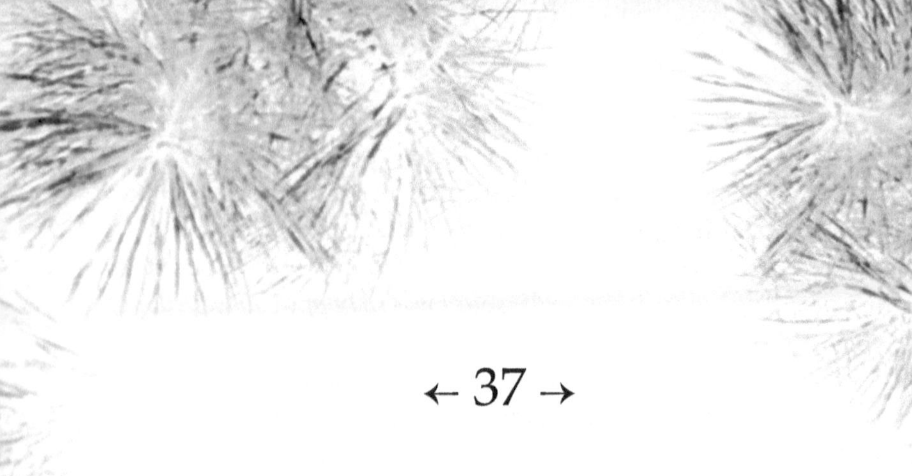

← 37 →

"The doors to Taggak," said the Face Stealer as they halted at the edge of a frozen lake, an opening in the otherwise dense forest cover, "can only be accessed by those who are made of it."

"And you are made of it," Apaay clarified.

The fur of his parka hood rippled like grass in the wind as a gust howled from the mouth of the trees at their back. "I wasn't always."

They had used the cairns. The miles had vanished like stars on a clear dawn, shivering in the bitter cold. They were somewhere in the Northern Territory along the eastern coast. She had smelled it: brine and the salted earth. Naga lay beyond the snow and trees, where a wash of gray lightened the world's eastern wall. The deepest blue-blacks were gone.

Apaay found herself asking, "What changed?" She thought of the war, Kenai's imprisonment, the Wolf Kingdom's downfall. Each a piece of some greater whole that had sharpened over the days and weeks, yet Apaay knew it was not the entire story, not even close.

Remoteness touched his features. The lake was a sapphire blue, deep and painfully abyssal. "Many things," he said. "Many things."

He stepped onto the ice.

Apaay glanced at the small air bubbles trapped in the lake. "I'm named after my grandmother," she said, not making any move to follow.

To trust the beauty of the North was to let the fire lull you, let it coax you toward its burning heart. Beneath its façade lurked something far more deadly. "She fell through the ice as a child and nearly drowned."

He paused where he stood, searched her eyes. "Are you afraid?"

"Of drowning? Not anymore." It was perhaps the only positive outcome of her imprisonment.

Leading Apaay to the center of the lake, the Face Stealer removed one of his mittens and explained, "The doors to Taggak have already been made. My blood brings them from beyond the veil." Using a needle, he pricked the pad of his finger, squeezing a single drop of blood onto the ice sheet.

Shadows ribboned upward from the drop, gathering like a cloud above their heads before knitting into an amorphous doorway, a hole in the fabric of the world.

A rush of ice crested in her chest, pooled, trickled away. The inside was black as pitch. A long breath wavered in her.

At the Face Stealer's grave stare, Apaay explained, flushing, "I still— That is, the last time—"

The pad of his thumb drew a line down the center of her forehead, smoothing the tension that had gathered. She blinked in surprise, her fear quieting at his touch.

Numiak dropped his hand. "Do you want to go back?"

"What about your heart? The blood oath?"

"Do you *want* to go in?"

To go into Taggak willingly? To surrender herself to the shadow fold, the waiting place for the dead?

Apaay reminded herself why she was here: to cast off the oath that had bound her to him. They would find his heart. That would be the last she owed him.

She nodded.

"Once it detects you," he said, "it will try to shove you out. Don't let go of my hand." He clasped her fingers tightly.

Together, they stepped through, sinking into the substance of the world before. The absence of air acted as suction to draw her inside. Once over the threshold, she was within the void, the substance like shredded bits of fabric fluttering against her skin, dry as old bones. Again, that prickling sensation of sweat rising up through her pores. She could no longer see in front of her.

Each step was more difficult than the last, like pushing against a green sapling, fresh in spring. The dark tunnel opened to an inhospitable stretch of land, a slab of gray rock tossed in dusty, colorless soil. When Apaay could move no farther, something jerked at her legs with immense force. She screamed as she fell backward.

The Face Stealer yanked on both of her arms, his body straining with the effort of keeping her in place.

The force was too strong. "Don't you even think about letting go of me," she choked out.

His eyes flickered. His hands tightened. "I won't."

The coils constricting her legs snapped, and she flew forward, crashing into his chest and sending them both sprawling in the dirt. Her heart gave a sickening thud. "It didn't do that when I was in the library," she said, needing a moment to settle her nerves.

"Taggak works in strange ways." She felt the rumble of his voice from where her cheek pressed into his shoulder. "Whatever it wanted to show you was more important than keeping you out."

Apaay rolled away. Her arms shook from the lingering adrenaline as she levered herself up to brush the dust from her legs, the fur of her trousers coated in a fine powder. Then she looked around.

The land itself was formless, with the horizon more of an idea than a reality. A fine mist hovered over the ground. Apaay, who was used to the tundra, felt a distinct lack of connection to the earth. The sky was papery and dark as if suffused with blood. There was no moon.

This was Taggak: a place without wind or breath.

"Does anyone—" Apaay winced and lowered her voice. The sound was vast and full of echoes. "Live here?"

The Face Stealer came to stand beside her, brushing off his hands. "Aside from the Raven and his subjects? No."

The Raven decided when a spirit passed into the spirit world, though strangely there were no spirits in sight. They were alone.

"I guess Taggak decided I wasn't so bad a guest," she said, hoping to distract herself from the desolation.

"What?"

"It's not trying to shove me out anymore."

"That's because I'm using my power to cover you." Glittering darkness appeared long enough for Apaay to notice it cloaked her from head to toe. "You're not that special, sadly. It thinks you're me." He started forward and didn't see the scowl Apaay sent to his back. "No time to waste."

Aside from their hurried pace, the desire to rid him of the curse and herself of the blood oath, nothing was particularly threatening. Apaay, however, had the uneasy sense that they were not, in fact, moving, for the landscape never changed.

"Have you been back here since . . . ?"

Pebbles rattled underfoot. "Since the curse? No. When Yuki hid my heart, I was not allowed to enter unless I brought someone who knew of the curse." He glanced around in mild curiosity. "I can't say it's changed much."

She had the sudden urge to ask him how he had become this person. He'd had a life before, traded for power, but also for abhorrence and darkness and isolation. No one would choose this. What, then, had pushed him here?

"Yes," she whispered. "It is rather dead."

He frowned, as if unsure of whether that had been a joke. Apaay wasn't sure, either.

A dark shape fluttered in her peripheral vision. She snapped her head to the side, taking in the barren plateau. "I saw something."

"A spirit?" he drawled, pulling ahead of her.

"Funny." It was gone now, whatever it was, leaving them to mist and smoke and dust. She took another step forward before spotting movement again. "Something's out there."

He stopped with a sigh of exasperation. "What did it look like?"

"It was small and dark."

"I imagine it was a raven." He tilted his head, scanned the area. "We must be getting close."

Taggak was a blurred, hollow place, and death curled in the pockets she could not see. Violet spilled across the ground, the color of shadows in dusk, and the dust lifted with their footsteps to catch the ambient light like small flakes of snow, or ash on a breeze. Only when the burn in her calves traveled to her thighs and her breathing tripped into a ragged beat did Apaay realize they were scaling the side of a sizeable mountain, the path cutting switchbacks through the rock.

Two black pillars loomed from out of the mist. A third had been laid across their tops with even smaller slabs of stone placed atop that. The cairn was the largest she had seen, overarching a set of wide, curving stairs of pale stone that shone like painted moonbeams. Beyond the stairs, more mist.

Apaay lingered near the Face Stealer's back, even going so far as to grip the back of his parka. He didn't seem to notice as they climbed the steps to a raised stone platform, the mists retreating enough to allow a narrow pathway through. She bumped into his back when he stopped at the top, then moved to the side to get a better view.

A tall, skeletal man in all black stood at a table, his back to them. What she had believed to be mist trailing along the ground was actually a flock of ravens. Hundreds of them, moving about and perched on the dead black trees, the branches so twisted they appeared to be roots, as if the trees had been ripped from the earth and turned upside down.

The figure spoke without turning around. "To what do I owe this pleasure, Numiak of the Wolf Kingdom?"

The air pulsed in response to his voice, which was as bare and insubstantial as an icy wind.

Then he turned, and Apaay gasped. His eyes, which were without iris or pupil, were the charred red of a fire's burning core.

One of the ravens perched on his shoulder. The tattered ends of his cloak were of deepest ebony, reflecting blues and greens on occasion. With not an ounce of fat on his body, he looked like a bird of prey.

"Can I not pay a visit to an old friend?" the Face Stealer asked, smooth and careful.

"That is assuming we are friends" was the Raven's reply. "You come without your usual consort."

"I'm afraid I no longer keep the company I once did."

"Yes, I can see that." His eyes, like two pinpricks of blood, perused Apaay's face. "Who is this?" he wondered, coming closer. The bottom of his cloak hissed along the ground. Leaning forward, he sniffed at her delicately. "Why do I smell—" He sniffed again as Apaay tamped down a shudder.

She sensed the Face Stealer's mounting tension, how it rose against his skin. His expression remained bland.

The Raven stepped back. "A thorough job." He looked to the Face Stealer. "I imagine Yuki hadn't a clue."

"What is he talking about?" Apaay asked, unable to relax even though he had put space between them. His mouth was obscenely wide. She wondered if he had teeth.

The Face Stealer's gaze remained steady on the Raven's. "Nothing. Ignore him."

She could not *ignore* the Raven. The Messenger. It was he who decided who passed over the Sky Bridge and who remained behind based on the deeds of one's life. The naaluet were his hellish fiends. They shared the same eyes.

The Raven turned back to the table. Bowls cluttered its surface. "I don't have time for useless small talk. Tell me why you're here or leave."

"I came to ask you for a favor."

The Raven, who had begun separating the objects held in one of the bowls, cocked his head. "Really. As I recall, when I last asked *you* for a favor, you ignored me."

"The circumstances have changed."

"Not interested."

Upon closer inspection, Apaay realized the objects were teeth: shark teeth, polar bear teeth, lemming teeth. The small piles linked together to form a sprawling mountain range across the table.

"You haven't even heard what the favor is," the Face Stealer bit out.

The teeth clattered as the piles grew. Pushing the empty bowl to the side, the Raven began to sort through the teeth in the next one. These appeared to have belonged to a canid. A fox, maybe. "Oh, I have a vague notion." His hands stilled as the Face Stealer crowded his shoulder. "You're blocking the light."

Although there was no outward change to the Raven's tone or body language, something had altered in warning. Apaay sensed the mist brushing her ankles and winding up her legs.

Scowling, the Face Stealer stepped aside. Then he narrowed his eyes. "Where did you get that tattoo from?" He gestured to the collection of lines and dots covering the god's chin and jaw, the ink blue-gray and faded. "That wasn't there the last time I saw you."

A new stiffness entered the Raven. Apaay guessed he wasn't used to careful scrutiny, especially from someone as keen as the Face Stealer. As for the tattoo, she found it unusual. Only Analak women participated in the generations' old tradition of tattooing. She hadn't considered finding it elsewhere. Even the gods, it seemed, utilized the art form.

Reaching out, the Face Stealer hovered his fingertips a few inches from the tattooed jaw. Sparks erupted, and he snatched his hand back as if burned. "This is how Nanuq bound you."

Those red eyes regarded him, flat but bright with intelligence. He scooped the pile of canid teeth into an empty bowl. "You're correct." He touched his jaw in contemplation. "I cannot, however, remember the details of ever receiving it."

The Face Stealer tracked one of the birds as it drove another from its perch in the tree. "Now, what do you know that Nanuq wants to keep hidden?" he murmured.

"Let me know when you find out, will you? It's been a nuisance having no recollection."

"Help us fight Yuki and Nanuq, and I will find a way to remove that tattoo and free you from this imprisonment."

A peculiar stillness came over the Raven. She saw the bird in him, in the tilt of his head and in his bones, fragile and narrow. "I see."

Apaay was quite certain there had not been any air movement since entering Taggak, yet now that feeling intensified, as if the atmosphere was not only still, but absent.

The Raven said, "I last saw you two weeks prior to the invasion. Nanuq found me shortly after. I don't recall our meeting. When I came to, I was back in Taggak with this tattoo, no memory of what had occurred, and no ability to leave." The Raven abandoned his teeth, crowding the Face Stealer's space. They were both not quite men, born of this dark world. "I called for your aid then. You never answered."

The Face Stealer wiped a bead of sweat from his brow. "I had my reasons. The curse, which you were well aware of, meant I was barred from Taggak. But even if I hadn't been, I was not ready to forgive your actions. You played your part in the death of my people. Why should I have come to your aid when you called? Two decades later or not, I'm here, and I'm offering you freedom in exchange for your loyalty."

"You are wasting your time. My loyalty is to the dead."

"So you choose imprisonment?"

"Did you ever consider the idea that I like it here? After centuries of dealing with you and your ilk, I rather enjoy the solitude."

A little smile tugged at the Face Stealer's mouth. "There was a reason Nanuq bound you," he said, shifting his body so it cast a deeper shadow across the piles of animal teeth. This time, he didn't move. "Whatever it is you know, he wants it to remain a secret. It is a weakness to him."

"You think this secret could unravel Nanuq's plans."

"I don't know, but it seems like a promising path to explore, yes?"

With the teeth finally separated into their respective piles, the Raven dumped them into their individual bowls and walked them to a second table piled high with raven feathers. "Things are never that simple."

The Face Stealer waited. "You will not help us?"

"No." He didn't sound the least bit regretful. "I daresay I have better things to do with my time." Then he left, and the mists swallowed him up.

The Face Stealer stared at the place where the god had vanished, chillingly quiet. Then he swore—succinctly, viciously—before settling on the steps to wait.

"Is he coming back?" Apaay wondered, sitting beside him.

"Who knows?" He sighed and dropped his face into his hands. His hair slipped forward over his shoulder and hung there, the water vapor like small crystals intertwined with the black. "I don't know what to do." The words were muffled.

His display of uncertainty hit her harder than she expected. These were not the words of a demon, but a man. It almost felt as if they were back in Sinika, sharing mushrooms side by side, letting the other in. The thought did not frighten her as it used to. "Is there something else you can offer him that might change his mind?"

"I'm already offering him freedom and the promise to remove his tattoo."

Apaay snorted. Unsurprising, really. Sometimes she wondered how aware the Face Stealer was when it came to power. Either he was too convincing of a liar, or he was completely oblivious.

He looked at her with piercing eyes. "Something funny, wolfling?"

"Offering him freedom is something you want. While it indirectly benefits the Raven, he would ultimately be in your power. What is something *he* wants?"

"I know what he wants," he said. "I'm not going to give it to him."

Apaay fought her exasperation. Kaan was far better at dealing with stubborn men than she was. At this point, the weapons master probably would have shoved him down the stairs. "Look, we didn't come all this way to leave empty-handed. If this trade will get the Raven onto our side, I think we should consider it. Unless he wants your power—"

"That is exactly what he wants."

Her mouth snapped shut.

"My power," he explained, "is the only thing standing between the Wood and outside forces. It is the only protection I have, and it is the only thing able to potentially stand against Nanuq. Sacrificing it would be the one foolish thing I could do."

Which made her wonder. What did the future hold for them? If the Raven was their one chance at survival, shouldn't they do whatever it took to call him to their side? If they didn't, might he eventually be swayed to Nanuq's cause?

"If you did give him your power," Apaay said, scanning his profile, "what would that entail?"

His bewilderment was borderline comical, in an uncomfortable way. "You're not serious."

She held up a hand. "Answer the question." Even if the Face Stealer didn't give away his power, she thought it important to explore all options, even the dangerous ones.

"Let's see." He started ticking things off with his fingers. "The Wood would fall, though I suppose that doesn't matter, considering it's forfeit. The protection around the Analak village would also fall. Yuki would be able to track me. I would have no way of protecting myself. I would essentially be useless to the Avi, which might cause him to retract his vote in the alliance." He growled out a sound of frustration. "It's a terrible idea."

It was. Still, she went on. "How would your power be transferred to the Raven if you agreed to it, and could it be replenished?"

The press of his mouth told her how much he disliked the direction of her thoughts. "A dark oath. It's similar to the blood oath, except that my word is bound to my power, not my blood, and by giving the Raven my power, he would have complete control over me. If I kept a portion of my power, then yes, that remaining bit would replenish itself if I burned through it. It would take longer, though. I would have only a fraction of my strength."

Despite the Face Stealer's every effort to refuse this idea, a plan began to form in Apaay's mind. She said, "What if you gave him your power but kept enough to protect the Wood and the Analak village? You could require the Raven to give aid to them if they ever needed it as one of the terms. You could give him a time frame when he would have your power, and once it passed, it would return to you." The dark oath could be worded in the Face Stealer's favor. It would be a sacrifice, but in the long term, having the Raven on their side would go far in increasing their odds of survival when they marched to war.

His gaze was cool as he said, "I'll consider it."

It was all she could ask for.

A droplet of sweat rolled down the Face Stealer's temple, across the new paleness of his skin. All around, the ravens worried at the dirt. The sky held a sickly tint above.

"You don't look well," she said.

"It takes a lot out of me to be here. Taggak always seeks to call its children back." He dragged a hand across his face. "It's hard enough keeping myself from giving in to the call, especially since I'm so close, but I have to keep a barrier around you as well. The combination of the two drains my power far more quickly."

A tremor rolled through him, and she asked, "What does the call feel like?"

"It's not a calling, per se. I don't hear a voice. It's a *need*." His eyes were near colorless. "Because I am partially made of this place, it always seeks to be whole. It calls me to its heart."

From the corner of her eye, Apaay watched three ravens fly a woven basket between them and set it on the table, their wings disturbing the mist. The Raven strode after them, and his presence drew Apaay and the Face Stealer to his side.

"What's in the basket?" she whispered.

The Raven lifted a tiny fledgling free, a fluff of downy feathers cupped in his palm. The baby bird shrieked, as if offended that its peace had been disturbed.

"Hush, now." A worm appeared in his hand. The bird opened its beak with another demanding screech until the slimy invertebrate dropped into its mouth. Satisfied, the chick fluffed its feathers, blinked it beady eyes, and went to sleep.

"My kin tell me they are cutting down large swaths of forest in the Southern Territory. The wildlife are fleeing north." He ran a finger through the chick's soft feathers, preening it. "War is horror and terror and destruction, and Nanuq is very good at it."

"What do you know?" The Face Stealer stared at the chick. Orphaned, Apaay assumed, and homeless.

"I do not know why Nanuq is felling the trees. He keeps his intentions close. What people do not know, they fear. Fear is mankind's greatest weapon."

"Nanuq is no man."

At this, the Raven set down the chick. "You are right." Thoughtful. "He is *almost* a man."

He paused. "But it is not enough for him. Nanuq has always been curious of man. You know this, Numiak. The need to be stronger, more powerful, to be as the Iskra were long ago, when they drove the animals from their homes. As long as man lives, Nanuq knows he can never equal them in power. In his eyes, there is not world enough for both."

"What are you saying?" said the Face Stealer. "He plans to wipe man out?"

"My friend." The word was spoken with much irony, alluding to the notion that they were not, in fact, friends. "Nanuq does not seek to wipe man out. He seeks to *become* them. To become fully man."

← 38 →

"What are you talking about?" Apaay snapped. "That's impossible." One born an animal could not be made into a man. The species were separate. Even the Unua, whose lives spanned two worlds, could not choose one or the other. Their nature was both, or neither.

"How do you know this?" the Face Stealer demanded.

A fluttering of ebony wings was all that stirred as a bird came to land on the Raven's shoulder. He smoothed a finger down its breast. "How do you think? The spirits talk."

Apaay was caught in the deep snow of her memories. She and Papa watching the pale men from Across the Sea tear down the coniferous forests. What had the Face Stealer told her? Nanuq had disappeared for ten long years before returning with knowledge of man's warfare. She imagined those were the men Nanuq had learned from, and those were the ones he sought to become.

The Raven sighed and pushed away from the table. "The object he seeks will give him the means to unite the North under one ruler. His intention is to use it to enslave both animal and man."

Apaay's attention jumped to the Face Stealer. A look of revulsion stared back at her. As if sensing the tension in him, one of the ravens cawed and took flight. Dense mist rolled toward them, shrouding all but the stone platform and veiling the shadowy land beyond.

"How—" No. That wasn't the right question. The question was, *Why?* But that seemed pointless to ask. The idea of conquering was as cold and remote as the stars, and as foreign. Why did anyone desire power? Why did anyone desire anything?

The Face Stealer turned away with a barely concealed snarl and strode a few steps into the fog, the edges of his form not fully clear. "This is why we need your aid," he said. "Nanuq wiped out my people in the last war. He won't stop. But we can't fight him alone. We're not strong enough. If he discovers the object of power, there will be no free will left in this world."

"You've already come forward with your offer. This changes nothing."

"My terms have changed."

Her stomach dropped. The Face Stealer would never give up his power, but the situation had gone from desperate to dire in the span of minutes. His eyes, when he turned, burned yellow-gold, fierce and frightening, utterly inhuman. "I offer you the dark oath."

Sucking in a breath, Apaay awaited the god's reaction.

"I see." The Raven sent the bird from his shoulder and came forward in unabashed curiosity. It was the first emotion she had seen from him. "This does change things." He swept out a hand, and the table cleared. Two pieces of blank parchment appeared in place of the teeth. "What are your terms?"

The Face Stealer closed the distance. No hesitation. He had made his decision. Apaay hoped they would not regret it. "I offer you the dark oath in exchange for your loyalty, until I either perish or am incapacitated indefinitely, or until the conflict ends." As he spoke, writing appeared on the papers. "During this time, you will do everything in your power to protect those who stand against Yuki and Nanuq. You will give your loyalty to the cause. You will hunt only those who seek to hurt you. You will tell the enemy nothing of our plans, whereabouts, or intentions."

The Raven listened carefully to the terms. It was far more official than the blood oath, and with each term listed, the air tightened around them, as if binding.

"In exchange for your loyalty, I offer you the following: my ability to enter and leave Taggak at will, my promise to remove the tattoo Nanuq placed on you, and lastly—" He and Apaay exchanged a look of understanding. "I offer you half of my power, until the dark oath is met, by which all terms will be nullified."

The Raven's cloak whispered as he stepped forward, his eyes deep wounds that promised violence despite his mild, "That is quite generous of you." He tapped the tips of his spindly fingers together. "But I want *all* of your power."

The Face Stealer's mouth twitched. Apparently the topic was too serious to warrant one of his sleek smiles. "Half. I need enough to protect the refugees, and that means ensuring the Wood remains safe long enough for me to get them out."

"I will have all of it, or nothing."

"What about everyone who depends on its protection?"

The Raven stared calmly. "The protections you have in place will remain, as will the enchantments. Anything that has been done with your power prior to this oath will not be altered." A new line appeared on both documents. "Your power will be returned to you when the tattoo is removed."

Apaay watched the Face Stealer come to terms with what he would be giving up and who he would be when it was done. Who *would* he be without his power? More than a man, less than a god. She'd always seen him as such. Maybe now he'd just be a man.

Apaay murmured, "You'll get it back. We'll find a way to remove his tattoo." Of course, she couldn't know that for sure, but it felt like the right thing to say to ease his doubt.

"Are you offering to help me break his curse?" His attempt to make light of a situation that was anything but.

"I was trying to make you feel better," she said, "since you'll be weak as a newborn after this."

"Your belief in me is positively inspiring."

The Raven looked utterly bored. Apaay sighed. "It won't be forever," she said with more reassurance than she felt. "You know as well as I that this is our best chance for the future." When he did not respond, she asked, "What do I need to do to get you to agree to this?"

"Help me find a way to remove his tattoo."

Apaay grimaced. Although it wasn't a blood oath, it felt too similar to being trapped. Still, the consequences if she did not help were far more dire. "If it will get you to agree to the dark oath, fine."

"Then I accept those terms of the dark oath," the Face Stealer told the Raven.

The parchment vanished. The men stepped closer, facing each other, each a child of Taggak.

Apaay rushed to say, "I could be lying, you know."

Numiak didn't look at her as he said, "I know."

It was as if they came to the decision all at once, a demon and a god, to cut into their palms and draw blood, reach for the other, and clasp hands.

The Face Stealer screamed.

His knees buckled, their hands still clasped as the ravens took flight, the writhing cloud flinging thunder across the barrenness, a current of air sending Apaay out of their immediate range. The Face Stealer's power twined with the wings as it was pulled from his body, before being sent into the Raven's. The god's eyes glowed brighter, and still the Face Stealer screamed, the air cleaving itself in two.

And then it stopped. Their hands fell. All was silent.

Apaay's ears rang as the ravens flew off. After an agonizing moment, the Face Stealer pushed into a standing position, using the table for support. His skin was pale and his eyes had dulled.

"I assume," said the Raven with much knowing, "you didn't come here to serve a dark oath. The curse will not allow you to take your heart. Someone else must give it to you of their own free will."

Moisture from the fog clung to Apaay's eyelashes in cool, clear droplets as the demon's heart materialized in the Raven's possession.

With a wordless nod, the Raven passed it into her cupped palms. Its strong current could be felt in the slow throb, a pulsing of flesh and blood.

The Face Stealer was slow to approach her. "Apaay."

She stared at the delicate organ. The heart of a demon. The Face Stealer was all but immortal, could live for centuries. Yet if she were to toss his heart onto the ground and crush it beneath her heel, he would perish. Apaay wondered if he could feel it—the power. *Her* power. To choose.

"Curious," she said, touching a finger to the pink flesh. "For some reason, I thought it would be black."

The skin around his clover-green eyes pinched.

Apaay thought to torture him a little while longer. A part of her whispered that he deserved it, but its voice was small, faded, and Apaay knew that to leave the dark place behind she would need to come to terms with all that had been done to her. Acknowledge it, then move past it.

"One last thing." With the heart held out of reach, she watched a muscle jump in his jaw, subtly. "I want to make another deal with you."

"There is already a blood oath between us."

"You're saying we can't complete another one?" Her lips curled dangerously. No matter how far they had come, Apaay never again wanted to feel powerless in his presence. The favor itself did not matter. With the Face Stealer in her debt, it acted as a barrier of safety should anything go wrong in the future. "You demanded a favor from me. Now I'm demanding a favor from you. At my convenience, of course."

He matched her smile, teeth for teeth, and came forward. "You want to play, is that it?" Leaning forward, he put his mouth to her ear. "Perhaps you don't know what's good for you, either."

The suggestion sent heat sliding through her. Before she could think about shoving him away, he stepped neatly back. "Give me your hand."

She did, the other tucked against her stomach so she wouldn't drop the organ. The Raven sighed and wandered to a far table, giving them privacy. The fog thickened, cold and ancient on her tongue. They were left to the sound of rustling wings, muffled and distant.

The Face Stealer sliced into both of their palms, pressed them together, and this time, Apaay did not scream. She looked at herself through his eyes, felt the emptiness of his body from the power draining. Heat flared, and she felt a thread pull taut between them. It lasted half a second. The Face Stealer broke contact, stumbling back, his palm clutched to his chest.

"What was that?" Apaay asked.

"I suspect you will find out soon enough," came the Raven's disembodied voice.

The Face Stealer looked nowhere but at her. "My heart, wolfling."

With only a small trace of regret, she passed the organ into his hands. Whatever curse he'd been subject to, it allowed him to press it through his clothes into his chest. His shoulders bowed. His head hung.

He breathed.

"The First Man," said Apaay quietly. "That's where Kenai and I went, to ask where you had hidden the face of the woman he loved."

Slowly, the Face Stealer unbent from his waist. His face was paler than it had been before. "Apaay." Her name held such gravity. "Tell me that's not true."

Her throat bobbed as a strange, creeping guilt grabbed hold of her. She couldn't.

"Did the First Man reveal the location to you?"

"I really don't see why—"

"Apaay!"

"Yes," she snapped, her apprehension spiking. Something was very wrong here. "It's not like you would have given him the face anyway. He isn't going to do anything with it."

A swift jerk of his head brought her next words to heel. "You're wrong. That face isn't who you think it is. He's leaving with something far more dangerous than you realize, and he's not coming back."

"He wouldn't." Not without letting her know. And not without saying goodbye.

Right?

The Face Stealer caught her wrist, though gently. "You don't see it. This was his intention. This was *always* his intention." He looked at her with more understanding than she was comfortable with. "I know it hurts. Believe me, I know what it's like to put your trust in someone because they *see* you."

Apaay jerked from his hold. It frightened her how he knew that when she had never told him.

The fog parted, letting the Raven pass into their space. "How long have you been gone for?"

Apaay looked to the Face Stealer, her pulse a jagged beat. "Two hours, maybe."

"Then I suspect you are already too late."

The Face Stealer shook his head. "Since I'm unable to fashion a doorway back to the living realm without my power, we'll use the cairn." But when he strode toward the massive stone formation framing the platform on which they stood and placed his palm to its smooth face, nothing happened.

Apaay's heart gave one painful thud. "Why isn't it working?"

With a troubled expression, he lowered his hand. "The connection to the other cairn has been severed."

"It doesn't even look like you're trying."

"I am trying. There's nothing I can do."

"Well, try harder." Something was being set into motion. She remembered Kenai telling her he hurt those who had stood in the way of his happiness.

"I can't draw from a well that is empty," he snapped. "But even if I could, this isn't something I can control." His hand swept the cairn's face. "The cairns draw their power from the rocks. This is how I'm able to travel by cairns, because the origin of power, the earth, is the same for all. Thus, they are linked. Kenai must have destroyed the cairn we need. Without its shape, the connection is severed."

She glanced over her shoulder, scanning the area. Beyond the point where the mists became opaque, the Raven's glowing eyes pierced through. "Then what are we going to do?"

A sound of exhaustion. He shut his gaze. "Under any other circumstances, I would never ask this of you," the Face Stealer said to no one in particular, though they both knew the Raven was watching, listening. "But if my brother reaches the coast with the face he seeks, the world we know will see change as it has never seen before."

The Raven said, after a pause, "What is it you ask of me?"

"Is it possible we could use the Sky Bridge to reach the Wood?"

The Raven considered the request. When the Analak left their physical bodies, their spirits went to Taggak to await judgment. It was here they crossed the Sky Bridge to reach the spirit world. Though his expression did not shift, his voice held reluctance. "I would have to ask the spirits. One moment."

The edges of his frame glimmered with soft light. In fascination, Apaay watched as the Raven's form lost its color, turning translucent. He was a shroud, wraithlike and insubstantial. The Messenger.

"They will allow it," he said, "just this once."

Light flooded the platform, shoving back the colorless patches and hanging curtain-like before them. Fern green and violet blue and streaks of pale yellow formed bands that rippled across the sky. The colors merged, became one, then split apart, two long strips solidifying into handrails, a curved staircase stretching upward. The shifting light was all the colors of the sky and sea. She could not make out their shapes, but she felt them—their souls.

"This is where I leave you," said the Raven. "We will see one another again. Farewell, Numiak of the Wolf Kingdom."

The god disappeared into the mist, and they began their hurried ascent. Color flared where their feet touched the steps, fading the farther they climbed. It took Apaay a minute to realize how quickly they were traveling via the Sky Bridge. Miles vanished with every step. The Aatu Forest spread below, and seconds later, the terrain morphed into hills, the hills into mountainous peaks.

In no time, they reached the bridge's apex, momentum pulling them faster and faster toward the earth until they reached solid ground, Apaay jumping the last few steps into ankle-deep slush. In the gloomy half-light, the conifers threw spiked shadows atop the snow. Wind skated across the ground and dragged up the flakes from where they had settled, whipping them through the air. The Face Stealer still had not spoken of what would occur should Kenai reach the sea.

They passed through the barrier into the Wood. With the enchantment restored, they reached the waterfall after only a few steps.

The Face Stealer swore, bolting ahead. His office door was ajar. As was the bookcase the First Man had mentioned, revealing an open doorway at its back and a set of stairs leading down into the darkness.

Down, down they went, their footsteps ringing against stone. Apaay kept one hand on the wall so she wouldn't trip and break her neck. They reached another door, shut, but it blew open to uncover a massive room deep underground. The air breathed green mist. The floor was crushed leaves, damp and rich in their scents. In the center of the room, a display case sat atop a stump, showcasing one face, two, three, four—

But the fifth face was already gone.

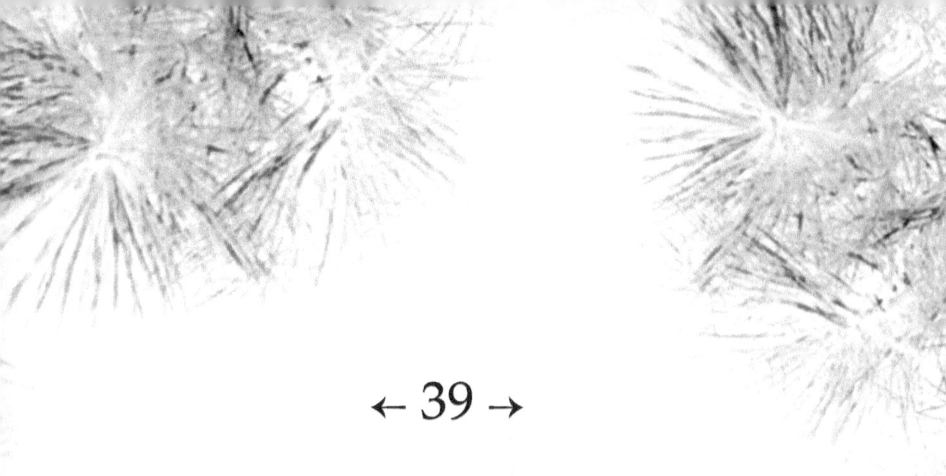

← 39 →

Ila told no one where she was going. It was the only way to ensure she would not be followed. The dying light flamed red on the highest branches of the birch and poplar trees. It was the last she would see of the Wood for some time, and she wanted to remember it exactly like this: a brightness, a star.

First, Ila went to her bedroom. She shed her lighter summer skins and dressed in the heavier furs needed to face the winter, placing the underlayer fur-side down and the parka hair facing outward. She traded her slippers for waterproof boots. The heaviness of the fur quickly drew sweat from her body.

Kneeling at the chest located at the end of her bed, Ila pushed open the top. Her belongings were few. There was a satchel made of caribou hide, which she stuffed with her summer clothing. At the very bottom of the chest were her animal carvings. She took her favorites—the wolverine, the goose, and the lemming—and left the rest.

Then she went to the breakfast chamber. The lamps burned low on the empty table. One of her favorite things had been to eat here each morning as the world came awake. Trailing a hand along the wide, rounded mushroom cap seats, Ila moved to her favorite table by the window. Light streamed across the table's cracks, creating shadows so black they looked to be lines of soot.

One of the Keepers of the Wood hopped onto the table. It was the haughty one from before. Ila sighed.

"Dinner is over," it said, its tiny leaf hat set lopsided on its head. "Come back tomorrow."

I won't be here tomorrow.

"Then I cannot help you." It didn't appear the least bit sorry about that. Unsurprising, really.

Yes, you can. She plopped her bag onto the table, and if it landed a hair too close to the Keeper, then so be it. *I need to fill this pack with as much food as you can spare.* Who knew how long she'd be traveling for.

The creature's beady eyes widened in outrage. "Do you think we have food to spare for you?" It stamped its foot, and the hat slid off its head. "You are not my master."

Her irritation surged to life. She was emotionally and mentally exhausted and hadn't the patience to argue with a leaf . . . thing.

Let me rephrase, she said calmly enough. *I am leaving, and I'm not coming back. Help me fill my pack with food so that I don't die in the cold, or I remain here.* Ila paused for dramatic effect as she glared at the tiny Keeper. *Forever.*

At this, the creature puffed out its chest in sudden excitement. Suddenly the table groaned beneath the weight of meats, roots, and berries. Ila fought a smile as she stuffed her bag full. She would miss the Keeper despite its rudeness. As it was, she would miss a lot of things.

Using the map she'd taken from Apaay as her guide, Ila left the Wood by way of a back exit through Kaan's workroom. Without the Wood's protective barrier, it was nearly five miles of battling the wind and cold. Apaay and Masuk's previous tracks had been cleared, and she thought it fitting that she'd have to forge her own way. Ila wondered how Tulimaq had known all those months ago of her weak heart. Learning how to fight had never been about becoming strong. It had been about taking control. The truth was, she hadn't been ready to face her fear of abandonment until she'd stepped beyond the barrier, map in hand.

After passing the lake, she knew she was getting close. The chill invaded the inside of her mittens, and frost collected on her lashes, pinching the skin around her eyes. It didn't matter how much effort she was exerting. She would never be warm.

Minutes later, the wind died and the cold ceased to be. Lifting her head, Ila found herself inside a ring of trees, a rock formation in its center. There was an ethereal feel to the place. A compelling, god-touched land. This, she thought, must be the First Man Apaay had mentioned all those months ago.

His eyes were gouged orbs. The chip of his chin and jaw, the high brow, suggested a visage that had once been handsome, though time and wind had eroded it. A prickle of power rolled along her skin, intermingling with the air as she shuffled forward. Whatever resulted from this meeting, she was still glad she had come.

Hello, she signed, figuring politeness would grant her favor.

A touch of warm air smoothed her cheek, like the pad of a curious finger.

Her heartbeat thrummed in her mouth. *I've heard you are the Keeper of All That Lives and Dies. I was hoping you might help me find what I'm looking for.*

The face was unmoving. She felt silly signing to what appeared to be little more than a large rock. If Apaay had received answers for Masuk, then logically, Ila could, too. Learning about her past, she might finally understand her future. A future not shrouded by fog or fear.

My entire life, the only thing I've known is a cage. At least, that is what I believed. But recently I've learned that wasn't always so. I was free as a child, though I do not remember it. A recollection of flames seared her mind. She swore she smelled burning wood.

And now, the truth. *I've come to you because I need to know where I come from.* More than that, if there was any place or anyone she could return to. Her parents were dead. Had they been her only family?

The stone figure remained as it was. In its motionlessness, Ila dropped to her knees, head bowed. *I don't understand. Is it because I'm not worthy? Am I so unlovable that I am not even given this grace?* Something rigid and immovable took residence alongside her heart. It felt like all the maybes she'd never discover, the possibilities out of reach.

Who am I? she wondered. It was tearing her apart.

As she stared at the weathered carving of a face, inert and without answer, she knew only the unfairness of it all. She did not ask for the world, or even half of it. Merely a piece large enough to hold all that she was, all that she could be. But Ila was coming to know the world, and it owed her not a thing. The world didn't care who she was. She'd come all this way. For nothing.

In the warm summer heat, Ila dropped her forehead against the curve of the stone's shoulder, sweating, too defeated to move.

"Hello, Matilaqaa," said a voice inside her head as ancient as the scarred, rutted earth. "I've been expecting you."

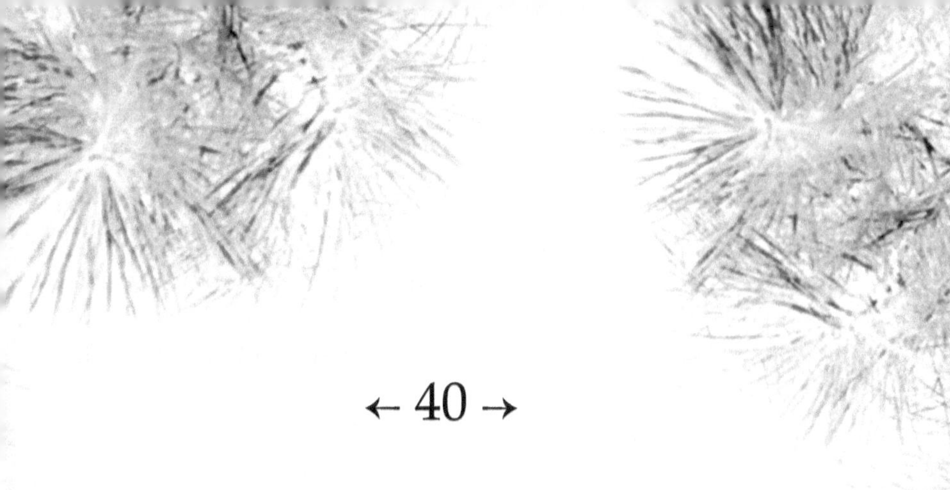

← 40 →

"We can't let him reach the shore," the Face Stealer said as he and Apaay tore down a slope somewhere in the Western Territory.

After discovering the face gone and Kenai along with it, the Face Stealer had collected the four remaining faces and told her they were leaving. A cairn had sent them south of Talguk, a port city of the former Wolf Kingdom. Five miles later, they traveled northwest, their bodies pushed to the brink of exertion, yet with no choice but to continue their brutal pace.

We can't let him reach the shore. He'd said that twice now. She wanted to ask why, and couldn't. The air was so cold the words froze in her chest.

Apaay slipped as they descended into a valley and would have tumbled down the incline had the Face Stealer not caught her arm. She was her body and her breath and the trip of her heart, each pulse knocking the next forward in dread of what awaited them once they reached the coast.

The sea hit when they topped the rise, the sound of earth sundering beneath the power of Naga's western brother, gray-green waves breaking upon the shore. The Face Stealer was already halfway down the slope, winding through the massive conifers with the wind at his heels. Apaay pushed her leaden legs harder to close the gap, focusing on remaining upright as the descent steepened before leveling off. In the distance, Kenai was a dark speck in human form. He, too, stumbled as he fled. Five miles of hard travel through the taiga would drain even the strongest of men.

"Ma— Kenai!" She slid in a muddy patch and nearly collided with a tree. "Kenai, wait!"

He reached level ground. Less than a half mile separated him from the water. There were so many trees that she lost track of the Face Stealer, but then she spotted him closing the distance. Apaay called to Kenai again, her voice lost to the pounding of the sea.

The first snarl split the air. She hopped a log, winding down, down, down. This near the coast, the trees were dwarfed, spindly, grotesquely bitten from the salt spray. The beach came into view, and then two wolves, one black and one gray, shot into her line of sight and crashed into a tree. The gray wolf, Kenai, struggled against the Face Stealer's hold with his lips curled back, snapping at his brother's throat. He howled as flesh tore, but then their positions reversed and it was the Face Stealer trying to avoid Kenai's dagger-like teeth.

Breaking free of the trees, Apaay slowed. The brothers had returned to their human forms, bleeding from multiple wounds, though the Face Stealer's looked far worse. Spite thickened the air, made the hair on her arms stand on end. Keeping Kenai in her field of vision, she asked the Face Stealer a question with her eyes. *Are you hurt?*

He worked his jaw from side to side and shook his head.

Facing Kenai at last, the fury now shredded through her. This was what Apaay had wanted: to help him find his beloved's face. To *fix* someone's life, even if it could not be her own.

She managed through her labored breathing, "Why?"

His gaze darted to the Face Stealer, who had moved to stand behind her in solidarity. Though she hadn't verbalized it, the Face Stealer seemed to understand she had her own reasons for confronting his brother.

"There was no other way, Apaay," Kenai said. "I saw a chance to leave, and I took it. I won't apologize for that."

"What about lying to me?" He had taken advantage of her vulnerability and goodwill, twisting what she thought was friendship into something unfeeling and cold. She would have forgiven him for keeping his identity from her, but not for abandoning her, using her. "You tricked me," she whispered.

"You always knew my intentions. I never planned on staying here. One day, I was going to leave."

"Yes, but with me."

There was a different quality to the pause, a new tension to the demon standing at her back. He hadn't known.

Kenai considered her in a knowing way. "Were you still planning on leaving the Wood? To my knowledge, you had changed your mind." He pushed away from the tree, a slip of brown skin clutched tightly in hand. Waves beat at his back. "I did what I had to do to save someone I loved, just as you did for your sister."

"It's not the same."

"Don't tell me it's not the same!" he snarled, taking an aggressive step toward her. She heard the Face Stealer shift in warning, and after a moment, Kenai retreated. "It is exactly the same. You did whatever you could to find your sister's face. You *killed* for her."

Blood flew to the edges of her skin as her past failures resurfaced. "I told you those things from a place of shame," she rasped.

"Maybe you regret your actions, but you don't regret that they brought you to your sister." His breathing stuttered, streams of sweat pouring down his temples, his black hair a tangle. "I know I hurt you, but you have to understand why I did what I did. Nearly twenty years in solitude, and I didn't know whether I would ever see the face of the woman I loved again. I know you don't believe me, but I do value your friendship. I've never had someone believe in me the way you do."

"He's lying to you," said the Face Stealer.

Kenai bared his teeth, the tips of his canines sharp. Spray spewed the rocks nearest to shore. "Yes, because we all know the infamous Face Stealer would never stoop so low." Though he responded to his brother, his agitated gaze never left Apaay's. "You see what he's done? He's pitted you against me."

"Apaay." Numiak's deep voice drifted to her ear. "Think of why Kenai was locked up. Nanuq's invasion was because of him. The death of our people was because of *him*."

"He's planting doubt in your mind," returned Kenai steadily. "These past months he's deceived you into lowering your guard, convinced you to trust him without quite knowing what you're doing."

This was where her story had led her to: a choice between brothers. Kenai had lied, but the Face Stealer had lied long before. And what of the actions that had yet to be carried out? Apaay didn't know how this would affect her family until it was too late.

"Kenai." She dared to step forward. He took a step back, closer to the sea. Apaay stopped, knowing something terrible awaited them should the woman's face touch the water. "If what you need is forgiveness, then I forgive you."

Something flickered in him. Apaay watched it crest, watched it cloud his eyes, before it retreated. "I stopped seeking forgiveness a long time ago."

"You don't have to leave."

"Come with me." It was both a plea and a demand. "That's what you said in the very beginning. We would leave this place, start a new life elsewhere, someplace *free*." The feeling in Apaay's chest tightened. "Don't you still want that?"

She had wanted that. In some ways, she still wanted that. But she could not shake the feeling that this man, his boots growing damp from the tide rushing in, was in many ways a stranger to her. He was leaving. That, she finally accepted, had always been his intention. Whether or not she was with him had never mattered. She had chosen not to see it.

"I don't know what the Face Stealer has said about me," he went on, as if sensing her doubt, "but the demon right there?" He pointed. "That is what becomes of someone who grew up in the shadow of our father's hatred. You want to know the real reason our sister died? Because Numiak made a choice, and he chose power over family."

The air at her back stirred as the Face Stealer stepped up to her shoulder.

"Ask him," Kenai urged her. "Go on, ask him."

This was exactly what he wanted: to erode the uncertain lens she now viewed the Face Stealer through, and in its place, allow knowledge to settle, of who the true monster was. She couldn't help but wonder.

"How," she whispered, still not looking at the man beside her, "did Sita die?"

The Face Stealer practically vibrated with leashed tension, all his emotion strapped down.

Kenai's expression was an awful combination of grief and cruelty. "I will answer for my brother, since it seems he cannot find it within himself to speak the truth." There was no triumph in him, only the purest form of detestation. Hatred was personal. It bore dying weeds, and hurt, pain, love, those were the roots from which it grew. "She was found dead at the bottom of a ravine, his dagger shoved through her heart."

The face Kenai held shook in his hand. He retreated another step, nearing the water as it rushed in and dragged out in a long, drawn-out hiss.

Apaay concentrated on keeping her voice level. "How do you know for sure it was him?"

"The weapon was forged from his blood. No one could have wielded it but him."

All she could think of was little Mika, motherless, and not by choice. With rising dread, Apaay looked at the Face Stealer. Revulsion twisted his features, a sickness of his own actions, which she now saw, horribly, as truth. "Did you—"

"Yes." Low. "But it's not what you think."

"I think it's exactly what she thinks," Kenai tossed back.

"No," said Numiak, the word so low it grated. "I was trying to fix the mess *you* made, the war *you* played a hand in. I loved Sita."

"You hated that Father loved us. You despised that he hated you. Admit it, Numiak. You were always jealous of the way Father treated Sita and me."

"Maybe I was," he said, and the strained tone left him naked to how torn he was over the favoritism, even to this day. "But at least I knew my feelings of love were true, not twisted by Father's grief. It killed you that, even when he loved you, you could never be what he needed, brother."

Kenai's eyes flashed rings of white. His rage culminated, narrowing to a point. "Brother?" he spat. "You stopped being my brother the moment you took everyone I loved away from me." Waves splashed as he at last stepped into the white foam. "Farewell, Numiak."

Gently, Kenai lowered the face to the water. Then it sank beneath the sea.

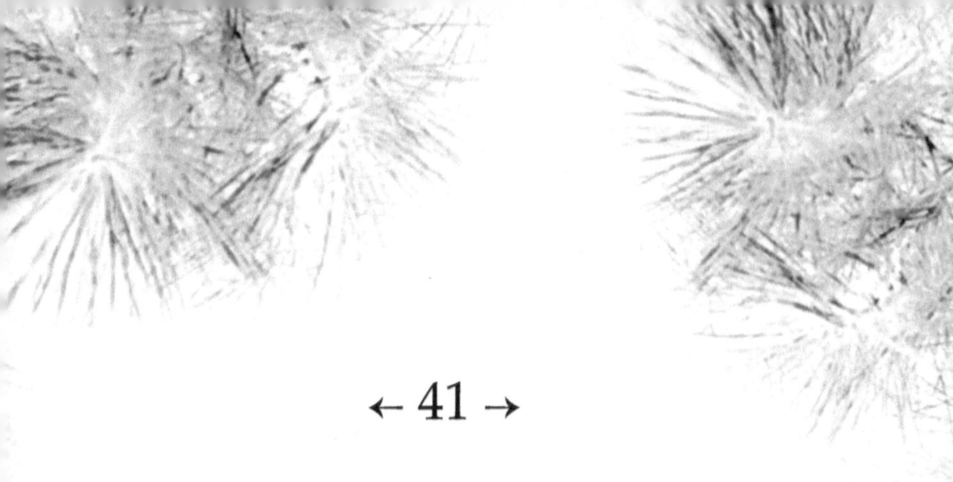

← 41 →

Tor went as flat and placid as a lake. No waves, no shifting of the tides. The white ruffles settled in the distance, and the ice floes no longer bobbed in the current. It all happened in a matter of seconds.

The Face Stealer froze. "Run."

Grabbing Apaay's hand, he dragged her back to the forest. Mud, pebbles, and snow streamed down the incline, having been shaken loose from the tremors running underground. They were halfway up the slope when sound ruptured at their backs.

The ground jerked so forcefully it threw them forward, and Apaay didn't have time to process their trajectory. She felt hands on her body, turning her in mid-air. Numiak tucked Apaay against his chest, one hand cupping the back of her neck and the other arm banding across her shoulders, and took the brunt of impact as they slammed into a tree and a column of gray-green water erupted skyward. The force ripped through her spine, but the sound of the air being punched from the Face Stealer's lungs was far worse. They hit the ground. Snow dislodged from the branches and pounded atop their bodies.

Apaay wheezed, "Are you hurt?" The soft ice encasing them gathered the warmth of their breath.

His arms twitched around her. "I think one of my ribs is broken."

Apaay helped push the snow off them. Pain gave his skin a slight sheen. She scanned his body, aware of the gushing water at their backs and time slipping through her fingers. "Can you sit up?"

A vein throbbed in his temple. He managed to prop himself onto his elbow. "Reach into my parka for the stone there. Hurry."

Apaay fumbled for his pocket, casting a look over her shoulder. Kenai had disappeared. The sea was angrier than she had ever seen it. It dragged huge piles of sand from shore back into the water's deep.

She closed her hand around the stone, felt its hum through her mittens. Apaay had never seen the Face Stealer so weakened. She wanted to demand a plan from him, but from the tightness of his features and the distance of his gaze, Apaay knew he didn't have one. They had meant to stop Kenai, yet they had failed.

"Here." She shoved the object into his hand. It sounded like the gushing water was beginning to calm.

Touching the stone to his mouth, the Face Stealer said, "Kaan, Ro, Tulimaq. Come to Tor, three miles southwest of Talguk. Hurry." He dropped his hand, as if it took too much energy to hold it up. "Even if they receive the message, they might not make it in time. They're moving the refugees. We'll have to stall."

Apaay's stomach churned as the consequences of what she had demanded from him in Taggak became known. "You don't have your power."

"You forget I was a soldier before I was a demon. I can still wield a weapon."

That made one of them. Apaay hadn't a weapon on her and would rather not kill someone else if she could help it.

She followed his gaze to where it settled over her shoulder. The water had cleared, and Kenai stood where he had moments before, unharmed, as a creature rose from the depths, held aloft by foam that concealed the lower half of her body, but left her upper torso exposed. It was indeed a woman. Her nut-brown skin held the palest tinge of yellow-green, as if strands of seaweed existed beneath its surface. She was a small thing, but not without presence. Netting covered her narrow shoulders. Red kelp banded around her breasts. Water beaded along her arms, her neck a balanced column supporting a face that was both arresting and cruel.

Slowly, the Face Stealer pushed to a standing position, frigid control encapsulating his features. Apaay got to her feet as well, and the first stirring of disquiet pulled at her. The woman wore sleek black gloves.

"Hello, Numiak," said the woman in a voice that was both the one Apaay remembered and yet harsher, wilder, and so terrible it took an enormous effort not to cover her ears. Though soft, it held all the intensity of an enraged shriek.

Apaay looked to Kenai with dread. He took no notice. His attention was only for the woman, whose features were not those of the girl-child she had been in the labyrinth, but someone ageless. Long, seaweed-tangled black hair fell in ropes over her shoulders and back. The cut of her bone structure was like broken coral. The blacks of her eyes glistened wetly. That red gash of a mouth.

The Face Stealer dipped his chin. "Yuki." His voice was cool.

Smirking at his acknowledgment, Yuki turned to Kenai. Impossibly, something in her face softened. The water rolled her closer, splashing Kenai's chest and darkening the caribou fur on the front of his parka. "Hello, Kenai." With light fingers, she touched the edge of his mouth where the heavy scarring dragged it down to one side. "It has been a long time."

His throat bobbed as she lowered herself so they were at eye level. "It has."

Apaay didn't know what was worse: the obvious love he felt for this woman, or the revulsion she felt as Yuki lowered her head and pressed a kiss to Kenai's mouth.

"Yuki," she began shakily to Kenai, "is your beloved?" The question came out garbled. She realized the Face Stealer had rested a hand on her shoulder. It trembled faintly. "I thought you said her name was Ain."

"That was the name I gave him, long ago," Yuki explained, still looking at Kenai. "I could not risk anyone discovering my identity."

She touched his scarred cheek and murmured to him, "I hope you understand."

His gaze never turned from hers. "Yes—Yuki."

Apaay remembered how she had reached through the bars of Kenai's cell to save him, and all this time he had loved the woman who had dashed Apaay's life onto the rocks.

Except she studied him again. During their escape from the labyrinth, he had *seen* Yuki, yet there had been no recognition. Because she had worn another's face, Apaay realized. He hadn't known that the woman he loved was the same one who had crushed Apaay with her cruelty.

Again, Apaay looked to Yuki's gloved hands as a new awareness took hold of her. "Who are you?" The material was supple, like sealskin. "If the Sea Mother—"

"You stupid child." Yuki bore a truly horrendous grin of serrated teeth. "I *am* the Sea Mother."

← →

The grim, sweat-darkened features of the Face Stealer told her that what Yuki said was true. Impossible, but true. Apaay only wondered how she hadn't seen it before.

Yuki's mastery over water. Her fish's teeth and the netting draped across her shoulders. How she had always smelled of the sea. She supposed the idea of the Sea Mother being anywhere near land was so outlandish she had never considered it.

Inevitably, Apaay's gaze returned to Yuki's hands. The slender, unusually short fingers concealed by the shiny black material. Because they had been severed at the joint, she realized. It was as the stories said. Yuki's father shoving her overboard in sacrifice, her fingers catching the edge of the umiak. Then a blade swinging down.

"I was telling you the truth before," Yuki asserted with bitterness, her chin lifting a fraction as the water rippled from movement beneath the surface. "I was trapped, you see. Given the face of a human child, doomed to remain on land until my true identity was returned to me." Her gaze touched upon the Face Stealer, wild with hurt. "It was a horrible life. The sea suffered while I was gone."

The Face Stealer's expression etched into a cold mask of fury. He growled, "Tens of thousands of people suffered because of your actions. They didn't have a choice. You did."

"And what did I choose?" she said with a high-strung laugh. "Loneliness? Separation from my children, who believed I had deserted them?" Even in hurt and sadness, she was fierce. "You forced me to abandon my purpose."

"You abandoned your purpose the moment you joined Nanuq's cause."

"You're wrong." The claim must have touched upon a weakness, for the words were sharp.

"My dear Yuki. You made it your life's work to prove to your father your power and might, then handed it over to the first man who swayed you with pretty promises."

Apaay had thought Yuki cruel, thought her power-hungry and vicious, but she was a woman among men, armoring herself in a man's world, and so she must be shrewd and knowing, in the way of old things.

Her eyes were hard and cold. "You think you can manipulate me, but your plan didn't work, Numiak." Yuki spat his name, her black hair choked with brown and red kelp. "One cannot tame the sea."

"That is the difference between Nanuq and myself," he said. "I have no desire to tame you. I had only hoped for you to have a change of heart."

"It doesn't matter," Yuki went on, in a way that suggested it mattered very much. "Now that Kenai has helped me return home, I don't need you anymore. Nanuq and I have joined forces. He, at least, welcomes me."

"He's using you."

"Save it," she hissed. "You might not think very highly of me, but I had plenty of time to reflect on my actions while I rotted in that prison. And yes, Numiak, it was indeed a prison. Believe it or not, I thought you and I could band together: two people the world had cast off." Her huff of breath was sharp as a pin. "You disappoint me. You always disappoint me."

"I didn't disappoint you," he said, his attention sliding to where Kenai stood beside the Sea Mother in silent support. In another life, he might be standing with them instead. "You did that all on your own."

Her lips parted in surprise. She whispered, "I'm through giving you chances."

Sleek heads of mottled gray skin breached the surf. Round, liquid eyes caught the frail moonlight and gleamed like wet stone.

The seal Unua were too many to count as they swam forward, transforming into their human skins upon reaching the shore. It was a siege. A wave of dark bodies, animal, then man. They bore tattered netting, bits of seaweed clinging. Their pointed black boots, flipper-like. Their disregard for cold.

They came, a heave of flesh onto the shore, bearing weapons: staffs caked with hard coral to catch and tear skin. Urchins attached at the tips, their spines filled with venom. Barnacle-encrusted blades that pulped flesh even as it cleaved it in two.

Apaay pressed into the Face Stealer's side, dizzied by the sheer number of opponents. Had the Face Stealer possessed his power, the gathering would not be so daunting, yet she felt incredibly mortal watching the Sea Mother's children heed her call. "Have you heard back from Ro or Kaan?" she asked him.

The hand he had placed on her shoulder slid to the back of her neck, his fingers curving around the base. "Not yet."

"And Tulimaq?"

Uncertainty flickered in him as he slowly shook his head. The mass had split to flank them as Yuki and Kenai discussed something with each other. There looked to be a few hundred soldiers at least. "I don't know. He should be here."

"Children." The Sea Mother's voice rang out. At once, her followers lifted their weapons.

Apaay tried shifting closer to the Face Stealer but found their bodies already as close as they could get. Her stare bored into the side of Kenai's head. He refused to meet her eye, the coward.

"I don't know how long I'll be able to hold them off," Numiak said under his breath, drawing a knife from somewhere on his person. Again and again, the seal Unua emerged from Tor's waters and streamed across the shore. "Can you make it to the edge of the tree line?"

"What about you?"

The demon stood stiff-backed, sharp-eyed. He looked to Yuki, then the soldiers, then his brother, then Yuki again. Their opponents stood in rows of ten with twenty columns total. Two hundred soldiers.

Apaay was well beyond fear at this point. "This is the part where you tell me you're very hard to kill." He had no power. More than that, he was weakened by his lack of it.

"I would be, had I not gotten my heart back." There was a distinct lack of humor in his voice. "Now I'm much easier to kill."

"That's not helpful."

His mouth twisted with the irony. "I can give you thirty seconds," he said, shifting to position himself in front of her.

She grabbed his arm, startling him. What could she say? And why was she hesitating? Surely she would allow the risk of his life. He was giving her an opportunity to flee.

"Take them!"

The soldiers descended before Apaay had the chance to formulate an answer, and a wall of power shot from the Face Stealer's palm and slammed into the nearest row, hurling them back into the sea.

Apaay gaped as they sank beneath the waves and re-emerged. He'd given his power to the Raven, hadn't he?

Yuki rose on her pillar of water, foam bubbling around her waist, and shoved a wave toward them. It hit the Face Stealer's semi-transparent barrier like the most brutal of hammers. The shield quaked.

This was when Apaay should have run. She had thirty seconds to seek safety in the trees. But five seconds came and went, and then ten. A third of her time gone. Her feet had yet to move.

"Apaay," he warned.

She stayed.

Sand churned with the water's agitation, and the trees groaned, bowing beneath a crushing wind. The second column of soldiers rammed into the barrier with a horrible *crack*. The wall of power flared, causing momentary blindness. Yuki rose up, magnificent and unearthly, and called to her children. The seal Unua, whose ancestors had been born from the severed tips of her fingers. Apaay shrunk from the budding, roiling power.

When the third wave hit, ripples spread from the force of impact. To Apaay's horror, thin fissures spiderwebbed across the barrier. "Numiak."

"Kenai's right, you know." He spoke through his teeth. Apaay wasn't sure if the pain came from his confession or from trying to maintain their only form of protection. He wavered like a flame in the wind. "I killed our sister."

His eyes were feverish. He felt too far away to call back in this moment.

"Did you kill her on purpose?" It was an important distinction.

Numiak blinked sweat from his eyes. "I loved Sita. I would have died for her, but I was weakened from fighting and couldn't return home fast enough." He grunted, pressed bloodless lips together. *Listen,* the words pleaded. *Listen to what I have to say.* "Yuki had my heart, had power over me."

Apaay felt the agony of his memory as if it stood between them, as if the confession was wrenching open her chest and reaching claws inside.

"By the time I reached Unana, Nanuq's forces had already arrived. A poisoned arrow had hit Sita in the arm. It was too late to save her. She was . . . in a lot of pain," he gritted out, jerking as Yuki bashed the barrier repeatedly, but the water could not penetrate it, and neither could her children piling at its front. "She told me to take care of Mika. It was her final wish. I ended her pain and sent her to the spirit world with my blade."

With the last word, he pressed an object into her hand. Apaay looked down at the knife, then lifted her gaze as his eyes snapped wide, revealing irises of the most piercing yellow: his wolf eyes.

"You'll burn out," she said, tugging on one of his arms.

The Face Stealer shrugged her off. His arms, held out on either side to reinforce the weakening blockade, trembled, and Apaay's fear twisted into something unrecognizable. He would kill himself in order to maintain the barrier until reinforcements arrived.

"Numiak, stop!" Apaay threw herself at him as his eyes rolled into the back of his head. The barrier vanished the moment he crumpled to the ground. "Numiak." She tapped his pallid cheek. The skin was cool. "Numiak!" Harder, the flat of her palm stinging as it made contact.

Apaay fumbled to check for a pulse when someone snagged her arms and yanked her backward. The dagger slipped from her fingers.

She was still screaming his name, kicking out at her captor's legs. The smell of fish oil rotted her nose as the crowd closed in, and it was no longer the smell of comfort and home, but stagnant and waterlogged, a seal corpse stinking in the sun. Thrashing her head, she caught the back of it against a hard surface. Pain erupted as her captor cursed. *Kenai.*

Wrenching her arms behind her back, Kenai forced her to her knees, rocks digging into the torn pelt of her trousers.

Water splashed across the shore at Yuki's approach, a skirt of kelp swaying as she moved. She was a woman. She was a god. Apaay bared her teeth while fighting nausea. It was not the first time she had been on her knees in Yuki's presence.

The deity tilted her head in contemplation. "I see your hair has grown back." Light, gloved fingers stroked a chin-length strand.

The taste of metal lay heavily on her tongue. She was afraid to open her mouth for fear of retching all over Yuki's bare feet.

"As much as it angers me that he left," Yuki said with a look of consideration at the Face Stealer's collapsed form, "I don't want him dead. Numiak is a useful tool, at the very least."

"Kenai does," Apaay tossed back.

Yuki's brows lifted. "Is that true, Kenai? You wish to kill your brother?"

With a mien of unfeeling cold, he came to take his place at Yuki's side. "Our father always claimed I was too soft. No matter what I did to please him, it wasn't enough. It never would be, with our mother gone. Ten years of my life I cared for Numiak. No matter how I tried, I couldn't break free."

"He's your brother," Apaay said, furious on Numiak's behalf. Did Kenai not see his brother as the little boy who had adored him? Kenai had been his entire world.

"*Was* my brother."

Yuki's shriek interrupted Apaay's reply. The Face Stealer, who had been on the ground seconds before, was gone. Apaay's head jerked around when she suddenly felt hands curving around her waist, power sizzling against her skin. Her last glimpse was of Kenai's eyes—haunted, betrayed—before they disappeared.

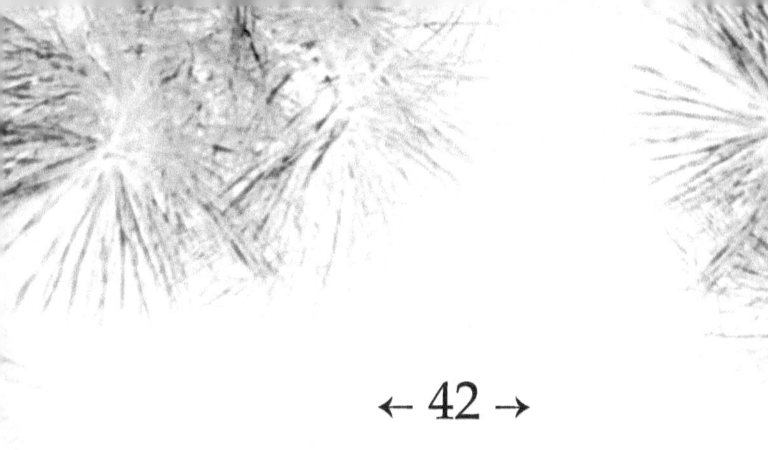

← 42 →

Her story began, it seemed, with a name.

Matilaqaa.

Said once, inside her head.

Matilaqaa.

Again, captured in the space between her hands.

Matilaqaa.

And lastly, a song in her heart.

I know that name, Ila signed in confusion. *Why do I know that name?*

The First Man's face shifted the barest inch. She realized she needed to touch the stone in order to maintain their connection. "I have the answers you seek," spoke the voice, filling her skull and vibrating inside her ears. It was deep and vast, of a different, older world. "However, I require payment. One secret in exchange for another."

A secret? She had none. She had done nothing in her life worth hiding. He must know this, which made her think he was looking for something else. A different truth, one quietly tended all these years.

Ila stared into the absence of his eyes. It was time. *My secret is this: I have been afraid all my life. I am afraid that I am unlovable, that I am broken. I am afraid that I am not important enough to remember. But to learn of who I am?* Her fingers dug into the green earth. *Of this, I am not afraid.*

The First Man considered her with his vacant gaze, one that would eventually witness the death of this world, and perhaps the world after. "What do you want to know?"

She said, *Everything.*

← →

"Numiak came to me many decades ago," the First Man began, "concerned that the Polar Bear Empire's civil war was reaching its end and that it might morph into an even greater conflict down the line, should victory fall into the wrong hands. Nanuq had returned from his absence ten years before, having brought with him war tactics his people had never before encountered. Knowledge of strategy and weapons, forms of torture. That was the first time people began to speak of him as almost a man."

Snow spiraled beyond the domed barrier and piled higher and whiter and deeper, ensconcing the bases of the trees. Beyond the broken peaks of the Atakana lay an eastern sky lightened faintly by a sun that would soon rise.

Ila listened with acute focus, sensing the fragility of what he said. This information gave context to her identity. She took every word and imprinted it onto her heart.

"Nanuq fought like a man and took as men did, pillaging and slaughtering the earth. For those in the outlying regions, who only heard of his deeds through word of mouth, he became almost a myth."

The First Man's voice held no emotion. For him, this was history. He was the repository of so many stories and lives. His job was to house them until they were meant to be passed on.

"When it was learned that Nanuq had assassinated his king, Numiak came to me. He was worried Nanuq would fix his attention northward, extending the war beyond the empire's borders. I told him what I knew. Nanuq sought an object of power called the Creator. No one knew what it was or how he had learned of it."

The stone figure's gaze seemed to search deep into her soul. Ila felt pinned. "He believed it to be hidden somewhere in the North."

This wasn't the first time she had heard of the object of power, but it was the first time she could put a name to it. The Creator. Ila hadn't any idea of its meaning. Whatever it was, Nanuq continued his search for it.

The First Man went on in his inflectionless, gravelly tone. "Numiak returned home and told his people to prepare. The Owl Clan did the same. The Caribou Nomads went underground and were not heard from. The Seal Colonies aligned with Nanuq's forces."

As the First Man painted this picture of history, Ila was struck by how huge this conflict had been. To have involved all the Unua nations, Nanuq must have been an immense threat. Powerful beyond measure.

"A year passed, and during that time, Nanuq built his army. People were afraid. Some traveled to Across the Sea, seeking safety in an unknown land. Nanuq believed the Creator to be located in what is now known as the Western Territory." A pause. "That was the second time Numiak came to me."

They were getting somewhere. With each step into this hole, Ila could feel the walls reaching higher, pressing closer, the pinhole of light squeezing into nothing. Her heart knocked inside her chest. *Now,* she thought. Now she would learn.

What did you tell him? she asked, her hand quickly returning to the rock so she would not miss his reply.

"He wanted to know the best course of action. Invasion was imminent." A softer breeze, as if he sighed into the air. "But it was a bad time for the Wolf Kingdom. The Vaal—their female leader and mate to the Narg—had recently given birth to their second daughter." For a moment, all was quiet inside her head. "Their first daughter," he said, "they'd named Matilaqaa."

The resonance inside Ila's skull gradually faded as she leaned back. She could not fully grasp what was happening. *I'm sorry?*

The earth rumbled as the First Man drew himself farther aboveground. "You, Matilaqaa of the Wolf Kingdom, are heir to a once-great nation. This was your fate from birth, though it was taken from you too soon."

Her hands dropped into her lap, clenched, the nails gouging the fleshy part of her palms through her mittens. At first, Ila thought he was making fun of her, yet she knew he was not. Heir to a once-great nation? He was mistaken. He must have her confused with someone else. *I don't believe you.*

"Believe me, Matilaqaa, for I am never wrong."

A trembling spread outward from her core. She did not feel like herself. It wasn't sickness, but a vast disconnect between her mind and heart, between what the First Man informed her and what she had previously believed of herself. So many things did not make sense, like why she'd been a prisoner in Yuki's labyrinth if Yuki had sided with Nanuq to invade the Western Territory, or why she was alive when the rest of her people were dead.

It can't be.

"And why is that?"

The question asked for no more than a simple explanation, yet every logical reason sounded like an excuse.

"Where you are and who you are now has no bearing on your birthright," the stone figure explained. "Whether you are young or old, lost or angry or deeply unhappy, you are the firstborn to the Narg and Vaal. Their blood runs through your veins."

This destiny was too large. It didn't fit her. The cramped bars of the cell—those fit her. Or maybe they didn't anymore. Maybe she had believed such a thing because she hadn't known she had the power to choose otherwise. Ila had chosen nothing of her life before. Which made her wonder: Had it ever been her life, or had she been living someone else's *idea* of her life?

Kaan had told her the history of the Unua nations. The Wolf Kingdom had deep loyalty to its people. It was deeper than blood, deeper than the bedrock of the North. To learn she was a part of this community . . . She'd never had that before. It was so much more than a gift. It was a piece of her identity returned to her, a purpose and a place.

Who am I? she'd asked herself.

It was time to stop smothering her own potential.

When Ila lifted her eyes, she swore the world burned a touch brighter.

Tell me the rest, she demanded. *Did Numiak save me during the invasion?*

His tone lessened in intensity, thankfully. "Yes. It was a dangerous time. Numiak came to me asking for a place to hide you. I told him the best hiding place was the one closest to harm. As far as I'm aware, the one you know as Yuki did not know your true identity. If she had, she would have killed you. You were pronounced dead on the day of the invasion."

What do you mean, the one you know as Yuki? Isn't that her name?

A pause as he considered the question. "Her current name, I suppose. But her history is as long as her names, and there are many."

Wait. She frowned, having remembered something. *You mentioned I was the oldest daughter. That means I have a sister. Is she alive?*

"She is."

Ila shuffled closer on her knees. The ground was soft. The air smelled of green things. *Please. What's her name?*

Rock cracked as the ancient being shifted his head an inch. "I'm afraid I don't have an answer for you. When the invasion occurred, she was but days old. Your parents had yet to name her, and no one has come to me with the information since then."

But she was out there somewhere. Perhaps waiting for Ila. *And my parents?* Though Ila already knew, she wanted to be absolutely certain they were gone.

"I'm sorry," he said, "but they were killed during the invasion."

It should not have mattered, in the end. She didn't remember them. Yet Ila felt the loss as if it were happening for the very first time.

Ila tilted back her head so her eyes were full of the stars scattered thick as green grass across the sky. Hope and disappointment, life and death—each fought for space in her chest. War sparked in some far-off corner to the south and would soon burn. It had already touched them in the Wood, in the Central Territory, in the long-since abandoned Western Territory, the land of . . . of her people. The world thought they were gone. If there was one labor camp, might there be more? She could go to them, free them. It was a start.

As this newfound purpose replenished her soul, Ila asked her final question. *Where do I go from here?*

"Return home, Matilaqaa, and set your people free."

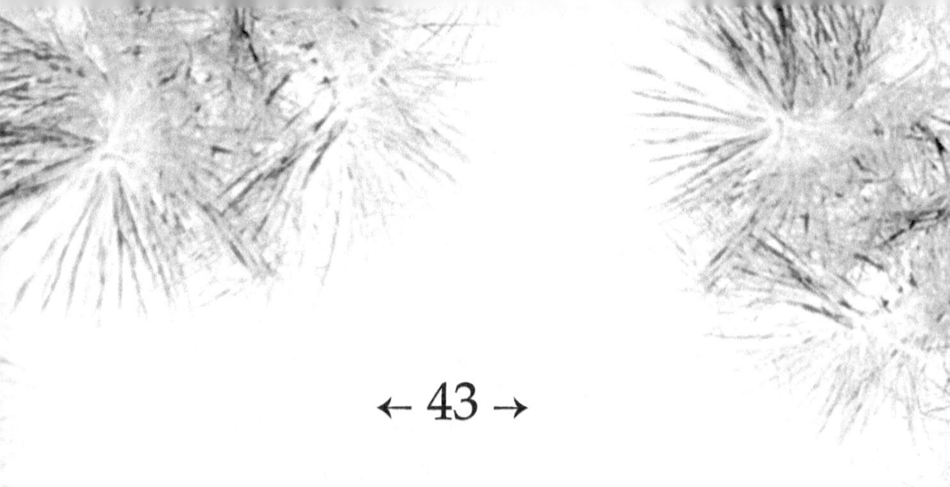

← 43 →

Apaay and the Face Stealer materialized in the middle of the woods moments before Yuki's furious scream reached their ears. Seconds later, he collapsed.

Apaay dropped to her knees. He wasn't moving. She pushed him onto his back, cursing his weight, the paleness of his skin. They had gone a few miles, if that. Far enough from immediate danger, but near enough to still be concerning. It wouldn't take long for the seal Unua to find them.

"Don't you dare die on me," she hissed, her grip tightening on his arm. "You're the one who got me into this mess, and you're going to get me out of it." She slapped his face until he groaned.

"Trying to kill me, wolfling?" he mumbled, his eyes still closed.

Apaay bit back a broken laugh. She was so damn tired. "If it gets you standing, then yes."

He sighed, as if this was an inconvenience to him. "Help me up."

She did, brushing the snow from his front and back. "Where did your power come from?" It had been a silvery white rather than the usual black. "I thought the Raven took it from you."

The Face Stealer stumbled to a tree and slumped against it, sweat pouring down his face. The damp would chill his skin and lower his core body temperature. It was grounds for hypothermia. "Doesn't matter. It's almost gone." He braced his hands on his knees, his hair hanging around his face. Apaay glanced around the wooded area and found it empty. "Listen to me." His gaze, though dulled, still managed to maintain its piercing quality. "You need to get to Talguk. Head north about three miles. There's a harbor where the city once stood. The most important thing," he said, "is that they don't catch you. Understand?"

You, he'd said, not *us.* Apaay studied his face and knew only confusion. She *didn't* understand. "What about you?"

"It's me they want. I'll draw them away. You focus on getting to Talguk."

This sounded like a terrible idea. Splitting their forces meant half the overall strength. He could barely stand. Apaay looked back through the trees. "Isn't it better to stay together, especially since you don't have your power?"

"They don't realize my power is gone, and Yuki doesn't know I have my heart back. If I can draw her away from the sea, she'll be weaker."

She wasn't convinced. "And when they realize you're powerless?"

A shiver racked his build. "I can still fight with a weapon."

One he could barely hold. But she bit back the worry. Despite everything that could go wrong, his voice was steady. Apaay had forgotten the Face Stealer was used to war. It was she who wasn't.

"Get to the port," he repeated. "There's a building with a blue door at the harbor. Take the stairs down to the lowest floor. There will be a tunnel that connects to a small village in the mountains. Take that tunnel as far as you can. Don't stop, understand? Do not stop no matter what."

What's going to happen, Apaay wanted to ask, *if this doesn't work? If they kill you or me or both of us?* She feared what he did not say. This wasn't a plan. This was crazed desperation, a shot in the dark. She didn't know if they would see each other again.

His gaze narrowed at her lack of reply. "Apaay."

"I won't stop," she whispered.

Numiak hesitated, looking down at her. For a moment, she thought he might say something.

He turned and fled in the opposite direction.

Apaay went north. Three miles didn't seem like a long distance—she had trekked farther distances during a hunt—but she had never been so worn down. Apaay did what the Face Stealer had told her to do. She did not stop.

In some places, the forest thinned to patchy clearings, as if whole swaths had been knocked down or burned. She passed ruins poking through the drifts and gasped with every step, every mile taken. If she could not run, then she would walk, and if she could not walk, then she would crawl. Apaay was sweating so heavily she had half a mind to abandon her parka, but that would be completely idiotic. She didn't want to die from exposure.

Apaay reached the edge of what must be Talguk. Ahead, ice hugged the low stone wall surrounding the harbor. Stone structures dotted the area, most collapsed into rubble and swimming in snow, but a few still stood with their peaked roofs hammered of shiny volcanic rock. It was a quiet scene, soft, with most of the buildings buried, yet a violent tinge infiltrated the area, a lingering memory of how brutally the city had been ransacked. Decades ago, Talguk had run red.

Apaay targeted the structures farthest from the water first. *Blue door,* she thought. The words tattooed into her mind. Even as she searched the rubble, much of which she believed had been homes, she did not feel entirely alone.

After checking every building on the city's edge, Apaay moved toward the harbor. It was there, only yards from the harbor wall, that she spotted three soldiers emerging from the forest.

Apaay ducked against a crumbling structure where the dark was thickest. Her breath made hot mist of the air. She covered her mouth with her hand and did not move.

Snow crunched beneath the women's boots. Their green-and-black garb marked them as seal Unua. Liquid eyes and shaved heads. Another shared characteristic, if not of their people, then the army.

They murmured to one another as they studied the crisscrossing trails Apaay had made, all fresh.

The tallest of the women scanned the area with a keen eye. Apaay immediately designated her as the leader. "We'll split up and reconvene. She can't have gotten far."

While her fellow soldiers headed off, the leader crouched to examine the ground more closely. She touched the edge of Apaay's boot print, rubbed the snow between her fingertips.

Whereas the other soldiers had taken off eagerly, this woman ambled toward the harbor. She stood where Apaay had earlier and looked out at the ruin of the city.

"I know you're there," she called, and Apaay realized the soldier was speaking to *her*. "And I *will* find you."

Apaay shrank against the shadows, trembling from exhaustion and looming peril. If she couldn't find the door, her only hope was to return to where she and the Face Stealer had parted ways. It wasn't really a hope, though. These women would hunt her down before she ever reached the Face Stealer.

"Our mother sent us to end you. There is nothing we would not do for her." The woman's eyes passed over Apaay's hiding place. "I will give you a head start. It has been too long since we've given chase."

Moving as quietly as possible, Apaay fled deeper into the city, terror closing its fingers on her throat and taking control of her emotions. She no longer had the luxury of time to dig among the ruins.

With the promise of death looming, Apaay darted between two of the larger structures, squeezing through a narrow space to an empty clearing surrounded by four walls on the other side. It may have once been a central square, back when there had been people to utilize it. There wasn't another exit, so she turned, thinking *hurry*, and found herself staring into the eyes of the lead soldier, the other women flanking her.

Apaay stumbled back, hands raised. "You don't have to do this," she whispered. "I'll run. You can claim you never saw me."

"Our mother doesn't care for you," said the leader.

From the corner of her eye, she spotted an unusually high snowbank. There might be rocks under it she could use to defend herself. She began inching toward it. "I'm aware of that."

"You've stolen Numiak away from her."

Stolen him away? As if. "If the Face Stealer left Yuki, it's only because she's insane." Seriously, there was something not right in the head with her.

The soldiers fanned out. They each bore a sword studded with sharp barnacles.

The shortest of the women lunged as Apaay scrambled to the other side of the mound. She was cut off by the second woman, whose eyes promised so much more than the first. The blade was a granite gray beneath the black barnacles, screaming as it swept toward her shoulder, devouring the air and space like it was nothing, and Apaay knew what the pain would feel like before it hit, knew the bite of a weapon burying itself into bone, knew how skin didn't tear neatly, but ripped open and spat blood. Apaay tried twisting out of range, but she was too slow. The blade embedded itself in her upper arm.

She screamed and lurched sideways, clasping her wound. Blood poured over her hand. The first woman darted toward her again. The tallest—the leader—stood back and observed.

Apaay did the only thing she could think of: She ran.

The first soldier cut off her escape and swung. Apaay ducked the blow and fell onto her backside. She scuttled backward like a crab and narrowly missed being impaled. The second woman appeared on her right. Apaay evaded the first woman's swing, but the second woman yanked her backward. Instinct screamed at her to pull away, but instead, she turned and rammed into the woman's stomach.

They crashed into the wall. Apaay forgot about the door, forgot about the Face Stealer. Her only concern was taking that weapon for herself. To be a predator, she must think like one.

But then the woman kneed her in the stomach. Then she slammed Apaay's skull against the stone, again, again. The sword speared down.

"Wait."

The barnacle-encrusted blade halted three inches above Apaay's forehead.

One look at the leader's cold, thin face, and Apaay knew she had run out of time. "Let me."

The two women gave them room, moving to stand along the wall. Apaay felt the world gape at her back, all that space to run. So it was to be this, then? Fine. One to one was far better odds than three to one.

The woman hacked at Apaay's side, forcing her back. Apaay lunged, grabbing hold of the leader's arm, and brought her down to the ground where the odds weighed in her favor. They rolled, grappling for leverage, each trying to render the other immobile. Apaay had grown up wrestling Eska and the other kids in her village. Muscle memory had her pinning the woman's legs, twisting her arm behind her back at an angle that pinched the nerve between shoulder and neck.

The woman was slippery though, and strong. Each time Apaay got close to pinning her, she broke free of the hold and reversed their positions. An elbow to the temple. A knee to the back. The bruises and sprains multiplied in the passing minutes as they hooked their arms and legs around one another, kicking up snow as they went.

Apaay shoved the woman hard enough to scramble away. The soldier, however, had tired of the games. She unsheathed her sword.

A scream in the wind as the weapon came down. Apaay dove to the side and rolled, hearing the thud as the blade stabbed the ground where her head had been seconds before. Apaay managed to wrap an arm around the soldier's neck, restrain her legs. She clasped the woman's wrist and slammed it as hard as she could against the ground. There was stone beneath the snow. Bone cracked.

The woman barked in pain and punched Apaay so hard the girl felt blood fill her mouth and her teeth rattle loose. She ducked her head to protect her eyes and clamped a hand around the soldier's broken wrist, digging strong fingers into the slivers of bone. A backhanded slap stung her cheek. Apaay shook the wrist, hard. The weapon flew out of the woman's hand.

They dove for it. Apaay grabbed it first, tried to toss it farther away, but the soldier wrenched her arm back with a growl, forcing Apaay to drop the sword unless she wanted a dislocated shoulder. The woman reached for the sword, Apaay shifting in retaliation, their movements a reflection of the other. In her focused state, she didn't notice the soldier pull something from her boot. Didn't see the knife in her hand.

The blade plunged into Apaay's gut.

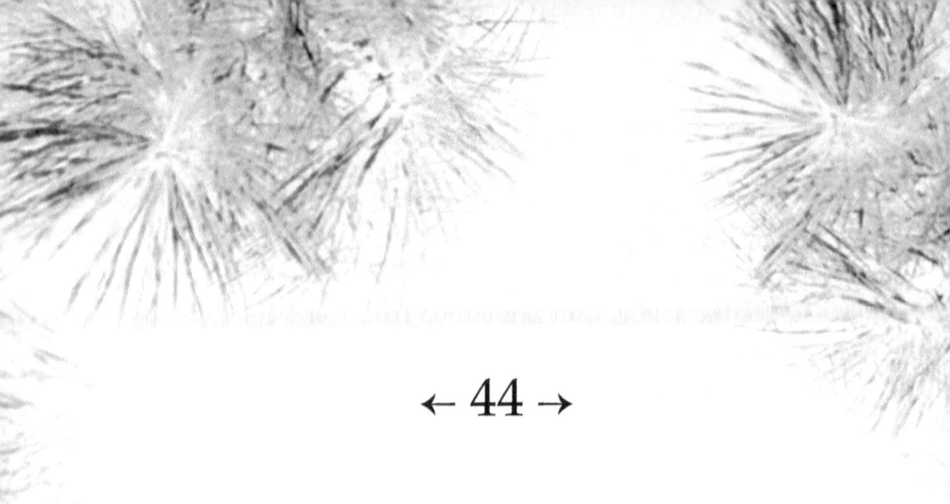

← 44 →

Apaay staggered, looking at the weapon sticking out of her stomach with horror and slow confusion. Blood soaked the front of her parka as she wrapped her fingers around the mother-of-pearl hilt. She didn't feel the pain.

The woman stared with onyx eyes, her expression empty of emotion. The other soldiers held back. "May your death come slowly."

They fled.

Apaay fell to her knees. The snow was soft, but the stone beneath was hard. Her hands shook. Apaay was never more aware of how alone she was, how alone she'd been these long, arduous months, and how she wished for company as her blood flowed across the muddied slush. If she was to die, she wanted someone to say goodbye to, and to bless her spirit as it passed on.

She stared at the hilt. It was the only thing keeping the wound closed, and wasn't that funny? Apaay tipped back her head and laughed. The taste of copper filled her mouth. She choked and spat it out.

Why was killing so difficult for her yet so simple for everyone else? Was it a flaw? A weakness? Was she too soft?

The pulsing in her ears drowned out all other sound. The blade had likely punctured a vital organ. If that was the case, she didn't have long.

Apaay didn't want to die. She wanted to live, ferociously. The Face Stealer had told her to find the blue door, the tunnel, to keep going and not stop no matter what. Well, did a *knife* in her gut count as *no matter what*?

This was exactly why she hadn't wanted to split up. If they had stayed together, maybe this wouldn't have happened. She couldn't say what had become of the Face Stealer. He'd given her a chance to flee. She wouldn't squander it.

It felt like years before Apaay gathered the strength to push to her feet. The adrenaline wouldn't last. When her body flushed it from her system, she'd feel the weapon as she'd felt the arrow sawing through her arm. Apaay wanted to cover as much distance as possible before that happened. The blade wasn't smooth. It was made of barnacles, its unrefined edges catching on soft flesh.

Gripping the hilt in one hand to prevent the dagger from shifting when she moved, Apaay stumbled from the square. Ten seconds later, she sagged against the side of a building and gasped as agony ripped through her. Her panting broke the quiet of the abandoned city. Blue door. She needed to find a blue door under all this snow. The backs of her teeth creaked as she clenched her jaw. Apaay felt woozy with pain.

One portion of the city remained that she had yet to investigate. Apaay used some of the freestanding structures for support as she stumbled her way to the huddle of small homes located on the opposite side of the frozen harbor from where she'd first emerged from the forest. With the stomach wound, it was almost impossible to brush the snow away from the rubble, so she resorted to using her feet.

Building after building, Apaay shuffled down the deserted path, her breathing growing more erratic with every step. The city's appearance didn't register. Stone and snow and rotting wood from collapsed roofs. Anything beyond that was lost to the waves of agony scouring her insides.

It was luck, she thought, that the next structure featured a blue door, the paint faded to nearly gray on dark-grained wood. She worked faster, clearing the way. Not that she had doubted the Face Stealer, but two decades was a long time for a door to remain standing in a place that had been ravaged beyond recognition. The only problem was, a large chunk of the adjacent stone wall had fallen and crushed the door in its center, blocking her way in.

The blood in Apaay's ears crackled like static from an electric storm. She took a few deep breaths, yanked on the door handle, and promptly passed out.

When Apaay came to, the gray sky curved above, and the ground chilled her back. Wet snow seeped into her hair. Blood oozed sluggishly from her stomach, her upper arm. It was difficult to move.

She closed her eyes, heard a shout. Apaay lifted her head, listening. Something about its tone gave her pause. It didn't come again.

Rolling onto her side, Apaay pressed her cheek into the dirty snow. The cold helped clear her wooziness. The terror, too, which pulled her heart in two ways. Fear that she would perish before help arrived, and fear of what would happen if she reached the end of the tunnel. Hope was such a fragile thing.

The next time she stood, she wrapped both hands around the door handle. Bracing one foot on the door, Apaay put all her strength into her legs and *pulled.*

The wood groaned. The blade sawed through her insides, and she bit back a scream. The stone shifted toward her an inch, then another. Apaay coughed up more blood, blinking away the black spots. One more heave. The stone fell back, and the door flung open.

Darkness awaited her in the tunnel. A mouth, a black chasm. She took the first step forward. Apaay was not afraid.

Another shout brought her to a halt, followed by a scream. She felt the hair rising on her nape.

The Face Stealer.

Apaay gripped the handle tighter. She was here. At the tunnel. Bleeding out with maybe an hour left before collapse.

Instead of all the reasons that pushed her toward the tunnel, she thought of all the reasons that held her back. When the Face Stealer had cast a protective barrier over her as wildfire erupted through the Central Territory. When he had fallen to his knees before the

Avi as she dangled hundreds of feet above the ground. And then his apology to her. It had been needed, and it had been true.

Apaay closed her eyes, resting her forehead against the door. He had his heart back, and this time, he *could* be killed. If that happened, she'd die in this tunnel. Without the Face Stealer standing between Nanuq and her family, they would die as well.

Death was a powerful motivator, but truthfully, it was not her main reason for hesitation. That vindictive streak called to her. If the Face Stealer died, she would never get the satisfaction of him carrying out the blood oath. For a favor of *her* choosing.

In the end, that's what got her feet moving in the opposite direction.

Power.

Over *him*.

← →

A trail of blood marked the three miles she had traveled from Talguk. Apaay had traded open sky for forest cover, salt for evergreen, and tentative safety for what would most likely be her death. *Fool, fool, fool,* pounded her heart. Her stupid, weakening heart. At least the frosty air had finally clotted the blood around her stomach wound.

Apaay heard Yuki's voice before she saw her. The sound, like animals dying a slow death, was unmistakable, as was her laugh. Apaay shuffled quickly in the direction it came from, as it often signaled pain.

Using a large conifer for cover, Apaay peeked around the trunk to take in the scene, and froze. Yuki and Kenai stood together among the trees, their backs to her, the Sea Mother's children arranged in tidy lines.

Apaay covered her mouth in horror. Numiak was on the ground. Multiple protrusions stuck out of his body. She thought they might be harpoon shafts, broken off with the heads still inside. One was buried in his stomach. Another two gouged his legs, one in the thigh, another in the calf. Kenai held a fourth harpoon in his hand.

She stared and stared, yet the Face Stealer didn't move. Her heartbeat ratcheted higher, and she had to physically turn away from the sight to steady her breathing. Not dead. He wasn't dead. Apaay had to believe it.

It had taken nearly an hour to get here. And during that time, they had tortured him. She felt the bile rise and pressed a sweat-slickened hand to her cheek, the hairs of the mitten scratchy. She should have come sooner, walked faster.

When she peeked around the trunk again, she watched Yuki kick the Face Stealer in the side. He groaned. "Stand up and fight. Or do you no longer have anything to fight for?"

Kenai's hatred of his brother was never more evident than in the hand that held the weapon. His fingers, curling around the staff in suffocation. The grip that was not quite steady, though Kenai's expression was as unfeeling as ever. Apaay didn't understand. What else had the Face Stealer done to Kenai? He'd taken Yuki's face, but was there more? What hadn't Kenai told her?

"Does this remind you of something, brother?" Kenai snarled. "Perhaps if you imagine not yourself in this position, but our father. Do you remember?" He leaned forward, as if daring him to answer. "Do you remember how they found him, just like this?" He was panting from the force of his words. "That's how it happened, isn't it?"

"That's not how it happened." He sounded exhausted beyond all measure. "Not really."

Kenai laughed. It was a horrible sound of grief, and it ran claws down Apaay's spine. "You're right. I'll tell you how it happened. How I was woken up in the middle of the night by the men who had come to our home claiming you murdered our father. I told them it wasn't you. I *defended* you. But they showed me what you had done to him after you were taken away. Sliced into his neck, right where the artery was."

The Face Stealer said, "You taught me that."

"I did." Kenai looked seconds away from a complete breakdown, but he managed to rein in his emotions long enough to say, "Why did you do it? Was it because of Yuki? Were you afraid I would leave you for her?"

Yuki glanced between the brothers, though her attention lingered on the Face Stealer as he said, "How could I be afraid? You had already left me—for someone who doesn't even love you."

Apaay used their distraction to duck behind the next closest tree.

"You have no idea what you're talking about," Yuki cried. "Of course I love him."

He shook his head, the motion sloppy and slow. "You don't know how to love, Yuki. I don't think that word is in your vocabulary." A fit of coughing stole over him. "You obsess. Too much. It eats at you, the obsession."

Apaay needed to figure out a way to distract Yuki, Kenai, and the soldiers long enough to get the Face Stealer away. How long had it been since he had called Ro, Kaan, and Tulimaq for aid? Someone should have come by now.

Kenai shook his head, looking far into the distance. Apaay wondered what he saw. "You're wrong, Numiak. Yuki does love me. She loves me the way you never could." He lifted the harpoon. "You took Father away from me."

"He was my father, too. When will you stop blaming me for his actions? I had no control over his hatred of me, nor of his withdrawal after Mother's passing."

"You wanted to punish him, and me," Kenai spat, his face darkening as the remorse bled free and the rage built. "So you took him away." He flipped the harpoon and aimed the tip at the Face Stealer's chest.

"You took our people away from *me*! If it wasn't for you, Sita wouldn't have died. It was Nanuq's men who killed her. The only thing I did was stop the pain."

"Lies. It's always been lies with you." But Apaay thought there had been a delay to the response. "Stand up, *brother*," he snarled, and Apaay noticed the glint of canines sinking into his lower lip. "Show me that you are more than your darkness and deceit. Show me that you still have the honor to fight for your life."

Kenai's kick jarred the harpoon staff sticking out of the Face Stealer's stomach, and the sound that came out of his brother's mouth was like nothing she had ever heard before. An animal scream.

Apaay bit the inside of her cheek so hard she felt flesh split beneath her teeth. He should never have made that dark oath. It was her fault they were in this situation. If there was a way to save him, she had to at least try.

"Stand up," Yuki snapped, but the demand didn't have its usual bite. She stared at his wound, then turned away.

He didn't move. "Why are you doing this, Yuki? This won't make your father love you. Fathers who love their daughters don't toss them into the sea as sacrifice."

She took two steps toward the Face Stealer, her eyes huge and black, and Apaay shrank against the side of the tree. "So that you will know what it's like for your own blood to turn on you. So that you will *understand*." She blinked to clear the sheen from her eyes. "Get up!"

Despite the obvious exhaustion, the deepening lines around his mouth, the Face Stealer's words were as coolly dangerous as she remembered. "The Raven sends you his regards."

Her nostrils flared. "So you got your heart back, did you? Was it the girl? Did she return your heart to you?"

"It doesn't matter. It is done."

The Face Stealer struggled to sit up. He managed to, finally, using a tree to help him stand. His body listed to the side. "I don't see how this is a fair fight, considering I'm mortally wounded."

"It wasn't a fair fight when you locked me up," Kenai responded, unnervingly calm as he watched his brother bleed out. "Take up your weapon."

With a near feral smile, the Face Stealer pulled a dagger from his waist sheath. He swung, but he was weakened, weary, drained. Kenai knocked aside the blade. It went flying. He shoved his younger brother against the trunk and pushed his face close.

"Tell me you hate me." The words were a choked whisper.

Numiak stared him in the eye.

His mouth remained shut.

"Say it." Kenai was trembling. Their pain was in the earth and in the air and flowing through their bodies, and Apaay felt it, too, felt the bond that had long ago been severed. Her heart cried out for Kenai, for them both. If her sister was half of her heart, what did that mean for the brothers?

"Say it!" he demanded.

The Face Stealer bared his teeth. They were outlined in blood. "No."

"Damn you, just say it!"

"You were my brother, Kenai." A pause. "And you were my father, too."

"Stop saying that," he spat.

"If you expect me to hate you, you're looking at the wrong person."

Apaay approached them from behind. She didn't know what she would do once she reached them. She didn't have a weapon.

"Don't listen to him," said Yuki. "When you return with me, you'll leave all this behind. Numiak had his chance to side with us. He chose not to. Now finish it."

The Face Stealer's eyes sharpened with clarity, briefly, before they dulled. "Kenai."

"You already made your choice," the Sea Mother said into the elder brother's ear. "With me, you will never want for attention. You will never want for love."

Kenai pulled back the harpoon as if to shove it through his brother's heart as Apaay came to a realization.

She did have a weapon.

Tears poured down her face as she slowly pulled the blade from her body. A new wave of blood spilled down her front. Apaay stumbled forward, trying not to vomit. She thought Numiak's eyes were closed, yet she caught the glimmer of his gaze beneath his lowered eyelids. He froze as their eyes locked.

Yuki noticed the change and whipped around. Apaay lifted the dagger. The Sea Mother screamed.

Apaay plunged the knife into Kenai's back.

A white wave surged toward her with a roar, slamming her into a tree. Water gushed into her mouth and eyes and nose, clotting her throat. Apaay sucked in a breath, choked. The air had gone. She tried wiping it from her face long enough to breathe, but there was always more to take its place, the salt scouring her nose and open wounds. Apaay was drowning on dry land.

A second roar came. It was someone's voice, so deep she felt it rumble through her. Something was broken. Her wrist, no, her body—spine, ribs, arms, knees. Apaay couldn't move even as she heard the sounds of battle, or animals, or men, or all of it—all of it wrapped together and pulling apart with vicious force, like the clashing of two white storms.

The black place she'd gone to grew even darker as the last of her air ran out. She heard thousands of beating wings.

Then Apaay was floating, rocked from side to side. As her head lolled, she caught the person's scent. Kaan. But they were running. How could this woman possibly be running while also carrying Apaay?

She must have blacked out, because when Apaay came to, she heard Kaan and the Face Stealer arguing nearby. The pressure in her stomach, a continuous agony.

"I only have enough power for one," Kaan was saying, the whisper fraught with fear. "It wouldn't make sense, Numiak. She's too close to death."

"I don't care how close to death she is," he snarled. "You *save* her, Kaan."

Apaay cracked open her eyes, found them deep in the forest with the shadows huddling at their backs. The heaviness on her abdomen turned out to be Ro pressing a soaked cloth to the wound.

Kaan and Numiak faced each other in a seated position. Or rather, Numiak was propped against the tree roots while Kaan leaned over him.

"Kaan." A warning.

"The poison will eat through your skin."

"You'll figure something out." It sounded like he spoke through his teeth.

She shook her head as, with a grim expression, she glanced at Apaay. No one noticed that she had woken. "You put too much faith in me," Kaan whispered.

"Not faith. Fact. You are the best healer I know."

"He's right," said Ro. It felt like years had passed since Apaay had heard his calming voice.

It will be all right, Apaay would have said if she'd had the ability to speak. The darkness was close and hovering.

The woman sighed. "I will heal her, but not before I tend to the poison. It will reach your heart within the hour."

"Kaan—"

"Don't argue with me on this," she snapped. "You're in no position to."

As Apaay's grasp on the here and now finally slipped, she became aware of her body, of soft hands on her stomach, then the dark fabric of unconsciousness.

← 45 →

High in the mountains, a single rucksack pulled across her shoulder, Ila navigated the perilous Atakana alone. The wind beat upon her hunched back. The granite, jutting and exposed on the cliff faces, grew smoother the higher she climbed. She had left the First Man behind hours ago and was now so deep into the impenetrable range no one would find her should they come looking.

The silence inside her head had become treacherous. It bred further apprehension of walking into this plan blind. She didn't know how she would get the prisoners out of the labor camp or where she could take them. The Wood had been the obvious choice, but with the breach, it was no longer safe. She'd overheard the Face Stealer talking to Kaan and Ro about moving its inhabitants to one of the Analak villages. Ila supposed the village could house the prisoners, but that was over two hundred miles of distance in the cold, traveled by people who had been beaten, whipped, and starved. There was also the matter of killing the guards without them taking notice, finding food, treating their injuries, which she imagined to be numerous. Ila didn't know a thing. But she had to try.

Snow gave way beneath her boots. Sopping clouds heavy with precipitation dragged across the glinting peaks. Ila counted her steps. Right foot and left foot and right foot and left foot.

She climbed.

Ila had never done something so dangerous or so full of potential. Matilaqaa. Heir to a once-great kingdom, and hers to claim.

The idea of leading people was so ridiculous it gave her heart palpitations. She didn't completely dismiss the idea, though. She needed to get used to it, that's all. Maybe she wasn't leadership material in her current state, but she could be, given the opportunity. Someone needed to piece her broken nation back together.

Picking her way carefully across the slope, she checked the stars, following the four-point cluster Tulimaq had shown her during their travels to the labor camp. On the next switchback, she sensed a stirring in the air. The hair along her body rose on end.

She reached a place of shadows clotted at the tree roots. But there—a flash of eyes, yellow and sharp, then shuttered, gone. Ila stood stiffly, her attention darting to every hollow and cranny. Slowly, she turned.

A large, dark shape darted toward her. Ila stumbled backward, and suddenly there was nothing under her feet. Her arms wheeled. Her back hit the earth, then her head, and the world flipped upside down. She tumbled down the mountainside, bashing into logs and roots, a battering that spread from her back to her front. She finally crashed into a snowdrift.

Ila's body gave one long throb. A low moan cracked in her throat. Nothing felt broken, miraculously, though her right ankle might be twisted. She fumbled to touch her thigh and found blood pouring out.

She applied pressure, too shocked to do anything but lie there. Then vibrations skittered up her legs and spine, all the places where her body touched the earth. Someone or something was approaching.

Keeping her hand pressed to the severed flesh, Ila stumbled to her feet. Her right leg buckled under her weight. She grabbed the branch of a nearby tree, holding herself up, and peered into the dark. It looked to be an animal on four legs skittering down the hillside.

Ila thought of the women and children digging holes in the permafrost, half-clothed and underfed, and the men somewhere farther, separated from their families. That vision guided her as she kept to the rooted, rocky areas so she wouldn't accidentally drop through a snowdrift. Upon reaching a large clearing, she quickly skirted the open space. A glance back showed the gray veil of night, a shroud that masked sight save for the patches of moonlight.

Ila leaned heavily against a tree, her breathing uneven and shallow. This seemed as good a place as any for shelter. She crumpled on the torn soil.

Ila tried not to move. The panic wasn't far off. Apaay would not be coming to save her. That was fine. It was time to stand on her own two feet.

As she drifted, Ila imagined herself as a child in the fire of the Face Stealer's memory, soot-stained and terrified. She imagined what would have happened if her mother had walked through the burning door instead. How she would have tugged Ila into her arms and rubbed soothing lines down her back. *Hush now,* she would have said. *It will not always be this way. You are frightened now, but one day, you will become strong.*

She smiled a little at that.

← →

A hand on her arm jerked Ila awake, her instincts coming alive under the firm grip. She was already swinging her talq when the hand tightened, stilling her movements. Ila looked into Tulimaq's haggard face, blood sliding down one side of his neck, and blinked away the fog of confusion.

Brushing Ila's bloody hands aside, he applied pressure to her thigh wound. Heavy grime caked his chin and cheeks. Streaks of sweat cut through the dirt.

Ila's throat tightened to the point of pain. It felt like hope and relief and gratitude and everything she knew she shouldn't feel when it came to the distant combat master. The first choked exhalation wavered as it hit the air. *What are you doing here?*

The skin around his mouth pulled taut. "Stop talking."

Ila tried sitting up. Tulimaq gripped her arm with rigid fingers. "Stop moving. Stop talking. Just stop. Sit there while I look at this wound."

His anger was more than anger. It transformed, outgrew its cage, and became something else: danger.

In the close darkness, her eyes adjusted. Their meeting was no coincidence. He'd tracked her all this way. To bring her back? His fury radiated against her body, though his expression was composed. After a few minutes of examining the wound, Tulimaq said, "How did you get this?"

What was worse: the mortifying truth, or a flimsy lie? Tulimaq, she decided, was livid enough that lying would be a mistake. *I kind of . . . fell down a mountain.* It sounded even worse outside of her head.

He paused, looking at her through his spiked eyelashes. "If for once in your life you did what you were supposed to, you wouldn't find yourself getting hurt every time I turned my back. You're lucky you didn't break your neck." He tied off the wound harder than necessary. Ila bit the inside of her cheek and bore it.

"Why are you here?" he demanded after a lull. "You should be at the Wood."

Pain clawed at her leg as she shifted, and dizziness swept her up and carried her away. Ila blinked a few times before her vision came into focus. *I'm free to go where I please.*

He wiped the blood from his mittens. "I understand that. It still doesn't answer the question."

She replied with complete honesty, *I wasn't planning on returning.*

He didn't ask why. Somehow that made it worse. Emotion rose in her throat and eyes.

"Stop crying," he snapped.

Don't— She faltered. Don't what? What did she want? A reaction. Something more than his dismissiveness. Feeling. She wanted that. *Don't do that. Don't belittle me.* She couldn't go on. *Don't act like you don't care* was what she wanted to say. An angry swipe of her face smeared tears across her cheeks. *Why does it bother you if I cry? Why are you so hard on me for being upset?*

A muscle slid in his jaw, and the smooth skin of his neck bobbed with his swallow. "Because the world is cruel. It will harden any softness you show it."

Is that what happened to you? she wanted to know. What did she know of Tulimaq aside from his name? She didn't know his heart. But she knew that how he decided to live was his choice, and how she decided to live was hers. *I choose to forgive when I should not. I choose to be soft when the world wants to harden me. That's my choice, not yours.*

"And when you are crushed by the enemy? When they capture you and torture information from you? Will you choose mercy when they show you none?"

Something about his expression made a chill creep across her skin. *You're trying to scare me. It won't work.*

"I'm trying to show you the world as it is."

No. Their gazes locked, their bodies near enough to share heat and their breath hot as smoke in the frost as it hazed between their eyes. *Your world is not the same as mine.* His perspective wasn't, either. When one sought the darkness, it was all they would ever see.

Uncertainty flickered in him. Four heartbeats passed before he repeated, "Why are you here, Ila?"

She let the anger go as more pressing matters took hold, then gathered her courage. Knowing she had a history, a sister, was every gift she had never been given. *I know who I am now.*

Dark eyes regarded her steadily. There was curiosity amidst the confusion. "Go on."

She was too full of the newfound knowledge to hold back. *I told you that I never knew where I came from, but I went to the First Man to ask him of my heritage. And he told me.*

Tulimaq did what he did best: He waited.

My full name, she said, recalling how the First Man's voice had shaken her awake, *is Matilaqaa. I am heir to the Wolf Kingdom.*

A peculiar stillness fell over Tulimaq. It was as if the world he knew was reshaping itself around this information.

She studied him warily. *Why are you looking at me like that?*

"You're supposed to be dead."

I know. Yet here she was, alive and well and whole.

"The First Man told you this?"

Yes. And the First Man could not lie.

The brief moment of Tulimaq's curiosity flickered. There was some thoughtfulness to his features now, a possible study. Then he turned away from her unexpectedly. Ila began to wonder if she had said something to offend him.

She caught his arm, waiting until he looked at her in that watchful way of his. *Did I do something wrong?*

"No." He shook his head, distant. He always had been. Walking a few feet away, he rested a hand on one of the trunks. Ila's confusion gave way to concern. She couldn't imagine he was upset with her, as she hadn't known of this information previously, but Tulimaq worked in mysterious ways.

A few minutes passed before he returned and reached into his pack. "How is the pain?"

The change of subject threw her. *Bearable.* Sort of. She didn't want him viewing her as weak.

"Here," he said, passing her a small cup full of liquid. "This will help dull it."

She took a sip, found the taste sweet, and downed the rest.

"Matilaqaa," he said. Just her name.

Ila blinked as her vision splashed with shades of gray. Time smeared in the spaces between her breaths. That smell, faint as summer on a breeze.

Moonflower.

The cup slipped from her grip. She was out before it hit the ground.

← 46 →

"You foolish, reckless woman."

Peeling open her eyes, Apaay whimpered in pain as her surroundings came into focus. A small, one-roomed structure constructed of stone slabs surrounded her, cloaked in gray light. Though the ceiling was caving in, the space was relatively insulated with the walls intact, the cracks filled in with snow. Numiak sat in the opposite corner, watching her. Ro and Kaan had gone.

"Where are we?" she croaked.

"Talguk." A crisp sound. "In one of the old port homes."

She sighed as the tension in the room rose a notch. "If you're going to yell at me, can you do it while I'm sleeping?"

"Of course. I wouldn't want to inconvenience you." That silken tone, brimming with danger. Anyone in their right mind would flee. Apaay shivered and waited for the rest.

"What the hell were you thinking coming back? I told you to go to Talguk and to *not stop*."

Apaay ground her teeth together. She was too fatigued and in too much pain for an admonishment.

"If Kaan and Ro hadn't arrived with reinforcements, you would be dead."

"So I was supposed to let you die?" She let that comment settle, uncomfortable with how furious he was at her decision. "I heard you screaming."

"That was over three miles away."

Apaay shrugged. "I know what I heard. And if I hadn't come back, you'd probably be dead, not me." Which reminded her . . .

She took him in. The harpoons no longer protruded from his body, but blood had seeped through his parka and trousers, sullying the fur. He looked worse than she had ever seen him. The skin beneath his eyes was very dark, paling the brown of his face in contrast. Sweat beaded on his upper lip. "Are you dying?" A whisper.

Numiak pursed his mouth, as if debating whether to allow the change of subject. "Technically, yes." He didn't sound put off by it, which made her think it was worse than it sounded. "The harpoon tips were poisoned. Kaan managed to slow the process, but the poison will eventually reach my heart, antidote or not."

"How long?"

"A month, maybe two."

Her throat bobbed. He had demanded Kaan heal her before himself. Apaay almost asked him why, but she wasn't ready to open that door yet. "Where is everyone?"

His mouth pulled as he shifted position. In the gray half-light, the blue of his eyes was as cuttingly bright as the stars. "Ro, Kaan, and their brethren returned to the Central Territory with a message."

"What message?"

He leveled a gaze at her. "To prepare for war."

Her stomach dropped and kept dropping. So it had come to that. The last few months they had, of course, discussed the possibility of war, but it had always felt distant, something that would take years to unfold. They'd had time, then.

The Face Stealer went on. "I imagine Yuki is returning to the Southern Territory to regroup with Nanuq."

"I need to warn my family."

"The Raven will keep them safe," he said at her panicked expression. "You don't have to worry about that."

Against all odds, Apaay believed him.

With the future so uncertain, her thoughts spun out. What came next for them, for the North? The Wood was forfeit. Was there no safe place left?

Everything was so much larger than it had been, the scope of the world magnified to her. It was one thing to understand her place with her people. Apaay's purpose had never strayed beyond feeding her village, caring for her family, building herself into a respected, dependable member of society, one worthy of recognition. But who was she outside of that structure? How did she fit into the greater whole?

The Face Stealer said, "I heard from Tulimaq while you were resting. He and Ila are safe, in case you were wondering. They will reach Sinika in a few weeks."

It was the best news she had received all day. "Should we meet up with them?"

"No." He tried to straighten against the wall and ended up sliding down lower. "Right now, our safety depends on disappearing. Yuki and Nanuq are searching for us. Well, me. And now that my brother has gone to their side, we have him to contend with as well. The more inconspicuous the group, the better."

In blatant incredulity, Apaay shook her head, unable to understand why he insisted on splitting their strength. "You're dying. You have no power. You barely have the strength to stand."

"Go on," he said dryly.

Apaay thought she would have enjoyed seeing him like this: small and weak. But she didn't. She finally realized that his past was perhaps more complex than he let on, and becoming who he was, the reputation preceding him, had been a difficult choice to make, if it had been a choice at all. "What's next?" she asked. They had tasted what the future held today, and it had not been pleasant. Anything could have gone differently.

"You and I will travel to the Northern Territory."

"For the hot spring," she clarified.

"Partially. It will rid my body of the poison, but our main task is to secure an alliance with the caribou Unua. Ro will act as our contact for the Owl Clan while we are gone."

Apaay considered their current location and the distance to the Northern Territory. Then she considered the Face Stealer's physical state, and hers. His lack of power. "How are you going to reach the Northern Territory in your condition?" It was over a thousand miles away. The poison would take him slowly. What if they reached a point when his body gave out, leaving her to go forward without direction? "It will take at least two months of travel. The poison will reach your heart before then."

A corner of his mouth curled. "You could call in your blood oath and force me to tell you."

Her eyes narrowed, though Apaay felt a little pleased at having taken advantage of the situation. "Didn't like that, did you?" *Well, good.*

"I never said I didn't like it. On the contrary, I was pleasantly surprised." His eyes brightened, and they were almost as sharp as she remembered. "People do not get what they want by asking. They get what they want by taking." He dipped his chin in a rare display of admiration. "You wanted power, so you took it back."

In the future, she wouldn't hesitate to do it again. "The antidote?"

Sighing, the Face Stealer held up a small vial. "It should last until we reach the Northern Territory."

She looked at the pale pink liquid and asked, "What if you run out?" If it came to that and there was nothing to stop the poison from reaching his heart?

"You can give me mouth to mouth."

Drat it all, she flushed. "You really are full of yourself, aren't you?"

His laughter, while pained, was the only warm thing in this cold room.

"Bastard."

He only laughed harder.

She was done with this conversation. Tomorrow was another day, and she would face it with eyes wide open.

"And by the way," Apaay tossed back, too exhausted to put any real heat behind it, "you're welcome." Turning onto her side, she shut her eyes.

Darkness was almost upon her when his low voice reached her ears. "Thank you," Numiak murmured, "for saving my life."

With a heavy exhalation, her body sank into the earth. She felt free. "I didn't save your life," Apaay said as sleep claimed her. "I saved mine."

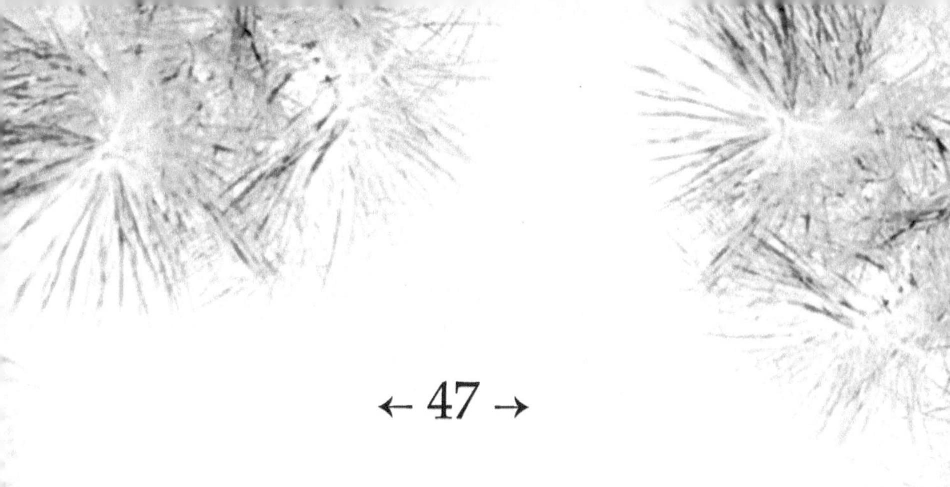

← 47 →

The first thing Ila noticed when she came to was the scent of smoke in the air. It tunneled into her mind, sent paralyzing cold down her limbs, beneath her skin, deeper, into the marrow of her bones.

Her eyes flew open, vision sharpening as her blood beat hot with awareness. A few shapes in the clearing's periphery, all swathed in near darkness. Trees, mostly, and scrub. Ila then realized it wasn't fear paralyzing her limbs, but rope binding her ankles together, her arms behind her back. She was lying underneath a granite outcropping on a stretch of ground brushed free of snow. Cold wind buffeted her face. The air was free of taint, which meant the burning had been inside her mind.

Tulimaq had betrayed her, tricked her and captured her and bound her like . . . like a prisoner.

How could that be? There must be some mistake.

From the corner of her eye, she caught sight of a slender figure moving toward her. Ila searched his face for a sign that something had changed, but to all appearances, nothing had. She sifted through past interactions for possible motives. He had almost reached her, a faint glow emanating from his staff in the dark. Ila considered feigning sleep before tossing the idea aside. She wouldn't cower. Her fury was so much greater than her fear.

Except when Tulimaq knelt in front of her, Ila couldn't help it. She recoiled.

He paused in reaching for her. "I'm going to untie your hands." His gaze was as remote as the snowy peaks. Tulimaq was someone who would always keep his thoughts close, but she saw him as she had not seen him before: a knife in the dark.

Tulimaq made quick work of the bonds, tucking the length of rope into his pack when he was done. With her hands free, Ila scrambled away from him until her back hit the stone. He hadn't untied her ankles. The tightness of the rope stung. *Who are you?* she demanded, pressure building behind her eyes. Ila vowed not to break in front of this man, though she had told no one of her whereabouts. *What do you want with me?*

He studied her as he had done so many times before. An eerie light glinted in his dark eyes. "I once told you my story, of a boy whose mother fled into the mountains and disappeared, as his father had hoped. But the boy wasn't satisfied with that life. He wanted to prove to his father that he was more than his bastardly status, more than the stain he was made out to be. So he planned. For years, he built himself a life that would one day allow him to return home. Recognition from Nanuq, the Great Bear, was all he had ever wanted."

Her heart kicked into a sprint at the mention of Nanuq. *I don't understand. What does Nanuq have to do with your father?* She dug her fingers into her palms, waiting.

Tulimaq watched her with quiet tolerance in his eyes. "You mistake me. Nanuq *is* my father. And you, Matilaqaa of the Wolf Kingdom, are the answer I've been looking for."

ACKNOWLEDGMENTS

This book. Man. It took a lot out of me. Over two years later it's taught me more than any other book I've written to date. Many thanks are in order.

First, I'd like to thank my editor, Rachel, for the most excellent feedback concerning character motivations and relationships, and for being Numiak's biggest fan.

Thank you, Beth, for your continued feedback, advice, and support in all things writing and publishing. I'm so glad we're still critique partners after all this time!

To all the book bloggers and bookstagrammers who have done so much to champion Apaay's story. You have my deepest thanks for getting the word out that these books exist!

Once again, my eternal gratitude goes to Faryn Hughes, who continually blows me away with the most beautiful covers ever!

And how can I forget my family? It's true love when you won't shut up about your made-up world and they just take it with a smile. Your belief in me keeps me going through the hard times.

Alexandria Warwick is the international bestselling author of the Four Winds series and the North series. A classically trained violinist, she spends much of her time performing in orchestras. She lives in Florida.